ALL THE GIN JOINTS

A NOVEL OF WORLD WAR II HOLLYWOOD

MARTIN TURNBULL

ROTHESAY
PRESS

This book is dedicated to

GENE STRANGE

*because his support, faith, enthusiasm, and nickpickiness
have never wavered.*

DISCLAIMER

This novel is a work of historical fiction. Apart from the well-known actual people, events and locales that figure into the narrative, all names, characters, places, and incidents are the product of the author's imagination or are used fictitiously. Any resemblance to actual persons, living or dead, events or locals is entirely coincidental.

1

---

*H*umphrey Bogart's face loomed thirty feet high, filling the screen with his sardonic grin. The Brooklyn Fox Theatre's sumptuous Spanish Baroque detailing fell away for the guy in the tenth row with the fistful of popcorn and bicycle clips around his ankles.

For Luke Valenti, all that mattered was the SPADE AND ARCHER sign on the window, the roll-your-own cigarette Bogart was filling from his muslin drawstring bag, and the blonde secretary announcing that a prospective client wanted to see him.

"Don't let her in," Luke murmured. "Her name isn't Miss Wonderly. She'll bring Joel Cairo to your door. And then you'll have to deal with The Fat Man, who will stop at nothing to get his paws on a statue of a black falcon from Malta."

He scooped up another handful of popcorn; the redhead at the concession stand always over-salted it. Luke didn't care. His eyes were now on Mary Astor spinning her yarn about how she'd traveled from New York to find her sister, who'd come to San Francisco with a dubious gent named Floyd Thursby.

Look at how she's telling Bogart they were never as close as sisters ought to be. Boy, she really knows how to sell that pack of lies she's dealing out.

But Sam Spade was one hell of an astute reader of people. He probably knew he had a world-class liar on his hands. Luke squirmed deeper into his seat. Cairo was about to offer Spade five thousand bucks to find a black figure of a bird. Don't do it. It'll bring you more trouble than it's worth.

The lobby stretched two stories high to a ceiling of sculpted marble, metallic accents, and six-foot chandeliers of frosted glass. A little overdone, perhaps, but there were worse ways a guy could spend a drizzling November afternoon.

The redhead stood at a circular counter assembling a display of paperbacks.

"These new?" Luke asked.

"The movie's done so well they're republishing it. Twenty-five cents apiece, if you're interested."

The cover featured a photograph of the black bird from the movie. "THE MALTESE FALCON" was scrawled along the top; Dashiell Hammett's name was in block lettering along the bottom.

Luke fished out a quarter from his pocket and slid it across the counter.

"You've seen this picture a bunch of times. Humphrey Bogart fan, huh?"

Luke wasn't especially a fan of Bogart. He liked him well enough, but no more than, say, Gable, Cagney, or Flynn. But there was something about this movie, this role, this Sam Spade. Until he'd figured out what it was, Luke wasn't prepared to admit anything to anyone. It was the safer choice.

He smiled at her. A bland smile. Intentionally uncommitted. She was cute, in a Shirley-Temple-Grows-Up kind of way. But he could see that familiar spark of recognition flicker through her eyes, which meant the "Say, ain't you . . .?" question wasn't far off.

He told her he'd better be going and headed for the glass-and-brass doors.

The cacophony of rattling streetcars and impatient car horns crowded Flatbush Avenue. Luke zippered up his jacket to keep out the bitter wind blowing from the Navy Yard. It hadn't been this cold when he'd walked into the Fox, but oh boy, there was no way to ignore that Thanksgiving was coming. He turned right. The German deli next door must have been fixing sauerkraut; the sharp smack of vinegar saturated the narrow alleyway beside the theater.

He always figured that one of these days he'd get to the end and his bike would no longer be there. Some wise guy with bolt cutters would have seen him park in the shadows beneath the fire escape. Not that Luke cared. He hated the damned thing. But that was okay. Only eight more weeks and he wouldn't have to slog around Brooklyn avoiding paint trucks and pushcart vendors, runaway mutts and old ladies with walking sticks.

He unlocked the chain from the back wheel and snaked it into the leather pouch attached to his bicycle seat. Fifty-six days. Yep, he could do that.

The pop of chewing gum caught him off guard.

Luke didn't move.

Another pop. Louder this time.

He turned around.

There were four of them. Street punks with their arms crossed, weight on one foot, tapping the weather-worn cobblestones with the other. Raggedy dungarees. Home-knitted sweaters unraveling at the elbows. One kid wore a pork-pie hat that was too pristine to be his. Seventeen or eighteen years old, maybe nineteen at most. At twenty-two, Luke wasn't much older than they were. But he was outnumbered, and by the looks of them, they knew how to land a punch better than Luke ever could —or would want to.

A pudgy ruffian with a crew cut stepped forward. "Nice bike."

Luke knew better than to break eye contact. "It's okay."

"Better'n okay." The ruffian took another step closer. His gang followed suit. "Which is why I'm gonna do you a favor." His three acolytes snickered on cue like it was their job, which it probably was. He bunched his right hand into a fist and punched it into the fleshy palm of his left with a lazy rhythm.

Talk about a cliché move. What's next? Calling me a dirty rat? "Wo-o-o-o-ow." Luke stretched the word into five syllables. "We've only just met and already you want to do me a favor. I should introduce myself." He pulled his bike forward until the sign attached to the rear rolled into a patch of sunlight.

Luke gave them a good, long chance to read it.

VALENTI FAMILY CONSTRUCTION
BUILDERS – ALL TRADES – HANDYMEN
No job too large or too small!
We'll treat you like family!
Come see us at 18th Ave & 70th Street
Telephone JEfferson 3-4411

The rhythmic palm-punching stopped. "You work for the Valentis?"

Years ago, Luke had learned to leave a ponderous pause before replying, "I *am* a Valenti." Emphasizing the 'am' did all the heavy lifting.

An acolyte with dirty fingernails took a step backward. He looked like the dimmest of the bunch, but he knew when to beat a hasty retreat.

Mr. Pudgy looked Luke up and down, not ready to admit defeat. "You? A Valenti?"

Dirty Fingernails said, "He's the other one. The runt of the litter."

Luke had often wondered if people called him the runt of the Valenti litter, but this was the first time somebody had said it to his face. It wasn't an inaccurate description. Luke had five older brothers—much older. Sal, the bricklayer, had twenty-two years, eight-and-a-half inches, and fifty pounds on Luke.

So, yes, he was the runt. But still, to hear someone say it out loud stung worse than a hornet. Not that these low-rent punks needed to know that. The vinegary air prickled Luke's eyes, but he dared not blink. "Be smart and walk away while you can."

Luke didn't draw another breath until he could see the backs of the Dead End Kids of Flatbush.

Walk away while you can. That was rich. Sometimes it was good to be a Valenti. Rarely, though. Hardly ever, in fact. But it came in handy when you were outnumbered four-to-one in a dark alley where nobody would hear your screams for help.

Luke was a block from home when he heard the roar blasting down 16th Avenue. He was tempted to keep pedaling and go— where? The Bay Ridge Candy Shop for an egg cream, maybe. But that would only put off the inevitable.

Closing the gate behind him, he leaned his bike against the brick wall and covered the Valenti Construction sign with a tattered blanket. Pop's voice barreled through the open windows along the side of the house.

"WHAT HAVE I BEEN SAYING ALL THIS TIME?"

Gauging from the full-throated response he got, all five brothers were there, braying like a Greek chorus. And if the brothers were there, the wives were, too, and their thirteen children. Running, screaming, jumping, crying, laughing, whining, arguing. God forbid one of them should sit quietly in a corner.

Luke entered the house and stepped inside the dining room. The Valenti dining table was a six-hundred-pound mahogany behemoth. Pop sat at the head, a *Brooklyn Eagle* spread in front of him. "I've been saying it. Over and over. Something's gonna happen." He tapped the paper with his finger. "Sooner or later those damned Krauts were gonna take a shot. And now we've lost the *Reuben James.*"

Luke positioned himself at the periphery of the family crowding around the table. "What's the *Reuben James?*"

"It takes balls to strike a U.S. destroyer." Sal thumped the table. "Especially after they torpedoed the *Kearny.*"

"Roosevelt didn't declare war when they sank the *Kearny,*" Pop thundered. "But two destroyers in two weeks? More'n a hundred deaths? Roosevelt's gonna order the Navy to attack any German vessel in the safety zone. After that, Congress will repeal the Neutrality Acts. And *that* means merchant vessels are gonna be armed."

"You predicted it!" Tony leaped to his feet. Luke wasn't sure why. Then again, he could rarely figure out why any members of his family behaved the way they did. "I remember!"

Enzo Valenti stroked his chin like he was the Oracle of Brooklyn. "We'll be wearing Army uniforms by Christmas—oh. Luke. You're home."

That's when you notice me? When you bring up the sorest subject possible? And now I feel like a deer caught in the headlights of a Valenti Construction truck barreling along the Sunrise Highway.

Silence had fallen over the dining table. Luke smiled weakly. "War's inevitable, huh?"

"You heard Pop," Rico said.

It was a safe bet that Old Man Lombardi over on 63rd Street had heard Pop—and that guy was deaf.

"I hope you're not hungry." Luke's mother, Sara, swiped a lock of her blonde bangs to one side. "Dinner'll be late. Just meatloaf tonight."

"But I like your meatloaf," Luke told her.

She pulled a tight smile. No teeth. No warmth. "I'll call you when it's ready."

In other words, none of this concerns you. You with your 4-F status and your "Exempt from War Service" card. What an embarrassment to the Valenti name. You'll never be fitted for a U.S. Army uniform, so go do whatever it is you do when you're not outside pedaling that infernal "We'll treat you like family!" sign between here and Bedford-Stuyvesant.

Luke retreated through the kitchen to the back door, where he stepped back into the November chill. The Valenti backyard stretched the width of three houses. It wasn't so much a yard as a field.

When the Valentis had got off the boat from Italy in 1881, they had looked for cheap land to buy. Manhattan was out of the question, so they'd crossed the bridge to Brooklyn, where they found a block big enough for six houses, three facing 16th Street and three facing Ovington Court. Enzo Valenti had had a plan when he got married: five boys in ten years. Sara had held up her end of the bargain: one after the other, right on schedule. Sara Valenti was nothing if not efficient.

Enzo had set out to teach each rambunctious kid a different skill. The oldest, Sal, was allocated bricklaying, drywall, and wallpaper. Next came Tony, whose fate was to become a carpenter, roofer, and layer of outdoor paving. Rico was the electrician. Carlo, a.k.a. Cal, was the plumber. And Vic was taught carpeting, tiling, counters, and indoor fixtures.

The reward for learning a trade was a house. One per son, built from scratch, was the best advertising that Valenti Construction could get. Who wouldn't go to the guy who'd built his sons' homes?

It was a grand plan. And it had worked exactly as intended.

Until a surprise baby had come along twelve years later.

Let's not give him an Italian name to help him fit in, though.

Let's not call him Lucca so that we can shorten it to Luke, like we did for his brothers. Let's call him Luke because growing up knowing there was no actual place for him wouldn't make him feel enough of an outsider.

Luke parked his butt on the wooden bench below the kitchen window. The communal backyard was blissfully free of the usual semi-feral nieces and nephews running around like savages. He slid the paperback out of his pocket and traced the silhouetted falcon with a fingernail.

"Thank God for cool air!" Cal's wife, Patty, stood at the open window above Luke. "I can only take so much brawn and bravado."

"Our Valenti menfolk," Mom replied. "Put 'em in a room together and they could warm Ebbets Field in February."

"They're sure looking forward to marching off to war."

Mom sighed. "Boys and their guns. Whatcha gonna do?"

"I kinda feel sorry for Luke, though."

"Why?"

Luke craned his neck to hear better.

"That hang-dog look; it was the same one he wore when he came home from the enlistment station. He could barely say 4-F out loud. It was like Father Bernard had told him to scream the worst curse word inside St. Athanasius."

"You talking about my baby brother?" Tony was son number two in the pecking order and Luke's least favorite. Mean when sober, nasty-mean when drunk. "Did you see what he had in his pocket? It was the book of that movie he goes to see all the time."

"The one about the falcon statue?"

"Twice in the past couple of weeks I've seen him coming out of the Fox. I pass it on the way to that job up near the Navy Yard. Jesus Christ, what kind of dud goes to the movies by himself? Everyone knows you only go to neck with your favorite girl in the back row."

Patty giggled. "Do you think he's queer?" Neither Tony nor

Luke's mom replied, so Patty's question hung in the air like soiled laundry. "He's, what, twenty-two and never had a girlfriend. Okay, so he's quiet and shy and 4-F, but he's no hunchback from Notre Dame."

"I really don't wish to think about it." A disdainful sniff had crept into Mom's voice.

The oven door gave off a metallic clang, which meant that Luke's mother had yanked it open with more force than it needed. Had she wondered if Luke was a homo? Had everybody else in the family? And everybody in Bensonhurst, too?

Luke jumped off the bench. If he reached the inside stairs unseen, he could sneak into his bedroom with nobody the wiser.

Luke's bedroom had five uneven walls, a sloping ceiling, and a window that overlooked the driveway. He'd left it open that morning, so now the room was freezing cold. He hooked the latch with his pinky finger and closed it.

I could tell them about the crushes I've had. All of them girls. Yes, that's right. *Girls*. But none of them returned the affection once they learned that I'm the runt.

He dropped *The Maltese Falcon* on his bedside table next to *Why England Slept*. Whoever this John F. Kennedy fellow was, he knew a thing or two about the crumbling situation in Britain. Luke would have suggested those gun-happy Valenti fellas read it before they rushed off to war, but it would have been a waste of time. When was the last time any of them had voluntarily cracked open a book?

The hullabaloo floated up from downstairs. Luke caught "Iceland" and "convoy" and "torpedoes," but the rest was the same old tumult of aggression and bombast. He pulled a shoebox from under his bed. Digging past the pencils and charcoal strips, subway tokens, his Edward R. Murrow autograph, and a *Lone Ranger* mask, he reached his East New York Savings

Bank passbook beneath a battered program from the 1939 World's Fair.

He looked at the total. Not that he needed to. He knew the exact amount: $179.36.

Eleven dollars from next month's pay would take him to $190.36.

Another eleven dollars from the following month would push him past the magical two-hundred-dollar mark.

Two hundred dollars meant freedom.

Two hundred dollars meant escape.

He gazed up at one of the few pictures on his wall: an 1850s etching of Anacapa Island. Sheer, wild cliffs banked downward to the Pacific Ocean. It was the sort of illustration he loved to draw for the unalloyed pleasure of it. He had shown his efforts to only his Aunt Wilda.

He retrieved a cardboard tube from under the bed, popped open its lid, and coaxed out the sheet of paper coiled inside. Anchoring it on his desk with four large stones he'd found on Brighton Beach, he straightened out the edges and examined his progress.

He had drawn Montauk at the far end of Long Island a bunch of times, always the same composition: Fisher Tower rising eight stories on the far left, the Montauk lighthouse on the right. And in the dead center, a huge bonfire lighting up the shore.

He selected a charcoal strip from the shoebox and shaded the flames licking the sky, brushing the paper in light, upward strokes, giving them depth and intensity. He worked at them until the aroma of meatloaf filtered into his room. He figured he had at least fifteen minutes before he had to return downstairs and face the hollering hordes. Once, just once, wouldn't it be nice to sit down to a family dinner where nobody raised their voice? Pipe dream, Luke told himself. Nothing but a pipe dream.

He reinserted the drawing into its tube and returned it under the bed. Back at his desk, he opened the drawer and withdrew a secondhand map he'd discovered at a junk store. He unfolded it and ran a finger along the fancy lettering at the top:

DETAILED MAP OF LONG ISLAND,
NEW YORK STATE, 1937

"Nearly there, bucko. Eight more weeks."

He picked up a pencil and drew a small lighthouse at Eaton's Neck, Shinnecock, and Fire Island. He shifted the map until Montauk sat in front of him. Gripping the pencil more tightly, he sketched another lighthouse, much larger than the other three. It allowed him to include more detail, like the windows in the two-story house at the base and the thick band of dark paint striping the middle of the lighthouse itself.

Mom's voice rang up the stairs. "Five minutes."

He glanced at the book on his nightstand, then back at the map, and added an extra detail. To anyone else, it looked like a nondescript bird. But Luke knew it wasn't just any old bird perched on top of the Montauk lighthouse. It was a falcon. More specifically, a Maltese falcon.

2

_L_uke lifted his feet off the bicycle pedals and coasted the last block of Argyle Road as oaks and elms scraped the sky overhead. This tradition was part of his Saturday afternoon escapes from the pandemonium of the Valenti compound to the welcoming sanctuary of Aunt Wilda's apartment.

She was a friend-of-the-family type of aunt, not a blood relation, and was the person he ran to when he got a straight-A report card or had finished a new lighthouse drawing he'd been particularly proud of. She was the only one who made a fuss.

He pulled up at number thirty-five and hitched his bike over his shoulder. Up three flights, he knocked twice, paused, then twice again.

Her voice chirped through the paneling. "Who is it?"

"Emperor Theodosius the Second."

He'd been biking to Wilda's every week since he'd received a Sun Racer for his eleventh birthday. Like lifting his feet off the pedals, he enjoyed dreaming up a new name every time he visited her.

The door flew open. Aunt Wilda threw her arms out wide,

causing the edges of her cape to flap like the mainsail of an overly theatrical pirate ship. "Theodosius! You *do* look well!" She enveloped him; he inhaled her gardenia eau de toilette. Unlike Luke's sisters-in-law, Aunt Wilda always applied "enough to enchant but never too much to choke."

As she released him from her embrace, her dozen silver bangles jangled. "Remind me who Theodosius the Second was."

"Byzantine emperor who built the walls around Constantinople."

"Inspired choice, my dear."

He tugged the corner of her cape. "What color is this?"

"I call it 'Moroccan Tangerine.' Does it suit me?"

"Everything you wear suits you." Luke halted in the center of the living room. "What's changed?"

Aunt Wilda shrugged an evasive shoulder.

The Egyptian sphinx sat on the upright piano. The peacock feathers burst from the elephant foot. The poster for the 1893 Chicago World's Columbian Exposition still hadn't been dusted since Coolidge was in office. The mummified African pygmy head was as repulsive as ever.

"I give up. What is it?"

Wilda pointed to the wall behind the sofa. "I got bored with the Vermeer print of the woman seated at the virginals and put up The Four Blooms instead."

The Four Blooms was a quartet Wilda had chaperoned around the vaudeville circuit. It had been a halcyon time for her, escorting four pretty girls: Violet, Lily, Jasmine, and Rose. The poster depicted each of them as a Gibson girl silhouetted against their namesake flower, with *THE FOUR BLOOMS* composed in a swirly Art Nouveau typeface.

Wilda lowered the Victrola needle onto a phonograph record. A glissando of harp strings filled the room, followed by Rudy Vallée warbling about how a kiss was just a kiss and a sigh was just a sigh.

"As Time Goes By" had been Luke and Wilda's "our song" when she had taken him to his first Broadway show, *Everybody's Welcome*. Afterwards, Wilda had bought Vallée's recording. Whenever Luke came to visit, he would insist she play it for him. Nowadays she did it as a matter of course.

"I played this for Irina Dashkova yesterday. Her father was a former *premier danseur* with the Bolshoi before the Revolution drove them all the way to the Lower East Side, the poor darlings."

It was hard to keep track of Aunt Wilda's social circle: Romanian counts, polo players from the Argentine, Turkish poets married to Swedish flautists—or was the Turk a flautist and the Swede a poet? An endless mélange of colorful characters with exotic accents and tongue-twister names. Luke had long since given up asking how she met these people. It was usually some variation of "A cocktail party at the Bolivian consulate thrown by the Cuban ambassador for that up-and-coming Dutch tennis champion." Not that it mattered. She was the conduit through which Luke glimpsed the outside world.

He headed toward the piano. "Could we start with that Beethoven piece? I was humming it the whole ride over here."

"There shall be no lesson today."

Luke's fingers twitched at the thought of missing out on his time at the keyboard.

At home, all they talked about was building, demolishing, and baseball. Nobody read books, nobody played an instrument, nobody saw Broadway shows. They didn't venture into Manhattan unless they had to. It was Wilda who had recognized that Luke had inherited his father's dexterity with his hands and had suggested he might be a natural at the piano. She'd been correct: he had taken to it immediately. With no piano in the Valenti house, however, progress between his once-a-week lessons had been a slow but steady ascent toward fair-to-middling competency.

"I have a glorious surprise instead!"

"You know how much I look forward to our lessons."

"Enough with the gloomy face." She took off for the kitchen. "We're going next door at three o'clock. Meanwhile, you'll find the Met's new recording of *Tannhäuser* on top of the gramophone."

Luke dutifully replaced "As Time Goes By" with *Tannhäuser*. As the Met's French horns, clarinets, and bassoons wafted through the apartment, he joined her in the kitchen where she was preparing their traditional British afternoon tea: tiny cucumber sandwiches, two-bite scones, slices of Battenberg cake, and a pot of Darjeeling tea.

He scooped out a fingertip of clotted cream. "I'm finally seeing inside Irving's place?" Aunt Wilda and Irving Kovner had been neighbors for as long as Luke could remember. A diffident gent with an academic air, he was conspicuously different from Wilda's usual parade of European artists and South American horse breeders.

The silver teaspoons rattled as Wilda placed them on the Wedgwood china saucers. Her eyes normally danced with boundless *joie de vivre*, but Luke stood close enough to see how uncommonly bloodshot they were.

"You okay?" he asked.

"Irina brought a bottle of Moskovskaya and we ended up skipping the lesson altogether, and listened to music instead."

Luke planted his hands on his hips. "You sat on the sofa knocking back vodka shots and now you're hungover like a sailor on shore leave. Let me guess. Rimsky-Korsakov's *Legend of the Invisible City?*"

"*Rigoletto*, which shows how much little Mister Wisenheimer knows."

Her histrionic pout triggered tiny alarm bells. Wilda wasn't the hangover type. Whatever she was shrugging off, he'd worm it out of her eventually. "I love you, Aunt Wilda."

She patted his back. "Of course you do, because I've seen to it that you're a young gentleman of taste and discernment. Now, take the sandwiches and scones and let's eat up. I promised Irving we'd be prompt."

As he went to take his usual spot on Wilda's dining table, he noticed an envelope sitting in front of the place setting. A circular logo with a pair of inter-crossing anchors filled the upper left corner. "The U.S. Coast Guard! Is this my surprise?"

Wilda placed the teapot on a small rattan mat. "I already told you. It's at Irving's."

Luke ran a fingertip along the envelope's edge. "You know what this is, don't you?"

"So open it already."

He picked up the butter knife. "I didn't think I'd be this nervous."

"Your future depends on what's in there." She poured the Darjeeling into matching blue teacups. "I'd be concerned if you weren't nervous."

Luke slit the envelope's edge. "Here goes nothing."

Dear Mr. Valenti,

Thank you for your application to join the U.S. Lighthouse Service training program. If you are successful in making the next round, we will be in touch no later than December 31st, 1941, to set an appointment for an in-person evaluation at our Manhattan location. Meanwhile, please accept my congratulations.

With best regards,

Stuart Perkins,

Chief Recruitment Officer

United States Lighthouse Service – Northern Atlantic Division.

"I'm on to the next step!"

Wilda lifted the cup to her lips. "As though there were any doubt."

Luke dropped into his chair.

This was it. His way in. Or more accurately, his path out of being the Valenti family embarrassment. Okay, so if the regular military forces wanted to kick his sorry 4-F'd ass to the curb, maybe the Lighthouse Service might accept him. Since the age of ten, he'd been drawing lighthouses, studying maps, reading books about them. Ask him anything—*anything at all!*—about the life of a lighthouse keeper, and he'd have the answer right there at his fingertips.

"Your tea's getting cold."

Luke dropped the letter on the tabletop, his heart sinking an inch or two. "You don't seem very excited for me."

"Of course I am, you silly boy." She tried to weave an encouraging trill through her voice.

"If we go to war, the Atlantic will be teeming with U-boats. Lighthouses will become frontline defense—"

"Don't cross any bridges before you come to them, is all I'm saying."

Luke's stomach churned with the sort of apprehension he usually had to deal with at home. "You don't think I'll get in?"

"Didn't I just say you'll be there doing your bit?" She lifted the plate of scones. "We've got twenty minutes till we're due at Irving's. Eat up."

Wilda rapped on her neighbor's door and swung it open. "YOO-HOO!"

Irving's voice rang down the hallway. "Come on in."

A floor-to-ceiling bookcase ran along his longest wall. Volumes about chess filled an entire shelf. He had a few pieces of artwork: a poster of the Reubens exhibition at the Metropolitan Museum of Art from a few years back, a still-life painting of bananas and apples, and a pair of ferocious African tribal masks, which Luke suspected Wilda had given him to liven things up.

Irving extended his hand. "How nice to see you again." He turned to a tall cardboard box sitting on his circular dining table. "You didn't tell him, I hope."

Wilda shook her head, frowning as though his question were an insult.

"I understand you're a fan of that Humphrey Bogart movie, *The Maltese Falcon*." Irving placed his flattened palms on the box. "You'd better brace yourself."

Wilda added, "It'll be better if you close your eyes."

Luke pressed his hands to his face and listened to what sounded like bunched-up newspaper. "Can I open my eyes now?"

"In three, two, one—OPEN!"

It was a statue of a bird, around twelve inches tall, and coated in black paint. Its feathers had been fashioned to look like diamond-shaped scales. The eyes had no pupils, but scowled over a beak that narrowed into a point sharp enough to gouge out an eyeball.

Something that had only ever existed on the Brooklyn Fox screen was now standing right in front of him. Close enough to touch. If he dared. "This isn't . . .?" He couldn't keep his voice from quivering.

"You can pick it up if you like."

It was heavier than he expected. Over five pounds. Seven, maybe eight.

During none of the times he'd watched the scene where Kaspar Gutman rotated his prize had Luke ever noticed how neatly its wings were folded behind it, one tucked sleekly beneath the other, or how its claws gripped the edge of the base, as though the bird were hanging on for its life.

"Did your aunt ever tell you I am a fairly skilled chess player?"

Wilda snorted. "That's like saying Jesse Owens is a fairly fast runner."

Was it any wonder that Sydney Greenstreet, Mary Astor, and

Peter Lorre had chased it across the globe? The Maltese falcon was mesmerizing. "She's mentioned it."

"I keep my game fresh by playing chess-by-mail. I make a move, write it on a postcard, mail it off, and wait until I receive one in return telling me what my opponent's next move is."

"Doesn't that take forever?"

"I'm in no rush." Irving pointed to an open doorway. "In there you'll find four games in progress: London, Prague, New Orleans, and Los Angeles. You may have heard of that fourth player. His name is Humphrey Bogart."

"You're kidding!"

"I most certainly am not. My brother, Simon, runs the props department at Warner Brothers. When Mr. Bogart learned that I'm a decent chess opponent, he asked if I would be interested in playing chess-by-mail. He has been coming along nicely since we started three years ago, and was very pleased when he check-mated me while he was finishing up on *The Maltese Falcon*. My sixtieth birthday was not long after that, so imagine my surprise when this package arrived." Irving tapped the statue's head. "There was a note enclosed saying how Mr. Bogart had never enjoyed anything in his life more than winning our game, and to enjoy the falcon prop as a token of his appreciation and birthday gift."

"Gee willikers." Luke picked the statue again. Bogart had touched this!

"Or at least that was the story Simon told him," Wilda put in.

Irving stroked his jawline. "Simon has a somewhat elastic relationship with the truth. A letter arrived yesterday in which he confessed that he had pilfered this falcon. It's one of four they made for the movie. The picture's been out for a few months, so Simon figured that nobody was going to notice."

"It's stolen property?" The bird felt as though it had doubled its weight; Luke returned it to the table.

Irving chuckled. "Jack Warner is stridently anti-Nazi and anti-isolationist. If we get sucked into war, he plans to mount a nation-wide fundraising tour using movie props. *The Maltese Falcon* was a tremendous hit for them, so he wants to include one. If that happens—"

"—the theft will be discovered," Wilda finished for him. "It'll be curtains for Simon. He's got a wife and four kids to support."

"It sure was nice of you to let me see it before you send it back," Luke said. "It's not every day we get to touch a real-life movie prop."

Irving and Wilda exchanged a glance that Luke couldn't decipher.

"Therein lies our problem," Irving said. "I work at the Navy Yard. The day after the Germans sank the *Reuben James*, ship production got boosted to around the clock. I can't get away."

"And we daren't send it by the post," Wilda added. "It might get broken, or damaged, or lost, or stolen."

"So you're taking it?"

She looked like someone on the verge of a confession, but courage deserted her at the penultimate moment. "We were hoping you could do it."

Luke reared back. "Me?!"

"I'm sure Simon could arrange for you to meet Mr. Bogart. Wouldn't that be exciting?"

"He's already wired me your train fare," Irving put in. "And has reserved a room at the Hollywood Hotel."

Aw, jeez, really? Luke shifted from one foot to the other. For a long, seductive moment he considered saying yes. After all, how often did a guy from Brooklyn get offered a cross-country railway trip all the way to California and back, a room at the Hollywood Hotel, *and* the chance to shake Humphrey Bogart's hand? But the thought of the letter on Wilda's dining table pulled him up short. "I'd love to help you out. Really, I would. But the Lighthouse Service. I have to stick around for the interview."

"Oh, that." Wilda waved away his concern, sending her

bracelets into a clanking turmoil. "You'll only be gone a week. Three days on the train to get out there, a day or two to return the falcon, see a few sights, and three days back."

"What if the summons comes when I'm gone?"

"I'll explain you were called away and that you'll be back shortly."

His dream was so close that he couldn't bear the thought of it slipping through his fingers. And why was Wilda so dismissive? He could take that sort of reaction from anybody else, but not from her.

He turned away from the table. "You'll have to find somebody else."

"There isn't anyone."

The air felt close and stuffy. Luke needed the fall sun on his face and the feel of the November breeze whipping against his cheeks. "Thank you for the chance to see the falcon, Irving. It was a genuine thrill, but I have to be going. I'll see myself out."

Back inside Wilda's apartment, he seized the handlebars of his bike, but a grip on his shoulder prevented him from moving.

"You've never been farther west than Hackensack. What a grand possibility for adventure! Goodness gracious me, Luke. I thought you'd leap at the chance."

He shrugged her hand away. "You know what this lighthouse opportunity means to me. It's a shot to join the Coast Guard. To contribute."

"If the regular military turned you down, isn't there a more-than-decent chance those lighthouse people will as well?" She had tempered her dismissive tone, but her words still smarted.

"I've got to try."

"We're offering you California, Warner Brothers, the actual Maltese falcon, and even Humphrey Bogart. When does anybody around here get this sort of chance? Don't forget, Luke, there's always next year. I'm sure a good percentage of applicants realize they can't tolerate all that solitude like they thought they could.

There must be a sizable turnover. And anyway, I don't understand why you're so stuck on this ridiculous lighthouse business."

There it was again, that uncharacteristic derision. If he wanted to be treated like that, he could stay home. He picked up his acceptance letter and shook it in her face. "Of course they could very well turn me down, which is why I have my backup plan."

"You're not still thinking of moving to Montauk, are you?"

"By the end of the year, I'll have saved up two hundred dollars."

"But there's hardly anything there. More importantly, hardly any people."

"That's kind of the point."

"Oh, Luke." She brushed his right cheek with the back of her fingers. "Montauk is not the solution." She pulled at his arm to get him to sit down, but he refused to budge. He knew what that pinched look on her face meant: *I'm about to tell you something you won't enjoy hearing.* He wanted to be standing up when she did.

"Why not?"

"Because you'll be running *away*."

"I'm sick of the noise, the constant commotion, conversations at the tops of people's lungs, the endless jabbering about baseball and bricks and faucets and a hundred other things I don't care about."

"You're sick of being ignored in your own home."

"Do you blame me?"

"Not in the slightest."

"Why are we having this conversation, then?"

"Wouldn't it be better if you were running *toward* something?"

"But I am. Toward a new life."

Wilda tsked. "You've never fitted in any more than I have, but if you think hiding away in an isolated lighthouse is the answer, I say you need another plan."

"Montauk *is* my other plan."

"But why Montauk? Because of that family vacation the

summer before the stock market crashed and everything went to hell?"

Luke breathed deeply for the first time in what felt like hours. Finally, she saw it.

"It's so tranquil there. Nobody yells, nobody throws things, nobody gets into brawls over DiMaggio's batting average. Until Montauk, I thought all beaches were like Coney Island. Over-cooked hotdogs, gaudy music, tacky kewpie dolls—and then I arrived at Montauk. I swear I could almost hear the Hallelujah Chorus."

She was smiling now. "The beach in those charcoal sketches of yours—it's Montauk, isn't it?"

Luke nodded.

"All this time I thought it was the Little Red Lighthouse at the foot of the George Washington Bridge. You'd think at my age, I'd be capable of putting two and two together, but apparently I'm dumb as a box of baseball bats."

He kissed her soft cheek. "Ah, but you're my favorite box of baseball bats."

"So, this trip to California—"

"I'm sorry, Wilda. I can't."

"But—"

"I'll see you next week at Thanksgiving, yes?"

Her shoulders sagged in surrender. "What's the latest I can be there and not be considered late?"

"Two p.m."

"I'll be there at one fifty-nine."

"I'll save you a seat."

"As far from those barbarous children as possible."

"Montauk is one hundred and fifteen miles away. Is that far enough?"

She screwed up her nose like Clara Bow's grandmother. "Touché, you little stinker."

3

*L*uke sipped at his Pabst Blue Ribbon and tried not to wince.

Wilda kept her eyes on Tony's youngest daughter as she asked Luke. "If you hate beer so much, why drink it?"

"It's not that I despise it."

"Do you not hear that pained whimper you make every time you swallow?"

Trailing a twelve-foot paper streamer behind her, little Carol was completing her third circuit around the backyard. It was a wonder she hadn't tripped over Vic's Newfoundland puppy or the water hose curled outside Rico's back door.

"You can't talk." He tapped Wilda's glass with his beer. "You enjoy Pimm's Cup as much as I enjoy this swill."

She held it up to the wan November sun. "If only they would replace Pimm's Number One with gin, throw out all that garnish garbage, and fill the remaining space with tonic water."

"Wouldn't that just make it a gin and tonic?"

"But instead, I must suffer through this revolting concoction with the dopey grin of an opium addict prostrate in some smoky den of iniquity in Hong Kong."

Little Carol's right foot caught itself under the exposed root of her mother's lilac tree and she plummeted face down in the dirt. A piercing wail rang out. The closest adult was Sal's wife, Faith, who stopped organizing her eight dishes of Thanksgiving stuffing and helped the brat to her feet.

"That frightful child has nobody to blame but herself," Wilda said. "Just like I have only myself to blame for bringing up Pimm's Number One in conversation once, and now they think it's what I drink."

Carol's shock at falling into the dirt evolved into a regretful howl at having spoiled her new gingham Thanksgiving dress and scuffed her shiny white shoes. Tony turned from the barbeque, where he was grilling six steaks the size of dinner plates and tossed his empty bottle of Pabst at a trash can. He missed by a wide margin and hit Sara's rose bush instead.

"For cryin' out loud, Carol," he yelled, "quit your damned whining."

"My dress was brand new and now it's muddy."

"Mommy will wash it tomorrow. It'll be fine."

"But Daddy! I—"

"MAYBE YOU SHOULDN'T HAVE BEEN RUNNING AROUND, YOU LITTLE DUMBASS!" He turned back to the grill, leaving his soiled daughter gaping like a beached halibut.

"Oh, my stars and garters," Wilda murmured. "Does your brother always talk to his children that way?"

"Only after the third drink."

"How often is that?"

"Most nights."

She pulled the hem of her dress over her knee. "I still say Tony has a chip on his shoulder because he's the second son."

Wilda tilted her head toward Enzo, who was sitting on the steps of his back porch shoulder to shoulder with Sal. Both were heavy across the forehead and barrel-chested; the two were father and son right down to the tufts of coarse hair sprouting from the backs of their fingers. Luke had inherited the Valenti physique, too. There was no denying he was a Valenti, but his mother's northern Italian heritage had tempered his body somewhat. His skin wasn't quite so Mediterranean-olive as his siblings', and his dark-brown hair contrasted with their asphalt-black. He was also a foot shorter and fifty pounds lighter than his siblings. The 'runt of the litter' epithet wasn't so completely out of line, after all.

He couldn't hear what Pop and Sal were talking about, but he didn't need to. The U.S.'s imminent entry into the European conflict was all the Valentis had talked about since the sinking of the *Reuben James*. Uniforms, firearms, battalions, basic training. Lend-Lease. The Battle of Moscow. Would the neutrality pact between Japan and the Soviet Union hold?

What would the family say if Luke showed them his lighthouse letter? Would they be impressed? He doubted it. In their eyes, the Coast Guard barely counted as military. Not that Luke had any intention of telling them of his application. At least not until he was accepted.

The aroma of the three fifteen-pound turkeys that Luke's mom and two of her daughters-in-law had been cooking since nine filled the yard.

"I'll say this for your mother," Wilda said, nesting the untouched Pimm's Cup in her lap. "She may not be the warmest person in the world, but she sure can roast a delicious bird."

Luke attempted another sip, but the beer soured his mouth. If he tipped the contents into the daisy bed behind them, would anyone notice? "Mom swears by Leonetti's on Eighteenth Avenue. She always says, 'If there's one thing Bruno Leonetti knows, it's his meat.'" He stifled a little chuckle. "I don't think she's ever caught on how dirty she sounds." He waited for Wilda to volley back a witty retort, but instead she sat upright, stiff as a statue, her face drained of color. "You okay?"

"It's. Nothing. Really." Her words popped out in terse, blunt gasps as she lifted her Pimm's Cup and pretended to take a sip.

Rico's wife and Vic's oldest son were singing "You Are My Sunshine," unaware how wildly off-pitch they were as Cal plucked what sounded like a whole different tune on his ukulele. "Distract me."

Luke cast about for inspiration, but her face was so ghastly pale he had trouble landing on a topic. He decided on Broadway; theater always excited her. "Did you see that *Times* article about what a heyday Broadway is having right now?" She shook her head. "Ethel Merman in *Panama Hattie*, Lillian Hellman's *Watch on the Rhine*, Eugene O'Neill's *Ah, Wilderness*. And that guy in *Pal Joey*. They're saying he's really going to be somebody. I forget his name, though."

"Gene Kelly."

"And the comedy about the two little old ladies who murder their gentleman callers—the producers searched all over for a Boris Karloff type to play the brother, and in the end, they said, 'Why not just cast Boris Karloff?'"

"Luke, dear, I think I'll go." She gulped at the air.

"What's the matter?" Luke asked. "And don't say 'nothing.'"

"It'll pass, but I prefer to be in my own home."

"I'll ask Pop if I can borrow his car."

"I'd rather walk."

"All the way to Prospect Park?"

"I feel better when in motion. Walk me home, please."

Audrey, T.J., and Cal were now slaughtering "When the Saints Go Marching In," and the rest of the family was cheering them on. "Let's just slip out the side gate. They won't miss us."

They were almost at Gravesend Park before Wilda spoke again.

"Luke, darling, there's something we need to discuss."

"If it's the Montauk thing—"

"Your choices are your choices." She waited until a couple of young girls in matching striped rompers skipped past them. She leaned more heavily on his arm and slowed her pace. "I have a request."

"I'll do anything for you. You know that."

"You won't like it, but I'm asking, anyway." The lights of the 18th Avenue Bakery threw a warm glow across the sidewalk. She stopped and looked earnestly into Luke's face. "Take Irving's falcon back to Hollywood."

Sweet Jesus. Anything but that. "The lighthouse people will be—"

"I'm going to insist." *Insist?* Wilda had never done that before. This was a bigger deal than Luke realized. She took him by the hands. "You need to go, Luke. *Now.*"

"Trust me, I get it. Irving's worried that his brother will get caught for stealing that statue. But I'm not the one—"

"Irving has been a wonderful friend to me over the years. Simon, too, when he still lived here. Every day he sends Irving a Western Union asking when the falcon is coming back. He's petrified of losing his job. Irving can't take the time, and I'm in no shape to travel. You're the only person I can ask." The stridency cracked her voice. "Please do this for me."

He softened his tone. "I'll know about the lighthouse situation by the end of the year. What if I went the first week in January?"

"Please, Luke. I don't mean to get all Ethel Barrymore melodramatic on you, but I want you to think of this as a final request."

The word 'final' struck a harsh chord through Luke's chest. "What does that mean?"

She looped an arm and set them in motion again. "My health isn't fabulous. I've got heart disease. Myocardial something-or-other. The other word is long and medical and has no meaning other than it's irreversible and there's no operation. So it's rather serious, I'm afraid."

He wanted to wrap his arms around her and tell her everything would be all right, but she was hauling him along 18th

Avenue with the determination of a sled dog. "How serious, exactly?"

"That's the thrill of it. I could go next week or next month, or I might still be around this time next year."

Wilda wasn't yet seventy. She was the most alive person he knew. He couldn't lose her. In ten, fifteen, twenty years, maybe, but not now. Not yet.

They passed the yeshiva on 55th Street. Luke was thankful the city was all but deserted. He couldn't have withstood this news amid the bustle of the crowds that usually filled the store doorways and curbs.

"So?" she asked. "Will you go?"

"Lookit, I feel bad for Simon." The sob in his voice burned his throat. "It's a tough predicament, but I can't leave you, not if your heart could fail at any time. I don't want to be more than a few blocks away."

"Oh, Luke, my darling boy, this isn't just about Simon's job. I fear that if you get into the lighthouse program or move to Montauk, you won't experience the world outside New York. You'll settle down into your routine, and life will march past your window. It rips at my heart." She drew a theatrically wobbly circle over her chest. "My weak, diseased little heart. At least give yourself a little adventure. One week and you'll be back. I swear to you on my freshly turned grave—"

"WILDA!"

"The chances of me dropping dead in the next week are very slim. The doctor talked in terms of months—"

"What is he, psychic? How about we consult Madame Zelda down on Riegelmann Boardwalk? Let's see if she can give us a more accurate schedule."

She threw him a withering look. "Months, plural. Not weeks. Not days. And what are the chances these lighthouse people say 'Now or never, bub'? And if they do, I'll use my irresistible charm. If I can't persuade them over the telephone to postpone your interview, I'll cast my magical spell in person. Meanwhile, you get to broaden your horizons before you settle down to live the rest of your life a measly hundred twenty miles from where you started."

Luke had thought that moving to the farthermost tip of Long Island was ambitious and daring; Wilda had made him see it wasn't that far at all. And it wasn't like she was asking him to *move* to California. Just to take the falcon to Warner Bros. and come home.

"This news about your heart is bad enough," he told her, "but the next week or two could determine the course of the rest of my life."

"And yet I'm asking you anyway."

"Insisting, is more like it."

"Lighthouses up and down the eastern seaboard will still be here when you get back. And if the Coast Guard says no, you have my unequivocal blessing to move to Montauk, because, let's face it darling, you have to get away from those people back there."

"Hey! That's my precious family you're talking about."

"They can be your family *and* awful at the same time."

She let out a snicker, as infectious as a tropical disease. It set him off and soon the two of them were giggling. He snuck a furtive side glance at her. The old broad had been the only person in his corner for as long as he could remember. He'd do anything for her. But travel to Los Angeles? Now? Of all times?

"So?" She prodded his ribs with a bony elbow. "You'll go?"

"I really don't want to."

"You can't deny me my dying wish."

"'Dying wish'? Now you're just playing dirty pool."

She looked up at him, a knowing smile filling her face. She had him and she knew it.

4

---

*T*he Atchison, Topeka and Santa Fe's Super Chief glided into Union Station amid a swirl of steam. Luke remained seated until the view outside his window cleared. A pair of men, each gripping a large camera, scuttled past. They were heading toward the locomotive end, which gave weight to the rumor that the first-class passenger who'd never left their compartment had been, depending on the gossipmonger, Sonja Henie, Ronald Colman, Ginger Rogers, or Janet Gaynor.

When Luke stepped off the train, a Pullman porter in a circular cap welcomed him to Los Angeles. "Suitcases still on board?"

He held up the two Boston bags Irving had lent him. "I won't be here too long. Where can I find a cab?"

The porter pointed to a ramp at the end of the platform. "Down there, turn right, and keep walking till you're outside."

Luke hefted his bags and set off. The ramp led to a wide concourse that was busy, but nowhere near as sardine-packed as Grand Central.

Gosh, had he been gone from Brooklyn three days already? The plains of Kansas, winding upward into the Continental

Divide, the barren deserts of Arizona, and the lush orchards around Pasadena. That trip had felt like a movie had unfolded outside his window.

The end of the concourse opened into a cavernous hall rising to a cathedral ceiling. A pathway of diamond tiles bisected rows of leather-padded seating, spacious enough to accommodate a canoodling couple. Dozens of travelers filled the waiting area, and yet a calming hush blanketed the air.

Where was the hustle? The bustle? The pushing? The shoving? Did nobody gripe and grouse here? Boorish people hurled themselves onto the streets of Brooklyn with a communal creed: Run or get run over. But here everybody was so gentle, so genteel, so *polite*. This was going to take some getting used to.

He stepped outside. The sun hit his face, playful like a friendly slap, its warmth tingling his skin.

Heat? In December? What kind of crazy, upside-down place was this? Where were the overcoats and wool-lined boots? The frozen rain puddles? The dripping umbrellas and the scarves that still smelled faintly of mothballs? Surely the come-to-sunny-California booster advertisements with their bathing nymphs and bronzed athletes only existed in travel brochures?

A row of palm trees, each of them upright like a soldier at attention, lined the driveway. Past them, across a wide boulevard, lay a circular plaza, ringed with wooden park benches, and exotic shade trees Luke didn't recognize. He lifted his hand to flag the taxi at the head of the line.

If I see an actual street paved with gold, he thought, I'm going to pass out.

Luke read the vertical sign in front of an Art Deco theater. "You have Pantages out here, too?"

"Where you from?" the cabdriver asked.

"Brooklyn."

"Long way."

Luke leaned back in the seat and started humming the song that had been buzzing around his head since leaving Union Station.

The year he turned eleven, Wilda had taken him to see Gertrude Lawrence at the Majestic. He had never witnessed anyone as graceful and poised as the star standing center stage, arms raised, her beaded gown shimmering in the spotlight. As he and Wilda rode the subway home, they'd sung what they could remember of the show's peppiest number. "On the Sunny Side of the Street" came back to him now as he watched the locals amble along the sidewalk: women in wide-brimmed hats, men in form-fitting three-piece suits, their shoes polished to a high shine.

The cab pulled up at the traffic lights. "Ever heard of Holly-wood and Vine?" the cabbie asked him.

A café called Melody Lane stood on the right-hand corner. Opposite it, an enormous neon sign, *THE BROADWAY-HOLLY-WOOD*, crowned a ten-story building. "Is this it?"

The driver pointed to a drugstore on their left. "The straw-berry blonde with the spit curls is Delores. She brews the coffee, and her husband bakes the best bear claws in town. Bar none."

The lights changed, and they moved forward past a succession of milliners, shoe stores, men's haberdashers, and beauty parlors. These streets were so clean, as though a battalion of janitors had spent the previous night on their knees scrubbing away every speck of grime.

Or maybe it was the air. Back home, a sharp edge tinged everything with icy rigidity. But here, the California sunlight had a benevolent haze to it, softening all the hard edges.

They approached a busy intersection where a sprawling building teemed with balconies and bell towers; a six-sided turret at one corner rose to a peak. The driver swung onto the Holly-wood Hotel's semi-circular driveway and braked to a stop. Luke paid the fare and climbed out of the car. A puff of sweet honeysuckle wafted past him. In December? He sniffed at the air again. And oranges?

A huddle of women, all hair buns and cameo brooches, crowded the check-in desk along with a flotilla of loaded luggage carts. Luke parked his bags near the end and looked around.

The foyer had low ceilings with pale wood rafters. Clusters of straight-backed seating dotted the long room. Vast rugs covered the floor, lending a welcomingly snug atmosphere. Luke took off his felt Homburg and fanned himself as an announcer's voice emerged through the speakers of the large cathedral radio that filled the end of the counter.

"And now, coming to you live from Carnegie Hall, the New York Philharmonic featuring Arthur Rubinstein at the keyboard playing the Brahms Piano Concerto Number Two in B-flat major, opus eighty-three."

Wilda would often play these broadcasts as they sipped Darjeeling together. When the first notes from a French horn wafted over him now, a pang squeezed Luke's ribcage. He clutched the edge of the desk to steady himself. A shocking thought socked him in the chest. Was this homesickness? For a place he was planning to leave? The pain abated almost as quickly as it had gripped him. The New York Philharmonic cascaded through the speakers as the concerto gathered momentum. Luke imagined Rubinstein's hands blurring as they skittered up and down the keyboard.

Without warning, the music subsided.

"With apologies to our listeners, we must interrupt this broadcast." A note of uncertainty underscored the announcer's voice. "We have received reports of attacks on Pearl Harbor."

The six women turned toward the radio. "How ridiculous," the one closest to Luke said. "Why would they break into their Sunday broadcast to talk about taxes?"

The woman to her right asked the clerk, "Where is Pearl

Harbor? Is it near Santa Monica? My nephew lives there. He's out of work. Ought I be concerned?"

"Not taxes," Luke told them. "I'm pretty sure he said attacks."

The old biddies crowded around him.

"We have confirmation from the Department of the Navy that Japanese forces have struck the U.S. Naval base of Pearl Harbor on the Hawaiian island of Oahu, four miles from Honolulu."

"I bet you five dollars this is another of Orson Welles' pranks," one woman said, "like he did with *War of the Worlds*. Why, the very thought of Japs attacking us—it's laughable."

"Initial details are sketchy," the announcer continued, "but early accounts indicate that the primary targets are Hickam Field, Wheeler Field, and Bellows Field, where the bulk of U.S. Army Air Force aircraft are parked. At least seven battleships are currently moored at or near Pearl Harbor. The surprise assault commenced this morning just before eight o'clock Hawaiian time. We shall now return you to our musical program."

"How far behind us is Hawaii?" The crowd around the radio had swelled to dozens of people.

"Three hours," the clerk replied.

"So the attack might still be . . .?"

One of the women whimpered. "My, oh my."

Another one joined her. "Whatever shall we do?"

The woman who had thought the whole episode was an Orson Welles prank clasped her hands together like a kindergarten teacher. "Ladies, I suggest we settle into our rooms and reconvene in the foyer at noon."

A trio of porters led the party away as Rubinstein continued to thunder through the Brahms.

The desk clerk wiped his forehead. "Checking in?"

"You should have a reservation under the name of Valenti."

He handed Luke a room key as applause from the radio audience poured through the speakers. *The Star-Spangled Banner* started up. Luke and the clerk stared at each other as the Philharmonic improvised its way through the national anthem.

Unpacking his bags took all of ten minutes. By the time he'd returned to the foyer, fifty or sixty people were gathered around the radio. The musical program had switched to The Ink Spots singing "When the Swallows Come Back to Capistrano."

Hunger gnawing at his innards, Luke set out along Hollywood Boulevard to the drugstore his cab driver had pointed out.

This was not, however, the animated thoroughfare he'd witnessed an hour before. It no longer buzzed with shoppers and Sunday strollers. Passers-by now marched, heads down, hats pulled low. A Jack Russell terrier trotted alongside his master, nose and tail down, not once stopping to sniff a tree or watch a squirrel.

The Owl drugstore was half full. A radio on a shelf over an Old Gold cigarettes display played a Glenn Miller tune, "Fools Rush In," amid the clatter of dishes and whoosh of the soda fountain.

Luke headed to a public telephone in the corner and dropped a dime into the slot. After ten rings, the voice of a harried housewife yelled, "This had better be my husband calling to tell me that he's had a change of heart."

"Mrs. Kovner?" Luke blurted out. "My name is Luke Valenti. I'm looking for Simon."

"Who isn't?"

"I arrived from Brooklyn this morning—"

Mrs. Kovner snorted down the line. "You've picked a hell of a day. Have you heard the news?"

"Yes, ma'am."

"Listen, kiddo, I got four screaming kids, a missing husband, and now we're probably at war. If you want to leave a message, you need to hurry it along."

"Please tell him I've checked into the Hollywood Hotel and assure him that I have the package."

"Package of what?"

He hadn't even told his wife? No wonder Irving had instructed him to speak only with Simon. "Just ask him—"

"GEORGIE! PUT THAT SKILLET DOWN! AND I MEAN RIGHT *NOW!*"

Luke waited until the muffled caterwauling stopped. "Have him call me at the hotel." He got a distracted "Sure" before she slammed down the receiver.

He took a seat at the counter and ordered a burger, fries, and orange phosphate soda. The place fell quiet when an announcer interrupted a Tommy Dorsey tune.

"We have an update from our Honolulu bureau on the devastation at Pearl Harbor. Battleships USS *Pennsylvania*, *California*, and *Arizona* have been hit, as well as cruisers *Raleigh* and *Helena*, and several destroyers. The U.S. Navy has acknowledged that the human death toll will be in the hundreds."

The spit-curled waitress strummed the counter with her fingernails. "Them dirty little Japs want a fight? They sure got one on their hands now. Ain't that right, Horrie?"

A thick-set bruiser with bushy eyebrows grunted over his bowl of chili two seats down from Luke.

On any other day in any other drugstore, Luke would have enjoyed the way this orange phosphate tingled his tongue. But its sharp, sour taste left him wishing he'd ordered something more soothing. More familiar. Like a chocolate malted.

If the Japs were brave enough to attack a U.S. Naval base, what would stop them from striking California? This place, Luke decided, might be drenched in golden sunlight, its streets scrubbed clean, and its air honeysuckle sweet, but it wasn't where he belonged.

* * *

In the dining room the following morning, Luke ordered buckwheat cakes, with a poached egg, a side of bacon, and a grapefruit juice, then asked the waitress where he might get a copy of the *New York Times*. She told him, "We've got our own *Times*," and produced a discarded newspaper from a neighboring table. He stared at the four-inch banner headline.

IT'S WAR!

His eyes ran down the front page.

Hostilities Declared by Japanese
350 Reported Killed in Hawaii Raid; 7 Die in Honolulu
U.S. Battleships Hit as Air Bombs Rain on Pacific Bases
Roosevelt to Address Nation at Noon

The waitress delivered Luke his breakfast as a loudspeaker on the wall hummed with indistinct chatter. At nine o'clock, a deep-voiced commentator announced, "The next voice you hear will be President Roosevelt live from the U.S. Congress."

Luke pictured Mom and Pop, all five brothers, their wives and kids jammed around the Philco. Mom would be bribing the children with snickerdoodles to keep them quiet; Pop would be predicting Roosevelt's next move. Luke didn't need to be sitting in that living room to know how this scene would play out, but he longed to be there as history unfolded.

"Mr. Vice President, and Mr. Speaker, and Members of the Senate and House of Representatives." Roosevelt's voice was low and deliberate, weighed down by the task at hand. "Yesterday, December 7, 1941, a date which will live in infamy, the United States of America was suddenly and deliberately attacked by naval and air forces of the Empire of Japan."

Luke's breakfast grew cold as Roosevelt laid out the country's position that negotiations to maintain peace in the Pacific had ended. He talked of the severe damage done to American naval and military forces, of deliberately false statements, and of reports that Japan was torpedoing American ships between San Francisco and Honolulu.

Luke stole a furtive glance around the room. None of the sixty or seventy souls near him appeared to be breathing as Roosevelt concluded. "I ask that the Congress declare that since the unprovoked and dastardly attack by Japan on Sunday, December 7, 1941, a state of war has existed between the United States and the Japanese Empire."

Seven minutes. That's all it had taken to usher the world into its bleak future.

In Luke's room upstairs, a falcon statue lay inside one of his Boston bags. He needed to drop it off as soon as he could and jump on the next train heading east.

The taxicab rounded a curve in the road; a long, pale building came into view. Three stories high and dotted with ventilator windows at regular intervals, it looked more like a warehouse than the glamorous movie studio Luke had pictured.

As they drew nearer, the words painted along the side sharpened.

Home of
WARNER BROS. FIRST NATIONAL PICTURES
and Cosmopolitan Productions

The driver braked at a sign: Gate Two. Luke paid his fare and climbed out, gripping the handles of his bag a little more tightly. A security guard stood at a window marked *Employees*. A brass "WB" shield pinned to his cap glinted in the morning light.

"My name is Luke Valenti. I'm here to see Simon Kovner in the props department."

The guard ran his eye down a typed list fastened to a clipboard. "Nope."

Luke had waited all afternoon and evening for word from Simon, but none had come. Despite the steamroller of history crushing everything in its path these past twenty-four hours, surely Simon was still anxious about his missing falcon?

"With what's happened lately, there's probably been a mix-up."

"Jap bombers could be heading right for us, so studios have been deemed a high-risk target. If you ain't on my list, you ain't getting in."

Luke landed Irving's bag on the counter. "Simon Kovner is waiting on this. A quick call could straighten everything out."

The guard didn't take his eyes off Luke as he picked up the telephone at his elbow and dialed three numbers. "This is Sid at Gate Two. Simon there?" Luke maintained his smile as the guard uh-huh'd several times before hanging up. "You're outta luck. Simon has enlisted as a seaman."

"It's not even been twenty-four hours!"

"Which gives him the distinction of being the first employee to sign up. And that's going to impress Mr. Warner."

Irving had told Luke to speak only to Simon. There had been no plan B covering the outbreak of war.

Impatience spread across Sid's face.

Luke retrieved the box inside the bag, opened the top flap, and pulled out the falcon. "I'm from the Burbank Glazing Company. Simon sent this to us for a professional polishing job because Mr. Warner wants to use it for some big roadshow he's got planned." Sid crinkled his forehead and strummed his fingers, but he wasn't saying 'get lost.' "My boss gave me strict instructions to deliver it into Mr. Kovner's—*only* Mr. Kovner's—hands."

"Sorry, kid, but I got my regulations."

"Do I look like a Japanese spy?" Luke attempted a buddy-buddy grin. Sid sucked at his teeth and bobbed his head back and forth. The sucker was softening. Luke spotted a folded *Brooklyn Eagle* lying on the desk. "I see you're from Brooklyn."

"Fresno." Luke pointed to the newspaper. "Oh, that. It's Burt's."

"Did someone say Brooklyn?" A second guard appeared. More weathered than Sid, he looked like an old-time whaler. "Which neighborhood?"

"Bensonhurst," Luke said. "Sixty-seventh Street at Sixteenth Avenue."

"No foolin'? I grew up just off Ocean Parkway. My dad used to run Steeplechase Park."

"Spent practically all my summers there." The only place louder than his family's house was Coney Island, so Luke avoided it as much as possible. "My dad's done a bunch of jobs there." Another bald-faced lie.

"What does he do?"

It was, on occasion, handy to be a Valenti. Like in a dark alley next to the Brooklyn Fox Theatre—or at the security gate of a Hollywood studio. "You probably saw our trucks. Valenti Construction."

The guard nudged Sid. "'We'll treat you like family.' That's their motto." He turned back to Luke. "A Valenti, huh? I'll be a monkey's uncle. Whatcha doing here?"

The guard from Brighton Beach nodded his head as Sid explained the situation. Nod by nod, his face took on the same we've-got-these-new-regulations frown.

"Brooklyn native to Brooklyn native," Luke said, trying to squash the desperation in his voice, "I give you my word that I'll deliver this bird to the prop department and be on my way."

The next few seconds stretched into hours until the guard

filled in a day pass and slid it over. "Take this road. Around the halfway mark you'll see the sign. Thirty minutes. Don't make me come looking for you."

Luke slipped it into his pocket and lifted his fedora. "Got it. And thank you."

A handmade sign in the door window read *Closed for lunch 12:30 to 1:15.* Luke checked his watch; it was 12:35. He tried the handle anyway; it was locked.

He couldn't just leave it sitting on the front step. Could he? No. This was *the* Maltese falcon, not a box of lemons from some neighbor's tree.

A corpulent figure in a three-piece suit lumbered toward him. When he spotted Luke, he lifted his Panama hat. "You look lost, young man." It was Sydney Greenstreet, right there in the portly, shambling, button-straining flesh.

"I'm supposed to deliver this package," Luke replied, "but they're at lunch."

"Isn't that the height of inconvenience?" Greenstreet fanned himself with the Panama. "You're more than welcome to wait in the shade of our soundstage." The idea of a warm sun in December was still a novelty, but who in their right mind refused an invitation from Kaspar Gutman? Luke nodded and fell in with the guy's heavy-footed gait. "Is that a prop you have there?"

If someone had told Luke two weeks ago that he'd be walking alongside The Fat Man, he would have laughed them out of the Brooklyn Fox. But while carrying the actual Maltese falcon? Luke would have asked the redhead to call the nearest nut house. He said nothing and kept walking.

Greenstreet let out a surprisingly high-pitched giggle. "Top secret, eh? These Hollywood people. They take it all so seriously. Not to worry." He held open a door for Luke. "I fear I need to revisit the makeup chair. Please excuse me. You'll find plenty of seats hither and yon."

The commotion of a busy studio subsided as the door closed behind them and Greenstreet waddled away. Luke moved closer to the movie set standing in the middle of the stage. It was like someone had taken a huge knife and carved out the deck of a ship. A thick mat lay at the end nearest Luke, the sort that a tumbling gymnast might use. To the right, a man in a white shirt with rolled-up sleeves sat slumped over a desk, his face pressed into the center of his crossed arms.

The light from the set slipped across the man's shoulders. Was it . . .? Could he . . .? . . .possibly be . . .?

Sydney Greenstreet in the flesh was one thing. But Humphrey Bogart?

Four men, roughly Luke's age, lounged against a wall lined with mattresses. One of them, beefier than his pals, swiped his hand through the air. "You deadbeats have never tried their Deluxe Corned Beef on Russian rye?"

"I'm telling you," the guy next to him insisted, "the Number Five Club-Style sandwich. There ain't nothing better at Schwab's."

For years, Luke had been hearing about Schwab's Pharmacy, but only in magazines, movies, and newsreels. It hadn't occurred to him that it was the sort of place regular folks ate at. If it was near his hotel, he could go there for dinner. What a story that'd make to tell Aunt Wilda when he got home.

"Hey pal!" The beefy guy jutted out his chin. "You need to speak with him?" Luke stared at the slumbering figure. "He ain't no dainty baby doll. Just shake him by the shoulder. He'll wake up quick as a firecracker."

Luke hated to awaken him, but maybe Bogart could slip the falcon into the props department with nobody the wiser. He had less than ten minutes before his half-hour was up. He nudged Bogart's shoulder. The actor moaned, but didn't move. Luke tried again, more firmly.

Bogart shot up to a sitting position, squeezed his eyes tight, then flung them open. "Was that you?"

The four men leaning against the mattresses now had their hands pressed to their mouths, stifling their laughter.

Bogart slammed a fist against the table. "Never—*never!*—wake me up unless the cameras are about to roll."

"No, sir, I—"

"Do you see the cameraman? The director?" Bogart pulled his mouth into a snarl. "Are the lights on, the extras in place, the clapperboard guy ready to go *snap?*"

"No, sir, I—"

"Get the *hell* out of my sight, the *hell* off this set, and the *hell* away from this studio. I don't want to see your bug-eyed puss around here again."

Luke backed away, disappointment crushing him. Where was Sam Spade, the laconic loner who rolled his own cigarettes, the terse gumshoe whose cynicism kept him from being duped by connivers and liars?

Humphrey Bogart was nothing more than a bawling, bellowing bully.

And Luke Valenti knew all about bullies. He'd grown up surrounded by them. Always shouting. Always throwing their weight around. There was only one way to deal with people like that.

"All right!" Luke yelled. "So you were asleep, and I woke you up. I'm sorry, okay? I haven't been to a motion picture studio before. And you, Mister Bogart, are the very first movie star I've ever encountered." Bogart opened his mouth to reply, but this yelling back business felt too good. "Frankly, if the rest of them are as ill-tempered, sullen, and crotchety as you, I'll be happy as a turkey the day after Thanksgiving if you're my last."

The nearest door led him back to the main roadway that took him to the exit. At the security gate, he tossed his pass onto the counter without breaking stride. Reaching the street, he charged toward the hills. He recalled seeing a streetcar line on the taxicab ride over and figured he'd come across it eventually. And if not, he would keep walking until he ran out of steam.

At the top of the hill, the tracks stretched in both directions. Left or right? He hadn't a clue. Eeny, meeny, miny, moe and hope for the best.

It wasn't until he was standing at the streetcar stop that he felt the weight of his Boston bag. Jesus! He still had this damned falcon.

5

---

*A*s the mellow California morning sun filtered through his hotel window, Luke stared at the box on the dresser. He couldn't go back to the Warner studios, not after he had lambasted one of their stars.

Disappointment still pressed against his chest. What a letdown Bogart had been.

Actors weren't their characters. Luke knew that, of course. Bogart wasn't a taciturn private eye any more than he was the truck driver he had played in *They Drive by Night*, or the stable master in *Dark Victory*. But gosh almighty, did he have to be such a foul-tempered, angry-eyed grouch?

There had to be some other way to fix this. And quickly. He had reservations on the train back to New York leaving at eight that evening. What if he cabled Wilda and told her to convince Irving to contact Bogart and explain what Simon had done? Oh, God. Eleven o'clock already? Two p.m. East Coast time. Short of a miracle involving divine intervention, he had no other choice but to move his reservation.

· · ·

Hollywood Boulevard had regained some of the vigor Luke had felt the morning he'd arrived. Had it only been forty-eight hours? Since then, the Japs had destroyed a U.S. naval base, the country had plunged into war, and he'd yelled at a famous movie star.

He spotted a vertical electric sign flashing the Santa Fe Railway logo. Inside, a line of passengers snaked out the door. An hour passed before Luke stood in front of a guy with the florid cheeks of someone asking himself if it was too early for a drink.

"I have a reservation on tonight's Super Chief."

"'Fraid not. They've all been cancelled."

"How is that possible?"

"New government rules give military personnel priority."

"But the attack on Pearl Harbor only happened two days ago."

The clerk arched a jaded eyebrow. "Almost makes you wonder if they saw it coming—not that I'm spouting rumors, you understand. These rules came down late yesterday afternoon and now everybody wants to leave the coast in case we're next. Trouble is, see, each train has an allowance of four civilian seats per departure. The first spot I can offer you is April twenty-fourth."

"I can't be stuck here till spring."

He stared at Luke, his face as deadpan as Buster Keaton's. "Unless you know President Roosevelt, the head of the Army, or the chairman of the Santa Fe Railway, there's not a lot I can do."

"I need to be back in New York by the end of the week."

"How do you feel about hitchhiking?"

Even Wilda's considerable charms couldn't put the Coast Guard off until April. "What about Greyhound?"

"They have only a two-seat civilian allotment. Now, if you have no further questions, I have the same news to break to a thousand other people before we close tonight."

"Western Union?"

The clerk pointed farther up Hollywood Boulevard. "Two blocks thataway."

* * *

Luke picked up the pencil.

STUCK IN LA STOP
SIMON IN NAVY STOP
STILL HAVE FALCON STOP
HAVE YOU HEARD FROM LIGHTHOUSE STOP

He had enough money to last him a week, maybe two if he economized. He could ask Wilda for a loan and pay her back out of his savings account. But it would have to come out of his Montauk stash, and he needed two hundred to make his escape. It had taken him so long to get this far; the thought of sliding back made him gag worse than the idea of begging mommy and daddy for a handout.

By the time he paid for the telegram, his stomach churned from hunger. "I'm not from around here," he told the clerk. "Can you recommend a decent place for lunch?"

"The Gotham Deli opposite Grauman's Chinese is pretty good," she told him. "And of course the Brown Derby over on Vine. Stars and bigwigs eat there."

"Sounds expensive."

"I wouldn't know." She giggled into her hand. "I'm never the one who's paying."

"And if you were?"

"Schwab's. Up on Sunset."

The word "Sunset" slugged the bruises around the memory of yesterday's skirmish.

"Can I walk there from here?"

"Take you about forty minutes, I guess."

"I hear the Number Five Club-Style sandwich is good."

"Number Three's better. And the Black Beauty sundae for dessert. You won't regret it."

Neon tubing silhouetted each letter.

SCHWAB'S PHARMACY

Luke pushed the glass door; a flurry of bright chatter and the clink of thick crockery flew at him. To the left, the usual pharmacy items—talcum powder, shoelaces, toiletries, hairbrushes, magazines, candy—filled dark wood display cases. On the back wall, another neon sign proclaimed SCHWAB'S – PRESCRIPTION DRUGS – FINE WINES & LIQUORS. A lunch counter ran the length of the right-hand side.

The honest-to-goodness real-life Schwab's Pharmacy in Hollywood, California, was a little more intimidating than he cared to admit. He sat on a stool and peeked over his menu so that he could study the place in the reflection of the mirrors filling the wall in front of him. Two gents in straw boaters were arguing over the merits of someone named Mank and whether he was the right scribbler for the Gehrig picture before they moved on to talking about a troubled RKO project called Ambersons.

A round face with sharp eyes caught his attention. The girl, around his age, was staring at him. She wore her hair in a Louise Brooks bob that brushed the top of her shoulders as she sipped her root beer.

The waitress approached him. "What'll it be?"

By the time Luke had finished giving his order, the girl had moved to the empty stool next to him.

The bottom of her glass cracked against the counter. "You sure can walk fast." Her cheeks dimpled when she grinned. "I followed you yesterday after your performance on Stage Seven."

"At Warner Brothers? You were there?"

"And real entertaining it was, too."

Her tone was more mischievous than malicious, but her words made him squirm. Had he not ordered his lunch, he might have stalked off rather than deal with this smart-mouthed Hollywood type, who probably knew if Mank was the right scribbler for the Gehrig picture—whatever that meant.

"Oh, gosh," the girl said. "I've offended you. I came over to compliment you, honest I did."

Luke twisted in his seat to face her squarely. "On how fast I walk?"

A tinkling "Ha-ha-ha!" bubbled out of her. "When you shook Bogie awake, I thought, 'Uh-oh! This rookie doesn't know the unbreakable rule.'"

"I was told that he wouldn't mind."

"You were misinformed." Her smile turned cheeky as the waitress set Luke's butterscotch malted thick shake in front of him. "You gave as good as you got, though."

He sucked down a mouthful of butterscotch. Equal parts creamy and sweet. Delicious. "The whole incident was thoroughly humiliating."

"Listen, if he thinks it's okay to yell, he shouldn't be surprised when he's treated the same way."

"It's just that getting yelled at by someone like Humphrey Bogart... It's—it's—"

"Disappointing? Disillusioning? Disheartening?"

"All of the above."

"You should have stuck around. He felt real bad about what happened."

The fast talkers in the boaters had moved on to Charles Boyer and was he right for *The Constant Nymph* as they paid the cashier.

"I doubt that very much."

"Most of the time he's a bang-up decent guy. He was just hungover, is all. He ran after you, but you'd disappeared."

Humphrey Bogart ran after *me*? As if that would ever happen.

"If you hadn't been so intent on breaking the four-minute mile, you would've received an apology."

The waitress appeared with Luke's club sandwich. He stared at it, feeling the resentment bleeding away.

The girl stuck out her hand. "My name's Nell Davenport."

"Luke Val—" That damned Valenti name. It came with the heavy yoke of history. Sure, it helped him in tight spots from time to time, but more often than not, it weighed him down like a sack of rocks. "Luke Vail."

He bit into his sandwich. The closest he'd ever come to an avocado was a photograph in *Life* magazine. The texture was like soft butter, but with a cucumber-y taste that enhanced the sharp zest of the bacon. "You work at Warner Brothers?"

"I'm a continuity girl."

"Which means what?"

"I make notes during each take so that it matches the next one, or the one after that, or the one shot five weeks later."

"You've got an eye for detail." She beamed as though nobody had ever complimented her like that. Maybe nobody ever had. "Why aren't you there right now?"

"The movie we're shooting revolves around the Japs sabo-taging our naval base at Pearl Harbor. That's too close to home now, so they're dreaming up a new plot line. Until they do, I'm a reluctant lady of leisure." She leaned a bit closer, her face suddenly serious. "Listen, I know Bogie will want to apologize to you in person. Let me see if I can get you onto the studio lot. Security is tight—" She gave him a curious look. "Say, how did you get onto the lot in the first place?"

This girl, with her brash smile and bold manner, was so different from the ones back home. They were brash and bold, but with a dog-eat-dog ferocity. This Nell in front of him exuded an irresistibly sunny confidence. *And* she worked at Warners, so maybe she was his way back in.

"Friend of a friend," he told her.

"Don't worry, I'll figure a way. Meeting Bogie can't look like a set-up. I'm thinking lunch in the commissary." She strummed the glass countertop with her fingernails. "Where can I reach you?"

"The Hollywood Hotel."

"The guy in charge of studio security, Blayney Matthews, he's put in a bunch of new regulations since the attack on Pearl Harbor. He just published a book called *The Specter of Sabotage*, so imagine how paranoid he is. What I'm saying is that it might be a week or two."

But that would take them practically through to Christmas. Another week after that and the chance to interview with the lighthouse people would have slipped through his fingers. An apology from Mr. Bogart would be nice, but it wasn't worth risking his future for.

"I don't know how much longer I'll be here."

"Good," Nell said, "because the *Times* had a big article about how, now that we're at war, the cost of housing is about to skyrocket." She sucked up the rest of her root beer and told him she'd be in touch. She turned to go, then turned back. "I really will be in touch. I'm not just saying it to be nice."

He nodded and watched her bound out the door and onto Sunset Boulevard.

Luke entered the hotel foyer. Dozens and dozens of people now filled the stiff-backed chairs and fraying sofas. He approached the front desk and asked for his key.

The clerk fetched it from a hook on the wall. "May I assume you'll be with us one more night?"

"It looks like my stay will be longer than expected."

His smile pinched at the edges. "We're able to extend the original rate for tonight, but after tomorrow, they're going up."

"To what?"

"Twenty-one dollars."

"That's triple!" Not to mention highway robbery.

"I could have already let your room out ten times over."

At twenty-one bucks a night, Luke had enough money for two more nights, assuming he ate nothing. "That puts a wrench in my plans."

The clerk passed the room key across the counter. "Out on the corner, you'll find a newsboy hawking the *Examiner*. There are tons of listings for boarding houses in the classifieds. But don't dawdle. Vacancies won't last long."

The clerk failed to mention how dreary most of the boarding houses scattered throughout Hollywood were. Luke didn't bother ringing the doorbell of the first two. A third one smelled like the tannery his Pop had once dragged him to out near Belmont Park. The room in the fourth one was a little on the dreary side but clean. However, newborn babies were crying their lungs inside out on both sides. The fifth had no screaming infants, nor did it have an actual bed. Just a mattress on the floor.

It was coming up to five o'clock when Luke trudged up the Whitley Avenue hill. The sun was slipping into dusk, the air cooling fast. If this one didn't work out, maybe he could go back to Number Five. Sleeping on the floor wouldn't be so bad if he gave the floorboards a vigorous scrub.

Nineteen-sixteen Whitley Avenue had once been a respectable Victorian mansion, big enough to house a family of six or seven, plus a valet for Father, lady's maid for Mother, a governess for the children, and a carriage house for the horses. But that had been some time ago. Its eaves were now weathered; the porch had a rotting plank and needed a coat of paint. Luke wouldn't have been surprised if every door in the place squeaked like a trapped mouse. But it didn't stink, and he could hear no crying babies.

A knock on the door brought a harried woman with large, moist eyes. Back in their heyday they had probably been camera-ready for luminous close-ups, but now they were more rheumy than radiant.

"My name is Luke Vail." How easily his new identity rolled off his tongue. "I've come about the room."

She took a step back and widened the door.

The vestibule was a perfect square. The walls to the left and right bore flocked wallpaper of an indistinguishable dark color. None of it was peeling away at the corners, and the rug underfoot looked a damned sight newer than anything on the outside.

The landlady started mounting the stairs. "I'm Edith Maine. Like the state." She pushed back the bushel of wayward hair that sprouted like a tumbleweed and regarded him oddly, almost hopefully, as though she rarely met anyone who'd heard of Maine. "Your birthday. When is it?"

Luke wasn't sure why that mattered, but this was already the most inhabitable place he'd seen so far. "February seventh."

"Aquarius. You're a deep thinker, aren't you? Books, books, books. I can see you surrounded by them."

Luke pictured the bookshelf in his room back in Brooklyn. If he told her yes, would he get the room?

She continued up the stairs. "You Aquarius types, you need to be alone to recover from the world, and that's fine. Don't forget, though. You're also a human being. People need people!"

They reached the landing, where a framed movie poster hung. Judging by the lurid artwork, Luke guessed *The Limitless Sky* was an early silent picture. Below the title ran the words *Starring Edith Marvelle*.

"Is that you?" Luke asked.

She sighed. "Marvelle was a ridiculous name when I already had a perfectly adequate one, but that's not how Hollywood works. I played an aviatrix who wants to be the first woman to fly cross-country but who runs into problems over Grizzly Peak."

"Were you good?"

She made another vain attempt to tame her unruly hair. "I was terrific!"

They arrived at a closed door. She pushed it open. "Look around."

None of the walls were of equal length. Luke guessed it had once been larger but had since been divided off. The paint job was intact, the striped rug was in passable condition, and the large window caught what was left of the afternoon sun.

"How much?" Luke asked.

"Seven dollars a week, including breakfast and dinner whether or not you're here to eat it. Breakfast at seven a.m., dinner at seven p.m. Sharp. Shared bathroom with a strict five-minute rule. If you become a bathroom hog, you'll be shown the sidewalk."

No fetid odors, no screeching newborns, a bed with legs, and at a price he could afford. For now, anyway.

"I'll take it," he told her.

"Pay a week in advance and you can move in any time you like."

* * *

Luke's sparse belongings fitted into the top drawer of the bureau with the pewter anchor-shaped knobs. He lifted the Maltese falcon out of its box and placed it on the wobbly bedside table. How the gosh-darned heck he going to offload this thing?

The smell of pot roast drifted up from downstairs. It was after seven now, and Edith had stressed how punctual he needed to be. He took the stairs two at a time and dashed into the dining room. A mismatched pair of crystal candlesticks holding half-used candles sat in the center of a lace tablecloth. The silver cutlery was tarnished but serviceable. There was, however, nobody sitting at any of the seven place settings.

A dull clanging pounded from behind the swing door, which opened into a kitchen where five people stood in a semi-circle. Edith lay on her back on the tiled floor with her head stuck in the cabinet below the sink.

A woman in her seventies looked over at him and said, "Are you our new lodger?" She had a sharp jawline to match her Teutonic accent.

Luke nodded. "Edith, it's Luke here. Plumbing problems?"

"This rotten pipe has clogged up again." She whacked it several times.

"Don't you think it sounds even more blocked now?" This question came from a girl around Luke's age. She was dressed in a matching skirt and jacket. The breast pocket featured an embroidered K.

When Luke joined the semi-circle, a vile stink punched him square on the nose. He'd smelled that same stench several Thanksgivings ago when Cal, the Valenti plumber, had been called out on an emergency. He had needed an extra set of hands, and his other brothers had been too blotto to be much use, so he'd pressed Luke into service.

"Pounding that pipe with a monkey wrench won't fix it," he said, stepping closer and rolling up his sleeves.

"I'm open to suggestions."

"Hand it to me. I'll need a bucket, a jug, baking soda, and vinegar."

Edith wriggled out from under her sink and let a pale chap in his thirties with white-blond hair and barely any eyebrows help her to her feet. She grabbed the four items Luke had requested and lined them up along the counter.

Luke placed the bucket under the curved pipe. He tightened the monkey wrench around the valve at the bottom and loosened it until it came away, releasing an even more fetid odor.

"Peee-yooo!" the K girl exclaimed. "Jeez, Edith, what've you been shoving down there? Human remains?"

Luke emptied the bottle of vinegar into the jug, then dumped in the baking soda. As soon as the mixture started to fizz, he drizzled it down the drain and opened the hot water faucet. His concoction ran free and his spectators cheered his success.

He put the whole contraption back together, mopped up the water, washed his hands and forearms at the sink. "Shall we eat?"

In the dining room, they took their places around the table. K girl was the first to introduce herself. "Beatrice Varney. Pleased to meet you."

Luke pointed to her pocket. "I thought maybe the K was your initial."

"I work at Kress's, the five-and-dime on Hollywood Boulevard. I've got to say, it's great to have a handyman in the house. Unlike these two." She wriggled her fingers at the pale fellow and a swarthy one, much older, with thick, dark hair graying at the temples. The swarthy gent held his hand out for Luke to shake.

"Seymour Black. And this is my wife, Minerva White."

"Black and White—get it?" Beatrice asked. "Stage magicians. Real big in vaudeville, they were."

"We're more of a comedy act," Minerva said. "Bits of magic and quick-change costumes, that sort of thing." She had the same moist eyes as Edith's, and had probably been a striking beauty in her prime. "But vaudeville's deader than a dodo bird, so now we do the rounds of Elks lodges, Moose lodges, Freemasons, high schools." She gave an airy shrug. "Anybody who'll have us."

"Don't forget the movie stars' kids' birthday parties." The pale guy waved. "Tristan Bannister."

"You in showbiz, too?" Luke asked.

"You could call it that." He gestured toward the older woman with the accent. "And this is the oh-so-talented Sabine Vogel."

Twenty years ago, she would have worn her hair in marcelled waves, but now it hung in loose ripples. "And you are . . .?"

"Luke Vail." The more he said his new identity, the more he liked it.

"Are you a screenwriter, Mister Vail?" Sabine asked. "You should be with a name like that."

Edith burst through the swing door holding up a bottle of Riesling. "The last of the stash our Napa Valley salesman left behind. Scrubbing out our notorious hellhole is reason to celebrate. Tristan, you'll find a corkscrew in the top drawer of the sideboard. Beatrice, you know where the nice glasses are." She placed her free hand on Luke's shoulder. "I'm so happy you've joined our little family. And not just because you've fixed the sink."

Tristan returned to the table with the corkscrew. Edith passed the bottle to him to wrestle with.

"As soon as I saw him standing there," she announced to the group, "I thought, 'He's one of us.'"

Edith's words—*He's one of us*—still rang in Luke's ears a half-hour after everyone had finished her pecan date pudding. Everyone said their goodnights and began retreating into their rooms. Luke, too, was heading toward the stairs when the doorbell chimed.

"Would someone get that?" Edith called from the kitchen. "I'm elbow deep in soapsuds."

A Western Union delivery boy stood on the porch, an envelope in his hand. "Luke Valenti?"

"That's me."

Luke took the telegram and, as the messenger trotted back along the garden path to the street, he spotted the Warners girl heading toward him.

"The clerk on the front desk at your hotel gave me your forwarding address." She jumped up the steps and planted herself on the porch, narrowly missing the rotted plank. "I was wondering if you've been to C.C. Brown's yet. They have the best hot fudge ice-cream sundaes."

If I could fix a blocked sink like Cal, maybe I could fix this plank like Tony.

She pointed to the telegram in his hand. "Good news, I hope."

They moved to the right until they stood under the porch light. Luke ripped open the envelope.

NO WORD FROM LIGHTHOUSE STOP
IS FALCON SAFE STOP
WHY ARE YOU STUCK STOP
WRITE ME AND EXPLAIN STOP
LOVE WILDA STOP

Nell flicked Luke's telegram with a fingernail. "I don't mean to pry, but is your landlord okay with you keeping a falcon?"

He crammed Wilda's telegram in his pocket and kept his hand there so that she didn't see it trembling. Back in Brooklyn, he was the Valenti who couldn't build walls like Sal, or carve wood like Tony, or lay wiring like Rico, or fit pipes like Cal, or cement tile like Vic. He had only ever been the surprise baby who'd never fitted in. Nobody had sought him out. Certainly not anyone as cute as Nell Davenport.

"I'd like you to come with me to my room."

She pressed her purse to her chest. "Why, Mr. Vail! You think I'm that kind of girl?"

And she was a kidder. Even better. "What makes you think I'm that kind of guy?"

She let her hands slip to her sides. "They say Hollywood is filled with rakes and leches, but I've yet to meet one."

She followed him upstairs to his room, raising an eyebrow as he closed the door behind them.

He pointed to the falcon on the nightstand.

"Holy cow!" She clapped her hands together in prayer and crushed them against her lips. "Is this the missing one?"

"People already know it's missing?"

"Just a few. I have a pal in Props."

She kept her eyes on the falcon as Luke described the serpentine route of unlikely circumstances that had brought him out to Hollywood.

"Jack Warner has been blathering on and on about his war-bond-selling roadshow. He's hoping that other studios will contribute their famous props to attract crowds all over the country. Your pal here—" she tapped the falcon's head "—will be in the center spotlight, so we need to get this back where it belongs."

"Could you sneak it in for me?"

"I wish. *Across the Pacific* has been shelved until they can replace Pearl Harbor with some other exotic locale. They've shifted me over to *The Big Shot*, but that doesn't start production till January. With Blayney Matthews' wartime restrictions in place, it's like getting in and out of San Quentin. Us small fry are persona non grata until we're working on a picture."

Luke sat heavily on the bed. "Wait until after the new year?"

"We can't. Mr. Warner takes a very dim view of pilfering."

She joined him. Leaning forward, she rested her elbows on her knees, cupped her chin in her palms, and strummed her fingertips against her cheekbones. She radiated Ivory soap. Luke's sisters-in-law used it, but on Nell it smelled sweeter. She jolted upright. "I might know someone who can swing it."

Luke threw himself backward onto the mattress. Moving to the boarding house had eased the immediate strain on his finances, but they wouldn't last forever. And there was a limit to how long the lighthouse people would wait. But he'd promised

Wilda he'd return the falcon. He'd come so far and now felt honor-bound to see it through. "How long will it take?"

"Hard to say. Why? You got somewhere you need to be—oh, I get it. Keen to spend Christmas with your family."

"Something like that." It was nothing like that. Those six strangers he'd eaten dinner with had made him feel more welcome than his own family had in twenty-two years.

6

---

*L*uke pressed a fingertip into his left forearm and watched the imprint fade. Who even knew December sunburn was possible? Still, it had been a marvelous day.

Like all Brooklynites, he was used to living near an ocean. As soon as April diffused the gray pall of winter, he had always jumped on his bike and escaped to Riis Park, Manhattan Beach, and Rockaway. But when Halloween decorations appeared in front yards and store windows, his Sunday escapes came to an end. It had taken a whole week before the idea of going to Santa Monica had found a toehold.

A nickel ride on the Red Car later, he'd been standing at the shadows of the pier, Californian sand squelching through his toes and cool blue water lapping at his ankles. The notion that he could romp around in it the week of Christmas filled him with the lighthearted joy he sorely needed.

He was pressing his skin a third time when a knock interrupted his reverie.

"Luke?" Tristan called out. "We have a tradition around here. Residents help trim Edith's tree with homemade decorations. Come join us. It's fun."

. . .

Five thick candles lined the top of the piano, lending the room a cozy glow. The dining table was awash with paper, scissors, and glue. Seymour and Minerva were sharing a story about a Christmas show in Niagara Falls with The Three Stooges.

"I failed to notice that Larry and Moe had commandeered the tree," Minerva said. "They kept moving it. I became so distracted that my daffodil-pattern tea dress that was supposed to transform into an emerald-green ballgown got stuck halfway over my head. Before I knew it, I was flat on my sweet patootie, with the Christmas angel pinned in my hair. I was beyond mortified until I realized the audience thought it was part of the act!"

"What about you, Sabine?" Edith asked, pushing popcorn along a stretch of cotton thread. "Did you and your family trim a tree together?"

"Jews do not celebrate Christmas, but we considered ourselves Germans first, and I remind you that Germans invented the Christmas tree." She was cutting trees out of thick cardboard with the dexterity of a dressmaker. "Our Berlin apartment had high ceilings, so we got an enormous fir. My mama, she would bake *Springerle*, so our home smelled of aniseed."

"I've had those." Beatrice held up a crayon she'd been using to color paper cutout stars. "My uncle fought in the Great War. He stayed behind long enough to marry a cute little Bavarian Fräulein. We called them Hannah's Christmas cookies. Say, Sabine, maybe you could make them for Christmas dinner."

Sabine nodded, her soft curls bouncing like bedsprings. "It would be my pleasure." She slipped the scissors from her fingers and took a spool of thread that was lying on the table. "And you, Luke? What is your family's Yuletide tradition?"

One year he had got a box of caramel marshmallow sticks from Williams Candy on Coney Island, which had rendered him speechless because the Valenti tradition had always been a predictable stack of handkerchiefs, scarves, and shoelaces.

"Luke, dear," Edith said before he could formulate a response, "it must be hard being away from family during the holidays, but maybe this time around won't be so tough, seeing as how it's your second Christmas here."

Everybody stared at their landlady.

"Edith," Beatrice said tenderly, "Luke's only been with us a week or so."

Edith blinked like an owl with cataracts. "Of course." The quiver in her voice gave her away. "I must have been thinking of our wine salesman."

Minerva murmured out of the side of her mouth, "That guy's been gone nearly two years."

Edith pushed sheets of reflective paper toward Luke. "How about you make us a festive chain? How's about alternating gold and red? Or green. Your choice. Build it long enough to wrap it around the tree from top to bottom. Fifteen feet ought to do it."

Luke hooked his fingers through a pair of scissors. Grabbing the two closest sheets of paper, he started cutting into them with the care of a surgeon.

"Gold and orange?" Beatrice asked, frowning.

"O Come, All Ye Faithful" spilled out of the mantel radio, filling in the silence left by Luke's panic. He had taken a chance that the two sheets complemented each other; evidently, he had picked the two least compatible colors.

Back home, everybody already knew about his condition, so it had been a very long time since he'd had to admit it out loud. Except for that awful day at the draft board. And now his six new neighbors were staring at him, the question *What the hell's wrong with you?* lurking behind their eyes.

He placed the scissors on the table and pressed his hands on top of them. This conversation never got easier. "I have a medical disorder called tritanopia. It prevents me from seeing colors."

"You cannot see them?" Sabine asked. "For you, life is the black-and-white movie?"

There it was. That wrenching, sickening tone. They always meant it sympathetically. Soaking their words with well-intentioned compassion. But no matter how they put it, nobody was ever skilled enough to disguise what they were thinking: *Imagine stumbling through this miserable life without being able to rely on the blue of the sky, the yellow of sunflowers, or the red of cranberries to cheer you up. You have my pity, but Jesus Christ, I'm glad I'm not you.*

The doctor at the draft board hadn't even bothered to try. "Well, shit," he'd sneered. "That's just about the most depressing thing I've ever heard." Luke had winced as the 4-F stamp struck his enlistment papers.

"I can distinguish black from white, but tritanopia makes it hard to tell the difference between blue and green, purple and red, and yellow and pink." Luke felt the heat of shame crawl across his face. "It also significantly dims colors."

"Are you able to see any at all?" Beatrice asked.

Luke thought of Wilda's cape. He'd have given anything to know what Moroccan Tangerine looked like; to him it was just dull gray. "In very bright light, I can make out a hint of color—if it's vivid. Most of the time, though, all I see is various degrees of gray."

"How frightful!" Edith clapped her hand on top of Luke's and gave it an encouraging squeeze. Not that it helped, but he appreciated the gesture.

"You make allowances."

"I'm guessing we won't be seeing you in uniform." Tristan lifted his mug of hot chocolate almost as a salute.

"No." Luke's voice was a whisper now. "They turned me down."

"We all have our flaws," Tristan said. "Personally, I have no sense of time. Two minutes feel like two hours to me. I'm constantly going berserk, thinking, 'What time is it? Is it the afternoon already? Am I late?'"

"Maps are my downfall," Minerva said. "Whatever you do, never hand me a map and ask me how we get to Pittsburgh. I guarantee we'll end up in Pocatello."

Seymour followed her with a complicated story about how he could memorize choreography but not lines from a script, which is why he had become a magician and not an actor.

It wasn't hard to see what they were doing. That issue about seeing colors, they were saying, it's not so bad. Everyone has some defect that holds us back. You're not so unusual.

As Sabine related how she couldn't tell them what asparagus tasted like if her life depended on it, Beatrice pointed out two sheets of paper. Luke presumed they were two colors that matched up better. She handed him a roll of adhesive tape and asked Sabine if she had ever tried putting salt on asparagus, because it brought out the flavor marvelously.

Hours later, with the tree loaded and the scraps cleared away, Luke had just reached the top of the stairs when a sharp "PSSST!" sounded in the hallway. Tristan beckoned Luke from his door.

His room was smaller than Luke's, with a ceiling that sloped toward the front of the house. He turned on a standard lamp in his window. "Has anyone explained to you about how Edith might be losing her marbles?"

"I gathered something was awry from that comment about this being my second Christmas."

"She's been saying that sort of thing more often lately."

"Going senile?"

Tristan see-sawed his hands. "Or simply getting old and forgetful. It's hard to say. At any rate, when it happens, we gently correct her, like Beatrice did."

A poster hanging on the wall over Tristan's bed caught Luke's attention.

EVA TANGUAY
THE "I DON'T CARE" GIRL
JOINS THE ZIEGFELD FOLLIES
COME SEE HER AT THE PALACE!

Below the headline, a young woman with a mop of unruly hair wore a gypsy scarf draped over her shoulders, a leather skirt that would have looked at home on a Roman centurion, and knee-high boots that showed as much skin as they hid. And below her feet were the words "Miss Tanguay's engagement starts May 9th, 1909."

"Eye-catching," Luke said.

"The crown jewel in my collection." Tristan flipped the lid of an old sailor's trunk at the foot of his bed. "With that accent, you must be from Brooklyn." He pulled out a handbill for the Morosco Burbank Stock Vaudeville Company that read *Starring that laugh-a-minute 300-pound barrel of fun, Mister Roscoe 'Fatty' Arbuckle.* "They played the Strand before touring China and Japan. I can't imagine what those Orientals thought of Fatty. You ever go to the Strand?"

"Sure. It's on Fulton. Vaudeville, mostly. Is that what you collect?"

Tristan was on his knees now, shuffling through the papers in his trunk. "Vaudeville is practically dead; all the more reason to preserve it."

"I don't suppose you have anything on an act called The Four Blooms?"

Tristan's face shot up, his eyebrows raised in surprise. "I was impressed when you cleared out Edith's drain, but now I'm positively dazzled that you've heard of The Four Blooms." He lifted out piles of handbills, posters, photographs, programs, and sheet music.

"My aunt was their chaperone when they were on the road."

"You don't say!" Tristan got to his feet, clutching a handbill. "This is from when they played the Trocadero in Philadelphia. It's a burlesque house now, but back then it was an important stop on the circuit. Nineteen-seventeen, maybe eighteen. The Four Blooms were a medium-time act. However, if you went over big at the Troc, New York producers would hear of it and bring you into the city."

Tristan's handbill was the size of a magazine. There weren't any photographs, but "The Four Blooms" were drawn amid an intricate nest of swooping lines and curly embellishments. A pang of homesickness stabbed at Luke's heart. He wished Wilda were with him right now so that she could see it.

"Did it launch them onto Broadway?"

"They went over great in Philly, but the act broke up not long after that."

Wilda had a bottomless pit of Four Blooms stories, but none of them had been about the act's demise.

"Marriage, I suppose?"

"You'd think so. Sadly, though, it was because one of them died."

Wait . . . One of The Four Blooms had died, and Luke was only learning about this *now*? "Of what?"

"Not sure." Tristan scratched at his thinning white-blond hair. "I believe I've got a souvenir from their last show."

He trawled through his collection until he reached a folded program of heavy linen cardboard. "This was from the Bijou in Boston." Back on his feet, he opened it and pointed to the lineup listed on the left side. "They were second on the bill. A very big deal."

Wilda had regaled Luke with so many tales of The Four Blooms that they felt like friends, but this Bijou program was the first time Luke had seen their full names.

Jasmine Howard. According to Wilda, she'd had the thickest hair.

Rose Primm—she'd had the narrowest waist.

Lily Osterhaus—the sweetest voice.

Violet Beaudine—the biggest bosom, and therefore the most stage-door Johnnies.

He turned to Tristan to ask if he had any other Four Blooms mementos and wasn't prepared when he found the guy's face inches away. He caught the yearning look in his eyes before Tristan leaned in and pressed his lips to Luke's.

Immobile with shock, Luke didn't move. Couldn't move.

Tristan took his quiescence as permission to press further and worked his tongue past Luke's teeth.

Luke shoved Tristan in the chest. What could the guy say to justify pulling a stunt like that? He vaulted toward the door, but stopped when his neighbor let out a sorrowful whimper.

"I'm sorry, I'm sorry, I'm sorry, I'm sorry . . ."

Luke turned back. Tristan was slumped over his piles of vaudeville memorabilia, now flattened into messy lumps.

"Don't be." Luke's voice came out so faint that he doubted Tristan had heard him. "This isn't the first time I've been mistaken for queer."

Tristan's head shot up, his eyes bloodshot and glassy. "You're in your twenties and not married, *and* the military rejected you."

"I told you. Because of the tritanopia."

"I just thought you made it up. You mean to say that you can't see colors? On the level?" Tristan blinked heavily as his mouth dropped open. "Oh my God, that's *terrible*."

"Don't I know it." In truth, though, he didn't know it at all.

Lacking the ability to see colors properly, Luke had had to associate them with other things. Blue was a big color because of the sky. Red was a passionate color because of fire. Green was soft because of grass. Black was a sad color because of funerals.

He helped Tristan to his feet and they sat down beside each other on the bed; it was firmer than the one in Luke's room.

"So, I'm not the only 4-F around here?" he asked Tristan softly.

"You're awfully nice not to punch me in the face." Tristan wiped away the viscous tears pooled around his eyes. "But you don't want to hear some poor, lonely faggot's woebegone story."

"I want to hear everybody's story." It sounded like a trite line, but Luke found he meant it. Sabine looked like she had lived the sort of life that would make a heck of a story. Edith, too, if that *Limitless Sky* poster was anything to go by. And here was Tristan, with a room full of theater programs, leaning in to kiss a total stranger right on the piehole.

Tristan straightened his spine and took a deep breath to collect himself. "I tried to enlist. I passed the physical and everything. But I knew I was in trouble when the doctor sent me into the tent on the right. I thought uh-oh."

"Why?"

"Because they sent all the other guys into the tent on the left."

"What was in the right-hand tent?"

"Different kind of doctor." Tristan tapped his temple three times. "Do you remember seeing a line on the draft notice that says 'Reason for rejection'? On my form the guy wrote 'psychologically or morally deficient candidate.' You know what that means, don't you?"

"Homosexual?"

Tristan nodded morosely. "When he grabbed his little rubber 4-F stamp, I stopped him. I told him that I can type like the dickens, so put me in the communications corps. And I can sew, so put me in the uniforms division. And I can play the piano. Sort of. So put me in the entertainment corps. I told him, 'I'm no conscientious objector. I want to do my bit. I'm as patriotic as you are.'"

"What did he say?"

"His sour old puss said it for him. 'We know what you'll get up to in the shower block. You'll corrupt our innocent Nebraska farm boys.' I can still hear his stamp hitting my application."

Luke flinched. He could hear that harsh thwack of rubber too.

"I concocted a story on the walk home. To save face, you know? I told them I'd been rejected because I was underweight. I'd been so worried about what was going to happen that I'd barely eaten that whole week. Everybody in Winnetka accepted the explanation. Nobody said, 'Fatten yourself up and apply again,' because they knew the real reason. And then I got angry. I have valuable skills, but they were too scared I might throw a bar of wet soap onto the shower floor and ask Oscar from Omaha to pick it up. I try not to think about it too much because it ticks me off."

"I get it," Luke said. "I really do."

His gaze landed on a headshot of a woman with a large halo of pale hair, rather like Marlene Dietrich in *Blonde Venus*, but with a squarish jawline and a steely look in her eye. Kind of a Gertrude Lawrence, but with a lot more makeup. He picked up the portrait. "Who's this?"

"Oh, brother." Tristan sucked in his breath. "This is the part where you run screaming."

"Who is she, Lucifer's sister?"

"Ha! You're funny!"

For a moment, the striking face in the photograph blurred. Nobody had ever said anything like that to him before. "No, really. Who is she?"

"As a matter of fact, she's based partly on Violet Beaudine from The Four Blooms. I saw her once in a third-rate touring production of *Helzapoppin'*. The show was frightful, but she shone like neon. So I put her into my act."

"You have an act?" Luke turned to stare at him.

The room felt silent. Tristan said, "Do you know what a female impersonator is?"

Luke tilted the headshot toward the lamp. "This is *you?*"

Tristan pursed his lips into a theatrical pout. "It's Miss Trixie Bagatelle."

"I would never have guessed."

"You're not supposed to."

"Where do you perform?"

"A few joints around town. Mostly in this nightclub down the trashy end of Vine Street. We cater to the curious crowd for whom the sight of a man dressed up as a woman is a novelty. They come to laugh at the freaks." A sly smile wriggled onto his lips. "But when Trixie Bagatelle steps on stage, they don't know what's hit 'em."

"I'd like to see Trixie in action some time."

"You're just saying that to be nice."

Luke thought of Nell. Would she be open to seeing a show like that? "What nights do you perform?"

A high-pitched scream punctured the air.

Tristan jumped up. "That sounded like Edith."

A second scream followed.

"That was Sabine."

They raced down the stairs and into the parlor, where Edith and Sabine clung to each other, rooted to the floorboards. Flames, bright as a streetlamp, were devouring one of the ratty old drapes framing the window.

"Candle!" Edith gasped. "I lit one for—must have fallen—"

Luke rushed into the kitchen. He grabbed the tea towel hanging from the oven door, doused it in water and threw it at Tristan. "Beat it with this while I fill a pot."

He pulled Edith's deepest frying pan off a hook on the wall and opened both faucets full bore. The water wasn't flowing fast enough. He snatched a large bottle of Coca-Cola and a half-empty

Dr Pepper out of the icebox and emptied them into the pan, then dashed into the parlor. "GANGWAY!"

He pitched the contents toward the drapes. The flames sizzled. Clouds of black smoke choked the air, filling the room with an acrid stink of shabby velvet and scorched cotton.

7

---

*L*uke took his day pass and thanked the Warner Bros. security guard.

What a difference a telegram made.

Nell's "a week maybe" had turned into ten long days. Not that he'd squandered the time. He had painted the front porch in exchange for a week's rent, and had driven Edith to a drapery store to replace the charred remains of that close call the night of the tree-trimming party.

There were, however, only so many times he could walk Hollywood and Sunset Boulevards, only so many streetcars he could ride, books he could read, and movie shows at second-string theaters he could see before restlessness stole his sleep. What if she couldn't get him back inside the studio? What if he never heard from her at all? And then Western Union had come calling.

GOT YOU IN STOP
GO NOW STOP
TODAY ONLY STOP

He bounded up the short flight of concrete steps. The props department smelled of dust and furniture polish. The guy behind the counter sporting a Friar Tuck haircut asked, "Production number?"

"Hi there. My name is Luke. I'm here to drop off a prop."

He deposited the box on the counter and pulled out the cause of his being stuck in Hollywood.

The clerk gripped it, his face widening like a party balloon. "Where the criminy's sake has it been?"

"Simon Kovner—"

"I've been dreading a call from Mr. Warner's office." Friar Tuck stroked the beak as though it were a real falcon that needed soothing. "Any minute now he'll be asking me to bring all four falcons so that he can choose which one he wants for the road-show. I did *not* want to tell him we were a bird short." He scrutinized Luke through narrowed eyes. "Say, wait a minute." The guy sifted through detritus crammed inside a drawer until he produced an envelope with Luke's name written on the front.

"From Simon?"

"That's his handwriting."

Luke ripped open the envelope and pulled out a folded note.

Dear Luke,

If you're reading this, it means you've returned the falcon. Thank God! I'm sorry I couldn't be here to take it off your hands, but I needed to get out of L.A. fast. (Some people shouldn't be allowed into Santa Anita, if you catch my meaning.) I know you're only in town for a day or two, but before you return home, there is someone you must see – Avery Osterhaus, 7711 Norton Ave, West Hollywood. Promise me you'll go, okay? It's important.

Good luck to you, buddy, and thanks for saving my bacon.

MARTIN TURNBULL

All the best, Simon Kovner.

"When did Simon leave this note?"

Friar Tuck shook his head. "He didn't. It was Mr. Bogart."

"In person?"

"Bogart and Simon were kinda pally. Used to go sailing together. Or fishing. Something about the ocean. It's how Bogart discovered Simon's brother was a chess player."

Luke tapped the note. "You ever heard of this Avery guy?"

"Nope. Then again, a couple of thousand people work here. I could name a hundred at most. Mr. Bogart might know him. Could be the three of them went sailing together."

The thought of repeating that ugly episode from last time made Luke's stomach churn. On the other hand, Nell had said Bogart felt bad about it.

"Where can I find Mr. Bogart?"

"Either his dressing room, or whatever soundstage he's shooting on, or Makeup, or Costuming. But if you want to catch him alone, he'll be in the commissary at twelve-thirty. He has a permanent reservation at a corner table. Turn left when you walk in. And be respectful. He prefers to keep to himself."

The soup of the day was cream of mushroom. Its buttery aroma permeated the brightly lit checkerboard of tables. Cowboys sat with slave girls, pirates with Victorian chambermaids. The din of chatter and laughter rose above the clatter of crockery and the "Yoo-hoo!" of people without enough time to table hop.

Luke felt like he'd wandered into a behind-the-scenes movie about Hollywood moviemaking.

Over to the left, past a quartet of jockeys shoveling tuna salad into their mouths, Luke spotted Bogart alone at his corner table, slicing into a ham steak with a book propped up in front of him.

76

As Luke drew closer, he recognized the heavy German gothic typeface.

There Was Once a King
Es War ein König in Thule

He couldn't have come up with a more perfect conversation starter if he'd had a month to plan it.

Luke shoved his hands in his pockets. "The second edition is better. It includes more poems from *The West-Eastern Divan*."

Bogart leaned back in his chair. Instead of a cursory nod for the sake of politeness, Luke felt the heat of a more considered review. "You don't say."

"It contains my two favorites: 'West Wind, How I Envy You' and 'Privileged Animals.'"

Bogart studied Luke's face as he closed *The Selected Poems of Johann Wolfgang von Goethe*. "We've met, haven't we?"

Luke bit down on his lower lip and nodded. "I'm the loud-mouth who yelled at you last week."

"You!"

Luke took a half-step backward.

"Have a seat."

Unsure if it was a command, a threat, an invitation, or a challenge, Luke did as he was told.

Bogart said, "There probably aren't thirty people on the entire West Coast who could've quoted the titles of two obscure Goethe poems."

"Are they the same thirty people who wouldn't believe Humphrey Bogart reads Goethe in his spare time?"

Finally, a warm grin. "Possibly." He rapped on his book with a knuckle. "You recognized it from ten paces."

"I studied ol' Johann in college. Practically know that text backward."

"What's your name?"

"Luke."

"Luke from the note that Simon asked me to drop off?" Bogart carved off a slice of ham steak. "You'll have to excuse me. I've only got another twenty minutes."

"I hear that you and Simon are sailing buddies."

The mood in the commissary shifted. A quiet hush muted the hubbub as half the eyes in the place followed Bette Davis to her table. She wore a simple dark dress cut low across the bosom, with sleeves to the elbows. The only adornment was a glittering bow halfway down her décolletage. It was unpretentious, but she carried it like a queen. The chattering didn't resume until she had seated herself with her back to the room.

"How do you know Simon?" Bogart asked.

"My aunt lives next door to your chess-by-mail partner."

"No fooling?" The world-weariness in his dark eyes dissolved as a wide grin spread across his face. "That Irving, he's one hell of a chess player. Did you know I checkmated him? Greatest day of my life!" Bogart slapped the table. "What brings you to L.A.? Irving's next move, I hope. He owes me one."

Luke forced a smile. Should he tell him? Bogart was the star of that picture, so would he feel like Simon had stolen his personal property? The affability he was showing now was so different from the cool loners he played on screen.

The truth, Luke decided, was easier to remember.

"Did you hear that one of the falcons made for *The Maltese Falcon* went missing?"

"Yeah."

"Simon took it. I guess he figured the studio didn't need four of them, so he sent it to Irving as a gift. But then Mr. Warner got the idea of putting together a war-bond tour using movie props to lure people in. To cut a long story short, Irving shanghaied me into returning it."

Bogart chewed on a chunk of ham steak longer than necessary. "But how could you have the missing falcon when *I* have it?"

Luke blinked rapidly. "You what?"

Bogart laid down his knife and fork, set his elbows on the table, and interlaced his fingers. "I had such a good time working on that picture that I was tempted to take a backup falcon as a souvenir. In the end, I didn't. But when the movie turned out to be such a hit, and propelled me into the big leagues, I changed my mind. So I snuck into the prop house and filched one out of the cabinet."

"But Irving told me they made four falcons."

"When it came time to take some publicity pictures, they found all three of them had gotten knocked around pretty bad during production. So John Huston commissioned a fourth one. That's the one I took."

"But—but if that left three, where the hell did mine come from?"

The question flew out of Luke loudly enough to reach Bette Davis, who looked over her shoulder at him. Those big Bette Davis eyes gave him a once-over, then returned to her lunch companion.

"Did Simon make the props himself?"

"No," Bogie replied. "His job was to keep track of them. Why? What did his note say?"

Luke retrieved it from a pocket inside his jacket and handed it over.

Bogie read it and slid it back to Luke. "Maybe that guy can clear it up."

* * *

7711 Norton Avenue was a one-story bungalow with a small yard and a flight of eight tiled steps leading to an arched front door. Luke rang the bell; chimes sing-songed deep inside the house. The door swung open to reveal a tallish guy with thin, light-colored hair.

"I'm looking for Avery Osterhaus."

"Okay."

"My name is Luke Vail." Osterhaus had no intention of shaking his hand. He let it drop to his side. "I'm a friend of Simon Kovner."

Another cagey "Okay."

"He joined the Navy," Luke persisted. "Before he left, he wrote a note telling me I should come see you. Said it was important." He searched the guy's face for a glimmer of—Luke wasn't sure what he was looking for. Recognition? Hesitation? Concern? Surprise? Fear?

Avery Osterhaus remained stoic. "I don't know why your friend sent you to me."

"He works at Warner Brothers. In the props department."

"I don't work at the studios. Somebody's made a mistake." He started rubbing his fingertips together. They were splattered with Indian ink. "You caught me in the middle of something and I've got to get back to it."

He turned away; the door closed behind him with a sharp smack.

8

_____

*L*uke stared at his bookcase. He had already read *Anthony Adverse, Goodbye, Mr. Chips,* and *The Age of Innocence.* And he was hardly likely to read *The Boston Cooking School Cook Book* or the volume of Edna St. Vincent Millay poems. Maybe *Me* by Charles Lindbergh? Maybe later. He turned over and faced the wall, where he outlined the poppy silhouette in the wrinkling wallpaper with his fingernail.

It wasn't like he'd had a lousy Christmas.

He had gone to bed Christmas Eve wondering if homesickness might kick in, but when he awoke the next morning, he felt only relief at not being forced to spend the day with an unruly horde of loud, in-your-face, ever-drunker Valentis who rarely engaged him in conversation, or made much of an effort when he initiated one.

That, in itself, would have been gift enough.

But then Edith had called him downstairs, where everybody had gathered in their bathrobes. She had prepared a feast of smoked salmon, orange marmalade pancakes, shirred eggs, and maple muffins. Later, he and Tristan had improvised Christmas carols at the piano until they ran out of songs.

All in all, it had been one of his jollier Christmases.

But that had been a week ago. It was now New Year's Eve, and a fog of disappointment weighed down on him like a sodden blanket.

New Year's Eve had been the lighthouse deadline. He had missed it. And for what? To return a fake movie prop that wasn't even missing. It was possible that Humphrey Bogart was mistaken and five had been made for the film. But really, four falcons, five, or five hundred. What did it matter now?

He jackknifed up in bed. It was eight a.m. in Los Angeles. Eleven in New York. Wilda's mail arrived around nine. A letter could be waiting for him right now. He threw back the covers. It was a slim chance, but not impossible.

In the Owl drugstore phone booth, he asked the operator to place a collect call to Windsor 6-4412. Time crawled until he heard someone agree to accept the charges. "Wilda? Are you there? It's me!"

"Luke?" The voice was too low.

"Irving?" He gripped the receiver more tightly. "Where's Wilda?"

What a relief to hear the chuckle in Irving's voice. In fact, it was comforting to hear any familiar voice. "She had to visit a friend over at Brooklyn Women's Hospital. But she had already called the plumber, so I'm here waiting for him. How come you're calling? Not in a tight spot, I hope."

Luke scratched his forehead. It suddenly felt hot and itchy. "I am a bit desperate. Today's New Year's Eve."

"Happy 1942 to you."

"I'm calling to see if Wilda's received any mail. For me, I mean. The lighthouse deadline is today. I'm hoping by some miracle I might have made it in under the wire."

Irving Kovner sucked in a sharp lungful of air as though to say,

I don't like your chances. "There is a stack of envelopes on her hallway table. Let me go check for you."

Luke tapped his toe against the phone booth's wood paneling. *Please let there be a letter. I'll do anything, be anything, give anything. Please, please, please, please.*

A rattling noise echoed down the line. "I'm sorry, my boy, but there's nothing here for you."

Those sorts of last-minute reprieves only happened in the movies. "Okay." His voice was barely above a murmur now. "Thanks for checking."

"I think I hear the plumber in the corridor."

"Wait! Wait!" Luke shouted. "Avery Osterhaus. What can you tell me about him?"

But Irving had already hung up.

* * *

Three sharp raps brought Luke out of Lucky Lindy's account of his Paris reception and how ten thousand over-excited Frenchmen had almost torn the Spirit of St. Louis apart.

Beatrice cracked open his door. "None of us have New Year's Eve plans so we're throwing our own little party." She eyed his untucked shirt and the brogues lying on the rug. "Care to join?"

"Haven't had a great day," he told her. "Not the best company right now."

"All the more reason. Put your shoes on and we'll see you in three minutes. Black and White start their act in five."

He closed the Lindbergh book. The lighthouse program was kaput, but he still had that savings account. Montauk would still be waiting for him when he got back East. Whenever that might be.

He walked into the parlor. Seymour and Minerva were standing in front of the Christmas tree. Seymour wore a black satin opera cape, which he held out like Dracula. Minerva was in a loose-fitting ballgown made of material that sparkled in the lamplight. He took a seat beside Edith, who whispered, "Glad you could make it."

"And now," Seymour said, "flowers. For you!" One moment his hand was empty; the next, a bouquet of paper roses filled it. Edith squealed the loudest, so he handed them to her. "And you!" Another bouquet, more like tulips, appeared, which he passed to Beatrice. "And Fräulein Sabine? Your favorite flowers are . . .?"

"Daffodils!" Her cigarette-ragged voice had jumped two octaves, and he produced a bouquet of daffodils. Sabine yelped, Tristan laughed, Edith clapped.

"But how did you know which flower she was going to say?" Luke asked. "What if she had replied—"

"Daisies?" A bunch of daises appeared.

"Calla lilies?" A bunch of calla lilies appeared.

"Roses?" A bunch of roses appeared.

"Sunflowers?" A bunch of sunflowers appeared that were so large they left Luke gaping in wonder.

"What a fine audience you are!" Seymour said. "And to prove there's nothing hidden in my cape, I shall take it off."

He raised it up, Dracula-style again, and with a flourish of his wrists, arched it over his head as he spun around and let it pool at his feet.

"Look!" Beatrice cried out. "Minerva!"

A tight silk dress had replaced her glittering ballgown.

The audience clapped and hollered its delight. After Seymour and Minerva had taken their bows, Minerva pointed to Sabine. "I believe our resident songstress is next."

Sabine stood up. "I was going to sing a favorite of mine. It used to get such applause, but alas, I could not find the sheet music this afternoon."

"What song is it?" Luke asked.

"'*Und Immer Noch Spiel'nse Blues.*'"

Luke crossed over to the piano and sat at the keyboard. "Whenever you're ready."

"*Mein Gott!*" Sabine pressed her hands to her chest. "You know it?"

Luke had come across the sheet music for that song when an Austrian lieder singer had left her music behind after one of Wilda's birthday parties. He'd only seen it once, but once was enough. "I'm willing to chance it if you are."

Sabine pulled at the lapels of her worn velvet bolero jacket. "*Bereit, wenn Sie es sind.*"

Luke closed his eyes a moment and pictured the notes playing across the paper. Yes, he decided. This shouldn't be too hard.

He started playing.

On Christmas Eve, Sabine had blended in among the others warbling along to the carols. But now her clear, confident voice filled Edith's parlor with yearning and angst. She had received formal training, that much was obvious. And she could project herself into the intimate crawl spaces of her audience's hearts—even if they didn't know what she was singing about. But Luke knew. Like all songs about the blues, she sang of the irretrievability of loves missed, lives lost, and a past strewn with regret and remorse.

The audience started clapping before she'd finished her final note. Luke went to take his seat next to Edith again, but she pushed him toward the front. "Your turn."

"I played a song whose music I saw once about a year ago. Isn't that enough?"

Sabine tilted her head to one side. Luke could tell what she was thinking. *Once? A year ago? How did you do that?*

"Come on!" Tristan called out. "A smart kiddo like you must have a party trick up his sleeve."

He could have told them that he only had one and they'd just seen it, but that would have been less than the whole truth. He had another. And he'd done it plenty of times, but only in his bedroom, alone.

Edith wagged a bony finger at him. "There shall be no supper for you until you do."

But this Hollywood family wasn't like those people in Brooklyn.

He stepped in front of the tree. "I'll need some paper and a pen."

Beatrice fished a pencil and small notepad out of her handbag. Luke tore off thirty pages, then wrote the numbers one through thirty, one per page. Next, he tipped them into Seymour's top hat and asked Edith to toss them like a salad, then pull them out and stack them.

"Hand me the pile, please."

He focused on the number written on the first sheet: 17.

Moving it to the bottom, he read the next one: 3.

Sending that one to the bottom revealed 25.

Next: 6.

Then: 14.

He went through the pile, relegating each sheet to the bottom, then handed it back to Edith. "I'm going to recite each number, page by page. As I do, I want you to take each sheet from the top so that the audience can see it."

Edith nodded again.

It was one thing to pull this off in an empty room. If he screwed up, nobody would be the wiser. But six people watching him with expectant eyes was a whole other ball of sticky, hot wax.

Luke took a deep breath. "17, 3, 25, 6, 14, 30, 1, 16, 27, 9, 2, 4, 22, 12, 19, 15, 26, 5, 20, 29, 11, 24, 28, 10, 13, 18, 7, 21, 8, and 23."

The parlor fell silent except for a car backfiring down the block.

Beatrice pressed her hands to her face. "I'm—speechless! That was—"

"Stupefying!" Minerva finished for her. "Astonishing!"

If Luke had ever drummed up the courage to do that in front of his family, they would have used words like 'freak' and 'weird.' Not to his face, of course, but he'd have seen it in their eyes.

"What's the trick?" Seymour asked. "I need to know!"

Luke shrugged. "It's simply a skill I have."

"Bravo to you," Edith said. "Bravo, I say!"

Sabine cupped her hands to her mouth. "*Wunderbar!*"

Beatrice stomped her feet hard enough to make the ornaments hanging in the tree behind Luke wobble and jangle.

He barely had any money; the whole reason he'd come to California appeared to be phony; he had no idea how he was going to get home; his dream of being a lighthouse keeper had dissolved. But as the applause washed over him, he realized that he didn't care quite as much as he probably ought to.

* * *

Luke prodded the vein throbbing in the middle of his forehead. He felt the blood pulse under his fingertip.

Thud-thud, thud-thud

He let his arm hit the mattress; his fingers felt the bedspread instead of sheets. For crying out loud, he hadn't even crawled under the covers. He wriggled his toes. At least he'd had enough sense to take his shoes off.

He remembered Seymour and his bouquets of paper flowers.

Sabine and her song about the blues.

Thud-thud, thud-thud, thud-thud.

He had wowed them with his memory trick—and then?

Hmmm. Oh, yeah. Beatrice. She had recited a Dorothy Parker poem. *Plenty of Rope? Enough Rope?* Something about rope.

After that, things got a little hazy.

He could picture Tristan waving his hands and giggling over a —parasol? The rest of the evening had dissipated into wispy scraps.

Downstairs, someone rang the doorbell.

Luke closed his eyes and prodded the vein again. Was that coffee he could smell? Or was it just a figment of his imagination, mixed with hope and desperation?

Plink! Plink!

Someone was throwing pebbles at his window. What was this, an Andy Hardy movie?

Plink! Plink! Plink!

Three. Two. One. He grunted as he swung his feet onto the rug. He crossed over to the window and pushed aside the damask curtain.

Nell stood next to Edith's hydrangeas. With her hair pulled back into inch-long pigtails and dressed in loose overalls, she looked like an Okie hopped up on cotton candy. "Happy 1942!"

Luke planted his hands on the weathered frame. "Not so loud. And not so early."

"It's nearly ten-thirty. You weren't still in bed, were you? You're a class act, Vail."

"I'm a *glass* act," he called back, "as in 'fragile.'"

"Schwab's make their coffee extra-strong on New Year's Day for chumps like you. The walk will clear your head. Come on. And no dilly-dallying."

"Thanks, but—"

"Please?" She clapped her hands together as though in prayer. "I need to talk with someone regular."

Luke had spent his entire life wishing he fit in with his surroundings. Being called 'regular' was pretty much the only enticement that could have worked. Groaning quietly, he reached for his shoes.

The midmorning sun held little warmth, but the air had an invigorating bite to it. Nell kept her chatter to a minimum until they had passed the seedy motel that looked like the sort of place mid-level insurance managers took their secretaries.

"Good golly, you're pale," she said. "Don't you fret none. Schwab's coffee will perk you up. Followed by a plate of ham and eggs—"

Coffee *and* ham *and* eggs *and* what else? His heart sank. If they were going out for breakfast, he'd be expected to pay. With what? He was down to a dollar bill, a dime, and a pair of nickels.

"I'll gratefully go for coffee, but I draw the line at fried anything."

She pulled at a pigtail. "We'll see about that."

"And anyway, where have you been lately? You got me into Warners—and then disappeared. I was starting to think Nazi spies had kidnapped you."

"I wish."

"What could be worse than them?"

Nell let out a sigh that ended up more like a snort. "The Davenports."

"That bad, huh?"

"I don't mean to sound like an awful harpy. I really shouldn't go around saying things like that." She stared morosely ahead of her and kept walking. "It's not like my family are horrible or anything."

Luke was intrigued. So there was someone walking around this world who felt about her family the same way he felt about his? A cute girl who looked even cuter in pigtails was a bonus. "I'll tell you my war stories if you tell me yours."

They arrived at Highland Avenue. The Hollywood Hotel looked almost deserted. Luke could see the lights in the foyer, but that was about it. They crossed the boulevard without waiting for a green light.

"I'm the youngest of five girls," Nell said. "They talk non-stop about dresses and hats and handbags. Makeup. Lipstick. Hair ribbons. Cold cream. Knitting patterns."

"You're a girl. Aren't you?"

"I am. Thanks for noticing. It's not like I *don't* want to talk about cashmere sweaters and pink kid gloves. But honestly, it never stops. And what's worse is we're only eighteen months apart from each other."

Luke thought about the twelve-year chasm that separated him and his nearest brother, and how he used to long for just one sibling he could relate to. "Is that bad?"

"The worst! They're in and out of each other's closets and beauty cases and bureaus borrowing jewelry and rouge and fascinators and shoes. It's like living in a Bolshevik commune. I spent the first twenty years of my life wanting one thing, just one damned thing, to call my own, that I didn't have to share. But no. That's considered greedy and selfish and covetous."

Luke almost laughed, but the girl was frowning too seriously to risk poking fun at her. "Did you say 'covetous'?"

"My mom's father was a Methodist minister. So it was all 'Thou shalt not covet thy personal property for it belongs to thy sisters!'" She caught the look on Luke's face and pointed an accusing finger at him. "You're laughing at me."

"It's just that I come from a big family too. I'm the youngest of six. But there's a dozen years between me and Vic, so instead of having to deal with everyone going through my things, I spent my childhood being left alone."

Nell groaned. "Sounds like my idea of heaven."

"It wasn't."

"So then, my mom and two of my sisters, Vesta and Ruth, decided to come visit me. They couldn't get on a train or a bus because they're full, so they drove out here before gas rationing kicks in. Did they think to let me know ahead of time? Heavens, no. Because everybody just loves having three uninvited house guests land on the front doorstep."

Nell's chatter about her intrusive sisters had done a great job of distracting him. Throw a few more questions at her, he figured, and maybe he could get through the rest of the day without thinking about lighthouses.

She let out a long, wet raspberry. "Maybe your situation is different, being boys and all."

Farther along the boulevard, Luke spotted the vertical *SCHWAB'S* sign. Seeing as how breakfast and dinner were included back at the boarding house, he shouldn't be spending anything.

He stopped outside a store called Parisian Florist. Poinsettias filled the window. Somebody had told him once that they were red, which he associated with anger, but these plants seemed so placid. "We're mirror images of each other," he told her. "You're the youngest of all girls; I'm the youngest of all boys. You feel swamped by your family's inability to see you as a distinct personality, whereas my personality is *too* distinct, so they've left me alone."

She leaned against the window, and a lopsided grin emerged on those full lips of hers. "You're kind of smart, aren't you?"

"It's interesting, is all. I suspect I understand you better than most people."

"You might be right." She pushed his shoulder with a friendly shove. "Now that Schwab's is in sight, I'm starving."

He didn't shift from where he stood. "Look, Nell, here's the thing: I'm running low on funds. I can't justify spending money on food when two meals a day are included in my rent."

"*I'm* taking *you* to breakfast. My treat."

"But you're the girl!" Luke protested. "I can't let everybody see who's paying our check."

She crossed her arms and contemplated him with brooding eyes. "Out of dough, huh?"

"Nearly."

"At the studio, men are enlisting by the carload. There's bound to be an opening somewhere. I can't promise you anything, but I can ask."

Work at a movie studio? With real-life movie stars? Luke snapped shut his gaping bazoo. "That would be terrific."

She popped open her purse and pulled out a couple of dollar bills. "And to save you the utter mortification of people thinking you're a breakfast gigolo—" She thrust them toward him.

He pushed the money away. "You've made your point."

"So you won't die of embarrassment when the check comes?"

"Please move your butt. I don't know about you, but I'm starving."

9

$\mathcal{L}$uke plucked *An Historical Atlas of Europe During the Middle Ages* from the bookshelf, flopped onto his bed, and turned over a handbill that publicized the recent march down Broadway to support Roosevelt's 'Four Freedoms' speech to Congress.

He had missed sketching. Missed hearing the staccato brush strokes of the charcoal along the paper or the feel of a pencil between his fingers. He began to draw. Pointed beak. Curved head. Feathers shaped like diamonds. Four talons curling over the block.

A slow, rhythmic thudding started up in the room next door. It wasn't the first time he'd heard it. It wasn't even the first time this week. *Bang, bang, bang, bang.* Luke waited for the tempo to pick up. It always did. Wait for it. *Bang-bang-bang-bang.* And now the bed springs. Any moment now. *Squeak. Squawk. Squeak. Squawk.*

He twirled his pencil around his fingertips. Had they been different sounds generated by any other activity, he might have continued to draw. But *bang-bang* and *squeak-squawk* were too distracting. Better that he waited for tonight's show to reach its inevitable conclusion. Those guys—Luke suspected it was never the same one—rarely took longer than ten minutes. Twelve, tops.

Bang-bang, squeak-squawk. Bang-bang, squeak-squawk. Good grief, this visitor had stamina. Nobody had lasted this long before. They'd been at it nearly half an hour. Evidently there was no end in sight.

He found Edith at the dining table stitching together swaths of dark velvet and took a seat opposite her. "What's all this?"

"Mandatory blackout curtains. The city sent me some thick cloth, but it's hardly sufficient for seventeen windows."

Her gardenia perfume wasn't the same brand Wilda wore. Edith's had a note of vanilla in it that Wilda's lacked, but it was close enough to remind him of her. A light ache pressed his chest. It would be her birthday soon; he'd hadn't missed seeing her for her birthday since the year he had received his first bicycle.

"I'd offer to help, but my skills with needles and threads are somewhat lacking. If you've got some black paint, I could cover the smaller windows."

"There's a clever idea!" She rested her fingers in her lap. "Why are you down here? Couldn't sleep?"

"Not tonight." He ran his hand over the swath of feather-smooth velvet. What a shame to waste quality stuff on blackout curtains.

"It's Betty-Sue, isn't it? I don't miss much. I know about her gentleman callers." Luke looked up, startled at Edith mistaking the name of her most longstanding resident. "I pride myself on not being an interfering sort of landlady. The personal business of my tenants is not my concern. After all, she's doing it for a good cause." She made it sound like Beatrice was selling Girl Scout cookies. "Oh my. Two o'clock! I must get some sleep. Would you mind taking Tristan some coffee? He's on the roof tonight."

"This time of night? What's he doing?"

"Volunteered with some organization or other. He'll be ever so grateful, as will my knees."

Luke filled a large cup from the pot on the stove. He was heading for the fire escape when the door to Beatrice's room swung open and her paramour du jour stepped into the hallway.

The guy was not the carnal stripling Luke had imagined. North of forty, he was graying at the temples and held himself ramrod straight. Definitely military, but no raw recruit. This one was in it for the long haul.

"Good evening," Luke said.

The officer nodded curtly. "I don't suppose you know the time."

"Just gone two."

His eyebrows shot up. "Four bells already?"

This was a Navy man. Stuck out at sea for weeks on end, his opportunities for getting laid were scarce and precious. No wonder he was up for an extra-long ride on the merry-go-round.

Luke was keen to get this coffee to Tristan while it was still hot. He bid the sailor good night and continued to the end of the hall, where a large window led to the fire escape. He climbed to the roof and poked his head above the gutter. "I have coffee!" He mounted the final five rungs and stepped onto the widow's walk.

"I was afraid Edith had forgotten about me." Tristan took the cup and wrapped his fingers around it.

"Edith couldn't recall which organization you're volunteering with."

He half-turned toward Luke and pointed to a badge sewn onto an armband. "Air warden with the Citizens Defense Corps. Sounds noble, huh?"

"Very."

"Don't get me wrong; I want to contribute. But honest to God, I just got sick to death of all those sour looks."

Luke knew what he meant. Judgmental and resentful to the point of hostile. And as more and more uniformed recruits appeared on the streets, those side glances were growing harder to ignore. He leaned against the metal railing. "I sat across from some old biddy on the Red Car the other day. She looked like she'd drunk a bottle of carbolic acid. I could tell what she was thinking. 'What's wrong with *you?*'"

"Or worse: 'What disease did *you* fake?'" Tristan said, nodding. "But I learned pretty quickly that speaking up only invites more questions and more judgment. When I get home from doing a show, I'm still wide awake. So I figured why not take on a task nobody else wants? And now I watch the night skies for enemy aircraft." He ran a finger around the emblem on his badge: a striped triangle inside a dark circle. "We're only supposed to wear it while on duty, but I slip it on whenever I leave the house. Believe me, it cuts down on the snide looks." He cast his eyes skyward. "The manual tells me to look out for Aichi D3A Type 99 carrier bombers like the Japs used at Pearl Harbor. Damned if I know how to tell the difference between ours and theirs."

"And if you do see one?"

"I'm supposed to contact HQ. Unfortunately, the nearest public phone is three blocks away, and I'm not the world's fastest sprinter."

They scanned the placid sky until Tristan asked Luke what he was doing up so late.

"Let's just say there was a ruckus going on in Beatrice's room."

Tristan giggled. "You should tell her to keep it down when she's entertaining. Not that I blame her. Captain Stamina is quite the dish—oh!" He turned and looked at Luke, his brow creased with concern. His skin, pale as marble, soft as marshmallow, shone in the moonlight. "Do you mind my saying faggy stuff like that?"

Once, when Luke was fourteen, he had stopped at a shoe store on Coney Island Avenue to admire a display of Keds. Not that he played basketball. He just liked the look of them and dreamed of the day when he'd saved up enough pocket money to buy a pair. But then a broad-shouldered shadow had fallen across him. He'd turned to see two thuggy street urchins leering at him.

The first one had said, "Nancy boys don't play no sports."

His buddy had added, "Fags hang around locker rooms hoping for a peep. Is that wotcha doing, you faggy-ass Peeping Tom? Salivating over the chance to sniff BVDs?"

Luke had enjoyed his fair share of wet dreams over boobs and soft, curly hair. But telling those two that he liked girls wouldn't have done any good. Brooklyn punks valued scraped knuckles and knife-fight scars. Those were the medals of honor that had currency, and Luke had possessed none of them.

"Say any faggy comment you like," he told Tristan.

Tristan faced the sky again, turning his head this way and that. "Who's the girl with the pigtails? The one throwing rocks around on New Year's Day."

"She's trying to get me a job at Warner Brothers."

"Does she know how cute she looks in overalls?"

Luke couldn't have agreed more. That breakfast at Schwab's had been loads of fun. They'd swapped sibling stories, laughed at each other's jokes, competed over who'd had the most miserable childhood, and split a slice of cherry pie à la mode. But was she interested in him, romantically speaking? Luke doubted it. If she had been, wouldn't she have made an effort to doll herself up? Overalls were nobody's idea of pulling out all the stops. "I'm no expert, girl-wise, so don't ask me."

"Me either. One thing I do know is make no assumptions. Take Beatrice, for example. Given her procession of recruits, I wouldn't have thought Captain Stamina would be her cup of tea."

Luke braced himself against a cool wind blowing in from the west. "I had not been picturing that gray hair."

"He must have twenty years on her."

"Gossiping old housewives!" Beatrice stood on the top rung of the fire escape, her hands gripping the side rails and her mouth pressed together in mock outrage. "For the record, he's twenty-two-and-a-half years older."

"Nobody's casting aspersions on your activities de la boudoir,"

Tristan declared. "I just assumed all your visitors were fresh off the farm."

She joined them on the widow's walk, where she took Tristan's cup and helped herself to a sip. "I suppose you think I'm a Victory Girl," she said, looking at Luke.

"I might if I knew what that was."

"For a smart cookie, you're still wet behind the ears, aren't you?"

Luke picked up no trace of insult in her tone and wasn't sure how to answer her question. Or had it been merely rhetorical? He stayed quiet.

Beatrice sighed. "A Victory Girl is someone who gives sexual favors to servicemen. Especially ones who are about to head off into war and may never know the pleasure of being with a woman." Well, that explained Edith's 'doing it for a good cause' comment. "Do you have a problem with that?"

"If I did," Luke said, "I would've banged on the walls to tell you to keep it down."

Tristan laughed. "He was okay with it when he thought you were just a floozie. Now that he knows you're a Victory Girl, you could step it up to four times a week. Or even five!"

She slapped him across the shoulder. "They won't allow us girls into the military, so this is how I do my bit. I'm standing the whole time at Kress's. When I'm not, I'm off my feet." She barked out a laugh. "It balances out."

Luke was glad for the night shadows that masked his shock. Maybe he was more wet behind the ears than he'd ever assumed. "I'd imagine guys like that are grateful for your generosity."

"They're very grateful." The cheerfulness fell from her face. "Or *were*."

"They don't even thank you?"

"Meaning I *was* a Victory Girl, but that's in the past now."

"Really? Because I encountered a certain sailor in the hallway."

"We gave him a name: Captain Stamina," Tristan added.

Beatrice's hands flew to her mouth. "He *does* have stamina!"

"Trust us," Luke deadpanned. "We know."

"It's different with him, though. It's—special."

Tristan nudged Luke. "You hear that? Our Beatrice is falling in love. But how can she know after one romp in the hay?"

"That wasn't our first time. Just our first time doing it here."

Although Nell looked to Luke like a long shot, he couldn't help but wonder what it would be like with her. He had little clue what to do with a girl once he got her into the sack. But maybe after three or four rounds he'd get the hang of it?

"Thank you for not judging me," Beatrice whispered, her voice suddenly serious.

Luke had been judged his whole life. Who was he to judge Beatrice for what she was doing? It was time to change the subject. "I was chatting with Edith earlier tonight, and she called you Betty-Sue."

She shot Tristan an *Oh, dear* look.

"We're lucky to be living here, and we're lucky to have her as a landlady," Tristan said, "but we need to start watching out for her."

Without warning, a siren rent the night air.

Tristan slapped the railing. "It's happening!" Lights switched on in the surrounding houses, winking like fireflies amid the blackout darkness. He threw his head back. "The manual says to focus directly overhead."

The breath in Luke's lungs escaped in a hot *whoosh*. "It's not the Japs, is it?"

"Damned if I know. It is clear out tonight, though." Tristan pointed to powerful searchlights strafing the western sky. Almost on cue, they converged on a single point in the sky. "What if it's a Kamikaze?"

"Where do you think it is?" Beatrice asked.

"My guess is Culver City—Christ on a cracker! Don't tell me they're bombing MGM!"

The wailing siren stopped; the air fell silent.

"Shouldn't we be hearing explosions?" Tristan dashed to the corner of the widow's walk and picked up a pair of binoculars. He trained them on the half-dozen crisscrossed spotlights. "There's an orange dot. Kind of fuzzy. Why would Japs paint their aircraft a bright color?"

"And why would bombers stay in one place?"

"Maybe it's a dirigible?"

Tristan leaned over the railing as though it would get him closer to Culver City. "My manual says Japs have no natural access to helium, so they don't build any."

"Maybe it's ours."

The words were barely out of Luke's mouth when the deafening *boom-boom-boom* of heavy artillery crowded the air. Trails of anti-aircraft tracer bullets blazed against the black of night.

"The Army's throwing everything they have at it."

People came out of their houses now, clutching bathrobes around them, to determine the cause of the thunderous barrage.

"Go back inside!" Tristan shouted down at them. "This might be the real thing!"

Nobody listened to him. Not that Luke blamed them. This was the first time Angelenos had witnessed anything first-hand, so naturally they were curious. Especially if it was playing out miles away.

The firing stopped as suddenly as it had started. The searchlights remained concentrated on the same spot as the night fell silent again. Luke felt his shoulders drop a full inch. "Can you still see the blob?"

"Too much smoke!" Tristan yelped with overheated excitement. "We sure showed 'em what to expect if they come back, though." He lowered his binoculars. "When I volunteered to be an air raid warden, I never dreamed anything like this would happen. Culver City is practically on our doorstep." He grinned at them both, his face flushed. "I'm going to need a shot of whiskey to help settle the nerves. Care to join me?"

Luke glanced at Beatrice, who didn't look like she would get any sleep tonight. He turned back to Tristan. "A shot sounds good. Two sounds better."

10

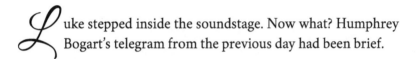uke stepped inside the soundstage. Now what? Humphrey Bogart's telegram from the previous day had been brief.

COME SEE ME TOMORROW STOP
STAGE TWENTY STOP
ANY TIME AFTER NINE STOP

A cheap restaurant stood in the middle of the cavernous space. Tables arranged in four rows; checkered tablecloths, and on one wall a sign: *Cardo's Italian dinner – 60 cents.*

The only person on the set was a crewman in overalls, a hammer in each hand.

Luke asked him where he could find Humphrey Bogart.

The carpenter poked the air with a hammer. "Back there."

The front of the set had looked like every Italian restaurant

Luke had ever been to, down to the breadsticks in jam jars. But from the back it was nothing but pressboard, rough enough to give splinters. Unvarnished. Unpainted. Untreated. Someone had stenciled *THE BIG SHOT - PRODUCTION 398* in dark paint.

Were they all this flimsy? Had Sam Spade's office really just been made of this gimcrack stuff?

He spotted a square tent set up in the soundstage corner. The entrance was a shabby door attached to a wooden frame by a pair of tarnished brass hinges. Luke knocked.

"Who is it?"

"Luke Vail."

"Come on in."

Bogart sat in front of a makeup mirror in an ill-fitting suit, a wrinkled shirt with the collar button undone, and a three-day growth. "I was hoping it'd be you." He pointed to a wooden chair next to the vanity. "I heard our continuity girl asking the gaffer how she could go about getting a friend of hers hired. It took me a while to realize she was talking about my old pal, the Goethe expert."

"I wouldn't call myself that."

"Anyone who can rattle off 'West Wind, How I Envy You' and 'Privileged Animals' like they're the names of breakfast cereals is an expert in my book." He picked up a brushed chrome cigarette holder from the makeup table in front of him, flicked it open with his thumb, and extended it toward Luke.

Luke had tried smoking a few times. But no matter how deeply he inhaled, they failed to give him the satisfaction other people reported. He could take it or leave it, so he usually left it. But it was different when Humphrey Bogart was doing the offering.

Luke reached for one and slipped it between his fingers. A Robert Burns cigarillo. Yuck.

Bogart took one for himself, lit it, and then motioned for Luke to lean forward and lit his as well. The air above them thickened with pungent smoke. "I've signed a new contract. Big jump up the salary totem pole."

Luke took a tentative drag on his cigarillo and breathed in the tobacco smoke as shallowly as he could. "Congratulations."

"Success is what we're shooting for, right? But with it comes more—" he waved the cigarillo around in tight circles "—everything. Fan mail, demands on my time, interviews, radio appearances, photo portrait shoots, invitations. It's . . ." His sentence trailed off into a sigh.

"A lot to deal with?"

"Especially seeing as how my wife is none too thrilled with my recent rise. The hotter my career grows, the more attention she demands, which gets to be a tricky juggling act because I now have less time to spend with her. I can't manage it on my own. So, what do you think?"

Luke was pretending to take another puff on his cigarillo and was glad for the excuse to put it down before the nausea gathering in the pit of his stomach had a chance to start calling the shots. "What do I think of what?"

"I'm asking if you want a job working for me. You'd be one part assistant, one part secretary, one part chauffeur, one part messenger, one part delivery boy, and one part whatever else needs doing."

"How much are you paying?" Anything over the twenty per week his family paid him would be enough to cover his rent, with a bit left over to impress Nell with a classy restaurant.

"Thirty a week."

"Deal."

"Can you start this time tomorrow?"

Just like that? He had a job? "I'll be here." He stuck out his hand before the guy could change his mind. "Thank you, Mr. Bogart."

The actor shook it warmly. "None of this 'Mr. Bogart' business, you understand? Just call me what everybody calls me."

"Which is what?"
"Bogie."

* * *

The woman behind the window at the Payroll and Personnel office blinked at Luke through cat-eye glasses. "You're not on my list."

"Mr. Bogart will be paying me, not the studio, but I'll still need an employee pass."

The women's mouth soured into a frown. "I can't go handing out passes like they're bags of penny candy."

According to the clock on the wall, Luke was already seven minutes late on his first day. "What do you want?"

"I *want*—" she emphasized the word "—you to send Mr. Bogart here so that I can get his personal okay."

Stuck behind her window, this shrew had probably never met any of the studio's leading lights. "Do you know how much it costs to halt production on a movie?" he asked her, mustering as much authority as he could. Old Miss Persnickety from Personnel would have had a better idea than he did, but Luke figured it was bound to be more than a buck or two. He looked at the clock again. "How about a compromise?"

She broke off her supercilious glower and started to tidy up an already-orderly pile of papers in front of her.

"Would a hand-written letter authorizing me to get a pass do?"
"It must be signed."
"Naturally."
"This window closes at five. On the dot."

A group of Indians ambled past in feather headdresses and leather loincloths. The two men bringing up the rear were arguing over Joe DiMaggio and Babe Ruth.

Luke fell in behind them.

The guy on the right was insisting the DiMaggio's fifty-six-game hitting streak from last year made him the best ballplayer in history. His pal was having none of it. Home runs and slugging percentages were his measuring stick. Luke was already composing the letter he'd write to Wilda that night: the way the feathers jiggled when they each defended their view by punching the air; the slap of their moccasins against the asphalt; the goose-flesh rippling along their backs in the January chill. Oh yes. Wilda was going to get a big kick out of this story.

Passing Avenue D, he caught sight of Nell—or rather, her hair, twisted into the same tight pigtails she'd worn to Schwab's. A burly guy over six feet tall emerged from a side alley. He snuck up behind her and wrapped his arm around her waist.

"Oh!" she squealed. "It's you!"

He pressed his hip against hers. "I love it when we run into each other."

That crewcut hair, those wide shoulders, that voice. It was the wisecracker who had assured him it was fine to wake up Bogie.

The guy slung his arm over her shoulder and whispered in her ear. Luke hoped she'd cringe away, but she let out a girlish giggle and allowed it to lie there like a sluggish python.

Don't be so surprised, Luke told himself. Someone as cute as Nell was bound to have a boyfriend. Did it have to be *that* guy, though? With his confidence, his swagger, his brawn? Luke retraced his steps to take the long way around to Stage Twenty. What sort of girl would be dumb enough to fall for the obvious charms of a lug like that? The type who had married his arrogant brothers, that's who.

Luke knocked on the door to Bogie's makeshift dressing room. No answer. He knocked a second time. No answer. Should he just walk in? Or would he be bawled out his first day on the job? After all, he was fifteen minutes late.

The door squeaked as he pulled it open.

The guy was slumped over his dressing table, his head resting on one arm, his right hand flopped over the edge. He was breathing heavily, an erratic mix of abrupt gasps and gravelly panting.

Humphrey Bogart was drunk.

Or hungover.

Or both.

A sour pall of whiskey and cigarette smoke hung over him. Welts and bruises mottled the man's arms. Had he come to work by way of a dockside bar fight? Luke pressed his thumb into the darkest bruise.

Bogie jolted awake and threw himself into the back of his chair. "Christ Almighty."

"A little worse for wear?"

"I want you to know this isn't normal. I pride myself on being a professional. I hate Jack Warner's guts, but he pays me a damned good salary for which he reasonably expects me to show up on time and ready to put in a full day's work." He closed his eyes, stretched and yawned. The yawn became a groan. The groan turned into a yelp when he hit a bruise against the corner of his makeup table. "Mayo and me, we've had some fine old fracases, let me tell you. But last night?" He whistled a low single note until his breath ran out. "We outdid ourselves."

On the set, someone shouted, "Hey, Jasper, switch to full."

Moments later, blinding light bathed the entire room. Bogie lifted an arm to shield his eyes.

Luke pointed to a bruise the size of a flattened golf ball. "Your wife's handiwork?"

Bogie prodded around it. "This must have happened when she pushed me through the back door. We sometimes end our fights that way." His grin was more mischievous than malevolent. "Sounds deplorable, doesn't it?"

Luke had spent many a Sunday morning watching his mother patch up his brothers' knife cuts and scrapes, black eyes, bleeding lips, grazed knuckles. As far as he knew, none of them had been pushed through a door. Much less by a woman.

"It kind of does," he told Bogie.

"I push her before she pushes me. She pushes me before I push her. Trust me, it's an even-handed fight." He winced as he rose to his feet. "You should see our back door. It's a pile of firewood now. Do you know where Holloway Hardware is?" Luke shook his head. "La Cienega and Holloway. Big hardware and lumber store. I'll need you to stop by there. Ask for Yancy. Tell him you're there to pick up the half-dozen new doors I ordered last week."

How often did these people go at it in hand-to-hand combat? "You order doors by the half-dozen?"

Bogart's mischievous grin resurfaced as he scooped up a shirt that lay crumpled on the floor. "Then go to my house. Do you know how to hang a door?" Luke nodded, hoping he knew how to hang a door like he knew how to unblock a drainpipe. "But for now, go find Lew Seiler. He's the director. Tell him I'm indisposed. He'll know what that means. They've switched on the key lights, so they'll be needing my stand-in. Tell Lew you're it. We're half an hour from filming. That should give me enough time to get my act together."

Seiler showed no surprise beyond a curt nod when Luke passed on Bogie's message. He pointed to an X taped on the floor of the restaurant and told him to stand on it.

Even on a set crisscrossed with shadows, the lights in Luke's eyes were blinding. There was more to this acting business than he'd ever supposed.

"Well, now, don't you turn up in the most surprising places." Twenty-four hours ago, the sound of Nell's voice would have thrilled Luke. But now? Not so much. "When I didn't hear from you, I figured things didn't pan out."

"It happened so fast." Nell was close enough for Luke to make out her silhouette. After the disappointment from earlier in the morning, her face was the last thing he wanted to see.

"And now we're work chums. How fun!"

Yeah. Chums. That's all.

"You okay?" she asked.

"It's these bright lights. I can barely see a thing."

"What in God's name is going on here?"

Another silhouette appeared next to Nell. Taller. Wider. Hands balled into fists.

Luke pointed to the X at his feet. "I'm standing in for Bogie."

"*I* am Bogie's stand-in." Nell's boyfriend made a big show of filling his lungs and pushing out his impressive chest.

Luke had seen his brothers make that move countless times. It was like the opening gambit in a game of chess—so commonplace it was almost a cliché. If this appealed to Nell, that was her problem. Bullies fed off alarm and distress, so Luke took a moment to calm his voice. "What are you? Six feet two?"

"Six one."

"Doesn't that mean you're three or four inches too tall? I'm Mr. Bogart's height, so it makes sense that I'm his stand-in."

"He's got a point, Gus," Nell said. "You're right for Errol, but for Bogie, you're just too tall."

"This palooka can't come in here and—"

"Of course he can," Seiler said, stepping out of the shadows. "Bogie's appointed this guy as his new stand-in. End of discussion."

"But—but—"

"Come on." Nell sounded as though she was talking to a recalcitrant kitten who refused to come in out of the rain. She took Gus's arm. "You need to step aside and let us get on with it."

This guy's face was a blank canvas of glaring light, but Luke could picture the pout, probably with gobs of spit in the corners, and the angry eyes glinting under furrowed brows. He raised his hand and waved. "Nice to meet you, Gus. And goodbye."

* * *

Luke turned into the driveway of the house on Horn Avenue, a block north of the Sunset Strip. He got out and opened the rear door of Bogie's Buick, then pulled out the top door from the stack piled on the back seat.

Bogie had told him the side gate was unlocked. "Take the path to the back yard. The tools you'll need are in the shed." When Luke had asked if he should first introduce himself to Mrs. Bogart, Bogie had said that he'd try to call her.

The flagstone path paralleled a bed of petunias and then opened to a backyard that sloped away from a large patio. The remnants of what had once been the Bogarts' back door lay scattered like fallen foot soldiers. Tools of every type hung in neat rows inside the shed. Luke selected what he figured he might need, as well as a broom, and headed outside again. He had swept up only half the mess when a pair of Scottie dogs scuttled over and began sniffing around his shoes.

"Who the fuck are you, and what the fuck are you doing?"

Mayo Methot leaned against the doorjamb, a cigarette in her left hand. She wore a housedress with a floral print faded in uneven patches, the bottom hem unraveling near her knees. She made a token effort to pull its lapels across her chest, but they fell back. In her right hand, she held a white coffee cup, but Luke could see no steam rising from it.

"I'm Luke Vail." He waited for recognition to filter through her eyes. It didn't. Luke pointed to the new door he had leaned against the wall of the shed. "Bogie said he'd let you know I was coming over to replace this."

"Yeah, well, he didn't." She gave it a cursory glance. "I suppose you think it's kinda nutty that we order our doors by the bunch. I mean, who does that, right?"

What was the most diplomatic response? Agreeing with her was tantamount to calling the Bogarts masochists. But disagreeing with her risked igniting the same sort of ire that had fractured their back door beyond repair.

The woman looked as though she hadn't run a brush through her peroxided hair any time in the past twenty-four hours. She pulled the sleeves of her ratty housedress to her elbows and thrust out her arms to show him welts and bruises the size of sea slugs. Luke had seen their twins on Bogie that morning. She turned and retreated indoors.

Was she coming back? Was she calling Bogie at the studio? Or the cops? Was that going to be the extent of their interaction?

He swept the debris into a pile and moved the new door toward an empty doorjamb. Except that it wasn't empty. Mayo had reappeared, holding a large pewter tray in front of her. The afternoon sun glinted into Luke's eyes. "Did you see the bruises on his arms? This is what I whacked him with. Just to knock him off his balance, you understand, before I shoved him into the door. Self-defense is what it was. I didn't clobber him until after he clobbered me with *Gone with the Wind*. And you know how much that sucker weighs."

The door grew heavy in Luke's hands. He let it slide onto the paving, wondering what kind of person tells a stranger that she struck her husband with a metal tray because he had hit her with a massive book? Was this just a game to them? A real-life Punch-and-Judy show?

He wished Nell were here so that he could ask her, "This is bizarre, even by Hollywood standards, isn't it?" But she was probably making goo-goo eyes at Gus the Goon. What did she see in him, anyway?

Mayo's eyebrows were halfway up her forehead now. She hadn't asked him a question, but she was expecting some sort of response out of him.

"This comes five years too late, but I thought you were terrific in *Marked Woman*."

"Thank you." Mayo lifted her chin, lips curled upward. As the creases gouging the corners of her mouth melted away, Luke glimpsed the vestiges of the fresh-faced Mayo Methot who had stepped off a train ten years before. "I met Hump making that picture." She blinked dreamily, then her shoulders dropped and the edges of her face hardened. "Bette Davis was the star of that movie. Look what's happened to *her*."

She retreated inside the house again without saying another word.

Was this why Bogie was paying him ten dollars a week more than his family was? Because he had to deal with a capricious woman who could switch from harridan to honey lamb in a trice? Whatever the reason, he gave silent thanks that she'd gone and turned his attention to the door. He'd once watched his brother Tony hang one, but that had been years ago. He didn't need an audience watching while he figured it out.

Twenty minutes later, he was twisting the last screw into place. Mayo reappeared, holding a portable typewriter. "He told me to give you this. If you're going to be answering his *fan mail*—" she coated the two words in caustic venom "—you'll need to type up the replies." She set it down on a narrow table just inside the door with a weathered top and wrought-iron legs. "Can you type?"

"Uh-huh." How difficult would it be to find a typing school in a town swimming with screenwriters?

"You look like that kind of chump."

Compliment or insult? It was hard to say.

"When you get back to the studio, tell him it's pork chops for dinner tonight. I'm fixing 'em just the way he likes 'em. Brined for an hour and lots of peppercorns. But if he gets home one minute after seven, he'll find 'em in the trash."

She let the door slam shut behind her.

11

A stagehand was painting a wall behind the jury box of the courtroom that had risen in place of Cardo's restaurant. "You're the new stand-in, right?" He kept his brush in motion as he flashed a look that qualified more as a flinch than a smile. "Sid needs you, pronto."

Luke found the picture's director of photography conferring with the cameraman. "Our first shot is where Bogie throws a left hook. Lighting-wise, it's a tricky one, so be warned. You'll be on your feet for quite some time." He pointed to the largest of three X's marking the courtroom floorboards. "Hit it, Mike."

A split second before light flooded the set, Luke caught sight of a couple standing near the perimeter. The girl held a clipboard in her arms; the guy stood behind her and to her left. Not close enough to touch, but close enough for her to feel his breath against her neck.

Great. Now he had to stand there for God only knew how long, with nothing to do and nothing to distract him.

Luke knew he could impress Nell with his memory trick. Or he could put a ton of effort into a sketch that would make her declare she *must* have it framed. Then he'd act all bashful. *Gosh, no.*

It ain't that good. Yes, she'd insist, it was the most precious gift anybody had ever made for her.

But six feet one of swagger? Two hundred and twenty pounds of congenital self-confidence? An ego the size of the Brooklyn Bridge? Nope. He couldn't compete with that.

A film of sweat coated Luke's face by the time they were ready for Bogie. Two-thirds of the lights went out; the temperature on the set fell ten degrees. Luke blinked away the glare as he headed for Bogie's dressing room without checking to see if Nell and Gus were still flirting.

"You all set?"

Bogie sat at his makeup mirror. A woman in her well-kept late forties stood behind him. She wore her hair—dyed black, Luke guessed—pulled back into a chignon. Bogie growled. The woman stepped to the side, blocking Bogie from view.

"Sorry," Luke said. "Should I knock first?"

"Oh, it's you. That's okay, Verita." She returned to her place behind Bogie. He waved his hand over his left shoulder. "Luke, meet Verita, my hairdresser. More importantly, the keeper of the toupées."

A smattering of sparse follicles flecked Bogie's scalp. He was far from bald, but Luke could see he was halfway there. He winced at his reflection. "Nobody sees Gary Cooper or Cary Grant worrying about turning forty-two and going the way of a cue ball."

Verita gave the hairpiece a final flick with her comb and slid it on. "Tell that to Fred Astaire. At least you don't have to pirouette in your movies."

"Nobody wants to see my pirouettes." Bogie jerked his Chesterfield toward a canvas bag sitting on the floor. "It's time you tackled that."

Luke pulled at the strings and opened up the top. There were hundreds of letters inside. "Do I reply to all of them?"

"God, no. Divide them into three piles. Most folks just want an autographed picture. Take those back to Publicity. The ones who have made some effort to personalize their letter, add them to the second pile. They'll get an autographed photo—or something."

"And third-pile people?"

"They're the ones with an unusual story. Could be they won a lookalike contest, or named their first-born after me." Verita tapped him on the shoulder. He rose out of the chair and put on his jacket. "They get an autographed picture and a letter, which you'll type out and I'll sign. That is, until you master my signature. It can get stuffy in here. You'll be more comfortable out there, so bring them with you."

Luke hesitated. Face Nell and Gus again? Bogie was on the move, though, so he followed his boss onto the set, dragging the bag behind him.

An assistant director had lined up half a dozen chairs near the camera. Luke took one and scooped up a handful of fan mail. The first letter was from Bismarck, North Dakota. He was unfolding it when Nell plunked herself down in the neighboring chair.

"Isn't it funny how things work out? When I asked around for potential jobs, I hardly expected you'd end up becoming Bogie's factotum."

Factotum. Now, there was a word nobody in the Valenti compound would use in a million years. And he had to get a crush on the one girl who could drop it into a conversation like it was 'cookie' or 'teaspoon.'

The fan letter was in pencil. Judging by the scrawl, Jamie Campbell was in grade school.

Nell clicked her stopwatch back to zero. "My pal in the mail-room told me Bogie's fan mail has doubled since *Maltese Falcon.* That's what a hit movie can do. It gives Bogie's agent ammunition when they renegotiate contracts. Three or four bags a day is hard to ignore."

Would Gus know the meaning of 'factotum'? Luke was willing to bet twenty bucks that he wouldn't.

"Say, is something wrong?"

Luke held up Jamie's letter. "This kid says his favorite Bogart movie is *The Return of Doctor X.* Isn't that the one where he appears paler than the Canterville Ghost?"

"He hated making that movie."

"So I shouldn't show it to him?"

"Maybe you should. He might be glad to know that at least one person enjoyed it."

As he opened another letter, Luke felt the heat of her stare. *Yes, I heard you, and yes, there is something wrong, but no, I'm not going to talk about it.*

"*Doctor X,* huh?" Bogie put on his suede loafers. "There's a publicity headshot of me in full makeup. They coated it on like paint and I was sweating buckets under the lights. How about you go over to Publicity tomorrow and ask around?"

Luke slipped Bogie's jacket off its hanger and held it. "Will do."

"You know, I've been thinking about that falcon of yours. When you turned it in to the props department, did they put it in the same cabinet with the others?"

Luke wondered if Nell had left the studio yet. For the rest of the day, he had pretended to be buried in fan mail, affecting a *Don't bother me* air. He couldn't keep up this cold shoulder routine forever, though. They were going to be working together. He'd get over this disappointment in time. A week or two. Or a month. Meanwhile, she'd catch on. She was a smart girl, but dammit, that was why he liked her.

"I didn't get any farther than the front counter."

"They only made four. And then you came along with an extra.

Suits me fine, because nobody misses the one I took. But where the hell did yours come from? Let's go see."

"Right now?"

Bogie fastened his watch around his wrist. "You got somewhere you need to be?"

Luke hadn't received his first paycheck yet. He didn't even know how Bogie planned to pay him. Cash? Check? Weekly? Monthly? Until he knew how this arrangement would work, he had to mete out his dwindling stash. "No," he replied. "Let's go."

The attendant behind the front desk opened his mouth, but Bogie waved away the words. "We know where we're going."

He led Luke down a corridor lined with vases, umbrella stands, picture frames, hurricane lamps. He stopped when he came to a tall metal cabinet. On the middle shelf of five, the four falcons stood in a neat row. Bogie studied them in turn, lifting each one up for a moment before returning it to its place. He plucked up the falcon second from the right and held it up to the electric light behind them.

"This is the one you brought." Bogie turned Luke's falcon around. "The others were shiny, so they photographed well. This has a matte finish. Simon must have known they didn't use this one in production. I'm guessing he made it and sent it to his brother."

The bird Luke had lugged clear across the country had been . . . a *fake*?

Bogie turned it upside down and squinted. Someone had carved a series of letters along the bottom. "Is this a q or an o?"

"Looks to me like a c."

"What do you think those last three are?"

The two of them stepped back until they were beneath the overhead light. Luke angled the falcon's base so that he could see the etching more clearly. The middle part was illegible, but the rest was clearer. "o n s."

"I'd have said e u s."

"That last letter could be a z."

"So it starts with an o or a c or a q and ends with either ons or eus. Unless the s is a z." Bogie chuckled. "What a couple of private eyes we'd make, huh?" Bogie returned the falcon to its spot on the shelf and closed the cabinet doors. "Could I get you to drive me home?"

"You feeling okay?"

He shrugged. "I thought I was done with second-rate pictures. Getting through this one has been a tougher slog than I bargained for. I'm wiped out and I haven't faced whatever scenario the missus has planned the minute I walk in the door."

Had this been anybody else but his boss, Luke might have been tempted to ask if this marriage was worth the effort. But who was he to dispense marital advice when he'd never even kissed a girl?

"Sure," he said. "Let's get you home."

Luke turned onto Laurel Canyon Boulevard. Soon they were heading up into the back of the Hollywood Hills. Bogie had said little since they'd left the studio, preferring instead to watch the world pass by outside his window.

"I gotta say, Luke, it's a relief having you around. I don't have to deal with answering fan mail, and hanging doors, and everything else I'll be finding for you to do."

"I'm glad to be of help." Would now be a good time to ask how Bogie intended to pay him?

"You impressed me that day at the commissary, knowing Goethe. Boy, that really was a kick."

"Like I said, I studied him in college."

"But can you finish this stanza? 'The world below the brine / Forests at the bottom of the sea, the branches and leaves / Sea-lettuce, vast lichens, strange flowers and seeds, the thick tangle, openings, and pink surf.'"

Bogie was quoting Walt Whitman, but who wanted to come off sounding like a wiseass? He hemmed and hawed a little. "Give me a second. I know this one. It's on the tip of—got it. 'Different colors, pale gray and green, purple, white, and gold, the play of light through the water.'"

Bogie slapped the dashboard in delight. "Dagnabbit! You *do* know it."

How ironic that of all poems, Bogie would choose the one Luke couldn't relate to, what with colors being largely theoretical to him and all.

"A favorite of yours?" Luke asked.

"I'm just an old seadog. There's nothing I like better than to take my yacht out on the open sea, and there's nowhere else I'd rather be than on *Sluggy*. They could pay me all the money in the world, but it wouldn't come close to the feeling of the water rocking my boat. Like swaying in a cradle. It's the only place I can truly relax."

"Speaking of pay—"

Bogie slapped the dashboard again. "What about this one? 'The debt is paid / The verdict said / The Furies laid / The plague is stayed.'"

"Ralph Waldo Emerson. 'The Past.'"

"Correct, Mr. Vail. However, can you complete the stanza?"

"'All fortunes made / Turn the key and bolt the door / Sweet is death forevermore.'"

"I'll have to work harder to stump you, won't I?"

They crossed the peak of the Hollywood Hills, where Mulholland Drive ran along the crest. It looked like the sort of winding country road where a fella could take a girl for some necking. If the girl was available and interested.

"What made you choose 'The Past'?"

"Because I thought I was done with it—and all those hoods and thugs and gamblers and crooks. In my first thirty-four pictures, I've been shot in twelve, electrocuted or hung in eight, and was a jailbird in nine. I've played more scenes writhing around on the floor than I have standing up. Now, I ask you, what kind of career is that? I'll tell you: a lousy one that no self-respecting man can be proud of."

"Is that what you want? A career to be proud of?"

"I thought I'd turned the corner with *Falcon*. I played a romantic lead. Before Mary Astor gets carted away by the cops, we had a couple of smooching scenes. And nobody plugged me full of holes. I read that script and thought, 'Finally, I survive to the end credits.' And now this *Big Shot* stinkeroo."

"You die in this one too?"

"Another loser. Another gambler. Another ex-con. I tell you, Luke, I'm reaching the end of my tether."

Luke was glad now that he had bought a map and had committed the L.A. streets to memory. Bogie was too preoccupied with his career crossroads to give directions. Laurel Canyon Boulevard meandered down the folds of the hillsides amid towering eucalyptus trees and manzanita bushes until it leveled off as it headed to the Sunset Strip.

"Perhaps it's just the last of the pictures they'd already lined up for you. What's next?"

"A load of tripe."

"Is that the title?"

"It'll be the slogan at the bottom of the poster."

"Do you die in the end?"

"No."

"Do you play a gambler, ex-con, or street thug?"

"It's some hokey story set in a place called Casablanca. I don't even know where that is."

"French Morocco," Luke told him.

"Where's that?"

"South of Spanish Morocco, which is south of Gibraltar."

"So it's in Africa?"

"On the Atlantic coast, about halfway between Gibraltar and Marrakesh."

"And you know this . . . how?"

"I took a college class in European expansionism." It had been a single class, so Luke had seen the professor's map of Europe and North Africa only that one time. "What's this new movie about?"

"It's based on an unproduced play written by unpublished playwrights, which is why George Raft knocked it back."

The evening traffic along the Strip had grown so heavy that they'd slowed to a halt. "Does it bother you knowing that you're their second choice?"

"He was stupid enough to turn down Sam Spade, and look how that turned out."

"Sounds like Raft might be your lucky charm."

"I'm yet to be convinced that a straight-up romantic melodrama is a good thing."

"Bette Davis has built a very successful career on those sorts of pictures," Luke pointed out. The setting sun was now shining in his eyes. "Hokey or not, wouldn't it put you on top of the pile?"

Bogie's "yes" was slow in coming.

They had reached Horn Avenue now. Luke rounded the corner and headed up the incline back into the hills. "Isn't that what you want?"

"It's what I've been shooting for ever since I landed at Warners. But now that I'm on the precipice, I don't know that I can pull it off. I mean, look at me. Not exactly Errol Flynn handsome, and as you learned today, I need a toupée. Whoever they cast opposite me, she's bound to be gorgeous. Who's going to buy that some glamorous star will find me attractive?"

Great Caesar's ghost, if that didn't beat everything. Bogie was within reach of the shiny gold ring, and he didn't think he deserved it?

"You probably think I'm nuts," Bogie said.

"Little bit." Luke took care to inject just enough of a chuckle into his response to soften the blow as he pulled into the Bogart driveway.

Stepping out of the Packard, Bogie rubbed his hands together. "Let me call you a cab."

A cab ride was the sort of extravagance Luke could ill afford. "I think I'll walk."

"Now that the sun's gone down, it's a little too cold out, isn't it?"

"Cold for California maybe, but I'm still fresh off the train from Brooklyn."

"I've lived in California too long. My New York blood's gotten too thin." He tipped his hat to reveal a white envelope sitting on his scalp. "Goodness! What's this?" He pulled the keys out of Luke's hand and replaced them with the envelope. "You didn't think I'd forgotten, did you?"

"Well, I . . ." Luke opened the flap and counted four ten-dollar bills. "We agreed on thirty."

"The extra is for the cab. It's six-thirty-five now. How else are you going to get home in time for dinner?"

1 2

*L*uke filled a metal bucket with Newport Yacht Club seawater and hauled it onto the deck. "What's next?"

Bogie pointed to the roof that covered *Sluggy*'s cabin. "I haven't given it a decent scour since the day I bought this tub."

"TUB?" Mayo called from the dining table. "I won't have you insulting our baby." She stroked the side of the porthole as though it were a cat. "Don't you listen to daddy. He don't mean nothing by it."

Luke dropped a scrubbing brush into his bucket. "Is the Coast Guard going to turn you down because of a slightly dirty roof?"

"Depends on how desperate they are. If I'm only one of four applicants to join their auxiliary, they won't be too fussy. But if I'm among seven hundred and ninety-two, and they turn me down because of my roof, I'll be mighty riled."

"Lemme tell ya," Mayo put in, "you don't want to be around this lug when he's riled."

Luke held his breath. Was this the moment when they started in on each other?

When he'd arrived home and told his fellow boarders about his first day on the job, they had filled him in on the "Battling

Bogarts." That was the name the press had bestowed on them when Bogie and Mayo had given up hiding their squabbles behind closed doors.

"All it takes is a couple of words," Beatrice had said. "Hedda Hopper wrote about how they were at Ciro's with Peter Lorre and his wife. Mayo called Bogie 'Calvin Coolidge,' which he must have found insulting because he smashed his glass on the table, brushed the shards into her purse, and threw the purse onto the stage. Right there in front of everybody!"

"I don't go in for half measures," Bogie said, "so when it happens around you—and it will—you have my permission to head for the hills."

"You won't need to hide out for long." Mayo joined them on the aft deck. "That's one thing I'll say for my Hump: he doesn't hold a grudge."

Bogie grabbed a bar of soap the size of a brick. "I thought you were going to quiz me on the skipper's exam."

"While you clean the roof?"

"Got anything else to do?"

"As a matter of fact, I'm in the middle of a cigarette."

"When you're done with that, m'lady, I'll be ready to field any question you might find in the manual."

Bogie and Luke climbed onto the roof and sloshed some water around.

"I know what you're thinking," Bogie said, swabbing the soap across the painted wood.

"You do, do you?"

"You're thinking, 'Where are the Battling Bogarts?'"

"I am, am I?"

"It's written all over your face."

"If your acting career ever goes down the drain, you could develop a stage act as a mind reader. Do you read palms, too? That'd pack 'em in." Luke dipped his brush into the bucket. "You seem like a regular couple to me."

Bogie panted as he put his back into scrubbing the grime away. "Being on the boat, on the water, in the open air, the sunshine and sea breezes, somehow all of it helps us to let that crap go. It just happens; that's the best part."

Mayo popped her head up. "Okay, skipper. Quiz time."

Bogie had applied as soon as the Coast Guard had announced they were forming an auxiliary force to beef up its operations. The Army Western Defense Command had deemed all coastal refineries and factories vulnerable to Japanese forces. There were too many for the regular Coast Guard to defend, so they were taking applications from civilians with small sea craft who wanted to be commissioned for wartime service patrol.

"I'm not a skipper yet." Bogie kept his head down as he pushed and pulled his brush across his patch of roof.

"You will be." Mayo opened the test booklet. "What's the difference between a rolling hitch and a marlinspike hitch?"

Bogie's brush stopped mid-stroke. "A marlinspike hitch is a temporary knot you use to attach a rope to a rod to make a handle. You use a rolling hitch to attach a thinner rope to a thicker one."

"Correct!" Mayo's piercing voice startled a pair of seagulls off *Sluggy*'s port side.

Bogie resumed his chore, a quiet smile dimpling his cheeks.

"Next question: what is the value of a weak link on an anchor, and where is it?"

"That's the last link in the chain. If you throw your anchor overboard, but the seabed is deeper than the chain is long, you might end up damaging the hull."

Mayo looked up from the booklet. "If the weak link breaks the chain, don't you lose your anchor?"

"If the damage is severe enough, you could scuttle the whole boat. Where would you be then?"

"I'd be bobbing around the water like a cork, yelling at you for being so damn stupid."

"Which is when I'd start swimming for shore and leave you to your own devices."

"You would, too, you nasty reprobate." She flipped the page. "When one sailing vessel approaches another, who has the right of way?"

"The larger one."

"Nope."

"The smaller one."

"It's the vessel with the wind on their starboard side. When both sailboats have the wind on the same side, the boat that is upwind has to yield to the other vessel."

Bogie's dimple faded away. "Trick question." He got to his feet and threw his brush into his bucket hard enough to slosh half the water onto the roof. He picked up a wrench he'd used to tighten the bolts around the portholes earlier in the day, wiped it against his sweater with *SLUGGY* embroidered across the chest, then turned it over and over in his hands. "Dammit. Dammit. Dammit."

"Two out of three isn't bad," Luke said.

"What's the next one?" His question was more of a demand.

"In which direction will the compass needle point when sailing south?"

"The North Pole," Bogie said straight away.

"Wrong."

"THE HELL I AM!"

"The hell you are. It's magnetic north."

Bogie hurled the wrench overboard. The three of them watched it splash into the water and sink from sight. He grumbled like a volcano getting ready to blow. Luke backed away, bracing himself for the torrent of invective he'd been expecting all day. Mayo kept her face blank. Was she rehearsing some wisecrack to throw at him? Luke eyed the dock. At least they weren't out at sea. If things got too nasty, he had an escape route.

Silence ticked by until Mayo said, "And that's my cue to go down to the galley to fix us some drinks."

Luke crossed the roof until he stood by his boss's side. "I guess I'm off to the hardware store now that you don't have a full set of tools to show the inspector."

"I thought I had this information down."

"You only got two wrong."

"That's the maximum you're allowed—out of fifty."

"So you keep studying."

"My exam's in three days, and the boat inspection is the week after that. I want this taken care of before I start filming *Across the Pacific* Monday after next." The two seagulls lowered themselves onto the same patch of water where the wrench had drowned. "Joining the Coast Guard means I'll be able to do my bit, even if it's only on weekends. Each of us needs to know that we're doing our part, don't we?"

They kept their eyes on the pair of bobbing seagulls. The question Bogie hadn't asked hung in the briny air: *Why aren't you in uniform?*

"Hey sailors!" Mayo called out. "Come and get it."

They followed her into the cabin, where Mayo had set out three highball glasses on the foldout table. "It's just iced tea. Our student needs to keep a clear head." She flicked a fingernail toward a plate of butter cookies. "Baked these myself. I should caution you, though—I'm not the finest cook in the world. I didn't burn them, so there's that."

They sipped the tea in silence. It was sweeter than Luke would have liked, but she was trying her darndest to leaven her husband's dark mood. To her credit, she hadn't fallen back onto booze, which, Luke imagined, was her solution of first resort.

The booklet Mayo had been reading from lay at the end of the table, face down. Luke spotted the chart filling the back page.

"How's your Morse code?"

"I sweated over this one. But, yeah, I think I've got it."

Luke ran his eyes down the grid, from A—one dot, one dash—

to Z—two dashes, two dots. He cast the book aside. "Let's start with spelling out your name."

Mayo looked at the booklet and then at Luke. "What were you, a Boy Scout?"

Joining the Boy Scouts might have been a way to build friendships, but Pop had been against it—and Enzo Valenti was not to be argued with. But for Luke to admit that he'd memorized the code so easily meant that he'd have to admit to having a bizarre memory. The folks back at the boarding house had taken it well enough, but he still felt like a sideshow freak sharing this information with anyone else. And besides, Bogie had struggled so hard to master it; Luke didn't want to make him feel even worse than he did. Would a little white lie be so bad?

"Yes, I was," he told them. "Using your knuckles, tap out Bogart."

"B." One dash, three dots.

"O." Three dashes.

"G." Two dashes, one dot.

"A." One dash, one dot.

"R." Dot, dash, dot.

"T." Dash.

"Six out of six correct."

Mayo clapped. "Now do 'Jack Warner is an ugly fathead.'"

"F." Two dots, one dash, one dot.

"U." Two dots, one dash.

"C." Dash, dot, dash, dot.

"K." Dash, dot, dash.

"J." One dot, three dashes.

"A." One dash, one dot.

"C." Dash, dot, dash, dot.

"K." Dash, dot, dash.

After they clinked their glasses, Mayo asked Luke, "Got yourself a girl yet?"

Caught off guard, he choked on his iced tea. "I—um—ah—"

"You're a decent-looking young fella. I'd imagine you'd do okay in the female department." She looked him up and down, and then seemed to come to some sort of conclusion. "Oh, I get it. Don't want to tie yourself down to one girl now that you'll be heading off to the front sooner or later?"

Luke stared at his drink, trying to wish away the heat creeping into his cheeks.

Bogie cleared his throat. "Speaking of Jack Warner, I heard this week he's on the rampage."

Mayo swirled the tea in her glass. "Since when *isn't* that man on a rampage?"

"You know that war-bond drive of his? He plans on using a Maltese falcon as a draw card and had the prop department bring them to him so that he could make his choice. Turns out, one of them has gone missing."

Luke's head jerked up. "But we were just there."

"Busted!" Mayo exclaimed, and turned to Bogie. "When you came home with that thing, I asked if you got permission. And you said that you didn't need it, that the picture's in the can, and nobody's going to miss one little falcon. How sore is J.W.?"

"Plenty."

"He'll blow his stack when he finds out."

"The only people who know I took it are on this boat." Bogie still hadn't blinked, but a wry smile had crept onto his face. "I think I'm safe."

"I'm sure Luke here knows how to keep a secr—" She cut herself off. "Say, why did you change the subject?"

"What subject?" Bogie said.

"We were talking about Luke not tying himself down to one gal before he ships out."

Luke cast his eyes on the tabletop and broke a cookie in half.

"What'd I say now?" Mayo demanded. "The kid's enlisted, ain't he?"

"Maybe it's none of our business," Bogie said quietly.

"We're at war. It's everybody's business."

It wasn't as though he could have this conversation once and be done with it. He was going to have to explain over and over why he wasn't in uniform, so he might as well get used to it.

"I have a medical condition that makes it hard to distinguish between colors. If you use a blue pencil to write on legal paper, I can't see it."

"You mean not even this gorgeous blue sky or my green dress?"

"I only know that things are blue and green because people tell me."

"What about Technicolor movies?"

"All movies are pretty much black and white to me."

"That's a tough break, kid." Bogie winced as though Luke had slapped him. "Real tough."

"I can't distinguish between a green light and a red one, so imagine me operating a submarine torpedo." Luke bit into the cookie. Its buttery smoothness melted in his mouth. "I could single-handedly lose us the war in the Pacific."

Luke had meant it as a joke, but Mayo frowned in genuine concern and sympathy. "They could make you a cook. Or the guy that types requisition forms."

"They sent me straight home with a big 4-F stamped on my card."

Silence filled the cabin, broken only by the tide slapping against the side of the boat, until Bogie said, "Do you suppose Gus O'Farrell is 4-F? He doesn't appear to be jumping into uniform any time soon."

Finally. A change of subject. "Isn't he the guy who used to be your stand-in?"

Bogie winked at Luke. "I suspect he's none too happy with you. He fancied himself my official stand-in and stuntman."

"Isn't he five inches taller than you?"

"Try telling him that."

"I did."

"Oh-ho!" Mayo slapped the table. "You said that? To Gus O'Farrell? How'd he take it?"

Luke shrugged. "He's not Humphrey Bogart's stand-in anymore, is he?"

Bogie reached behind him, where a pack of Chesterfields and a lighter sat next to an ice bucket. "If you're willing to tackle Hell O'Farrell's son, I dread to think what you'd be like with a gun in your hand."

"Hell O'Farrell?" Luke asked. "Who's that?"

"Elmore O'Farrell and Buster Wiles are the two big Warners stuntmen. O'Farrell's a genuine tough guy who'll fall off a horse, jump from a moving train, dive out of a window, swim across a raging river, or wrestle an alligator. He'll go through hell to give a director what he wants; hence, his name. Gus is his youngest son, and the only one willing to take up the family trade, which I reckon has deeply disappointed Hell. But Gus? He's a chip off the old man's block, that's for sure."

Mayo pulled the cigarette out of Bogie's fingers and took a drag. "You told an O'Farrell to back off. That takes guts."

"I didn't know who he is. Or his father."

Bogie lit up a fresh Chesterfield. "Hell O'Farrell is used to getting his way."

"Are you saying I've made an enemy of Hell Junior?"

Bogie blew a plume of smoke toward the ceiling as he contemplated his response. "It's safe to assume you have."

"What should I do about it?"

"Well, now, *that*," he said, rising from the table, "is a quandary you'll need to figure out on your own. Let's get topside."

Luke watched Bogie make his way aft. "It's like that, is it?"

"You haven't arrived in the movie biz until you've made an enemy." Mayo thrust out her hand for Luke to shake. "Welcome!"

13

*J*ohn Huston kneaded the muscles at the back of his neck. "Listen up, people." The cast and crew of *Across the Pacific* turned to their director. "We've got a problem. The actor we hired to play Sydney's manservant hasn't shown up. I've sent a studio messenger boy to fetch him. If he returns empty-handed, we'll have to scratch around for a replacement. Either way, we're now behind schedule, so I'm asking that no one leave."

Sydney Greenstreet raised his hand. "Can we pop outside? The air in this soundstage is suffocatingly oppressive."

Huston's standard grin was closer to a leer. "I wouldn't take any chances if I were you. J.W. is on a rampage over his war-bond tour. He's eight city blocks beyond furious over this missing falcon."

"Why not use Errol's *Robin Hood* tights?" Nell suggested. "God knows, he filled them so awfully well."

Mary Astor laughed. "The women of America will turn out in their thousands for a chance to touch them. The tights, too."

"J.W. busts a gut if someone wastes so much as a single nail,"

Bogie said. "He paid for four falcons, so that's how many there should be."

Luke felt the heat of Nell's mute *Know anything about this?* stare. His disappointment in her still chafed the rough edges of his confidence. He returned his focus to straightening the stack of headshots he had been handing Bogie to autograph.

"Anyway," Huston said, "let's hope that kid I sent to Little Tokyo doesn't return alone."

Greenstreet mopped his forehead with a limp handkerchief. "My goodness gracious me, in a city of a million and a half, surely there is one gentleman of Oriental origin who can play my manservant."

Bogie handed the last of the headshots to Luke. "You're not taking into account the effect of the Battle of Los Angeles."

Greenstreet waved his handkerchief like a grand old duchess. "It was a false alarm sparked off by a bunch of over-enthusiastic, trigger-happy volunteers. There was no enemy aircraft, just a balloon carrying a red flare."

"We know that now," Bogie said, "but at the time it was unnerving. I was at home charging through *For Whom the Bell Tolls*. It felt like all hell had broken loose."

"That book's on my nightstand," Mary said. "I want to finish *Mrs. Miniver* before Metro's version comes out. I bumped into May Whitty at the Brown Derby. She told me Greer is marvelous and Norma Shearer is going to kick herself for turning it down."

Luke gave up hiding his smile. Nobody was paying him the slightest bit of attention. Three months ago, he'd been watching *The Maltese Falcon* at the Brooklyn Fox. And now, here he was with the leads sitting close enough to spill coffee on. He wasn't planning on being in California forever, but until he figured out a way to get home, he got to listen to Sam Spade, Brigid O'Shaughnessy, and Kasper Gutman chatter about reading Hemingway.

"Has everyone's Japanese gardener disappeared?" Mary asked nobody in particular. "They've all gone on our street. My neighbor is some big mucky-muck at Paramount; I had to teach him how to iron his shirts because his houseboy's on the lam."

"Isn't that what Chinese laundries are for?" Greenstreet asked. He turned to Huston. "Does my valet have to be Japanese? My character is from Britain, so couldn't he have a British manservant?"

Huston cackled. "You corpulent son of a bitch! You haven't read the whole script?"

"My preferred method is to go through my scenes over breakfast so I can play them with freshness and spontaneity."

Huston raised his arms and slapped them to his sides. "Does anybody want to explain why we're waiting for a Jap actor?"

Bogie clapped a hand on Greenstreet's sloping shoulder. "Your Dr. Lorenz is a professor of sociology who admires the Japanese and therefore is very unpopular in the Philippines, where he lives. It's kind of central to the plot."

"That's all I needed to know. Does anybody have a deck of cards? We could play gin rummy—"

"I'VE GOT IT! I'VE FOUND IT! IT'S HERE!"

Gus O'Farrell marched into the middle of the soundstage like he was Johnny Appleseed. Gripped in his left hand was a Maltese falcon. "It was the damnedest thing." Gus's eyes darted around him. "I was in that alleyway behind the mill where the scenery department and the paint shop dump their trash."

Luke had stumbled on the alleyway when he'd lost his way during his first week on the job. It wasn't where the mill workers left their trash. The lane Gus was talking about was what the commissary used. Those cans were filled with half-eaten apples, leftover pastrami, melted ice-cream, and yesterday's chili. The whole place needed a vigorous hosing down.

"I happened to be walking through there." The hell you were, thought Luke. "I looked down and spied a glint of light." The hell you did. "And I thought to myself, 'That's weird.' Usually there's wood offcuts, and sawdust, and dented old paint cans." Okay, now

I *know* you're lying. "So then my curiosity got picked." The word is *piqued*, but don't let me interrupt your outpouring of tripe. "I kept my eye on this gleam because it was almost like this thing was calling me." Inanimate objects talk to you? Telephone the local booby hatch. "I climbed over buckets and greasy old canvases and balled-up wads of paper stained with I don't know what." For someone who's been crawling through trash, your shoes are awfully clean. "The closer I got, the more I could see it didn't belong there." *You* don't belong here, because I've replaced you. "I couldn't believe my eyes! It was the missing falcon that Mr. Warner's been looking for!"

To illustrate his point, Gus was now cradling the falcon like he was Joseph holding the baby Jesus. All he needed was a manger and some farm animals to complete the scene. He craned his neck and shifted the falcon to his other hand. "I sent word for Blayney Matthews to meet me here."

Bogie leaned over Luke. "Looks to me like it's got a matte finish."

Luke slid off his chair and approached Gus.

"You ever seen one of these up close?" Gus's question came out more like a taunt: *This is the one you brought with you—and I know it.*

Luke extended his hand. "May I?"

"So it's true!"

Gus turned to a trio of men in pressed suits who stood shoulder to shoulder at the perimeter of the set. "Mr. Matthews!" he called. "Over here!"

Luke returned to Bogie's side. "Who are the other two?"

"Charlie Einfeld and Alex Evelove from Publicity. Somebody sure knows how to milk this for all its worth."

"Mr. Warner will be so pleased to hear we have found the missing falcon," Matthews said. "He's been putting me through the wringer since he learned about the theft."

Gus adopted an aw-shucks pose. Shoulders hunched forward.

Hands clasped behind his back. "I'm just glad I saw it when the sun hit it at the right angle."

Einfeld lifted his Graflex press camera. "A little higher, Gus. Closer to your face." He took a bunch of shots. "You'll make the front page of the *Warner Club News.*"

Gus handed the falcon over to Evelove. "I sure wasn't expecting that."

Luke wanted to puke his breakfast down the guy's plaid shirt. Nell was a smart girl. She had seen enough of life to know how to tell phony from bona fide. How could she buy this baloney?

One of the studio bicycle messenger boys raced up to John Huston with news that made the director rub his hands together. "We've located someone to play Sydney's manservant. He's in Costuming, so let's get moving, people!"

The crowd began to disperse, and Luke turned back toward Bogie's dressing room. A bag of fan mail had appeared outside the door. Larger than the previous day's load, Luke guessed it contained four or five hours of work. He took a step toward it as Nell's hand closed around his elbow. "What's eating you, Mister Sourpuss?"

Luke jacked a thumb toward the bulging mail bag. "Until I saw this, I didn't realize how much work was ahead of me today."

"That doesn't explain why you looked like you wanted to slash Gus's jugular with a broken beer bottle. So spit it out. I've got a job to do in a few minutes, and I won't be able to concentrate if you don't tell me what's bugging you."

All right. Okay. Fine. She insists on knowing? Well, here it comes. "That performance we just witnessed."

"Performance? We haven't started filming yet."

"I'm talking about Gus."

She turned to watch Gus leave the soundstage with Blayney Matthews. "You don't believe him?"

"If someone went to the trouble of stealing a famous prop, why would they toss it away in the most foul-smelling spot in the studio?"

"Maybe they got scared they'd get fired?"

"It was never there. The falcon he paraded around, that's the one I brought to California. I returned it to Props before Christmas."

"Anyone could've—"

"Weeks later I showed it to Bogie, who confirmed it wasn't used in the movie. And then it went missing, and *then* Gus discovered it and rushed right over here, but somehow found time to alert the heads of Security *and* Publicity? His entire story is fishier than a river full of trout."

"You don't like him, do you?" Nell asked quietly.

"Posers like him are so desperate to be noticed. He should be in front of the cameras."

"If you knew his father, you'd understand."

"Bogie told me about Hell O'Farrell."

An Asian guy about Luke's age walked into the soundstage, dressed in the simple, conservative suit of a domestic servant. "Everybody!" Huston shouted. "Places, please."

Nell ignored him. "Hell O'Farrell is no reason to give me the cold shoulder."

"You need to be in your chair."

"They can't start shooting until I'm there, but I'm over here trying to understand why you're Mister Frowny Face just because—"

"Why are you dating a guy like that?" His question came out a long, acerbic hiss.

She drew back, like he stunk worse than the alley behind the mill. "We're not dating, per se." *Per se?* How impressive that she could stuff so much meaning into two little words. "We've gone out a couple of times—"

"Does the word 'dating' have a different interpretation here than it does in New York?"

She shifted from one foot to the other. "The O'Farrells are a big deal."

"I'm surprised you'd find that sort of thing appealing."

"Who says I do?"

"I might not be Errol Flynn, but I know flirting when I see it."

"When did you see it?"

"My first day here. He came up to you and put his arm around your waist."

"Did *I* put my arm around *him*?"

"You went soft and squishy like a cute little octopus."

"It's okay for you," she said, resentment rising in her eyes. "You're a guy. It behooves us career girls to get on the good side of people who wield power."

"By flirting?"

"Soft and squishy is what men like."

"Not all men, I can assure you."

"NELL!" Huston's voice blasted the air. "WE ARE WAITING!"

"Go," Luke told her. "We can talk about this later."

She poked him with the corner of her clipboard. "Were you jealous when you saw Bonehead O'Farrell trying his luck?"

"No."

"Even just a little bit?"

He tried to keep a straight face, but the effort was beyond him. "I was jealous a lot."

She tsked. "Of a lunk like him? You bet we'll talk about this later."

---

14

*L*uke pulled Bogie's new Packard Clipper out of its reserved parking and headed for the Olive Avenue exit in silence. Several weeks into filming *Across the Pacific*, he had learned that his boss exuded two different silences.

One of them was like a simmering cauldron, threatening to boil over given the slightest provocation.

The other had a plaintive quality to it, like a peevish child waiting to be asked, *What's the matter?*

It was the latter type that filled the car. Luke waited until the studio had disappeared from the rearview mirror. "It's John Huston, isn't it?"

"What is?"

"Is it because he has finished up on *Pacific*, and tomorrow he joins the Army Signal Corps to shoot documentaries for the war effort?"

"I'm jealous, is that it?"

Luke could tell he was on the right track from the way Bogie slumped into his seat, wound down the window, and lit up a cigarette. "He'll be shooting footage, not Germans."

They rounded the broad curve of Cahuenga Avenue and

headed into Hollywood. "You're in the Coast Guard," Luke reminded him. "It's not like you're spending the war sitting at home on your highly paid patootie doing sweet Fanny Adams, helping nobody."

"It's only the auxiliary."

"That exam was pretty tough, as I recall."

They drove six blocks before Bogie was ready to give an inch. "It was."

"You're out there patrolling the coastline practically every weekend. It's far from impossible that you could encounter Jap subs. And it's not like Huston's going to be leading the charge into Berlin."

"Don't bet on it." Bogie cracked a smile and flicked his cigarette butt out the window. "If there's a chance to be in the front row when the Allies roll in, that crazy asshole'll take it."

"Wouldn't we all?"

"I'd give anything to see the looks on the faces of those shitty Kraut bastards."

"You'll miss him."

"I know this picture's nothing much, but it's sure been good to get the *Falcon* team back together." He lapsed into silence again, the plaintive kind, so Luke kept his eyes on the road and let Bogie talk when he was ready. "That *Casablanca* movie I told you about —we start in May. Romance in the African desert, shot in Burbank." Luke could have cut the derision in Bogie's voice with a machete. "What's worse is that Hal's cast Ingrid Bergman."

Bogie said her name as though Hal Wallis had cast Lady Macbeth.

"But she's wonderful!" Luke exclaimed. "Didn't you see her in *Intermezzo*?"

"Who's going to buy someone who looks like her going for short, balding Hump?"

"Never assume what someone will find attractive."

Since that day Gus had pranced onto the set claiming he'd

found the missing falcon, Luke and Nell had ridden a Red Car to Santa Monica, shared a hot fudge sundae, and seen picture shows at Grauman's Chinese. They had reached the hand-holding stage, but only after the lights had gone down, or if C. C. Brown's wasn't too crowded. Never at the studio.

"We're professionals," she had told him. "And professionals don't behave like that." Luke had pointed out that affairs between actors and actresses were commonplace. Almost expected. Movie stars were a separate breed, she had reminded him. Answerable to a unique set of rules written in a book mere mortals had no access to.

Truth be told, he didn't mind her pumping the brakes. He was in no hurry to rush through the getting-to-know-you stage of his first romance. If nothing else, it made for a comforting contrast to the frantic hanky-panky going on in Beatrice's room.

"Thanks," Bogie said.

"For what?"

"Being my one-man cheerleading squad."

They were passing the Garden of Allah Hotel now, which meant they would be pulling into the Bogart driveway soon. More importantly, Luke would make it back to the boarding house in time for dinner. Wednesdays were meatloaf nights, and Edith cooked the best damned meatloaf in Los Angeles County. Crisp on the outside, juicy on the inside, not too salty, and made great sandwiches the next day if there were any leftovers. Not that there often were.

"How about you stay for a bite to eat?"

Luke gripped the steering wheel more tightly than he needed to. There were two versions of Mr. and Mrs. Bogart. There were the Bogarts Luke had seen on *Sluggy*, playing it for laughs, relaxing in the sun. The other version thought nothing of throwing drinks in each other's faces and filling purses with broken glass. Which one would be sitting at their dining table?

Luke wasn't sure he was up for taking the risk. Especially not on meatloaf night.

"Is that fair to Mayo?" he hedged. "Coming home with an unannounced dinner guest?"

"Probably not."

Luke turned onto Horn. "Some other time, perhaps."

Bogie sighed. "All right. I confess. I've got an ulterior motive. Mayo and me, we haven't been getting on so great lately. Doing a picture with Mary Astor is safe. Mayo knows she's no threat."

"Does she know they've cast Ingrid Bergman?"

"Why do you think I'm asking you to dinner?"

A melancholic, almost desperate tone underpinned his question. Luke bid a silent farewell to the meatloaf and pulled into the driveway.

Mayo gawked at Luke with slow-blinking bleariness. "We're drinking bourbon Old Fashioneds." She thrust a tumbler into his hand and gave him a look that said, *Catch up.*

Bogie threw back his drink like it was room-temperature water. "Luke looked hungry, so I invited him in for dinner."

"I hope he can cook, because I sure as hell haven't given it a second's thought."

"There must be leftovers in the ice box." Bogie fixed himself another Old Fashioned. "You'd be okay with a salad, wouldn't you, Luke?"

He'd have preferred Edith's meatloaf. "Anything's fine."

Mayo leaned up against their mahogany bar and crossed her arms, a drink in one fist, a lit Kool in the other. "Did you revel in playing Mister Big Time Movie Star today? Are you nearly done with *Across the Atlantic* yet?"

Bogie glanced at Luke. See what I mean? "It's called *Across the Pacific*," he said through locked teeth. "You're confusing it with *Action in the North Atlantic*, which they want me to do after—" He faltered. Luke guessed he was trying to avoid Ingrid's name. "The one in French Morocco."

"The Pacific. The Atlantic. Africa. By the time this war's over, you'll have conquered the entire world. I'm surprised they didn't use you as a model for that new comic-book hero, Superman." The word came out 'Supernam.' She took an extra-long pull on her cigarette, burning it down to the butt. She crushed it into the glass ashtray, withdrew another Kool from a gold case, and waited for Bogie to offer her a light.

He stood where he was and stared at her.

Luke wondered if he had walked into an argument they hadn't finished when Bogie had left for the studio that morning. One drink, he decided, and he'd be out as soon as a polite opportunity presented itself.

"The lighter's right next to you," Bogie pointed out.

Mayo turned her head to throw Luke a jaundiced eye. "I hope my loving husband is more of a gentleman at work than he is at home."

She hadn't asked him a question, so Luke wasn't sure if he should respond. Saying yes meant he was more considerate to his co-workers. Saying no would leave her with an opening to accuse Bogie of being an asshole to everybody, and why the hell did she marry an asshole?

The carriage clock on the mantel showed a quarter of seven. Whitley Manor would soon be sitting down to juicy meatloaf, peas and mashed potatoes—and peach cobbler à la mode for dessert. Getaway time had arrived. Luke gulped down his bitter apéritif, trying his best to fend off an involuntary wince as it burned his throat.

"How 'bout another?" Bogie jerked the tumbler from Luke's hand. "To answer your question, my dear, *Across the Pacific* is coming along fine. Tomorrow'll be a different story, though, when Vincent Sherman takes over."

"Ooooh, yeeeees." Mayo extracted every ounce of malice she

could out of two syllables. "Huston leaves for the actual war while you stay behind playing make believe in your fake one."

Bogie was at the bar now, his shoulders hunched halfway to his earlobes. He spun around, doubles in hand, and joined Luke on the sofa. "And your day? How was it?"

"Quite a day of gossip, it's been." Mayo lit the Kool herself and knocked back some more Old Fashioned. "A rumor's been running up and down the street that a Negro has moved into the neighborhood."

"What's wrong with that?"

"Did I say anything was wrong with it? This area could do with a bit of color. I'm simply repeating what the neighbors told me. And not just any Negro, but a woman. Young." Back at the bar, she poured out a heavy slug of bourbon and didn't bother dressing it up with bitters, sugar, and orange rind. "Mighty pretty, too. A singer, is my guess. Attractive enough to be an actress, though." The light above the bar picked up a ring where she'd slopped some booze. She ran her finger through it and slurped it down. "God help her."

"I think maybe it's time you took a seat."

She slow-blinked at him, the left corner of her lip curling into a jeer. "And I think maybe it's time you stopped telling me what to do."

"When did I start?"

In a peculiar way, Mayo reminded Luke of his second-oldest brother, Tony. The Valenti men were hard drinkers who knew how to throw the sort of punch that could stop an impending donnybrook—but not the family's ugly drunk. Tony rarely made it through his first drink before his words would slur and his eyes would blink slowly—just like Mayo's were doing now.

The second hand on the Bogarts' clock ticked toward the twelve. Drats. He was starving enough to eat Edith's entire meatloaf, but here he was, watching a Punch-and-Judy show play out its endless permutations.

"Let's ask Luke here." Bogie's eyes had reddened. "Do I tell you what to do?"

"You're his boss!" Bourbon slopped on the carpet as Mayo cast out her arms. "Or did you forget that, you madman?"

Bogie raised his glass and deepened his voice. "'Have you not heard of that madman who lit a lantern in the bright morning hours, ran to the marketplace, and cried incessantly: 'I seek God! I seek God!' As many of those who did not believe in God were standing around just then, he provoked much laughter.'"

Mayo raised her eyes to the sculpted ceiling. "Now I know he's lost his marbles. He's raving like a madman."

"Am I?" Bogie cleared his throat. "'Has he got lost?' asked one. 'Did he lose his way like a child?' asked another. 'Or is he—is he—'"

"Christ give me strength. One of his precious goddamned poems."

"'Or is he hiding?'" Luke finished for him. "'Is he afraid of us? Has he gone on a voyage? Emigrated? Thus they yelled and laughed.'"

Bogie raised his glass in admiration. "Not just Goethe, but Nietzsche, too?"

"I read Nietzsche in college as part of my philosophy degree."

"Reading Nietzsche is one thing; quoting him verbatim is another."

Luke felt light-headed as the bourbon hit his empty stomach. "To pass my German poetry class, I was required to memorize *Parable of a Madman*."

"Can you recite the rest of it?"

"Get me outta here!" Mayo pushed herself away from the bar. "We have cheese and crackers in the kitchen. Maybe some pickles." She headed out of the room.

Parable of a Madman was locked inside Luke's noggin, and no amount of bourbon-induced dizziness could blur it. "I think so."

Bogie got off the sofa. At the bookshelf, he ran his fingers along the spines until he arrived at *Nietzsche: A Selection of Works*. He flipped the pages until he found what he was looking for. "Pick it up after 'Thus they yelled and laughed.'"

Luke drained his glass. "'The madman jumped into their midst and pierced them with his eyes. "Whither is God?" he cried; "I will tell you. We have killed him-—you and I. All of us are his murderers."'"

Bogie followed along as Luke reeled off the next thirty-six lines.

"AMAZING!" Bogie wore the same expression that Luke's fellow boarding house residents had worn at their New Year's Eve party. "College must have been, what? Five years ago?"

Luke shrugged. "I have a strong memory."

"More than strong," Bogie replied. "That's a photographic one."

To Luke's way of thinking, there wasn't much difference between the parlor game with the numbers and reciting Nietzsche from his college days: they were just a trick. Photographic memory? Was that a scientific term, or had Bogie made it up?

"I don't know if it's *that* amazing," he said. "You quote poetry too."

"It was a stratagem that an acting teacher taught me. Committing poetry to memory helps with learning lines. But I can't recall whole poems I read five years ago. I can't do what you can do. Not even close."

Mayo appeared at the doorway holding a platter of cheese and crackers, pickles, and red grapes, and a bowl of martini olives. "It ain't much, but it'll have to do."

"You should've stuck around!" Bogie said. "Luke just recited *Parable of a Madman!*"

"You two still yapping about that junk?"

"Nietzsche isn't junk. Luke was word perfect."

"I'm standing right here. You don't have to yell. What are you, the town crier?"

"You missed one of the most astounding things I've seen all

year."

Mayo hoisted the tray to shoulder height. "Do you want this or not?"

"Philistine!" Bogie barked at her. "Would it kill you to get some culture?"

"OH, SURE!" Mayo screeched back. "I just love to sit around and listen to dead German guys prattle on about crazy nutcases."

"Nietzsche was Prussian."

"Prussian, Russian, German—who gives a crap?"

"The rest of the world cares so much they're willing to go to war for it." Luke regretted his words the moment he said them. This wasn't his fight. Why had he said that? He should have made a break for it after the first drink.

"Says the guy who isn't going to war for anything."

"Play fair," Bogie said. "He explained about his 4-F."

"You're two peas in a pod. Barking up a storm about wanting to join in a war the military doesn't want you for."

How different she was on *Sluggy*, Luke thought. That blonde hair now looked brassy and cheap, her genial smile sour with contempt.

"I qualify for military service," Bogie hissed.

"You barely make the cut-off," Mayo shot back. "They'll have to run through pretty much every guy in the country before they get desperate enough to call you up."

"He joined the Coast Guard Auxiliary, didn't he?" Luke said. "You saw how hard that skipper exam was."

"A minor offshoot from a military also-ran. It ain't exactly taking on the Nazis in the streets of Paris, is it?"

"You're skating onto paper-thin ice." Bogie was on his feet now. "You better shut your nasty mouth."

"Or what? You gonna shut it for me?"

"If I have to."

"You're only a tough guy on the screen. In real life, you ain't nothing but a mouse." She jiggled the tray still hoisted on her shoulder. "Hey there, little Humphrey Mouse. You want some cheese?"

She grunted as she hurled the food at him. Chunks of gouda and slices of Swiss scattered across the carpet along with pickles, olives, and crackers. The platter caught Bogie square in the chest. He gasped as it thudded against his ribs and crashed to the floor.

Luke felt something snap inside him as the platter fractured into pieces. "What are you, a child?"

"Oh, yeah, Joe College who doesn't have any kids? Is that what they do? Throw tantrums? Throw food?"

"Instead of nagging and needling and getting drunk, why don't you behave like an adult and say what's on your mind?"

Mayo pinned her hands onto her hips. "And what, pray tell, is that?"

The force of his own reaction surprised Luke, but he was part of this skirmish now. There was no backing off, especially not with an experienced brawler like her. Luke pegged his own hands to his hips, mirroring Mayo's stance back at her. "Ingrid Bergman."

She unleashed a high-pitched gasp as she staggered backward, hitting a wooden ladder-back chair and collapsing into it.

Pieces of broken platter lay at Bogie's feet. A Ritz cracker had landed on his shoulder. Luke brushed it off. "I'll see myself out."

He fled into the foyer, wrenched open the front door, and stepped out onto the porch, where the first hint of summer warmed the April night air. How badly he needed it after being trapped in that musty, closed-in living room, reeking of stale cigarette smoke and curdling bile.

Relief dripped off him like sweat. No wonder everybody ducked the moment hostilities began. He wouldn't make that mistake again. Maybe he wouldn't get the chance. Bogie could arrive at work tomorrow and tell him not to bother sitting down because he was fired. Maybe it was time he started figuring out how he might hitchhike home to Brooklyn.

But first, dinner. There would be no meatloaf leftovers in the icebox, but Carpenter's Drive-in might still be open. With dimouts and blackouts and brownouts becoming the norm, no restaurant could be counted on to be open past dusk.

The door behind him squeaked. "I'm glad you're still here." Luke heard the scrape of a match. A moment later, the familiar smell of Bogie's cigarillo filled the porch.

"Sorry about that," Luke said.

"What have you got to be sorry for?"

"That bit about Ingrid Bergman."

Bogie drew alongside him. "It takes a lot to put my wife in her place. I'm now even more impressed with you." Smoke drifted out of his nose as he chuckled. "With a memory like that, you must be able to count cards."

Bogie's comment nudged a long-buried memory about the week when the Valenti family's radio set had broken down. While it was in the repair shop, Pop had decreed they'd play gin rummy instead. Luke had been so excited to take his place at the dining table and learn about clubs and hearts, jacks and kings and aces. So grown up! So included! Those halcyon days had lasted less than two weeks. At the time, Luke had assumed it was because the Philco had returned to the corner once more. It wasn't until much later that Wilda had set him straight. "Your family didn't stop playing cards because the radio was working again," she'd informed him. "They stopped because you always won and they couldn't stand it."

"I've never consciously tried to count cards," he told Bogie, "but yes, I guess so."

"Can you play poker?"

The Pickwick Bookstore near Grauman's Chinese was bound to have a rule book. "Sure."

Bogie grinned. "In that case, you and me, we're gonna have some fun."

15

*B*ogie stopped Luke outside the costume building. "These ration books—you have to register for them?"

Luke glanced at the second story, where Orry-Kelly had his workroom. Bogie didn't know what the designer had waiting for him up there, but Luke did. "Eaten any beef lately?"

Bogie nodded.

"Did it taste like horsemeat?"

"I don't think so."

"Is Mayo a good cook?"

"Not especially."

"In that case, you haven't. My landlady served it last week."

"How was it?"

"Edible." Luke pictured his neighbors' tentative reactions as they took their first forkfuls of horsemeat casserole. "But only because she simmered it for hours and jazzed it up with a ton of salt and pepper, herbs, onions and tomatoes."

Luke followed Bogie inside. He drew in as deep a breath as he could and held it. Bogie was minutes away from hitting the roof. But, as Orry-Kelly had explained to him in his broad Australian drawl during a furtive meeting the previous day, there was only one workable solution.

"We're here to see Orry-Kelly," Bogie told the perky blonde twenty-year-old behind the front desk.

"Second floor."

They thanked her and headed to the stairwell.

"How long are the ration books supposed to last? What can you buy with them?"

"It's a point system. Different number of points for each item. They're mainly for staples like butter, shortening, meat, and coffee. Has Mayo stocked up on sugar? The ban goes into effect on Friday."

"What?!" Bogie halted on the landing, his voice ricocheting off the brick walls. "They banned sugar?"

How could Bogie not know this? Rationing had been part of nearly every conversation Luke had had for weeks now. It must be nice to hide away in a dressing room playing chess, unconcerned with mundane matters like where to buy coffee.

"The *sale* of sugar," Luke explained. "After that, it'll be regulated. Unless you get it on the black market."

"Buying sugar on the black market." They started up the stairs again. "Now I've heard everything."

"I overheard Bob Williams from Publicity tell Perc Westmore in the commissary how he supplements his income by selling black-market nylons. He meets his supplier in the Schwab's parking lot at midnight and buys fifty boxes of them for two dollars twenty a pair. He sells them in Beverly Hills for six sixty."

Bogie blew a raspberry. "You and I are in the wrong business."

The stairs opened onto a two-story atrium with tall windows of frosted glass. Unlike his female co-stars, whose fittings could take hours, Bogie could be in and out in under an hour. This fitting, however, wasn't about a tux, a couple of suits, and a fedora.

A seven-foot mirror stood against the far wall next to a rack filled with an array of dresses. To the right, a second rack held half a dozen suits.

"I heard you were on your way up."

Orry-Kelly was a tall gent with a plump face that had probably been handsome during his youth, but was now tending toward fleshy. He was thickening around the waist, too, but hid it with a dark jacket that featured vertical stripes. A trench coat hung over his arm, the cuffs of its sleeves frayed and ragged. A button was missing from the front panel, and it had no belt.

Without moving his head, Bogie let his eyes stray over to Ingrid Bergman's wardrobe. The first two items were suits, one with a floor-length skirt, the other reaching to just below the knees. They had sharply defined lines made in white fabric that would glow under the key lights. Next to them hung a creamy blouse with a soft paisley design and a wide belt—red? purple? Luke couldn't tell—teamed with a black skirt. It was all very crisp and clean.

Bogie held up the trench coat. "Where did you dig this one out of? Bottom of the trash?"

The smile fell from Orry-Kelly's face. "The script says life has battered Rick Blaine around. I spent hours yesterday searching for the right coat for the final scene at the airport."

Bogie dropped his arm, letting the dilapidated coat droop onto the wooden floor. "Are you telling me they've finished writing it?"

Bogie's concern that nobody would buy Ingrid Bergman falling for a schlump like him had been replaced by the stark reality that they were now four days out from start of production and he had yet to see a script. "And how the hell," he had asked Luke earlier that morning, "am I supposed to know how to play this guy if I don't know his character arc?"

Luke wasn't sure what a character arc was, but he'd shrugged his shoulders and muttered some bromide about Bogie's job being hard enough and didn't they know how much harder they were making it for him?

"And what's with the trench coat?" Bogie said. "Casablanca's in the Sahara."

"Try it, anyway," Orry-Kelly suggested. "It'll at least give me an idea of the fit."

"This must be the tenth movie we've made together. If you don't know my size by now . . ."

"People change, bodies change," Orry-Kelly said airily. "Humor me and put it on."

The coat hung from Bogie's shoulders in limp, lifeless folds. "I'm supposed to get the girl wearing *this*?"

Orry-Kelly sighed. "It was just a suggestion."

"Or do I not get the girl in the end?"

"Why wouldn't you?" Luke asked.

"I didn't get her in *Maltese Falcon*."

"She was a murderess!" Peter Lorre stood at the top of the stairs, his hands buried in the pockets of his loose-fitting gaberdine pants. "Of course you'll get the girl. The star always does—unless he's wearing *that*. Did they make it out of Miss Havisham's old drapes?" He joined them at the mirror. "For God's sake, Hump, take it off before I put a match to it."

Peter Lorre no longer wore his hair in Joel Cairo's tight curls, but the rest of him looked the same: apprehensive smile above a pair of heavy-lidded eyes bulging out of a pale, round face. But he was shorter than Luke had guessed. Five feet five at most. But his hand was warm and strong when Bogie introduced them.

Neither Bogie nor Lorre noticed when Orry-Kelly slipped behind a curtain next to the mirror. They were too busy talking about the size of Lorre's part and how he didn't care as long as he got to work with people he liked. He broke the news to Bogie that Conrad Veidt had been cast as their Nazi villain, Major Strasser. The three of them had shot *All Through the Night*, which had been directed by Vincent Sherman, who had taken over as director of *Across the Pacific* after John Huston, who had also directed *Falcon*, had left. *Pacific* co-starred Mary Astor and

Sydney Greenstreet, who were in *Falcon*, and Greenstreet had also been cast in *Casablanca*. These folks, Luke realized, looked at each other like an extended family whose lives crisscrossed over and over.

A letter from Wilda had arrived earlier that week, mostly about how the war had changed his old neighborhood. The focus of activity had shifted from Fulton Street to the Brooklyn Navy Yard, which was now operating twenty-four hours a day. "It's so gosh-darned crowded everywhere you walk," she had written. "Sharp elbows are *de rigeur* for those brave enough to take their chances on the sidewalks. I rarely go out anymore."

Her penmanship, once copybook perfect, had deteriorated into a spidery sprawl with loops plunging several lines. Along with ignoring his repeated questions about the falcon he'd brought to California, she had also neglected to share news of the family. Were his brothers now in training or en route to the Continent? Who was helping Pop run Valenti Construction?

"Those had better not be what I think they are." Bogie's voice had filled with venom.

Orry-Kelly held a pair of wooden platforms, three inches thick, with leather straps and brass buckles. "'Fraid so." He thrust them toward Bogie, who pitched himself backward as though he'd been slugged in the jaw.

Luke took them from Orry-Kelly and bounced them in his hands. Solid wood. Heavy. It wouldn't be easy for Bogie to walk around in these.

Lorre asked, "What the hell are they?"

"A death-blow to my masculinity and a knee to the groin of my dignity."

"So you have to—?"

"Strap them on like I'm Manfred the Midget from Tom Thumb's Miniature Circus."

Lorre giggled in that high-pitched, machine-gunfire way of his. "You're lucky they're only three inches. I'd need seven or eight. Not that I'll ever play a romantic scene." He shrugged. "Such is my lot in life."

"Look, Bogie, I know it's undignified," Orry-Kelly said. "It's not like I'm about to feature them in my 'Hollywood Fashion Parade' newspaper column. But there's a reason Hal ordered them."

"There are five million actresses in a two-block radius. Couldn't they have cast someone shorter than me?"

"How tall is Ingrid?" Luke asked, even though he already knew.

"Too damn tall," Bogie said.

"Five nine," Orry-Kelly said.

"It's only an inch difference."

"Yes, but she'll be in heels. Hal wants him five eleven when they're together. Especially in the love scenes."

"SHE CAN CROUCH DOWN!"

"Or," Orry-Kelly suggested, "you could make it easier for your co-star to convince the audience that she's still in love with you by giving yourself a little lift."

Luke approached Bogie. "I'm five foot nine. Why don't you strap these on—" he shot out a flattened palm to thwart another heated protest "—to see how the height difference is going to look on camera. And how hard it is to walk in them."

"Love scenes are two-shots. Just her and me standing there in a clinch. I won't be in motion."

"The script isn't finished yet," Luke pointed out. "There might be a scene where you and Ilsa walk through Rick's Café Américain."

Orry-Kelly tapped his foot against a stool a few feet away from Bogie. "Just try them on. Hal will be calling me soon. Don't fall into the cliché of being difficult to work with now that you're getting to be a big star."

That phrase—getting to be a big star—was Luke's cue. "Your director on this picture—remind me of his name?"

"Michael Curtiz."

"Didn't you tell me he's an authoritarian with zero patience?

How's he going to take it when his leading lady is towering over his leading man because you won't strap on a couple of wood blocks?"

Bogie snatched the platforms out of Luke's hand and parked his behind on a nearby stool. Ignoring Luke's offer to help, he strapped them on and stood up. Luke took his place, pressing his back against Bogie's.

"Yes, I think that'll work fine," Orry-Kelly said "Now, will you —oh, excuse me. I don't think I caught your name."

"Luke."

"Okay, Luke, turn around. We need to see sightlines."

Luke had to raise his face to look into Bogie's eyes, but only slightly. He clasped his hands together and batted his eyelids like Betty Boop sauced up on a love potion. "Why, Mr. Bogart." He raised his voice into a falsetto that somehow came out in a south-ern-belle accent. "Y'all my all-time favorite movie star!" He held his breath, waiting to see the ice break in Bogie's dark eyes. Luke knew his gamble had paid off when his boss's mouth crinkled at the edges.

As Luke took his seat with Bogie and Lorre at the usual corner table, he noticed the unblinking stares and whispers behind menus. Famous faces rarely stirred more than an indifferent once-over from studio workers, but the tectonic plates of celebrity had shifted. Admiration was now less guarded. Gazes lingered longer from the prettier girls in the room. And there were plenty of pretty girls peppering the Warner Bros. commissary.

Three tables away, a striking blonde in a Veronica Lake peek-a-boo abandoned any pretense of propriety. She stared at Bogie with naked determination to catch his eye. Was it any wonder Mayo sat at home, stewing in jealousy, drowning her mistrust in whiskey?

"Have you heard of it?"

Bogie's question pulled Luke into a conversation he had barely heard. "Heard of what?"

"The European Film Fund." He jabbed his menu toward Lorre. "Explain your pet project to my boy here."

"It's a charity established by Ernst Lubitsch and others to help bring refugees to America. We secure affidavits for movie people and provide them with a stipend so that the immigration authorities can see they're not coming to this country empty-handed, even though most of them are. The Nazi onslaught is forcing them to leave everything behind. But if they have an official-looking document and some money in their pocket, they're allowed in. Lubitsch is from Germany, so he knows what it's like."

"Where are you from?" Luke asked

"Born in Hungary, then moved to Berlin. I was happy there, but when Hitler came to power, the writing was on the wall." He sniffed, a touch dolefully. "Literally. So I bolted for England and ended up here. One of our major donors is our director. Mike's from Hungary, too. He didn't flee from Nazis, but he gets it."

Bogie signaled a waitress to no avail. She was the only female in the room not eyeballing Bogie like a bird of prey. "Pete's helping to organize a fundraiser. Sort of a cabaret revue."

"We're struggling to get some names to perform. We've got a few Americans, but if we can get a European entertainer, the Europeans are more likely to donate bigger sums."

"I know one," Luke said.

"Is she any good?"

"Very. In fact, you might know her. She used to sing in Berlin. Ever heard of Sabine Vogel?"

Lorre grasped the edge of the table as though it were the last life preserver on the *Lusitania*. "Sabine Vogel? Here? In Los Angeles? Alive?"

"Very much so."

"When I moved to Berlin, it was the height of the Weimer

Republic. The cabaret scene was the center of everything, and one of the queens of Berlin cabaret was Sabine Vogel."

Luke pictured his neighbor, rarely contributing to the dinner-table conversation, preferring instead to allow the others to talk about their day at work, war news, and what might lie ahead. If Edith hadn't owned a piano, Luke wouldn't have guessed she could carry a tune, let alone possess the singular talent she had for putting over a song to tear hearts in half.

Lorre pressed his fingertips to his cheeks, rocking from side to side with excitement. "If you can get her to perform, we can look for a bigger venue, sell more tickets, raise more money. This is *very* exciting." His gibbous eyes bulged with hope. "When you are likely to see her again?"

Edith's Thursday-night chicken and dumplings were almost as delicious as her meatloaf, so the Whitley Manor dining table was always full. "Tonight."

The waitress appeared. "What'll it be, gents?"

Lorre borrowed her pencil and wrote his telephone number on a paper napkin he had pulled from the metal dispenser. "Please, please, *please* ask her to call me."

"Sure."

Luke felt a tremor shudder through him. The Sabine he knew was a private person who now lived in a boarding house. If she had once been the queen of Berlin cabaret, would she even want anyone in America to know how far she'd fallen? Luke bit his lower lip. Maybe he shouldn't have opened his mouth.

16

Luke gazed up at the canvas ceiling of the La Belle Aurore Café set. It was so low that he was tempted to see if he could touch it, but disturbing it wouldn't be a terrific way to kick off filming on the first day of Bogie's new movie.

"Vail!" The lighting guy's bark shot across the set. "I can't light your face if you're looking at the ceiling, now, can I?"

Bogie coughed near the end of the bar, next to a four-foot replica of the Eiffel Tower. A half-smoked cigarette dangled from his lips as he mouthed his lines. Setting the loose pages of his script on the bar, he hooked a finger inside the collar of his white shirt and tugged at it. That meant he was getting antsy for the scene to begin.

Casablanca's director, Michael Curtiz, strode onto the set. A tall gent with thinning hair and a prominent, aquiline nose, he carried himself with an intense air, as though he had misplaced a winning lottery ticket.

"People, people, your attention I must have. *Now, Voyager* is running late two weeks. Mr. Rains will not be finished until June third. Mr. Henreid will be tied down for another month. It is okay for Mr. Rapper to take his time, but it makes messy our schedule."

He shrugged extravagantly for the benefit of the crew members in the rafters. "This is why we have switched to the Paris café scene. Miss Bergman has hurried into makeup, but we do not have a stand-in for her. A volunteer, if you please."

Nell raised her hand. "I'll do it."

Curtiz shielded his eyes with his script. "Fine, fine. I must make the conference with Epstein boys."

He retreated to a nook near the fireplace, where a pair of identical-looking men in their early thirties waited for him. They were in their shirtsleeves, no jackets, neckties, or hats, and sat slouched in the wooden chairs.

Jasper told Nell to stand next to Luke, who pointed toward the nook. "Who are they?"

"Philip and Julius Epstein. They're our *wunderkind* writers. When a movie's in trouble, they get called in."

"*Casablanca* hasn't started shooting and already it's in trouble?"

"My typing pool spy says Wallis has five scribblers madly scribbling. One of them works on the plot, another on the politics, another on the romance, and the Epsteins are polishers. They punch up the bits that are too slow, too mushy, or too complicated."

Nell wore a new dress—a subtle floral pattern, roses interspersed with ivy, with wide lapels that reached the edges of her shoulders.

"I haven't seen you for a while," he said.

Jasper told her to turn to the left. "Sorry to disappear on you. They've asked us to double up at my boarding house. I now room with a girl from Sioux City, who works at the Lockheed factory drilling bolts into airplanes. Her dad's a farmer and she's all gung-ho about turning our backyard into one of those victory gardens. We've gone from eight girls to sixteen. That's a lot of mouths to feed, so it makes sense." She struck a deadpan face. "Do you know how much work it takes to start a vegetable patch?" She blinked. "There she is!"

Ingrid Bergman stood on the edge of the set, her fingers interlaced and her palms pressed together. She took a couple of steps closer to catch Curtiz's eye, but he was too preoccupied with the Epsteins to notice. Left alone, she fussed with the cuffs of her blouse.

Nell said, "I was reading Kathryn Massey's column in *The Hollywood Reporter* yesterday. She said that Perc Westmore told her that Ingrid Bergman is one of the easiest actresses in Hollywood to work with because she doesn't need tons of makeup. I can see what he means. Women are so much more attractive with all that artifice stripped away, don't you think?"

She didn't strike him as the fish-for-a-compliment type, but didn't girls enjoy being told how pretty they were? Fussing over them the right way was a tough call when a guy was new to the game. "You're kind of like that, aren't you?"

She swung her head around. "Am I?" Jasper called out her name, and she turned away from him again.

"Glamor girls like Lana Turner and Linda Darnell—they're okay, I guess. But take away that makeup and the eyelashes and careful lighting, and what have you got?"

"I don't know. What *have* you got?"

"Natural girls, like you and Ingrid. That's what guys go for."

"Did you just put me in the same club as Ingrid Bergman?" Nell's voice had taken on a peach-fuzz softness.

Luke cupped his hands to his mouth. "PSST!" Bogie looked up from his script. "She's standing there alone. Maybe now would be a good time to introduce yourself."

"Nope."

"You're about to do a love scene with her, but you can't say, 'Hello, I'm Humphrey Bogart'?"

Bogie lifted his right foot to show he was wearing Orry-Kelly's platforms. "And risk falling flat on my face? No, thanks."

"So make a joke out of it."

Bogie's mouth fell into a pout; Luke knew he'd pushed the

limits of what he could get away with. He also knew that to break eye contact was a sign of capitulation. Bogie had once told him, "When Mayo looks away, I know I've won the fight." Luke forced himself to not blink until Bogie said, "Joke about what?"

"How hard it is to walk on stilts and not get a nosebleed."

Bogie rolled his script into a baton. "Fine."

His first steps in Orry-Kelly's workroom had been timid and wobbly. He had cursed each time he nearly tumbled over. Lorre's off-key rendition of "High on a Windy Hill" hadn't helped. After a few laps, Bogie had ripped open the buckles and kicked aside his "confounded instruments of torture." Luke had picked them up and deposited them between him and Bogie on the drive home. "You'll get the hang of it," he'd told him They hadn't spoken about them since.

Today, however, was an entirely different cakewalk. There was a slight waddle to his gait, and a reserve in his forward motion, but these were noticeable only to those people who had witnessed his first few attempts. For all his complaining and sulking, the son of a bitch had been practicing.

Bogie approached Bergman with his hand extended. She clasped hers in his, relief washing over her face.

"It's a weird job, isn't it?" Nell said. "Minutes after meeting, they have to pretend like they're deeply and desperately in love."

"You've already read the script?" Luke asked.

"Leads in Hollywood romances are always deeply and desperately in love. And besides, there's no set script. The typing pool has been retyping it from scratch every day for three weeks." Nell pointed to Curtiz and the Epstein boys, who were now clustered around Bogart and Bergman. The director's already-stern face looked like it had been carved from granite. "In four, three, two, one."

Bogie hurled his rolled-up script onto the floor. "ARE YOU FUCKING KIDDING ME?"

Luke took a step toward him, but Nell yanked him back. "Hold your horses. Part of this drama is for public consumption. Give the players their audience."

"I've just learned five pages of dialogue," Bogie said to Curtiz, "and now you come to me with five *new* pages? Right before shooting?"

Nell sucked air between her teeth. "This is going to be a rough ride."

"We want the script to be best," Curtiz said. "Some of the times, it takes more longer."

"I was handed these pages an *hour* ago." Bogie faced the Epstein brothers. "How can you have rewritten them already?"

One of them—it was hard to tell one pale egghead from the other—shrugged. "We knew we hadn't quite hit the bull's-eye, so we gave it another pass."

Nell poked Luke in the back. "Now!"

Luke half-walked-half-ran across the set, reaching Bogie as Curtiz handed him a stack of pages. Bogie snatched them out of the man's hand and told Luke to follow him.

"HEY!" Jasper's voice rang out. "I haven't finished lighting—"

"Get somebody else."

Gus O'Farrell stepped onto the edge of the café set. "Happy to help if I can."

Yeah, I'll bet you are. Luke tried to catch his eye, but Gus kept his focus trained on Curtiz. Luke felt a hitch in his stomach. I didn't think I needed to worry about you. I was wrong.

Bogie slammed his dressing room door and struggled to free himself from the platforms. Luke grabbed the script and read through the pages. He hadn't seen the previous draft, but this version read pretty well to him. Not that he knew a decent script from a bungled one.

Bogie leaned an elbow on his makeup table and scratched at his forehead just below the edge of his toupée. "Was I too much just now? I felt like I was Bette, chewing every inch of scenery in sight."

Telling Bogie he had overplayed the scene would win Luke no points. Not while the man was so steamed. "If this is the picture that catapults you into leading-man territory, doesn't that mean more money, more power, and more control? But not if you're a doormat, right?" He pointed toward the set. "You were signaling to the cast and crew that there's a new Humphrey Bogart in town, and he's no longer putting up with getting pushed around like furniture."

Bogie was grinning now. A cheeky, almost insolent grin, but tinged with—dare Luke hope?—admiration. "I want you to make me a promise."

"If I can."

"Always tell me the truth. I mean it. I want you to always be honest with me. Like you were just now."

The previous week, Luke and Bogie had been leaving a photo session when they'd spotted Jack Warner striding through the studio like he was General Pershing. A phalanx of Brooks Brothers suits trailed behind. "What a sight," Bogie had mumbled. "The Grand Pooh-Bah surrounded by his lackeys whose survival depends on how fast they say 'Great idea, boss!' I bet he hasn't heard a contrary view in twenty years."

Luke enjoyed this new job, but he worked for a hothead with a hair-trigger temper. It was easy to make a promise like that in the sanctuary of a dressing room, but Luke had seen Bogie scream at his wife so fiercely that she had thrown a platter of food at him.

"Even if I think you're behaving like a bum, or your drinking's gotten out of hand?"

"Especially then."

"On one condition: You can't insult me, yell at me, or fire me for it."

Bogie lifted a self-deprecatory shoulder. "I don't know if I can promise that."

"I reserve the right to throw this conversation in your face anytime I want."

"Deal." Bogie picked up the new script. "So. You and Nell. Have you made your move yet?"

At first, Luke had been all for a slow courtship, and was happy to let this romance blossom naturally. And it had. And that was all fine and dandy. But good golly, he was starting to see that there was such a thing as "too slowly." It was time to move things along at a brisker clip. But how? "I'm new at this sort of thing. How do you know when a moment's right?"

"I was bending Lorre's ear yesterday about acting with a woman who glows just by standing there. He gave me some nifty advice."

"I could do with some of that."

"He told me to stay still in the scene and let her come to me. You should do the same with Nell. Let her know that it's safe to move forward." He picked up the pages. "We should start rehearsing."

"Your first line is the one about watering gardens with champagne before letting the Germans drink it."

Bogie leaned back, reappraising Luke. "You can memorize lines from a single read-through. Jesus! You're getting to be more valuable to me every day."

When Luke walked onto the set, he wanted to turn around and walk straight back into Bogie's dressing room. It was bad enough that he'd had to relinquish his stand-in duties to Gus O'Farrell, but did he need to see that sycophantic apple-polishing bozo standing on a café table executing a one-armed handstand while the cast and crew looked on with undisguised admiration? Maybe at a New Year's Eve party. Maybe if it were someone else pulling off a stunt like that. But not this guy. Not this set. Schemers like Gus always had an agenda.

Curtiz rubbed his hands together. "Your stand-in was making

the entertainment, meanwhile you were calming down, Mr. Bogart." He pointed to the X on the floor.

Bogie stationed himself at the bar where the model Eiffel Tower now glowed in its own spotlight. In the background, Ingrid stood behind a piano about half the width of Wilda's upright.

Curtiz took his place next to the camera. "Where are my musicians?" A Negro in a natty dark suit sat at the keyboard. "You are Mr. Dooley, yes?" The man nodded. "And where is Mr. Carpenter?" When Dooley shrugged, Curtiz whacked his script against a chair. "They cast a drummer as a piano player. Okay. Fine. But now when everybody is waiting, my real piano player, he is nowhere."

"It's not Carpenter's fault." This brave statement came from *Casablanca*'s unit manager, Al. "We were supposed to be filming a whole other scene. But when we switched—"

"When will he be here?"

"He lives clear across town—"

"Who the hell is going to play 'As Time Goes By'?" An involuntary yip escaped out of Luke. Curtiz glared at him. "What did you say?"

Behind him, well off the set, O'Farrell stood with his arms crossed, a smirk plastered on his face. Luke ignored him. "The song that starts 'You must remember this'?"

"I don't like it," Curtiz snapped. "Max Steiner doesn't like it. But Hal Wallis does, so we are stuck with that cockamamie tune."

"My aunt taught me to play it after we went to see Frances Williams originate it on Broadway in a show—"

"I do not need to hear the life of your story." Curtiz pointed to a piano situated off-camera "You can play the *átkozott* song?"

Bogie slapped him on the back. "He's a goddamned champ!" The crew applauded as Luke made his way to the second piano. As he hit the opening chord, Luke glanced up at O'Farrell. The chump's face had darkened with impotent fury, his teeth biting down onto his lower lip. Keep that up, Luke wanted to say, and you'll draw blood. But he had, instead, a pithier response.

"Checkmate."

"And then this one," Nell elbowed Luke in the shoulder, "pipes up and says, 'Excuse me, Mr. Curtiz, but I can play'—what's the name of that song?"

Luke pushed away her elbow. "It wasn't a big deal." Except that it was. He'd helped the production save time—and therefore money—until Elliot Carpenter arrived.

At the last minute, Luke had invited Nell home for dinner. He didn't know if it was allowed; none of his neighbors had done it. But he wanted to hang on to the satisfaction of one-upping Gus O'Farrell for as long as he could. Edith hadn't hesitated to set an extra place.

"'As Time Goes By.' It's from a musical called *Everybody's Welcome*. It's a pleasant tune. I don't know why Mr. Curtiz hates it so much."

Edith tapped her chin with her spoon, leaving behind a bead of tomato soup. "Michael Curtiz?" She indulged herself with a wistful smile. "I haven't thought about that Hungarian in ages."

"You worked with him?" Beatrice asked.

"Years ago, I was at Warners and got assigned as Delores Costello's stand-in on *Noah's Ark*. An enormous production, it was. Million-dollar budget. Cast of thousands."

"I remember that one," Minerva said. "You'd have thought it was a Cecil B. DeMille extravaganza."

"Naturally the big climax was the flood. And what a flood it was, too. Hundreds of thousands of gallons of water. They needed every extra they could lay their hands on, so once I was done standing in for Delores, they got me to be one of the heathens. Let me tell you, nobody had fun that day. A falling column bonked me on the head and I nearly drowned. Oh, it was just awful. Even for poor Delores; she got pneumonia."

"Did they have a doctor on the set?" Nell asked.

"Not so much as a trainee nurse. A bunch of us got carted off to L.A. General. In the morning Mr. Curtiz checked up on how we were doing. Personally! He had this reputation of not caring a brass button for his actors. In fact, he could be quite callous, but very charismatic and charming if he chose to be. I was shocked when he came to visit. I mean, it was unheard of for any director to go out of his way—especially him. But I was thankful and flattered because I'd suffered a terrible concussion. It wasn't until later that I realized he wanted to sleep with me."

Sabine leaned over her soup bowl. "And did you?"

"Not right there in the hospital bed." Edith's voice had taken on a faraway tone, as though she were recalling a pleasurable summer day spent at a country fair. "But later. Several times. He was a very energetic lover. I would have enjoyed it more if he'd slowed down, though. Always in such a rush. Keen to get home to his wife, I expect."

"Your Mr. Curtiz hasn't changed," Nell said. "He has a terrible reputation for taking girls into his office during filming and making with the whoopee. The poor things believe they'll be cast in a movie, but we don't see them again."

Luke hated how shocked he'd been by this news of a director luring innocent lambs into his office. It wasn't like he'd lived a sheltered life behind the walls of some isolated monastery. Every day, the streets of Brooklyn handed out lessons in the School of Hard Knocks, but Curtiz's behavior made him feel like a rube. People out here sure did lead their lives according to a set of rules Luke never knew existed. The heat of embarrassment crawled across his cheeks, and he was relieved when the conversation moved on to rumors that blackouts around Los Angeles were to become more widespread and strictly enforced.

. . .

After everybody had finished Edith's ginger crumb cake, Luke and Nell stepped onto the front porch. It was late May now, and the evening weather had grown balmy.

"Your landlady sure is a sweetie-pie," Nell said, sitting on the top step. "Who'd have guessed she had such a wild past?"

Luke sat a little closer than he might have done a week before. "Her *Noah's Ark* tale—I don't think we ought to take it as gospel."

"You can tell she was a real looker in her day, though. It's exactly the sort of stunt Curtiz would pull."

"Has he ever tried anything with you?"

"Me?" She laughed. "I'm not the right sort of glamor-girl pretty to inspire those sorts of shenanigans. And thank God, too. I hear he's very strong, so it's easier just to let him have at it. The sooner he starts, the sooner it's over."

"*I* think you're pretty." He hadn't meant to whisper, but his compliment benefitted from the hushed way it floated into the night air.

She looked at him with *You do?* eyes. "I've been thinking about what you said today. About how I was the type who didn't need makeup." She landed a hand on his forearm. It felt warm, like freshly baked bagels. "You know what else I was thinking? Gus's handstand was the most show-off-y stunt he's ever pulled. Hard to do, I'm sure, but heavens to Betsy, talk about desperate for attention."

"You weren't impressed?"

"Quite the opposite." She kept her hand in place. He longed to put his hand on top of hers, but Bogie's advice came back to him: Let her come to you. But hadn't she done that by placing it there? The advice wasn't so clear as it had seemed in the dressing room. "What a bonehead. Ugh!" She tightened her grip around his arm, then realized where it was and yanked it away.

"You could have left it there," he told her.

She squinted at him. "Would you like to kiss me?"

"The question is, would you like to be kissed?"

"I've never met a boy like you."

She hadn't answered him; nor had she broken her gaze. "What kind of boy am I?"

"Most of the men here, they assume it's their God-given right to paw a girl any time they like."

Luke couldn't imagine his brothers asking the girls in the back row of the Brooklyn Fox if they'd like to be kissed. *Let her know it's safe to move forward.* "I've wanted to kiss you for the longest time."

She shifted closer. Her perfume had a honeyed undercurrent to it. That smile of hers surfaced. Cheeky and knowing, sassy but challenging, it felt like a gate swinging open. He closed those final three inches that separated them and hoped like hell he wasn't a lousy kisser.

17

*L*uke squinted over the steering wheel of Bogie's Packard and into the shadowy folds of Benedict Canyon Drive. "What number are we looking for?"

"Twelve twenty," Nell replied from the back seat. "She said she'd be waiting out front."

Bogie scoffed. "I've yet to meet a woman who stands on the sidewalk waiting for her date. Especially at night."

"Nell is *my* date," Luke pointed out, "which makes Ingrid yours." Bogie said nothing. "What did you tell Mayo?"

"That Jack Warner insisted I do some glad-handing at a stock-holders' meeting."

"What's your story going to be when she learns the truth?" Nell asked. "A high-profile charity event for the European Film Fund. Marlene Dietrich, Paul Henreid, Peter Lorre, Ernst Lubitsch. What'll you say when she throws tomorrow's *Examiner* at you?"

"I've got four years of experience figuring how to get around my wife. I'll tell her we went there afterwards."

Despite the brawling, the arguing, the jealousy, and the broken doors, Luke doubted Bogie had cheated on Mayo, but surely it was just a matter of time before some knockout sauntered into view?

Or maybe he couldn't understand Bogie's marriage because he was floating along on the sunshiny breezes of new love.

That front-porch kiss had been everything Luke had hoped his first proper kiss would be: alternating delicate and intense, hesitant and passionate, lingering and eager. When he'd stroked her cheek with the back of his fingers, her skin had felt softer than cotton balls. He had pressed his lips harder to hers; she'd responded in kind. Their breathing had shortened into gasps and staccato yips. They might have gone further if a dog-walking passer-by hadn't interrupted them with a teasing whistle.

Luke switched the headlights to high beam. Four houses along, a slim figure in an ankle-length gown of shimmering silk under a striped fur stole stood perched on the curb's edge.

Bogie murmured, "I'll be damned."

Luke pulled on the handbrake and jumped out of the car. "We weren't sure you'd be out here by yourself."

"The night is clear; the air is fresh." He opened the rear passenger door, but she didn't climb inside. "Thank you for inviting me." The moon slipped out from behind a cloud. It shone through the leaves of the oak tree above them, dappling Ingrid's face with shadows.

"You're very welcome."

She glanced at the car's roof directly above Bogie. "Am I?"

During the first week of filming, Bogie had been polite, professional, and courteous—and that was the problem. How was she supposed to portray a woman in love with a man she thought she'd never see again if the object of her cinematic affections only showed up to say his lines?

So when Peter Lorre had arrived on the *Casablanca* set and announced that Ernst Lubitsch had booked Romanoff's in Beverly Hills for the European Film Fund benefit, Luke and Nell had hatched a plan to get Bogie and Ingrid together outside of work. If she could see the witty and educated side of him, maybe it would make her job easier. And that was more likely to happen during a fundraiser at Bogie's favorite restaurant.

"Of course you are."

Luke handed her into the car, then slipped back behind the steering wheel, spun the Packard into a U-turn, and headed down the canyon toward Rodeo Drive.

"I've heard about the chap who runs Romanoff's," Ingrid said. "Claims to be a Russian prince, doesn't he?"

"That he does," Bogie said.

"But it's a fabrication?"

"My advice is don't believe a word that comes out of Prince Michael Dimitri Alexandrovich Obolensky-Romanoff. He's just Harry Gerguson from Lithuania, a petty criminal and forger of checks."

"You must like him, though," Nell said, "otherwise why would you be one of his backers?"

"He's the greatest storyteller I've ever encountered. Who cares if his tall tales are outrageous whoppers? Give me an entertaining conversation paired with a delicious meal, and I'm happier than John Wayne in a saddle."

Luke turned onto Rodeo Drive and headed south toward the cluster of stores and restaurants. "I hear the food is first class."

"The finest you'll eat in L.A."

"Any recommendations?" Ingrid asked.

Bogie faced the back seat. It was the most eye contact he'd given her all week. "Appetizer-wise, your best bet is the Terrine Maison or Baked Oysters Parisienne. If you start with the Terrine, have the Délice de Sole Veronique for your main course. If you have the oysters, go with the Rack of Spring Lamb Persillé. Are you a dessert kind o' gal?"

"I could be tempted."

"Most actresses I know wouldn't touch a dessert for all the haute couture in Paris."

"I don't mind suffering for my art; however, I draw the line at denying myself one of the greatest pleasures in life."

"In that case, order the Soufflé Grand Marnier. I should warn you, though: it's for two."

"We can share it."

Bogie let a silent moment tick by. "Perhaps we can at that."

They could now see the bold logo—a pair of wrought-iron R's, three feet tall, positioned back-to-back, painted black, and hung on a white wall. Luke glanced in the rearview mirror and caught Nell's eye long enough for her to wink.

Luke had been expecting Romanoff's to resemble the Russian Tea Room on 57th Street. Wilda had taken him there after seeing Marilyn Miller, Clifton Webb, and Ethel Waters in Irving Berlin's *As Thousands Cheer.* "The walls are green like salty olives," she had told him. "The carpet and upholstery are bright red, like those spicy pepper flakes your father showers his lasagna with. And the ceiling is shiny copper, just like the hair on that woman who runs the beauty parlor on Eighteenth Avenue, the one who's always wearing fur and pearls."

But Romanoff's was nothing like the Tea Room. Aside from another large double-R logo, the walls of Bogie's favorite restaurant were empty of decoration. The ceiling was painted white, with no chandeliers.

The room was already three-quarters full. Banquettes upholstered in a checkered floral pattern lined the perimeter. Nearer the center, tables of eight, ten, and twelve were filling up. A six-piece band sat on a low stage; their soft, nondescript tune underscored the lively chatter.

"YOO-HOO!"

Beatrice waved an arm encased in an opera glove that sagged at the elbows and drooped at the cuff. She had dolled herself up as elegantly as her five-and-dime paycheck would allow, and had brought along representatives from all branches of the military: Army, Marine Corps, Coast Guard, Army Air Force, Navy. "Captain Vance bought us three bottles of Mumm! We've finished the second one, but I insisted we save the third for our guests. Mr. Bogart! Miss Bergman! I can't tell you what a thrill it is to—" A loud belch popped out of her. "Excuse me! I'm a teensy bit pickled."

"We can always order more." It was the Navy officer Luke had encountered outside Beatrice's room the night of the Battle of Los Angeles. Captain Stamina, Tristan had called him. It was, Luke now knew, an apt nickname. If he recognized Luke, he gave no sign of it as they shook hands.

The servicemen had been detached models of military self-control when exchanging introductions, but as the champagne flowed, they inundated Bogie and Ingrid with questions.

"What are you working on now?" A tale of doomed love in the northern Sahara—unless the writers change their mind, which is likely.

"What's your favorite picture?" The one I haven't made yet.

"Do you enjoy living in the United States?" I would prefer my husband Petter and our daughter Pia weren't in Rochester.

"Do you miss Sweden?" It's awfully close to the Nazis. However, you gentlemen will fix that situation in short order.

Beatrice caught Luke's eye and jacked her thumb toward the dance floor. Soon the two of them were foxtrotting to "Night and Day."

"That's quite a harem you've got there," Luke said.

"They didn't want to come gussied up in their dress uniforms, but I talked them into it."

The Army, the Army Air Force, the Marine Corps, and the Coast Guard were talking to Bogie now, leaving the Navy to entertain Ingrid.

"If I had a uniform, I'd wear it every chance I got."

A frisson of excitement fluttered through the crowd. Marlene

Dietrich had positioned herself in front of the maître d's podium, where she was backlit by a standard lamp in the foyer. Buried in her shadow was lantern-jawed Randolph Scott, who was filming a Western with her at Universal. Luke wasn't sure that staging a publicity stunt at a fundraiser to benefit Europeans fleeing the Nazi regime was in terrifically good taste. Then again, her presence ensured that people across the country tomorrow would read about the European Film Fund, so maybe her movie-star entrance wasn't an altogether bad thing.

The band shifted to a livelier "Things Ain't What They Used to Be."

"So," Luke asked, "you and the captain?"

She pursed her lips in mock consternation. "Are we going to pretend you don't overhear us going at it?"

"I will if you will."

"I know what you're thinking. That he comes across as staid and conventional, but he's not like that at all. I shouldn't tell you this, but I'm too tipsy to care." She lowered her voice to a stage whisper "He's very high up in Navy intelligence."

"Does he share any of his secrets . . . afterwards?"

"Heavens, no. He's military through and through." They were passing the table again. She threw Captain Stamina a tender look. "Poor lamb. He's a widower. Wife died of kidney disease. He's got his war work to distract him, but he's been so lonesome. He came into Kress's to buy thread for some buttons that'd fallen off his uniform. He had no idea how to sew them back on, so I gave him a lesson. I nearly fainted when he asked me out. Took me to Sardi's, so that was nice. Walked me home, which was nice, too. And then he kissed me, and that was *really* nice. Those young bucks, they barely know one hole from another. So, when the good captain and I started necking, I thought, Finally, a guy I don't have to teach!"

The band drew "Things Ain't What They Used to Be" to a close. As Luke escorted Beatrice to the table, a drumroll hushed the crowd, who erupted into applause when Peter Lorre walked on stage.

"Save it for those who'll earn it," he said into the microphone. "I see faces of people who have been forced to flee, or have chosen to leave before they were given no choice. Ernst Lubitsch and Salka Viertel, please show yourselves." Two figures stood up at a table down the back of the room. "These two are like locomotives, working hard to rescue as many people as they can." Lorre let the ovation rise and fall. "And now, it is time I bring you the ersatz charms of Miss Trixie Bagatelle."

A tall, slender woman sauntered on stage to the sound of an unbroken trumpet blast. Dressed in a floor-length gown dripping with diamantes, she tilted her torso, leading with her hips, which she undulated with unhurried indifference until she had positioned herself at the mike. "Well, hello. And what a collection of humanity we have here tonight. Some of it remarkable. Some of it . . ." she landed her eyes on Marlene Dietrich and see-sawed her hand ". . . not so much."

Dietrich's roar was the loudest in the room, her applause the most raucous.

Trixie Bagatelle had fashioned herself into a facsimile of Dietrich, circa *Shanghai Express*. But she wasn't 100% Dietrich. She was also part Hedy Lamarr—the apathetic part unable to summon much enthusiasm—together with a generous dollop of Sophie Tucker-esque swagger.

Nell leaned over until Luke felt the heat of her skin pressing his shoulder. "Who is this?"

"Remember my neighbor with the pale complexion?"

"But it—but he's—oh my lord!"

As a man, Tristan Bannister was on the quiet side. Polite. Dependable. He radiated the air of someone who would reassure you on a three-a.m. ride to the hospital that it probably wasn't an appendix threatening to burst, but a far less cataclysmic malady, which the doctors would no doubt confirm in short order. Trixie

Bagatelle, on the other hand, was equal parts saucy and bold. She didn't give two hoots who she insulted, or whose ego she might bruise. Shooting season was always open, every two-legged creature was a sitting duck—and Miss Bagatelle was a hell of a crack shot.

She pointed to the bandleader and yelled, "Hit it."

Wilda had often played Al Jolson's version of "Let Me Sing and Be Happy" during their Saturday afternoon tea parties, but Trixie had transfigured it into a fist-to-the-sky anthem: "I Will Sing and You Will Be Happy to Hear Me, Dammit."

She had enchanted the crowd into awed silence, and when she ended on a high note that wasn't quite on key, she made up for it in power. It soared over an audience familiar with the perils of facing a tough crowd. Lubitsch jumped to his feet and pounded his hands together. Whatever he yelled was drowned out in the bravos and calls for an encore.

Trixie executed a deep, lady-like curtsy and held it until the acclaim subsided. "Thank you, my dumplings. Thank you, one and all. Raucous bunch, aren't you? I thought I'd be facing a crowd more sober than Sister Aimee's Sunday morning sermon. But what do I find? All liquored up and look like you're getting ready to pay a visit to Lee Francis." Trixie lifted an acerbic eyebrow and threw a side-eye to Dietrich. "I see Marlene knows who I'm talking about. You have to wonder, don't you," she tapped a finger with a long, painted nail "if our favorite Fräulein knows Miss Francis as a worker—or a customer." The outburst was deafening, the wolf-whistles piercing, and the applause thunderous. And again, nobody clapped louder than Marlene herself.

Trixie lifted a hand to shield her eyes from the spotlight. "Where's Ernst Lubricant—er, I mean Lubitsch? Oh my, what a Freudian slip of the tongue that was. Ernie? Ernie? Wherefore art you?"

"Over here, Miss Trixie! Worshiping you from afar."

Trixie dragged the microphone to the edge of the stage. "I

suspect you were hollering like a Canadian lumberjack, but I couldn't hear over the tumultuous adulation. Now that these inebriates—yes, Humphrey Bogart, I'm looking at you—have quietened down, would you repeat it?"

Lubitsch called out, "Please sing 'What Is This Thing Called Love?'"

Trixie pressed both hands to her mouth in mock surprise. "You want me to perform my signature tune?"

While applause fizzed through the crowd, Nell turned to Luke. "He even has a signature tune?" Luke shrugged his shoulders helplessly. Whenever he'd asked for a glimpse of Trixie, Tristan's response had always been that Miss Trixie Bagatelle demanded to be seen in full regalia or not at all.

The slow-tempo ballad sounded like a tune Dietrich might have performed early in her career. As she warbled about how love had made a fool of her, one of the musicians approached from behind and draped a voluminous white cape across her shoulders. As the number built toward its climax, she rippled it like the sails of a fantasy pirate ship from an Astaire-and-Rogers musical extravaganza, billowing it higher and wider until she hit her last note. Throwing her arms straight out, she flicked her wrists, sending the cape six feet out on both sides of her.

Without warning, she dropped to her knees.

The cape fluttered in the air for a moment.

It drifted to the floor.

The crowd gasped.

Standing in the spotlight, her hands clasped as though in prayer, was the singer everybody had really come to see.

Her gown, strewn with bugle beads, hung from one shoulder into a cinched waist, then spread out in generous drapes. She had marcelled her hair into the sort of coiffure that she would've worn at the peak of her cabaret popularity. This wasn't just her L.A. debut, Luke realized, it was a chance to recreate her glory days.

"Danke schön! Merci! And thank you!" Sabine Vogel let the applause splash over her, a broad smile splitting her face. "I'd like to start with a number that I sang first, but that my darling friend, Josephine Baker, made famous." She lifted her shoulders as though to say, *C'est la vie.* "It's called 'I Have a Message for You,' but I must sing it in French."

The violinist and saxophonist hit a long note, joined by the pianist and the clarinetist. Luke caught a glimmer of trepidation in her eyes as she tilted her face and sang the opening note.

Luke's jaw dropped open.

Maybe it was the stage, the warmth of the spotlight, or the safety net of a six-piece band. Or had that marcelled hair summoned her memories of halcyon days? Whatever it was, it filled Sabine with a grandeur that impromptu sing-alongs around the Whitley Manor piano hadn't hinted at.

Luke didn't know what she was singing about. It hardly mattered, though. She landed each note like a swan gliding onto the surface of a tranquil lake, wringing the appropriate emotion for the perfect length of time before taking flight again.

The last note wasn't an Ethel Merman belter, but an Edith Piaf plea. Sabine held it for as long as she could, then dropped her head to her chest.

The applause was deafening. But instead of milking it for every drop of adoration, she launched into a couple of songs by singers Luke hadn't heard of: Trude Hesterberg and Kate Kühl. She followed them with a brave choice, considering Marlene herself was sitting a dozen feet away.

When the audience recognized the opening bar of "Falling in Love Again," some members gasped, while others murmured, "She isn't!" But Luke figured that if Sabine could endure *Kristallnacht* with enough presence of mind to pack a suitcase the next day and flee Europe, this was a cinch.

She sang the initial verse in English, before switching to German. For the third verse she flipped to French. The fourth was

Italian, and the fifth was, Luke suspected, Dutch. Then back to German, and she finished in English. The applause swallowed the famous last line—"Can't help it"—so completely, she needn't have bothered singing it at all.

This time, she let the acclaim fill the room and didn't speak again until it had died away.

"For my final number—" Lubitsch cut her off with a shrill *NO!* She told him to hush. "—I'm giving you three songs for the price of one. I can only sing them in the original German. That won't be a problem for many of you."

She sang the opening verse of "Pirate Jenny" from Brecht's *The Threepenny Opera* before sliding into "Ballad of the Easy Life," treating her rapt audience to only one verse, then segued into "Cry from the Grave." Building on the deft skill she'd earlier demonstrated, Sabine wove the three songs together into a dense braid of love, strength, and redemption for a gathering that knew first-hand the rewards of perseverance in the face of insurmountable odds.

The medley ended with a pounding thump on the drums. The stagehand killed the spotlight, plunging the stage into darkness. He didn't switch it on again until the crowd was on its feet calling "Bravo! Encore!"

Sabine took five deep curtseys. "Well, well!" she exclaimed. "That was *très dramatique*, wasn't it? Time for some levity. I'm going to ask someone to join me up here. He's not expecting it, and I suspect he won't want to come up here so, ladies and gentlemen, *Meine Damen und Herren, Mesdames et Messieurs*, I need you to encourage to the stage my friend, Luke Vail."

Luke's heart skyrocketed into his throat. Since when was he part of the act?

Nell pushed him to his feet. Applause engulfing him like a flash flood, he joined Sabine. Her Cheshire Cat grin made his palms damp.

"You're wondering what you're doing up here, aren't you?"

Luke could only nod as Trixie emerged from the wings. She held a pile of cards, each about the size of a magazine. As she drew closer, he saw what was written on the top card.

Oh, God, no. His party trick.

Luke's mouth went dry. Performing for neighbors in a parlor had taken a handful of guts—but in front of *this* crowd? He forced down a raw swallow.

Sabine made a dramatic show of shuffling the cards as Trixie planted herself at the microphone. "We have thirty cards, each with a number. Luke will look through them. Just once. And when he's done, he's going to list them, out loud, in order, from memory." She gave the end of Luke's nose a playful tweak. "As you can see from the scared-rabbit-in-the-headlights expression on his face, he wasn't expecting this, were you, *liebchen*?" Luke shook his head. "Not only that, but we're going to make things interesting. For each number he gets out of sequence, he'll donate five dollars to the Fund."

Five dollars? Per card? He only had to get seven wrong and there went a week's salary, *pfffft!*, into thin air. He ran his hands down the sides of his trousers.

"Hold on!" Everyone in the room turned toward Bogie, who was now on his feet. "If Luke gets all thirty numbers right, I'll donate a hundred and fifty."

Peter Lorre jumped up from two tables across. "I'll match it!"

A tide of applause swelled through the room, but stopped when Lubitsch called "ME TOO!" followed by Bette Davis. "ME THREE!"

Six hundred bucks the European Film Fund could lose out on if he screwed up. Luke wanted to throttle Sabine. Or Tristan. Or whoever was responsible for this stunt. But five hundred people were looking up at him, expectation filling their faces.

"Ready?" Trixie framed her question in such a way that left only one response.

Luke extended his right hand. "Give me the cards before I lose my nerve."

The men's room at Romanoff's was a refreshing oasis of cool air. Square wall tiles the size of dinner plates. Marbled patterning to chest height, black to the ceiling.

Luke was unzipping at the end urinal when Captain Stamina marched through the door. He said nothing until he stood at the one next to Luke.

"Hell of an act you've got there."

"I did not see it coming."

Captain Stamina chuckled. "Trust me, we could tell. The fact you're not a stage performer made it all the more impressive."

"Thank you."

"As impressive as your neighbor, Sabine."

Luke's chance encounter with this guy outside Beatrice's room had been months ago. It had barely lasted a minute and the lighting in the hallway had been dim. Luke wasn't the only man in this bathroom with a sharp memory. He zipped up. "I knew she used to be a big deal in Berlin, but I didn't know she could do *that*."

"Her final number!" They were at the basins now, washing their hands. "I'm not familiar with the song, but it sure packed a wallop."

"It was three songs." Luke handed him a small towel from the pile at the end of the counter and picked up one for himself. "From *The Threepenny Opera*." The captain looked at him blankly. "Bertolt Brecht."

The guy bunched his towel into a wad and launched it like a basketball toward the wicker hamper in the corner. It flew in without hitting the sides. "Are you German?"

"I studied the German school of philosophy in college."

"So you're American? Born and bred?"

"Lived my whole life in Brooklyn."

The captain nodded as he leaned against the counter. "Tell me, that bit with the numbered cards—how'd you do it?"

"I memorized each one as I went."

"That's all it took?"

This conversation had started out as casual bathroom chit-chat, but it had now shifted into a more serious tone. Almost like an interrogation. To what end, though? "Humphrey Bogart told me I've got a photographic memory. First I'd heard of it, so I'm not convinced it's an actual thing."

"It is." He gave Luke the once-over. "You 4-F?"

Here we go. Again. Luke nodded.

"How would you feel if I reversed your status?"

WHAT? Did he say 'reversed'? "You can do that?"

"*I* can't, but my superior officer reports to someone who can. Maybe." He held up a cautionary finger. "Emphasis on 'maybe.' You interested?"

"Yes! Is there a number I can call you—"

"I'll be in contact if the opportunity arises. You still living at Bea's boarding house?"

When Luke said that he was, the guy gave a satisfied grunt and left the men's room.

Luke walked back inside the restaurant. How had he not noticed how noisy it was in there? And smoky. And so crowded. He headed out the front door and onto Rodeo Drive, where bougainvillea sweetened the cool June air. He strolled slowly along the front of the building, gulping in deep breaths of air and trying to clear his head.

How would you feel if I reversed your status?

Was that even possible? Once 4-F, always 4-F. Wasn't that the rule?

He's high up in Navy intelligence.

Not high enough to fix his 4-F, but he knew someone who knew someone. Maybe.

'Maybe' was good. He'd take 'maybe.'

He ran his fingers along the smooth plaster.

'Maybe' was better than he'd had half an hour ago. A heck of a lot better.

The lighthouse keeper program had slipped away like a moray eel.

He reached the end of the building. The wall was still warm from the summer heat. He pressed his palms against it.

Navy intelligence. Was that what Captain Stamina had in mind? It wasn't shooting Nazis across the Maginot Line, but it felt like a foot in the door. If not a foot, then at least a toe.

"Where's your uniform?"

The question, low and gruff, came from out of nowhere.

The five G.I.s were in uniform, but none of them wore it as intended. Two of them had lost their neckties. Only one of them wore his garrison cap. Another one had no shoes at all. They all stank of beer.

"Hi, fellas," Luke said, evenly. "Out for a night on the town?"

"My buddy here asked you a question." Shoeless Joe took a step forward. "It's only polite to answer him. So answer him already. We got drafted. How come you didn't?"

Luke stepped toward the curb. Maybe if he got around them, he could avoid the ugliness he saw coming. The first rule of dealing with drunks was to agree with them wherever possible. "I got drafted, just like you."

"Oh, yeah? Which branch?"

"I'm from an Army family. My dad, he served in the Great War."

"If you got drafted, why ain't you wearing your goddamned lousy uniform? You look healthy enough to take on Nips, same as us."

"That's what I told them." Luke stumbled over the edge of the curb.

The guy on the other end started punching his right fist into the palm of his left hand. "Daddy didn't want his precious little bundle going off to war? So he called a pal? Pulled strings to get stamped 4-fucking-F?"

They spread out into a semi-circle. Luke looked past the beefiest one to the Romanoff's entrance. Now would be a great time for someone to step out into the street. But the doors remained closed. "Look, fellas, I don't want any trouble." He raised his hands. "Let's not get into anything we might regret later."

The first punch landed on the back of his shoulder. It sent him staggering.

The second punch hit his temple with a sickening thwack.

The third one sank into the pit of his stomach.

His knees buckled. He dropped forward; the asphalt scraped his palms.

Chest. Shins. Left calf. Right knee. He lost count of the blows after that.

His face felt wet. He tasted metal. He closed his eyes and curled into a ball.

They kicked his back. His neck. His sternum.

They grunted like cavemen and swore like Vikings until he couldn't hear them anymore.

Until he couldn't see them anymore.

Until the blackness overtook everything.

18

*L*uke gingerly pressed the bruise flaring across his right cheekbone. It wasn't nearly as visible as it had been at the hospital, but holy smokes, it sure was tender.

His ribs screamed every time he breathed. Or sneezed. Or laughed. Not that there had been a lot to laugh about. Thank goodness that Puerto Rican busboy had seen enough brawling on the streets of San Juan to know how to scare off five resentful G.I.s.

Jasper's voice called across the Rick's Café Américain set. "That's it for now."

Luke eased himself into his canvas chair. Nell looked up from her notes. "You could've taken another week. Nobody would've minded."

"Truth be told, I missed this place."

She twirled her pen around her finger. "You're getting celluloid in your veins."

He pressed his cheek again. Why couldn't he leave it alone? He knew he was going to suffer. "Is that bad?"

"Ironic, is all. You came to this fair land thinking you'd only be here a couple of days."

He tried to turn, but his ribs radiated a blast of pain. He stiffened and kept his eyes on the café, where dozens of dress extras were settling into position. "I want you to know how much I appreciate you visiting me every night after work."

"Yeah, yeah. I'm a regular Florence Nightingale. Tell me, why *are* you back? This scene is real complicated. We're in for a tiring day."

In a phone call to check up on how he was doing, Bogie had mentioned that Gus O'Farrell had taken over Luke's stand-in duties. The guy had flattered and fawned his way into Curtiz's good graces. Every day Luke was away from production was another opportunity that jerk could ingratiate himself even more deeply.

But there was an equally important reason Luke had struggled out of bed this morning. "I couldn't miss watching them film this scene."

"What's so special about it?"

"Aren't you the girl keeping track of the script?"

Nell lowered her voice to a whisper. "Those Epstein boys deliver new pages in the morning, which Wallis decides aren't sharp enough, or droll enough, and orders them to take another crack at it. So now we're filming a scene that the actors haven't rehearsed, that Jasper hasn't set the lights for, and that we mightn't have enough extras for. No wonder Bogie's been holing up in his dressing room. Meanwhile, there's poor Ingrid."

"What's going on with her?"

"Ingrid's nervous about Paul Henreid. How can she establish rapport with the guy who's supposed to be her husband when she's only just met him?"

"She did it with Bogie."

"Doesn't make it any easier. She takes this acting stuff real serious, so it's the opposite of how she prefers to work. Even worse, she's got no idea if her character ends up with Henreid or Bogie, so she doesn't know how to play her scenes."

An exotic girl with black hair piled high on her head took her place in front of a decorative hinged screen. She held up the guitar in her hands and strummed it.

"Who's the gypsy?" Luke asked.

"Corinna Mura. She's the daughter of Edwin Schallert, the drama reviewer for the *L.A. Times*. If nothing else, this picture will get at least one decent review. Say, what did you mean about this scene?"

"Is this still where the Germans play 'Die Wacht am Rhein' and Laszlo fights back by getting the orchestra to play 'La Marseillaise'?"

"Unless the Epsteins have changed their minds."

"This is where Rick goes from being someone who has detached himself from life to the guy who realizes that he needs to pick a side."

Nell's mouth dropped open while she absorbed Luke's observation. "Boy, you really are one smart cookie, aren't you?"

Luke feigned nonchalance with a slight shrug. Back in Brooklyn, everyone believed the mildest praise would turn a shrinking flower into an unbearable swellhead, so compliments were rarer than a July snowman in Prospect Park. But these Californians handed them out like Halloween candy. Not that he doubted Nell's sincerity. But still, what was he supposed to do when somebody flattered him like that? He had no idea, so he looked away.

His eyes landed on Gus, who was talking with Lee Katz, the assistant director. Specifically, on Gus's white tuxedo jacket. It wasn't the one Bogie was going to be wearing in this scene, but it was close. Too damned close. Gus's services were no longer needed, and it was up to Luke to let him know. He had to be subtle about it, though. He couldn't get into another altercation. Not with his ribs throbbing like a son of a gun.

When Paul Henreid strolled onto the set in his cream jacket and dark necktie and stood inside the entrance to the soundstage, Luke bypassed Gus and approached Henreid.

"Mr. Henreid," he said, "my name is Luke Vail. We're glad you could finally join us."

"Thank you." Henreid shook Luke's hand. "Filming on *Now, Voyager* went on and on."

Luke swept a hand toward the Rick's Café Américain set. "*Und willkommen in Casablanca, wo die Vergangenheit früher oder später alle einholt.*"

Henreid blinked in surprise at hearing this stranger welcome him to Casablanca, "where sooner or later the past catches up with everyone," in his native tongue.

"*Vielen Dank,* Herr Vail," Henreid replied. "*Ihr Deutsch ist ausgezeichnet.*"

Luke was happy to hear that his German was excellent. Even better, he felt the heat of Gus's resentful scowl burning the side of his face. "Mr. Curtiz is busy with the screenwriters. They're always rewriting."

"Just once I would like to work on a picture where the script was set in stone before the cameras rolled."

"*Was mich nicht umbringt, macht mich stärker.*"

"'What does not kill me makes me stronger,'" Henreid said. "You can also quote Nietzsche."

"You'll find we're awash with your fellow Europeans." There was no need to continue in German; Luke had made his point. He led Henreid past Gus and into Rick's. "Ingrid Bergman is Swedish, but speaks German. As you're aware, Conrad Veidt is from Berlin. And then there's Peter Lorre and Michael Curtiz, who were born in Hungary."

"You've done your homework, I see."

"Does reading Hedda Hopper's column count?"

"I don't read her," Henreid snapped. "She's so virulently anti-Roosevelt. Personally, I believe he is all that's standing between us and Hitler."

Gus had skirted around them and taken a circuitous path toward the set. He was trying to be inconspicuous, but a chowderhead like that possessed all the discretion of Frankenstein's monster.

"The other day, Hedda talked about a humdinger of a scene you have in *Now, Voyager*."

"I do?"

"You light two cigarettes and give one to Bette Davis. Hedda said it's got sex written all over it."

Henreid smiled. "Ah."

Close by, Gus parked himself at a café table and pretended to be fidgeting with the collar of his jacket.

"Did I hear you speaking German just now?" Ingrid wore a loose, paisley blouse and black skirt. She winked at Luke. "Your accent is commendable."

"Ingrid Bergman," Luke said, "may I introduce you to your husband, Paul Henreid."

He clicked his heels together. "Victor Lazlo at your service, ma'am."

"I was telling Mr. Henreid that we have an international company. I've heard German, French, Italian, Spanish, and what I assume was Polish, but don't quote me on it."

"How marvelous," Henreid said. "It'll make me feel I'm like on the Continent once more. My wife and I got out just in time. Of course, being designated an official enemy of the Third Reich helped us decide. I never want to go back, but there are some things I miss."

"Such as?"

"Decent food. God help me, the food here. Such shoddy, second-rate fare." He turned to Ingrid. "You've been here a while. Any recommendations?"

"Last week Luke and I were at Romanoff's in Beverly Hills. Excellent menu."

"You had an enjoyable evening?"

Luke and Ingrid swapped hesitant glances. It had been wonderful—until Luke had stepped outside.

"Romanoff's is one of Bogart's favorites," Luke replied. Gus had given up feigning distraction. He was staring openly at them now. Luke wanted to turn his back on him, but it wasn't worth the pain. "Run by a guy who goes by Prince Michael; however, it's best not to question his lineage."

Henreid's face pinched into a frown. "Another Hollywood phony."

"Just enjoy his food," Luke said. *"Und wenn Sie nett fragen, könnte er sogar Sachertorte zu seinem Dessert Menü hinzufügen!"*

Telling an Austrian-Hungarian to ask Romanoff's to add Sachertorte to their dessert menu was Luke's attempt to ease the man's apprehension. Henreid had arrived several weeks into filming, by which time the company had fused into a well-oiled unit, and he was the new kid in school with no friends.

"Ah!" he said. "Ah! *Ich hab, seit ich Wien verliess, keine vernünftige Sachertorte mehr probiert."*

While Ingrid and Henreid consoled each other over not having tasted decent Sachertorte since they'd left Europe, Luke looked at Gus. This was no swift clandestine peek, but a full-faced, unblinking provocation.

Gus stared back, curling his lip into a sneer, but was forced to look away when an assistant director brought a foursome of dress extras in evening clothes to his table and asked him why he was sitting there. The feet of his chair scraped the wooden floorboards as he retreated.

When Luke rejoined the conversation, Henreid was telling Ingrid how the British authorities might have interned him had it not been for Conrad Veidt vouching for him. "Conrad's wife is Jewish and has long been an avowed anti-Nazi. And now here he is playing our Nazi villain. I was hoping to see him before we started shooting."

"He's with the German soldiers on the other side of the Moroccan screens."

This new voice, soft and feminine with a French accent, came from a pretty girl, no more than twenty. "Bonjour," she said. "My name is Madeleine LeBeau." She extended her hand toward Henreid with a hopeful, almost pleading smile.

"Enchanté."

"I have been a fan of your work since I saw you in *The Mystery of Carlo Cavelli.*"

Henreid's long, serious face softened. "Mon Dieu, mademoiselle. You must have been very young. Which part do you play?"

"Rick's mistress, Yvonne, who he discards when Ilsa comes back into his life." She threw Ingrid a cheeky *Thanks for nothing* look, but Luke could tell it was an effort. Nerves twitched at the edges of her lips.

"That's a very becoming costume they've put you in." Luke pointed to the off-white blouse that looked more like a jacket. Covered in tiny square beads that shimmered in the light, it fitted her perfectly.

"Merci," she said, running her finger along a sleeve. "Every time they rewrite a scene, my part grows smaller. I think Orry-Kelly has taken pity on me. When I went for my fitting, he told me he'd been saving this one."

Ingrid picked at the ruffle on her paisley blouse. "You'll certainly outshine me today."

"I'm glad to be in it at all!" Madelaine exclaimed. "My husband, Marcel, and I—he plays Emil the croupier—we fled to Paris, where we got transit visas letting us travel through Spain to Lisbon, where we booked a ship to America."

"Just like *our* characters," Henreid told Ingrid.

"We were stuck in Portugal for two months. In Mexico we learned our visas were forgeries."

"No wonder they cast you."

Madelaine fluttered a hand toward the crowded set. "Many of us have lived a version of this story." Her flicker of a smile suggested she'd prefer to not think of it again. "I wish to ask some advice."

Henreid raised his eyebrows. "From me?"

"This scene we're about to film might be my only good moment. I want to get it right. My character is French, so when they start 'La Marseillaise,' how should I play it? Proud and patriotic, even though it is reckless to defy the Nazis? Or timid like a little bunny rabbit because they have the power to ruin my life?"

"How do *you* feel when you hear 'La Marseillaise'?"

"Patriotic. And brave."

"Even with bad guys singing 'Die Wacht am Rhein'?"

The young woman's hands coiled into fists. "They were in Lisbon, too. Watching and listening and following. They cannot be too blatant because Portugal and Spain are neutral, so they threaten with their eyes. Waiting for you to stumble." Luke scanned the set for Gus. The guy was no Nazi, of course, but he always seemed to lurk in the background. Watching, listening, following. "Whenever I saw them, I hummed 'La Marseillaise' to myself."

"How did it make you feel?"

"It encouraged me to go on."

Henreid beamed. "You have answered your own question."

"But humming is not singing out loud."

"Everything in the movies must be exaggerated. The audience cannot see inside your head. In a crowded casino, they cannot hear you humming. You must display your determination. Your character is the first to stand up, *n'est-ce pas*? She shows the bullies they will not win in the long run. She shows the other French citizens in Rick's that they, too, must have courage."

All heads turned as Michael Curtiz strutted onto the *Casablanca* set in his boots and riding britches. The only thing he lacked was a stiff leather crop. "We start with the wide shot. Everybody on their foots, singing out of their lungs. But first we have rehearsal. You know the words, yes?"

Men straightened their bow ties and women fussed with their

hats as Jasper and his team adjusted the lights. The seven-man band picked up their instruments and ran scales.

Luke returned to his chair next to Nell. "I thought they were just actors."

"Curtiz insisted they be musicians, too. Give the scene a touch of realism." She nodded toward the spot where he'd been standing with Henreid and Ingrid. "Playing Welcome Wagon, I see."

"I figured if he heard some German, he'd feel less like an outsider."

"Did it work?"

Luke pictured the stricken look on Gus's face. "Yeah, I think so."

Curtiz's assistant approached the edge of the set. "Okay, people, we're going to run through 'La Marseillaise.' No improvisation. No focus pulling." He turned to the band. "In five, four, three, two, ONE!"

The trumpetist and trombonist lifted their instruments and blasted out the first notes. On cue, the extras started singing with such overwhelming emotion that Luke felt his chest vibrate.

Nell leaned closer. "Do you know what they're saying?"

One of Luke's favorite college memories was of his philosophy professor comparing the national anthems of France, Italy, Germany, Spain, and Austria-Hungary. The professor had proposed the theory that national anthems provide a window into a country's soul. Consequently, Luke knew the full lyrics of five European anthems.

"'Arise, children of the Fatherland,'" he quoted. "'Our day of glory has arrived. Against us the bloody flag of tyranny is raised. Do you hear in the countryside the roar of those ferocious soldiers? They're coming right into your arms to cut the throats of your sons, your comrades.'"

"Not exactly the dawn's early light and twilight's last gleaming, is it?"

Luke kept his attention on Madeleine's clenched fists and

resolute chin. He hoped the girl hadn't blown her emotional stockpile by the time Curtiz was ready to shoot. "They go on to sing about blood watering their fields."

Nell screwed her eyes up tight. "Gruesome!"

Henreid's words about showing the bullies they wouldn't win in the long run pinged inside Luke's skull as he spotted Gus slipping out a side exit deep in the shadows.

The cast was still singing about forming battalions as Luke stepped into the warm summer sunshine. He peeked around the corner in time to see Gus hurry down Avenue A past the garage. There was a skulking quality to the way he moved. The guy wasn't out for a stroll.

Sticking close to Stage Eight's wall, he followed Gus toward the truck shed that overlooked the L.A. River. A grove of six or seven ancient oak trees ran along the studio's southern perimeter. Gus headed for them, a sheaf of papers clutched in one hand. With the Epstein boys writing and rewriting every scene, discarded script sheets had become a common sight on the *Casablanca* set. What would Gus want with any of the superseded pages?

As the guy took cover behind the farthest tree, Luke positioned himself close enough to see Gus stare at the page.

"R-r-r-r-r-i-i-i-i-ck." He studied it some more. "Oh! Rick?"

He ran a finger slowly down the page and stopped halfway down.

"He."

It came out more like "Huh-ee?" as though it were a surprise appearing from out of nowhere. Then suddenly he growled, "Screw it," and thrust the pages aside, muttering "Too hard" as he stomped off in the direction of the woodworking shop.

Luke waited until he was out of sight, then darted in and scooped the pages off the withering grass. Why would Gus steal an old version of today's scene? Luke didn't have time to figure that out. He should never have left his post.

. . .

When Luke slipped back inside the soundstage, the dress extras were rehearsing "La Marseillaise" while the Nazis competed with "Die Wacht am Rhein."

Nell beckoned him to her. "Jasper's been asking for you." She nudged him toward the set, where Jasper stood next to Dooley's upright piano.

"Sorry," he said. "I had an urgent errand to run."

"Get up to the landing. Bogie's going to be leaning onto the banister with his hands spread wide apart."

Luke took his place on the steps to Rick's apartment. Competing anthems swirled around him. The French sang about the howling of fearsome soldiers; the Germans sang about crashing waves and the clang of steel; the French sang of how the day of glory had arrived; the Germans sang of how, as long as a drop of blood still glows, a fist still draws the sword.

But Luke heard little of it.

Did the guy have an intermittent stutter? Did he want to become an actor, but couldn't get the words out? Why skulk off into the shadows? He worked in a movie studio, for crying out loud. Half the people here were desperate to become actors. Or screenwriters. Had he been collecting discarded pages so that he could study screenplays? Gus O'Farrell was a hulking ox, hardly the type who wanted to write.

No. That wasn't it. Not even close.

All that bluster. All that bravado. All that bombast. It was just an act. No different from what Bogie was doing on Stage Eight, what Bette Davis was doing on Eleven, what Errol Flynn was doing on Fourteen. Luke wanted to kick himself. He'd grown up around swagger; he should have seen it for what it was: a camouflage for the guy's Achilles heel.

Gus O'Farrell couldn't read.

19

The striped awning extended from the front door to the corner curb, where Wilshire Boulevard met Rodeo Drive. Above it, large neon tubing told Luke that he had the right place.

The

BROWN DERBY

Restaurant

It would have made better sense for Luke and Nell to meet at the Derby on Vine Street. After all, it was only ten minutes from Whitley Manor. This one was clear across town in Beverly Hills. The walk had taken him over an hour, and his nice shoes weren't built for trekking God only knew how many miles. His feet ached like he was Moses climbing down Mt. Sinai, but who cared about that when he was about to escort Nell on their first proper date?

They had breakfasted at Schwab's. Lunched at the Nickodell.

Burgers at Delores' Drive-in. Desserts at C.C. Brown's. But not a *proper* date, where he would wear the one pair of trousers that didn't shine in the seat and she'd wear her new hat. Where the tablecloths were linen and waiters slung starched napkins over their arms.

But dinner dates at fancy eateries cost money, so he'd saved until he had enough to take Nell on a memorable date. She had chosen the Brown Derby. "But the one in Beverly Hills," she had insisted. "I've heard it's more refined. People don't table hop like Mexican jumping beans, telling everybody, 'Don't you look marvelous?'"

He shook his hands to ease his nerves. Did any of his brothers get this antsy before a date? Probably not. Valenti boys grew up knowing they were the flames and girls were the moths.

But Nell had never heard of Sal, Tony, Rico, Cal, or Vic. And that made all the difference.

He smelled Nell's perfume. "Chanel No. 5?"

Her dress was soft and wafty. It swirled around her legs like mist, floating in the warm June breeze. "I admire a boy who knows his perfumes."

"When your eyes don't work as intended, the other senses rise to fill the void." He sniffed at the air again. This time he detected an underlying tartness he hadn't initially picked up on. "Or is it?"

"There's a guy in Electrical whose father is an industrial chemist. He has a side business reconstructing expensive perfumes, which he sells in plain bottles for a fraction of the price." She wagged a wary finger at him. "I'm going to have to be careful around you."

The main room had high ceilings. World-famous faces gazed across the diners from the framed portraits arranged in neat rows along the walls. The waiter stopped at a circular table beneath the gigantic twenty-bulbed chandelier and pulled out a chair for Nell. They each took their seats and accepted the offered menus.

"I'm sorry I had to meet you here," he said.

"Where would you prefer to have met me?"

"A gentleman picks his date up."

"Hard to pull off when the gentleman doesn't own a car."

"I wanted to give you the full treatment."

"Relax, will you? This is wonderful. You look spiffy. Is that tie new?"

Luke had bought a new one especially for this evening, but when he arrived home, Tristan had pointed out it was "the color of diseased cabbage." He had disappeared into his room and returned a minute later with one of his.

Luke ran his fingertips down it. "Let's just say Tristan came to my rescue."

Nell laid down the menu. "If you can't see colors very well, how do you match your clothes?"

The Brown Derby menus were oversized. When Luke set his menu down, it covered half of hers. "My Aunt Wilda would take me shopping. I could pick whatever I wanted, but she had veto power. We would go back to her place and she'd stitch a little symbol on the label. One cross meant black, white, and gray. Two crosses meant dark purples, blues, dark greens. Three crosses for light greens, yellows, light oranges. Four crosses for dark oranges, reds, pinks, and light purples. And next to the crosses she'd stitch a number, five through eight, thus giving me a ton of combinations."

"How frightfully clever! But what have you been doing here in L.A.?"

"I have to rely on the clerk's good taste, which apparently this afternoon's haberdasher lacked."

Nell picked up her menu again. "I could be your Wilda—if you trust me."

The waiter arrived at their table and asked for their drink

order. When Luke suggested champagne cocktails, Nell nodded, then waited until the guy was outside earshot. "What's in a champagne cocktail?"

"Darned if I know," Luke admitted. "I saw Bette Davis order one in a movie where she plays a girl reporter. It sounded so sophisticated that I promised myself that I'd have one the first chance I got."

"And here you are."

"Here *we* are."

A faint blush shaded her cheeks. "Speaking of Bette, you know that war-bond tour Mr. Warner is spearheading? It's kicking off at the Pan-Pacific Auditorium. I sure hope we can get tickets, because he's pledged her *Private Lives of Elizabeth and Essex* gown. The one with the huge collar of stiffened lace and the bodice covered with pearls."

"She looked incredible."

"He's also pledged the Maltese falcon and Errol's Robin Hood bow and arrow. Selznick is lending them a Scarlett O'Hara dress, MGM's giving them Dorothy's ruby slippers from *The Wizard of Oz*, and Walt Disney has pledged an animation cel from *Snow White and the Seven Dwarfs*. Seems like every day one of the studios announces a new item."

Several tables behind Nell, a guy sat alone. He wore a jacket that was plainly a couple of sizes too big for him. It kept falling backward off his neck and he had to tug at its lapels to pull it into place. Luke couldn't see his face, just his profile. And barely even that. But he looked familiar.

"Don't you think?"

"I'm sorry," Luke said. "Don't I think what?"

"A real draw card would be the Rosebud sled from *Citizen Kane*."

"Hearst would burn the Pan-Pacific down before he let people see Orson's Rosebud."

"You know what I'd love to see? Wallace Beery's baseball bat from *Casey at the Bat*. Did you ever see it?"

"I must have missed that one."

In the entire time he'd been in Los Angeles, Luke had never seen a familiar face on the streets, at the studio, or in any of the stores—except that guy in the ill-fitting jacket with his folded newspaper and cracked crab.

"When it comes to baseball, I'm a take-it-or-leave-it kind o' gal," Nell said. "But I would love to have witnessed Joe DiMaggio set a new hitting streak record against the Red Sox. I bet you Yankee fans went bananas!"

Luke could picture how the Valenti family's communal backyard must have looked when DiMaggio broke his record. Pop would have spent the night barbequing platters of burgers and hotdogs and steaks. Tony would have served enough beer to fill Yankee Stadium twice over. Nobody loved baseball more than the Valentis, and they adored no other player more than the humble Italian boy who'd hit it big by hitting big. Good God, they must've gone out of their cotton-picking minds.

The waiter delivered their drinks and said he'd be back to take their food order. They clinked their champagne cocktails and took tentative sips.

Luke swirled his around his mouth and picked out the individual flavors: champagne, Angostura bitters with some sugar to balance it out, and a splash of brandy. "Say, this is pretty good."

"Have you been to Gilmore Field yet?" she asked.

"I don't know what that is."

"A baseball stadium at Beverly and Fairfax, home to the Hollywood Stars. It's the minor league, but the crowd's enthusiastic. We should go some time. Think of it as the Ebbets Field of L.A."

Luke felt his face flush. He lifted the menu to shield it from view. He would have kept it there until the heat dissipated, but Nell's fingertips curled over the top and drew it down to the table.

"We don't have to talk about baseball."

"Anything but that."

"Can we talk about why you don't want to talk about baseball?"

He stalled for time and took another sip of his cocktail. More like a mouthful. The bubbles tingled the roof of his mouth, but they didn't cool his cheeks.

Nell shifted her face into neutral. She was trying so hard to be earnest, but not too grave. Interested, without tipping over into prying.

Should he tell this no-nonsense girl the Ebbets Field story when he hadn't even told Wilda? He had no idea how it would come across. How *he* would come across. Hero, victim, or casualty? Then again, if this budding romance was going to go anywhere, she deserved to know all about him and not just the best-foot-forward parts. And if anyone could understand, it was this girl who had run away from home before she drowned in sisters.

He smoothed out the white linen tablecloth.

"Round about ten years ago, I was reading *Journey to the Center of the Earth* in my room when I heard our Woody station wagons back out of the driveway. I looked through my window and saw a line of cars along Sixty-Seventh Street. My five brothers are all married with kids, so if we wanted to go someplace, it took a convoy. I watched the whole lot of them take off."

"Without you?"

"Not so much as a wave goodbye."

"Did you run after them?"

"I was too shocked to move."

"Can't say I'm surprised. They left you behind!"

"Well, yes, that too. But just as shocking was how the house fell silent. I'd grown up around non-stop noise. Music playing. Kids hollering. People laughing. Or arguing. Usually arguing. Suddenly it was like somebody had cut off every sound in the world."

Luke had deliberately not thought of that day in years. But he could still remember how the silence had pressed in on him like a giant balloon, feel the cool wood on the steps leading downstairs, hear the tick-tick-tick of the kitchen clock.

"I tiptoed around the house calling out, 'Hello? Hello?' But nobody answered. I had the whole place to myself. Even though I was relieved to have some peace—my family has only two ways of talking: loud and louder—I kept wondering where they'd gone until I saw the calendar. There it was in big red letters: Baseball season opening game at Ebbets."

"Didn't you usually go?"

"Yes, but not because I wanted to. It was always so crowded and uncomfortable. But Jesus! It would've been nice to have been asked. Later on, I figured it out. Pop assumed Mom had asked me, and Mom assumed Pop had asked me. So it was just a miscommunication."

"They didn't even say goodbye."

Luke thought of the peanut-butter-and-jelly sandwich he'd made for himself that day, and the glass of extra chocolatey milk, and how he'd sat at that blissfully quiet kitchen table and recited to himself those same five words: *They didn't even say goodbye.*

Nell knitted her brows together and pulled her lips into a thin, stricken line.

"I know, I know," he said. "It sounds like the saddest tale since *Les Misérables.*"

"Pollyanna would have trouble seeing the bright side of that story."

Oh, brother. Never let it be said that Luke Valenti knows how to show a girl a good time. He needed to get this date back on track.

"There is one," he said. "I realized that I had two parents, five brothers and sisters-in-law, and more than a dozen nieces and nephews, but I couldn't count on any of them."

"If this is what you call a bright side—"

"I told myself, 'You're on your own, kiddo. The best path through life was to be self-sufficient, and from then on, I adjusted my expectations accordingly. It's the day I grew up, and that's a good thing.'" And that was all the wallowing in the past he was prepared to do. He raised his hand to attract the attention of their waiter. "Isn't this place famous for inventing their own salad?"

"Cobb Salad. But you have to like Roquefort cheese."

Luke didn't know Roquefort from Rod La Rocque. "I'm game if you are."

Their waiter made a three-act play out of mixing the spinach, tomato, eggs, bacon, avocado, cheese, and chives together at their table. As he created his culinary work of art, Luke sneaked another gander at the diner in the baggy jacket. He was now cleaning the melted butter and crab juice from his fingers. The longer Luke watched, the more he felt sure he knew him. If only he'd look in their direction.

The waiter finished his handiwork with a triumphant "Ta-da!" loud enough to attract the attention of the familiar stranger, who looked over at them.

It was that guy Luke had gone to see before Christmas, the one who didn't know who Simon was. Luke had given up asking about that in his letters to Wilda. Hers were full of news about Jascha Heifetz's violin recitals and cocktail parties for the Swedish ambassador at the Rockefeller apartment building in Beekman Place, but nothing about—what was his name?

It started with a vowel. Didn't it? How was it possible that he could recite a Nietzsche poem he'd read five years before, but couldn't remember the name of someone he'd met six months ago? His remarkable memory formed the whole basis for his party trick. He hadn't realized how notable it had made him feel—especially now that he was swimming in a giant pond filled with people endowed with distinct talents of their own. Had it just . . . gone?

Three loud knocks on the table arrested his flight of panic. "You look preoccupied. Is it the baseball thing?"

He stabbed at a chunk of avocado. "When I returned the Maltese falcon to Props, the guy handed me a note from Simon telling me to go see someone on Norton Avenue. But that someone didn't know who Simon was."

"What's his name?"

"I'm having trouble recalling it."

"Since when do you have trouble remembering anything?"

"Since five minutes ago—oh!" He snapped his fingers. "He's got the same last name as one of the girls in The Four Blooms. Throw some flower names at me."

Nell laid her fork down. "Hollyhocks. Sunflowers. Dahlias. Lilacs. Pansies. Lily of the Valley—"

"That's it!" Thank Christ. He wasn't losing his marbles after all. "Lily . . . Lily . . . Osterhaus." He looked at the stranger with the familiar face. "Avery Osterhaus!"

"Which one is he?"

"What's that Mexican dish of little parcels wrapped in corn husks?"

"Tamales?"

"Don't look, but he's three tables behind you, by himself, where the waiter is serving him tamales."

Nell wiped her mouth with her napkin. "I'm going to powder my nose via an absurdly protracted route."

She meandered twice past Osterhaus's table before she disappeared underneath the sign for the ladies' room. Luke was trying the Roquefort cheese—*Ugh. No thanks.*—when he spotted a second familiar face. The woman settled into a chair at a table across the room and let her evening wrap fall from her shoulders as the waiter removed the other place setting. She avoided eye contact by studying the menu like it was the American Constitution—not that anybody had noticed her.

They soon would, though.

MARTIN TURNBULL

Bogie wasn't a fan of seeing himself projected thirty feet high, so he'd sent Luke to sit in on the dailies. Even in their crude state, with no editing, no adjustment for light and shadow, no music or special effects, Luke could tell that after *Casablanca* came out, Ingrid Bergman wouldn't be able to slip into a restaurant incognito ever again.

And if Luke thought he might be intruding on one of her last anonymous meals, he mightn't have been tempted to approach her. But even from this distance, the forlorn air of solitude hanging over her was palpable. He crossed the room and approached her table.

"How nice to see you," she said. "Are you and Nell having an enjoyable time?"

"You saw us?"

She smiled, a touch enigmatically. "I'm an actress, Luke. It's my job to notice everything."

He gestured toward the empty chair. "Dining alone?"

"Tonight is my fifth wedding anniversary. Petter and my darling little Pia are still back East, so I had planned to grill a cheese sandwich in my kitchen. Then I remembered: I have a Brown Derby ten minutes away."

"You shouldn't be spending your anniversary on your lonesome. Would you like to join us?"

A flicker of relief glinted in her eyes before she buried it behind a cunning wink. "Aren't you on a date?"

Luke shifted his weight from one foot to the other and back again. This wasn't just any date. It was their first linen-napkins-perfume-nice-shoes-three-courses date. And it had been going well. Mostly. That story about the family forgetting him had sucked the fun out of the conversation for a short while. And Nell had had to rap her knuckles on the table to startle him out of his panic-induced dismay over forgetting Osterhaus's name. They had recovered, though, and were having a delightful date. But

208

how could they continue to enjoy themselves when Ingrid Bergman sat a few feet away, alone on her anniversary?

"We'll enjoy it even more if you joined us."

Nell had returned to her chair when they arrived at the table.

"Luke said you wouldn't mind a third wheel," Ingrid said, "but I want to hear it from you."

"Of course! We'd love to have you."

Luke relaxed when he saw no sign of resentment or disappointment as Nell shifted her chair to make room. The waiter appeared; Ingrid ordered the veal goulash and a glass of whatever wine he felt best paired with it. She unfolded her linen napkin and took great care to smooth it across her lap.

"I neglected to thank you both for what you tried to do that night at Romanoff's."

So much for thinking they'd been so artfully subtle.

"Have your scenes with Bogie gotten any easier?" Nell's breath came in quick gasps as though she'd sprinted from the ladies' room. Her fingers ran the length of her salad fork. Up and down and up and down. Luke looked across at Osterhaus's table; it was empty.

Ingrid made a brave attempt at a smile. "Not quite. But that's all right. I'm one of those hopeless actresses who'd prefer to stay at the studio twenty-four hours a day."

"You love what you do that much?"

"It's artificial, of course, but supplying my character with the emotions needed to fill the screen so much it spills into the audience—it comforts and fulfills me."

"Even when you're playing opposite someone who only shows up to do a scene and then disappears into his dressing room to play chess?"

"Mr. Selznick warned me about Bogie. How he can be standoffish—that's a word, yes? *The Maltese Falcon* was at a second-run theater on Beverly Boulevard, so I went to see it five times just to get an idea of his acting style and choices. If I didn't do that, I don't know how I could do this job. Please, Luke, isn't there anything you can share with me so that I may connect with him?"

Luke's mind flew back to the day he and Bogie had quoted Nietzsche, and Bogie had confessed that when he looked in the mirror, he saw only a craggy face with hang-dog eyes and a scarred lip. Had all of that been off the record? Probably. He hated the thought of betraying Bogie's confidence, but what would Bogie say if he suddenly found Ingrid looking at him intently, earnestly?

Ingrid wound her napkin around a finger. "Tell me, is it those wooden platforms he must wear?"

The platforms weren't it. They were close enough, though. And they gave Luke leeway to reply to Ingrid without stretching the truth too far.

"Put it this way: They don't help."

"You know men and their egos," Nell added. "The idea of going into a clinch and the woman towering over her leading man, well, it's more than they can handle."

"Such silly nonsense."

"Look at it from his point of view," Luke said, choosing his words carefully. "You walk in wearing barely any makeup, find your mark, and you're ready to go. That scene where you see Bogie for the first time? That longing in your eyes. The heartache. That desperate conflict of wanting to see him and dreading it as well. I don't know how you do it."

Ingrid leaned back in her chair as the waiter placed a glass of red wine in front of her. "It's one part acting, one part camerawork, and one part lighting."

Nell snorted. "More like one part camerawork, one part lighting, and eight parts acting."

Luke nodded. "People will weep in their seats when this picture comes out. You're breathtaking."

She laughed off the notion. "I wish they would tell me how it ends. Not knowing which man I walk off into the sunset with—it's torture for an actress like me."

"But doesn't Ilsa agonize over choosing between her husband and her great love?" Luke asked. "She's tucked Rick away in the distant past. And when he pops up, in some far-flung corner of the Sahara, no less, isn't it agony for her, too?"

Ingrid sipped her wine as she mulled over Luke's assertion. Not that he had any right to tell this talented woman with the luminous face and the self-effacing ego what to do in front of the camera. She let out a sigh. "At least this keeps my mind off María."

"Who's that?"

"Paramount starts filming *For Whom the Bell Tolls* with Gary Cooper in November. I desperately want to play her. Unfortunately, Vera Zorina is the favored choice."

"Never heard of her," Nell said.

"Losing out to a dancer from the Ballet Russe is like grinding salt into the wound." The waiter arrived with their main course: Hungarian Veal Goulash for Ingrid, Creamed Turkey Derby for Nell, and Scalloped Chicken a la King for Luke. "But let's forget about such nonsense." She raised her glass. "Here's to romance in the desert, to first dates, and to a prima ballerina falling off a stage and breaking her leg—not badly. Just badly . . . enough."

Luke and Nell waited on the sidewalk until Ingrid's taxi joined the Wilshire Boulevard traffic. "I was dreading the possibility that she'd bring up her salary," Luke said. "Do you think she knows Dooley Wilson is earning $375 a week more than she is?"

"ThankGodshe'sgoneIcouldn'tbearitoneminutelonger!" Nell hooked her arm through his and hauled him along the sidewalk like a tow truck.

"Sorry about that," Luke said. "I didn't want a third wheel on our date, but you should have seen how forlorn—"

She spun around beneath a streetlight to face him. "I can't believe you didn't mention what Avery Osterhaus looks like!"

"How do you mean?"

"I mean how he resembles *you*, you big dummy!"

Luke shook his head. "I think I'd have noticed."

"Are you kidding? The shape of his nose, his mouth, the way his eyes are positioned. I mean, it's not like you could be brothers. But cousins? Absolutely. And then there was his clothing."

"That jacket did not fit him."

"More to the point, nothing matched. They were odd, contrasting colors, like he doesn't know how to put an outfit together."

"Plenty of guys don't care about clothes."

"It's more like he can't see colors well enough to match them."

Luke blinked. "You mean—?"

"My first thought was, What is this guy, color blind?"

20

---

*N*ell and Luke hid behind a sycamore across the street from 7711 Norton Avenue.

"You sure about this?"

He nodded. But was he? Yes and no. Kinda sorta. Ask him in five minutes and he might give a different answer.

She looked down at his fingers; he had twisted them into a Gordian knot. "I'm not convinced."

"I don't know what's worse," he confessed. "Thinking we could be related and not knowing, or confirming that I have a relation that nobody's ever told me about."

"Which is why we came up with this." Nell pulled a sheet of legal paper from her purse. He knew she had scrawled *7711 Lexington Ave, West Hollywood* in blue pencil only because she had told him. Light blue writing on yellow paper was invisible to him. If Avery Osterhaus suffered from tritanopia, he wouldn't be able to see it either.

Luke interlaced his fingers against the back of his head. "It is kind of strange, what we're doing. If you'd prefer to bail—"

"Are you kidding? I feel like Nancy Drew in *The Mystery of the*

Weird Color Blindness That Only Two People in the World Have." She tapped her cheek. "A kiss for good luck, please."

He gave her a peck and, through the leaves on a low-hanging branch, he watched her cross the street. When Osterhaus answered his door, she held up the sheet of paper. He studied it for a moment, then shook his head.

Luke gripped the bark. Tritanopia was rare, but not unheard of.

"Just one of those things." That's what Luke's mother had told him when he was nine and the oculist's explanation had been double Dutch. And then one day at college he had wandered into the library's medical section and his eye had fallen on a textbook: *Conditions and Treatment of Diseases Afflicting the Human Eyeball.* He'd flipped to the T section, where he had read that tritanopia was hereditary. It wasn't just one of those things at all. But inherited from whom? He'd never been brave enough to ask.

Nell appeared by his side. "Bingo."

"What did he say?"

"And I quote: 'I've got this peculiar eye condition that prevents me from seeing colors the way normal people do.' He doesn't have your build. You're the thick-set type, whereas he's tall and reedy. But the two of you have the same facial features, *and* a weird eye condition."

Luke turned away from her. Reality was slapping him in the face, and it was easier to absorb the blows if he didn't have to witness the conviction that filled her eyes.

"Simon must have had his reasons," she said, taking care to soften her voice. "Did you tell him your name? And by that, I mean your *actual* name?" The conviction had mutated into provocation. "It isn't Luke Vail, is it?"

Oh, jeez. Oh, crap. This wasn't how he'd planned to tell her. Not that he'd formulated a solid strategy. If he had, it would've involved a sunset and a picnic blanket—or Don the Beachcomber's Coconut Rum Swizzles at the very least.

"How did you know?"

"That time you showed me your room, you threw your wallet on the bed. It bounced onto the floor, and when I picked it up, your New York state driver's license fell out. I wasn't snooping, I swear." He went to launch into an explanation, but she cut him off. "Let's save it for another time."

Avery Osterhaus gave them a *Say, what is this?* face. "You've got twenty seconds before I get my sledgehammer."

"I know this looks strange, but I can explain—"

"Fourteen . . . thirteen . . ."

"When I came to see you the last time, I told you my name is Luke Vail, but it's really Luke Valenti."

Suspicion remained etched across Osterhaus's face. "So?"

Nell waved her finger back and forth between the two of them. "So how come you look like each other?"

This guy's mouth, his nose, his eyes—they matched Luke's. How had he not seen that?

Osterhaus studied Luke for an agonizing couple of moments. "We do, at that." He widened his front door. "Maybe you should come in."

His living room was sparsely furnished, with two loveseats facing each other over a glass-topped coffee table. The Persian rug covering the wooden floor had frayed at the edges. There was very little art on the walls, just a few framed drawings, which was odd because the place smelled of paint and ink. Luke and Nell chose the sofa facing the door; Osterhaus took the other. He crossed his arms and chewed on the inside of his lower lip until Luke couldn't bear his silence any longer.

"Simon Kovner," he said. "You know him, don't you?"

Osterhaus cleared his throat. "I didn't know who the hell you were. I can't risk getting caught."

"Doing what?"

"Let's just say I have clients who prefer to deal with somebody who knows how to keep his mouth shut."

"Clients like Simon?"

"God, no. Simon's a straight-up kind of fellow. Outside of the Santa Anita racetrack."

"How do you know him?" Nell asked.

"I work part-time as a studio assistant to Fred Sexton. He's the guy who John Huston approached to sculpt a new Maltese falcon. I met Simon when I delivered the sample to Warner Brothers and we got chatting. Turns out we both have boats down at the Newport Yacht Club."

"That's where Bogie keeps his *Sluggy*," Luke said.

"Five docks down from where I keep my *Christabel* and three docks down from Simon's *Bonnie*. Anyway, a few weeks later Henry Blanke ordered four falcons. One screen-ready prop, plus a backup, and then two more for publicity. Fred carved a mold, and I made them. Two plaster, two resin. Then I made an extra."

A fifth falcon? Things were starting to make sense. "For Simon?"

"Uh-huh. Months later, though."

"Could you tell the fifth one from the others?"

"Sure. I etched a little telltale mark near the base."

"What kind of mark?"

"My name."

"Osterhaus!" Luke wanted to kick himself in the butt. "I couldn't read it."

"Did you find the trapdoor?"

Luke hunched forward. "The what?"

"Simon ordered a hollow falcon with a trapdoor. I knew those *Maltese Falcon* guys love to prank each other, so I figured they were up to some sort of caper."

Luke took a deep breath to calm the wooziness engulfing his stomach. If that statue he'd carted from Brooklyn was hollow, what the devil was inside it?

"But when did *you* see it?" Osterhaus asked.

"Simon sent it to his brother in Brooklyn as a birthday gift. But then he realized he might lose his job if the studio brass learned he'd stolen a famous prop. He couldn't take the time off, so they tasked me with bringing it back . . ."

The rest of his explanation trailed off because it no longer made sense. Simon knew they hadn't used it in the movie, which meant he had lied to Irving. Or Irving had lied to Wilda. Or had Wilda lied to him?

A montage of scenes from spy movies avalanched through Luke's imagination: Edward G. Robinson in *Confessions of a Nazi Spy*, Rex Harrison in *Midnight Train to Munich*, Conrad Veidt in *Nazi Agent*, Joel McCrea in *Foreign Correspondent*. FBI agents! Secret military plans! Clandestine meetings with codewords and passwords! Microfilm! Good God. Had Luke been the unwitting intermediary between Irving and Simon? Were they a pair of real-life *spies*?

Get a hold of yourself. You're not Robert Cummings, Nell's not Priscilla Lane, this Osterhaus guy isn't Norman Lloyd, and this isn't *Saboteur*.

Nell laid a hand on top of his. "One phone call can clear this up. I'm sure Wilda's explanation will be perfectly reasonable. By this time next week, we'll be having a good laugh over it. But for crying out loud, can we talk about this—" she drew a circle in the air around Luke's face "—and that?" She drew another air circle nearer to Osterhaus.

"I suspect I'm going to need a drink," Osterhaus said. "Care to join me? I've only got whiskey."

"On the rocks," Luke said.

Nell added, "Make that two."

He pulled a half-empty bottle of Four Roses bourbon from out of a chipped secrétaire. "Jesus! How did I not see it?" He returned to the sofa with three highball glasses half-filled with triples. "I suppose that business with the address was a test?" When Nell nodded, he turned to Luke. "Can you see blue writing on yellow paper?"

It was bizarre to see his own eyes staring back at him. "Nope." Luke waited as the Four Roses burned his throat, then forced the question out of his mouth like he was a cat with a hairball. "Are we related?"

"You're not *my* kid, that's for damn sure. I didn't start getting busy between the sheets until after I landed in California. Do you look like your father?"

"Me and my brothers, we all have his build. But I'm not quite so all-out Italian. I'm a little fairer than they are."

"More like your mother?"

"None of us looks much like her. You and I share far more similarities than . . ."

Another onion skin of reality peeled back, leaving Luke feeling raw and defenseless. Through an open swing door behind him, Luke could hear the slow drip-drip-drip of a kitchen faucet. His brother, Cal, could fix it in a jiffy. Cal looks like Pop. Just like all us Valenti boys.

"So, Osterhaus," he said slowly. "A German name, I take it?"

"Yep. We were all born in Homburg. You know, like the hat. It's near the French border. Not that I remember it. We emigrated right after I was born."

Luke's breaths came in shallow rasps. "Are you related to Lily Osterhaus?"

Avery flinched at the abrupt right-turn in the conversation. "You know about Lily?"

"My aunt escorted The Four Blooms around the vaudeville circuit."

"The goofy chaperone? The one who knows every duke and ambassador and avant-garde artist between here and Hong Kong?"

"I knew that one of the Blooms was called Lily, but I've only recently learned her last name."

Avery ran a hand across his two-day growth. "She was my twin sister—" Nell gasped. Luke probably would have too, but his jaw was clenched shut. "—and the Osterhaus family black sheep. Lily rarely played by the rules of social etiquette, which is what happens when you're pretty, and can sing, and know how to light up a room."

"So, if I look like you, and you and Lily are twins, does that mean—is—is Lily—" *Go on. Say it. You need to ask the question. Out loud.* "—my mother?" Luke held his breath. When Avery shrugged and told him that he didn't know, Luke let it out again in relief. News like that was too big, pierced too deeply to grapple with right then and there. "Were you and Lily close?"

"I hated my father," Avery said. "The day after Lily and I turned eighteen, I caught the next train heading west and landed in L.A. with a buck seventy-five to my name and a chip on my shoulder the size of the iceberg that took down the *Titanic*. By then, Lily was spinning around vaudeville. I'd hear from her from time to time, picture postcards usually, until they stopped coming."

"Didn't you wonder why?"

"Of course. But I didn't know any of her friends, and I sure as hell wasn't going to ask Father. I had to assume she died."

"In childbirth?" Nell asked.

Avery remained still as a statue, his eyes trained on his highball glass.

A wave of nausea rose from the pit of Luke's stomach, scorching his chest as it reached up through his neck and enveloped his head, leaving him dizzy and dry-mouthed. He lurched forward, landing his elbows on his knees and pressing his face into his palms. Nell's hand rested between his shoulder blades, the warmth of her skin seeping through his shirt.

Luke heard only the drip-drip-drip from the kitchen. He lifted his glass. "Could I trouble you for a refill?"

Avery returned to the secrétaire; Luke looked around the

room for distraction and landed on a sketch of a—yep. Of course it was. What else would it be?

Lighthouse—check.

Beach—check.

Seagulls—check.

Charcoal—check.

"You did this?" he asked as Avery approached with a freshened glass.

"Lighthouses are kind of an obsession of mine. I do them in charcoal so that I don't have to worry about colors."

"Here's a funny thing," Luke said. "I have a hundred just like it back home in Brooklyn."

The two men stared at each other. *Wow.*

"If you draw with charcoal, how come your house reeks of paint and ink?"

Avery curled a finger. He led them through the kitchen to a spacious workroom. Floor-to-ceiling shelving jammed with wooden trays covered the southern wall. Bottles of ink and tubes of paint filled each tray, and on the front of each one was a code in thick black letters.

"Some people might call me an art forger; however, I think 'duplicator' wouldn't be inaccurate. Most people can't afford an original Rembrandt or Botticelli. But they can afford someone who can mimic their work closely enough to fool most of the people most of the time. You name it, I can copy it."

Nell asked, "Doesn't your color blindness condition interfere with this line of work?"

Avery pointed to the code on the nearest tray. It had four X's, followed by a 7 and the letter N. "This color blindness of ours: Lily had it, too. Everyone said she had the most terrible taste in clothes until her chaperone came up with a color-coding system."

"Numbers and X's." Wilda had always maintained that she'd invented the system for him. But that was just another lie, wasn't it, Wilda? She'd invented it for Lily. "I use it too."

"I needed a more sophisticated technique, so I added numbers and letters to give me over fifteen hundred combinations."

Luke's limbs felt heavy as marble. His head swam—and not from the two bourbons he'd just thrown down his gullet.

"Thank you for your time." Luke thrust out his hand, but his uncle—*Oh my God, this guy's my uncle!*—didn't take it.

"You're welcome to stay a while."

Nell wrapped an arm around Luke's shoulders. "I think a long walk in the open air will do us a world of good."

They remained silent until they'd reached Fountain Avenue, where the late-afternoon shadows stretched across the sidewalk.

"He and I do look alike," Luke said, "so there was bound to be some sort of explanation."

"But to learn that your mother isn't your mother? I'm surprised you didn't collapse right there on the spot."

Maybe it would come later. He would sit bolt upright at three in the morning, fists clenched around the bedsheets, mouth stretched open in a silent scream.

Or not.

He had a version of that Valenti build: the stocky chest, thick legs, hairy forearms. But on the inside, he had always felt like a chimpanzee amid a troop of gorillas.

At the end of the street, a Bullocks delivery truck drove past a woman with a stroller. A couple of girls played hopscotch on the corner. A lanky teenager who'd outgrown his dungarees bounced a basketball against a brick wall. Luke's entire existence had turned upside down and yet life continued on its merry way.

Nell's fingers squeezed his elbow. "The best thing your aunt could have done was to send you out here."

"Why didn't she just tell me?"

"All we know is that Simon got Avery to make a hollow

Maltese falcon. How about you and me take a trip to Props tomorrow, pop open that trapdoor, and see what's inside?"

He stared at her earnest face. That earnest, eager, unquestioning face of hers. Had he finally found someone in his corner? Someone who had his back? And who said 'Let's do it' with no hidden motives he had to guess at? This was all so new, so overwhelming. A wave of passion surged up inside him. It threatened to engulf him so entirely that he didn't know what to do. Until he did.

He grabbed her by the shoulders, pushed her against the tall wooden fence, and kissed her passionately enough to taste Four Roses whiskey, Juicy Fruit chewing gum, and Lucky Strikes. The potent combination heated his ardor. He thrust his tongue deeper into her mouth and found it wet, warm, welcoming. Pressing his body along the length of hers, he drove her legs apart with his knees. He hugged her tighter. His groin swelled and hardened. Could she feel it, too?

The wail of a passing ambulance broke the spell. Nell pulled back her head. "Where did that come from?"

"Do you mind?"

"Hardly."

"I'm ready." His confession came out hoarse, almost gruff. "Are you?" She nodded. "You need to know that I've never done it before."

"You think I have?" She giggled softly. "Your boarding house—it allows guests, right?"

"I live next door to a Victory Girl. At Whitley Manor, the rule is: There is no rule."

* * *

Bogie peered at Luke in his makeup mirror as Verita slid a toupée over his scalp. "You haven't quit smiling since you got here."

Luke picked up a stack of fan mail he'd already responded to and shuffled through the envelopes. "I haven't?"

Of course not. He hadn't stopped smiling since he had waved Nell off at the Hollywood Boulevard streetcar stop at ten o'clock the previous night.

Now he got it! All the love songs, the movie romances—hell, even the magazine advertisements featuring alluring women and square-jawed men. They were hawking love and sex. Sex and love. Love masquerading as sex, and sex disguised as love. *Now* he knew why Rhett had pursued Scarlett. Why Glenn Miller was "In the Mood." Why Frances Langford had yearned "Once in a While." How Ginger Rogers had fallen for Fred Astaire in their movies. And why Edna Ferber had hit the best-seller list with every book she wrote.

Even now, twelve hours later, his skin tingled from the way Nell's fingertips had trailed over his body. How warm it had felt as she'd let his hands roam wherever they pleased. Her lips—so soft. Her tongue—so urgent. Her hair—so silky. He could still smell the roses in her soap, and he blissfully sank into the delicate tenderness of it all.

"If I didn't know better—hey!" A mischievous grin crept across Bogie's face. "Verita, sweetheart. Give us a minute?"

She slid her comb onto the makeup counter. "You kids take all the time you need to get that boy talk off your chests, but remember: it's going to be a scorcher today so I'll have to apply extra glue to keep it in place."

Bogie held off until she had closed the door behind her. "You dirty dog!" He punched Luke in the arm. "How did you seal the deal?"

Where in God's name should he start? The part where the guy who made the falcon he'd carried from Brooklyn turned out to be his uncle because the woman he thought was his mother wasn't? Or probably wasn't. The jury was still out. Or how that question might be answered once Luke and Nell pried open the hollow statue?

"The time was right," he said.

"And?"

"You know how in those Andy Hardy movies, there's always a scene where Mickey Rooney gets to kiss a pretty girl and he goes all goofy and wobbly-legged and bunches up his hat and plasters a dopey grin on his face three miles wide? It was like that multiplied by a hundred."

Bogie pulled a Chesterfield out of a packet next to Verita's box of makeup tricks and lit it. "That good, huh?"

"Multiplied by five hundred—no, a thousand."

Comprehension dawned in Bogie's dark eyes. "Jesus, boyo, this was your first time!" He yipped with delight. "We need to celebrate. After we finish work today, we'll go out. Don the Beachcomber. Seven Seas. Trocadero. Your choice."

"That sounds great, but first Nell and I have a special errand to run."

"There are a lot of hasty marriages going on these days. Tell me you're not—"

"Nothing like that. In fact, you should come with us."

"Count me in—as long as there's no lifting involved."

"Why not?"

Bogie pulled up the left side of his undershirt to reveal a large square bandage taped over an area the size of his fist. "The Missus got that 'Fuck you and everybody you've ever met' look when I told her about the party J.W. is throwing on the set today."

Casablanca's director was Warner's golden boy after his previous picture, *Yankee Doodle Dandy*, had spent the summer burning so brightly at the box office that it was on track to become Warners' biggest-ever success. Today marked Curtiz's fifteenth anniversary at the studio, and Jack Warner had planned a big celebration with cake, champagne, photographers—and Hedda Hopper.

"What happened?"

"She came at me when I said invited guests were any current Warner employees. She hasn't worked here since *Brother Rat and a Baby*. And even then, her billing was 'Girl in Bus.'"

"That must have stung, but—"

"—but first there was an hour of yelling and screaming and throwing things." He lowered the undershirt. "She sure is a pistol, that wife of mine."

"She almost took out a kidney because of a party?"

Bogie tossed him a world-weary look that said, *You don't know women, do you?* "She's talked herself into believing that I'm having an affair with Ingrid."

"You mean the co-star who you barely speak to, even after I told you what she said at the Brown Derby?"

"Hey, I've been making an effort, haven't I?"

He had—if making general chit-chat for a few minutes between scenes counted as making an effort. But it hadn't been enough to wipe away the loneliness that haunted Ingrid's face each time Curtiz called cut.

"If Mayo shows up, she'll have to face the agonizing truth that I spend all day looking at a beautiful woman who's ten years and ten thousand drinks behind her. Trust me, Mayo most definitely does not wish to see Ingrid. Still, let's not give Hedda any headlines. I want you to keep an eye out for her."

"You think Mayo will show up?"

Bogie flicked a finger toward the door. "Send Verita back in, then go find Ingrid and warn her about—" he pointed to his wound "—this."

By midday, the heat outside the soundstage radiated in waves. Luke located a patch of shade inside the elephant door, where he could observe the comings and goings without frying to death.

The reshoots on the La Belle Aurore Café set required only

Bogie and Ingrid with Dooley at the piano singing "As Time Goes By." Mr. Warner had commanded that the entire *Casablanca* company be present today, so one by one they had trooped in: Peter Lorre, Sydney Greenstreet, Paul Henreid, Conrad Veidt, S.Z. Sakall and his wife, Boszi, along with their lunch of Hungarian food because, as much as he loved America, Sakall refused to eat anything else.

As shooting got underway, and Rick and Ilsa professed their love to each other with new Epstein speeches, Luke drifted back to the previous evening. He'd been a little shocked at how readily Nell had peeled off her outfit. By the time he'd unbuttoned his shirt, she had already been standing in front of him, naked and unabashed. Modesty, she had declared, held no place in a house of five girls. As he'd shucked off his clothes, there had been no hiding his excitement. Bold as a burlesque queen, she had enveloped his pecker in her fingers and squeezed it ever-so-slightly. His knees had nearly buckled as his vision blurred.

"Young man?"

Luke saw the extravagant concoction of feathers and polka-dotted ribbons and smelled the cloying perfume before he recognized the face of the woman. "Miss Hopper!"

She threw him a withering once-over. "The jackass at the gate said Michael Curtiz was filming on Stage Eight. Is this it?"

"Welcome to Casablanca!" He raised a hand toward the interior, but the columnist didn't budge.

"Aren't you going to escort me to Mr. Curtiz and Mr. Warner?"

"I don't know that Mr. Warner is here yet."

"I was led to believe he would be."

Luke glanced up and down the street separating Stage Eight from Nine. He saw no sign of Mayo's powder-blue LaSalle, so he accompanied Hopper onto the set, where Curtiz was standing with his focus trained on the cameraman. His sourpuss expression, with a furrowed eyebrow shaped in a V and lips thrust forward into a pout, meant a rant was imminent.

"FINE!" Curtiz turned to Bogie. "Say whatever the hell line you want. Everybody else has written the script of this cockamamie picture. Why not you, also?" He stood next to the camera which was positioned low so that it looked up at the two stars. "Take it from Mr. Dooley's line. Action"

"This ought to take the sting out of being occupied. Does it, Mister Richard?"

"You said it." Bogie smiled and turned to Ingrid. "Here's looking at you, kid."

"And cut! Happy now, Mister Bogart?"

Bogie nodded.

"It's a cute line," Ingrid said. "I hope you don't edit it out."

"That's Hal Wallis's decision. My job is to keep filming the script until the Epsteins run out of ideas."

Luke cleared his throat. "Mr. Curtiz?"

"What now?" As the director whirled around, Luke stepped back to let him get a load of Hopper's absurd hat. The fury plastered across his face evaporated. He held out his arms. "Miss Hopper! How long since you were standing there?"

"Far be it from me to interrupt a master at his work." Hopper's voice dripped with treacle.

At the front of the soundstage, Luke saw no sign of Mayo's determined bulldog face. He thought of Avery. Wouldn't Wilda get a kick out of knowing what he'd done with her little clothing code? Luke could already hear her whooping laugh when he telephoned her.

The enormity of that call loomed bigger than the Empire State Building. Though he was fairly sure he knew what she would say, he doubted he could dial her number until he was ready for the answer. If Lily Osterhaus were his mother, it explained an awful lot. And that was a good thing, right? But it all seemed so farfetched, as though he'd stumbled into a Betty Hutton movie.

But first things first. There was a hollow Maltese falcon he needed to open.

Luke wished he'd had a chance to say hello to Nell. She hadn't been around when he'd arrived, and he'd spent the morning in Bogie's dressing room. He wasn't even sure what he'd say. *Thank you for making love with me three times last night. I didn't know I had it in me to do that. I didn't know anybody did.* Was that the Valenti in him coming through?

* * *

"There you are." Nell sidled up to Luke and ran a finger down his arm. It left a tingling track in its wake.

By the time Curtiz's two-hour anniversary party had broken up, Bogie's wound had started bleeding, and he trusted only Luke to change the bandage. He was now in his dressing room, resolutely working through a bottle of Canadian Club whiskey. Luke guessed it was a way to put off going home. For all he knew, Mayo had spent the day sharpening her carving knife.

"If I didn't know better," Nell whispered, "I'd have suspected you were trying to avoid me."

"No!" Luke exclaimed. "Far from it. But Bogie—"

"What was up with him?"

Would it be crossing a line if he told anyone, even Nell, how badly the Battling Bogarts' marriage had deteriorated? "I think he'll be glad when this picture'll be in the can. Can we go to Props now? I'm dying to see what's inside that falcon."

Ten minutes later they were dashing past the woman on the front desk with her nose in a *Hollywood Reporter.*

Luke flung open the cabinet doors. The Maltese falcons still stood in a neat line on the third shelf down. This time, however, there were only three.

Luke lifted the first one, turned it upside down, and angled it toward the light. There was no *Osterhaus* etched into the base. Nor into base of the second. Nor the third.

"They can't have lost yours again," Nell said.

All those weeks Luke had kept the falcon with him, he hadn't suspected there might be something inside—let alone the key to solving a mystery he never knew existed. And now the blasted thing had slipped away.

The clerk looked up from *The Hollywood Reporter* spread out on the front desk as they approached.

"Humphrey Bogart asked me to check on the Maltese falcon props. There's only three of them. Do you know what happened to the fourth one?"

"Mr. Warner's secretary took it for that 'Stars Over America' tour."

Panic gripped Luke's chest, choking off words. He forced himself to keep talking. "Took it where?"

"The Pan-Pacific, I assume. That's where the fancy kick-off gala is happening."

"Tomorrow night, isn't it?" Nell asked.

"Good luck getting in. Stars only, from what I've heard." The woman returned to her article about *The Song of Bernadette*. "Or accompanying them."

Luke looked at Nell. "Are you thinking what I'm thinking?"

21

$\mathcal{T}$he taxi turned off Beverly Boulevard and into a vast parking lot. The building on the left featured four streamlined turrets, each with a tall flagpole reaching into the July dusk. Along the front entrance, five-foot letters spelled out *PAN-PACIFIC AUDITORIUM.*

"We performed here a few years back," Minerva said. "A national Chrysler convention. Or was it Dodge?"

"Both," Seymour said. "I remember thinking how those men looked dull as dishwater, but they sure enjoyed our act."

The driver pulled to a stop. "That'll be eighty-five cents—is that Humphrey Bogart?"

Bogie had said he'd be there, "assuming Mayo doesn't give me any crap." After that knife fight, anything was possible and nothing ought to be assumed. But there they were, talking to Ann Sheridan and her husband, George Brent.

Luke handed the driver four quarters and they got out of the taxi. By the time they reached the Bogarts, they were waving Ann and George goodbye.

"Evening, all." Bogie extended his hand toward Seymour, who flung aside the edges of his opera cape. "Mayo and I saw Black and White at the Navy Relief Ball at the Ambassador a few years back."

"You're by far the best quick-change artists I've ever seen," Mayo said. "I assume you're tonight's distraction?"

A handbag dangled from her elbow, big enough to hold a fifth of scotch. The woman was capricious when sober, let alone at a soiree where waiters would be circulating with trays of drinks from an open bar. Luke knew he'd have to be one lucky duck to get away with this longest of long shots, but he had to take the chance. What was the alternative? Spend the rest of his life wondering what was inside that hollow falcon? But they needed to sneak Bogie's bird into tonight's shindig somehow, and Mayo's pocketbook was their ace in the hole.

The Pan-Pacific was longer than a football field and nearly as wide. Halfway down one side, the Cocoanut Grove's Gus Arnheim Orchestra was playing "Tuxedo Junction" on a raised dais. A few couples swayed together on the dance floor, but most of the crowd had gathered at the display along the other wall.

Nell hooked Luke's arm and dragged him to a gown with a profusion of ostrich feathers around the neckline. "It's the velvet dress Scarlett wore to Ashley's birthday party."

"What color is it?" Luke asked.

Her fingers wriggled as she battled to keep herself from touching it. "Burgundy."

"Can you describe it using one of the other senses?"

She gazed at the Scarlett O'Hara costume longingly. "Think of red wine. Rich, full, deep, and not for the faint of heart."

A woman appeared next to them with a nightclub photographer camera slung around her neck. "For a five-dollar war bond, you can have your picture taken with any of the items in the display."

Bogie thrust his head between Luke and Nell and whispered,

"You can take a photo of Errol's bow and arrow any time you want." He turned to the photographer. "For twenty bucks, will you let my friend here put Scarlett's costume on?"

Nell snorted. "As if I'd fit. Look at that waist."

"Sorry, Mr. Bogart, but Mr. Selznick wouldn't allow that."

"Is he here tonight?"

"He and his wife were looking at the oversized bottle of Jungle Red nail polish from *The Women*. They were having a fine old laugh over it with Norma Shearer."

"So if I get David's permission—"

"Stop!" Nell cried out. "Honestly, Mayo, how do you get your husband to quit kidding around?"

"I wouldn't mind trying on that dress myself, so I say let Hump schmooze all he wants."

"In case my schmoozing skills aren't up to snuff . . ." Bogie pulled out his wallet and handed over a five-dollar bill. "Where's *The Maltese Falcon*?"

The photographer pocketed the money. "Halfway along, past *Dr. Jekyll and Mr. Hyde*. If you've reached the Carmen Miranda tutti frutti hat, you've gone too far."

"That's terrific advice, honey," Mayo said, slapping a heavy hand on her husband's shoulder. "My husband rarely knows when he's gone too far."

As Luke positioned Nell in front of the Scarlett gown, Mayo rubbernecked for the nearest circulating waiter. "They're serving champagne, whiskey, and some sort of rum concoction. I hope it's a Zombie. I'd kill my grandmother's dog for one of those."

"Not just Fido," Bogie said, "but Grandma, too."

The photographer snapped Nell's picture and handed her a numbered receipt. "You can collect yours at the souvenir booth near the entrance."

Somewhere between Katharine Hepburn's toy yacht from *The Philadelphia Story* and a *Little Caesar* Tommy gun, Mayo had procured drinks for them. She handed them around and then took a deep gulp from her own glass. "Not Zombies but close enough."

Luke sidled up to Bogie. "Can we get the falcon away from her before things get out of hand?"

Bogie raised his voice. "Hey Mrs. B., let's go visit my old pal."

He jostled her forward, nodding to people gathered around the props and costumes until they reached Bette Davis standing in front of her elaborate Elizabeth I dress, flanked by her husband and Orry-Kelly.

"Well, if it ain't the fourth Warner brother," Bogie said.

"Bogie! Mayo!" Bette exclaimed. "We were just talking about you. Remember when we were filming *Marked Woman* and Lola Lane told us about the time she scandalized her local congregation by dancing the Charleston after a dreadfully boring Sunday service? She had me in absolute fits."

"There would've been no danger of that if she'd been wearing . . ." Luke pointed to the gown.

"It was torture!" Bette said. "And I lay the blame fully at the feet of this miscreant from Down Under."

"Just following orders," Orry-Kelly said. "Wallis and Curtiz told me to be historically accurate."

"Your abomination weighed sixty pounds!" Bette backhanded Orry-Kelly's shoulder. "Damn near gave me a hernia." She eyeballed Luke. "Say, aren't you the kid who saved half a day's filming on *Casablanca*? You knew how to play some song Curtiz hates?"

"Yep, that was me." Everybody in a twenty-foot radius turned toward Luke. Flattered as he was that Bette Davis knew of him, the Maltese falcon loomed over her left shoulder. The sooner they made the switch, the better. He threw Nell a look, imploring her to distract Bette so the rest of them could move on.

"It's the collar that caught my eye." She ran a fingertip along the stiffened lace. "It must have dug into your neck something awful."

As Bette ranted about the difficulties of attaching the collar, Luke, Bogie, and Mayo slipped over to the next display.

The falcon sat on a shiny box painted black with a lobby card glued to the front. Bogie canted his head toward Luke just as Arnheim's trombonist pierced the air with a note that launched the orchestra into "Stairway to the Stars." Several more couples hit the dance floor—one of them was Beatrice's Captain Stamina. Or might have been. There were several uniformed Navy officers scattered throughout the crowd, so maybe not. Beatrice had commented that he'd been away a lot lately, which Luke hoped explained why he hadn't contacted him after that encounter in the men's room at Romanoff's.

Luke's eyes flickered from the falcon to Captain Stamina, then back to the falcon. Focus! Focus! One thing at a time.

He felt a heavy weight press against his hand.

Bogie murmured, "You going to take it, or what?"

Luke wrapped his fingers around the bird's neck and furtively nodded at Seymour as he rounded the back of the display.

Seymour and Minerva executed a series of tight spins that flared Seymour's cape behind him. Reaching the center of the dance floor, he hit what he had warned Luke was his famous high C. "Trust me," he'd said back at the boarding house, "they'll hear it next door at Gilmore Field."

The note soared like a comet. Seymour cocooned his cape around Minerva, rippling it in the air before he pulled it away. Minerva thrust her hands up. Their audience needed a moment to realize she wore a different outfit. What had been a billowing tea dress with a roses pattern was now a floor-length bold-striped gown. The crowd gasped.

As applause thundered, Seymour spun around her, his cape splaying out behind him. Once again, he enveloped her in the black silk and hit his high C. Minerva called out, "Three! Two! One!" Seymour yanked the cape away. The gown was now a flapper-style dress, six inches above her knees and covered in long strands of onyx beads that shimmered in the light. The audience cried out in surprise and renewed its applause, which filled the cavernous room.

Luke looked to his left and to his right. "Once they see my Minerva go into her act," Seymour had bragged, "nobody will give two figs about what you're up to." It was a cocky boast; nonetheless, the plan to swap the Maltese falcons undetected hinged on Black and White's ability to capture attention.

Minerva had told Luke that she would save the most spectacular one for the third metamorphosis. "Swap them out on the third *arriba*."

Seymour whipped around like a whirling dervish until his cape paralleled the floor. Minerva snapped her fingers as though they were flamenco castanets, then clapped three times. He sheathed her once more in his cape and called out, "*Arriba! Arriba! ARRIBA!*"

Luke grabbed the falcon on display and replaced it with Bogie's. Stuffing it inside his jacket, he raced toward the far end where Nell was waiting.

"This way," she told him. "There's a staff exit."

With everybody's attention glued to Minerva's spectacular ballgown of white egret feathers, nobody paid the slightest heed to the kid with a peculiar-shaped lump on his belly.

The door led to a long corridor with doors evenly spaced on both sides. The first four were locked, but the fifth opened into a sparsely furnished office with a desk, chair, and matching pair of filing cabinets.

Luke flipped the falcon over. The Osterhaus signature was obvious now that he knew what it was. He ran his finger around the edge of the base until his nail caught on a rectangular bump that stuck out a sixteenth of an inch. "You'd think I'd have noticed." He placed the bird on the desk.

"Aren't you going to open it?"

Luke stared at her, his mouth sandpaper dry. "It's just that —what if—"

"What if there's a microfilm detailing Japanese war planes? Or the location of their next attack? Or what about the names of Nazi double agents—"

"I was thinking more like a photo of Lily Osterhaus."

Jaunty music from the orchestra in the main hall bled through the walls and into the office.

Luke picked up the hollow falcon and flipped it over. "Irving and Wilda must have had an excellent reason for asking me to bring this across the country." He pushed against the latch until he felt a delicate click. "Ready or not." He turned the statue right side up and waited for the contents to slide out.

But the top of the desk remained bare.

He peered inside. "There's nothing there."

Nell gasped. "EMPTY?"

The pent-up anticipation that had fueled him all week drained away, leaving him heavy with disillusion.

22

*L*uke studied his cards. Two jacks and three eights. He'd been memorizing the cards that Bogie, Lorre, and Greenstreet had been throwing down. They had seen all the queens and all but one king. The only ace to show up so far had been a heart. The chances of the other three showing up in the same round were minimal.

He dropped a five-dollar chip onto the pile at the center of the table near the entrance of the Blue Parrot, which Sydney's character owned and which stood across the street from Rick's.

Bogie folded and crossed his arms, their prearranged signal: *I'm letting you have this one.*

Luke squirmed in his seat. Even though he was going up against crackerjack whizzes with years of experience at five-card stud poker, counting cards was still cheating. "Nah," Bogie had assured him earlier that morning. "This memory of yours levels the playing field, is all. Besides, Pete's sharp as a cleaver, but he'll be preoccupied with his own prank today. That bug-eyed midget won't even notice."

"I'll see your five," Greenstreet purred, "and raise you five." He threw in his second-last chip.

Lorre followed suit, then blinked twice.

According to Bogie, two rapid blinks were Lorre's tell that he was bluffing. Greenstreet would have to have four of a kind or a straight flush to beat Luke. Possible, but not likely. Luke threw another five-dollar chip into the pot. Greenstreet matched him.

When they revealed their cards, Greenstreet had a three-four-five-six-seven straight. "Damn you, boy! You've won five out of the last six rounds."

"Beginner's luck?" Luke herded the stack to his side of the table. He now had twenty-six chips. A hundred and thirty smackers. More than a month's salary with enough left over to telephone Wilda. Calling collect didn't feel right. It'd be forcing her to pay for a phone call she didn't make in order to force her to tell him a secret she didn't want to share.

"Mister Lorre!" Greenstreet boomed. "I suspect we've been duped like a couple of Barbary Coast suckers."

Lorre picked up his boater and fanned his sweaty face. "Good lord, it's hot today. And they haven't even switched to full lights." He twisted in his seat and looked at the large ceramic urn sitting in front of a wooden pole. It was interesting enough—dark glaze, circular handle, topped by an Ottoman crescent-and-star—but Luke wasn't sure why Lorre kept eyeing it.

"Mister Lorre," Greenstreet repeated. "Did you hear me?"

"We're all suckers." John Huston stepped up to the table and threw his arms out wide, like he was Noah welcoming the animals, two by two. At six foot one and lean as a strip of bacon, he cut an imposing figure spruced up in his captain's uniform.

Bogie took him in with a slow-motion review. "You shitty dog."

"A fine how-d'you-do. I thought you'd want to take a gander at my get-up. I'm heading off to Alaska soon to film *Report from the Aleutians*." Huston clapped his hands over the gold buttons of his breast pockets. "I cut a dashing figure, don't you think?"

Bogie jumped to his feet. "I know what I'd like to cut."

"He means the deck." Lorre's declaration convinced nobody.

Bogie tossed the cards to him. "Give 'em a damned good shuffle and deal in Captain Dashing while Luke and I—" He couldn't think fast enough to finish his sentence.

"We ought to run through those new lines." Luke pushed back from the table. "The Epsteins churn out pages every hour on the hour." Mercifully, the crew buzzed around the Blue Parrot set, busy with their individual tasks. "It looks like Curtiz is getting ready for a take."

Luke followed Bogie into the dressing room.

"I love that guy like a brother." Bogie paced the floor. "But God, he can be an asshole. Shoving that Army uniform down my throat."

"The Signal Corps is hardly the frontline infantry. The Aleutians aren't even Alaska. They're on the outskirts."

"They're two seconds from Russia."

"Russia's our ally, so—"

"I thought he'd get a kick out of witnessing this prank that Pete and I are playing on our tyrannical director. If I'd known he'd show up wearing that fucking thing, I wouldn't have invited him."

"Is that why Peter keeps looking at the ceramic urn?"

Bogie wrenched the jacket of his costume off its hanger. "I want you to take Huston to the cleaners. Count cards like you've never counted them before."

Until today, Luke had never counted cards at all.

A pair of knuckles rapped on the dressing room door. "Mr. Bogart? We're ready for you. Mr. Curtiz told me to tell you—"

"Tell Mr. Curtiz he'll be there shortly," Luke called out. He turned to Bogie. "This isn't what I signed up for."

"What isn't?"

"Cheating at cards."

"It's not cheating when it's just a lark."

"You look like you want to take a machete to that guy you love like a brother."

Bogie slipped into his jacket and fastened the top button. He swiped his fedora off a toupée stand. "We're going to let those bums in on the joke afterwards."

"You promise?"

"How about this: we'll use the pot for a fancy night out at Romanoff's."

The site where drunken G.I.s had kicked the stuffing out of Luke wouldn't have been his first choice, but the cast and crew were waiting. This was neither the time nor place to argue the point. Or maybe there was no point. In anything. He still couldn't get the image of the empty falcon out of his mind.

They stepped back onto the Blue Parrot set as running footsteps slapped against the soundstage floor. "A terrible accident! On the set of *Gentleman Jim!*"

"Errol?" Curtiz cried out.

"It's Buster Wiles," the bicycle messenger said. "He's had an awful fall."

"Isn't that the guy who does Errol's stunts?" Luke asked Bogie.

"One of the best in the biz."

Curtiz's stoic face corrugated with dismay. "Is he in a badly way?"

"I was passing by Stage Four—"

"Go back and find out, you imbecile you!"

"Does this change our plans?" Lorre whispered behind them.

"Hell, no," Bogie told him.

"He almost looked worried about a human being."

"It'll pass. Soon enough he'll be ordering us around like Rommel. We're still going ahead."

"That's all I need to hear."

The Blue Parrot set was a shambolic mishmash of hookah pipes, ceiling fans, and waiters in fezzes designed in a long sweep so that when Bogie made his entrance near the silhouette of a belly dancer, the camera tracked him past downtrodden citizens of Casablanca.

"And action."

Bogie marched toward the beaded curtain. He was halfway to his second mark when Curtiz yelled, "Cut the goddamned cut."

Bogie executed a slow blink that Luke knew was a put-on. "I'm giving this scene some pep. It's a long walk to Sydney's entrance."

"I am building the atmosphere, Mr. Bogart. I want the audience to see what a second-rate dive Ferrari runs."

"I HEARD THAT!" Greenstreet poked his head through a beaded curtain. "It might not be the Ritz, or even Rick's, but it's mine, by thunder, and I will not have you cast aspersions on the good name of the Blue Parrot."

Curtiz stared at him. The man could barely string a proper sentence together; there was no chance he knew what aspersions were.

On the second take, Bogie sauntered through the Parrot's doorway and took the steps at a more leisurely pace.

Too leisurely, Luke thought. He's up to no good.

Bogie ambled past two men seated at a low-slung table pretending to puff at a hookah pipe and an Oriental woman in a tight Chinese dress sipping tea. He had barely made it to the urn before Curtiz ordered the cameraman to cut the goddamned cut again.

"Now you are on a Sunday stroll along the Venice Beach?" he spluttered. "Are you trying to put me in the cuckoo nest?"

"You said that you wanted to get this marvelous set in the shot."

"*Jézus Krisztus!*" Curtiz slammed his script onto the floor. "It is only Tuesday. How will I survive the rest of the week with such fooltommery?"

Luke bunched his hand into a fist and pressed it against his mouth. Of course! Today was Tuesday. He looked at his watch.

MARTIN TURNBULL

Right on eleven-thirty, a.k.a. Hopeful Starlet O'clock. Any minute now . . .

"She's over there."

Nell pointed to a pale-skinned redhead in a neat two-piece tartan suit and matching beret tilted at a perky angle.

Luke had assumed that the casting department sent over these Tuesday Girls, but nobody had ever confirmed that. The first time it happened had been the second week of filming on *Casablanca*. That week's Tuesday Girl had been a platinum blonde. Her eyes had been too narrowly spaced and her hair too stringy to make it in the movies, but that hadn't mattered because she'd been smart enough to squeeze herself into a dress that accentuated her curves.

Without warning, work on the set had stopped. Bogie had disappeared into his dressing room. Crewmembers had busied themselves with patently unnecessary tasks.

Over chicken soup in the commissary, Nell had explained Curtiz's habit of "entertaining" a girl in his office every Tuesday. "Jack Warner adores Michael Curtiz." Nell had snapped her cracker in half and bitten down on it with undisguised rancor. "So it just happens. Not that he's the only one, mind you."

Curtiz's assistant recited his standard speech. The redhead nodded, as the Tuesday Girls always did, and followed him to meet her fate.

Nell fanned herself with her clipboard. "How many telegrams have you sent to your aunt?"

"Three in four days."

"Maybe she's ill?"

"Wilda Doyle smokes and drinks and eats however she likes, and never has to pay the piper. She sails through life like she's the Queen Mary plowing the North Atlantic."

"Sounds like I'd adore her."

"You would."

Luke thought of Wilda's myocardial something-or-other. Had she taken a turn for the worse?

A low, gravelly grunt filled the Blue Parrot set.

Nell gripped her armrests. "What the heck was that?"

"Our illustrious director."

Bogie and Lorre stood behind them, shoulder to shoulder, hands jammed deep in their pockets. Another groan. Longer this time. Deeper. It tapered into a series of panting shudders. They snickered like a pair of incorrigible schoolboys.

And now a third groan, much louder than the first two. Luke turned toward the Blue Parrot and spotted a speaker on the floor in front of the urn. "You didn't! A microphone? In his office? On a Tuesday?"

"What better day?" Lorre asked.

Curtiz's voice blasted out of the speaker like a grenade. *"Ja, mehr, ja, mehr!"*

"Is that German?" Nell asked. "What's he saying?"

"Yes, more, yes, more."

The company coalesced around them, drawn by the magnetic force of a shared disgust. They had a film to make, and a damned fine one from what Luke could see, and yet there was the man on whose shoulders this endeavor rested, screwing some misguided optimist too young or too witless to grasp what was really going on.

One of the grips said, "He'll die of embarrassment when he learns about this."

"If he was embarrassed over us hearing this sort of carry-on," someone else added, "he wouldn't do it in the first place,"

"Ooooh! Ooooh!" Curtiz's voice had flipped into falsetto. "Ooooh, *igen!* Ooooh, *igen!*"

"Did he say *igen?*" Nell asked.

"It's Hungarian for 'yes.'" Lorre wasn't even bothering to stifle his sniggering. "As in 'yes, yes, yes, give me more, more, more.'"

"You gotta hand it to anyone who can hump in several

languages, but do you think he's close?" The question came from a lighting guy who spent most of his day in the rafters. "I'll need to get back to my perch."

"Ooooh!" Curtiz cried out. "Don't stop! Don't stop!"

"WHAT IN GOD'S NAME IS HAPPENING HERE?"

Bette Davis stood with her feet wide apart, her hands planted on her hips, one eyebrow arched.

Bogie and Lorre ducked behind a camera, leaving Luke and Nell to face Bette on their own. "Hello, Miss Davis," Luke said. "How are the reshoots on *Now, Voyager* going?"

Bette kept her eyes on the speaker. "We just finished. I didn't get a chance to thank Paul for his gentlemanly contribution." She leaned heavily on the last couple of words as Curtiz toiled toward his goal.

"He'll be sorry to have missed you," Nell said. "He's not in today's scene—"

Bette thrust her hand out like she was a traffic cop. "Is that who I think it is? Blasting through the speaker like a back-alley mongrel?"

On one of their banana-split-sundae dates, Nell had told Luke about the raging clashes between Bette and Curtiz on the set of *The Private Lives of Elizabeth and Essex*, made worse by his affair with her stand-in. She sure must have been fond of Paul Henreid, Luke thought, if she had voluntarily walked onto another Michael Curtiz set.

Luke stepped forward. Oh brother, did that rotten Bogart chicken owe him a big favor for taking the brunt of Bette's wrath. "Yes, it is. You're hearing our director indulging in—" a breathy Curtizian croak cut him off "—his Tuesday routine."

"Thank you—remind me of your name?"

"Luke Vail."

"If I'd realized what day it is, I wouldn't have bothered." She winced as Curtiz continued to pant and wheeze. "I assume somebody rigged up a microphone in his office to capture this—" she waved a hand toward the speaker "—performance? Don't get me wrong. I'm all for it. That man's advances are as welcome as the Spanish Armada. I'm worried about the poor girl. It's humiliating enough to be put in that position, but for the whole sordid ordeal to be broadcast. It's too much. Tell me, Luke, where's his office?"

He pointed to the northeast corner of the soundstage.

The *Casablanca* company formed a semi-circle as Bette marched up to the door. Luke expected her to barge in, but she waited until Curtiz was close to orgasm. She pulled off her left shoe and banged the heel against the wood. "Mike?" she sing-songed. "It's me, Bette. I must talk to you about a movie called *Old Acquaintance* that J.W. wants me to do. I'm ambivalent, though. May I come in so that we can discuss it?"

A strangled sound, halfway between a squawk and a whine, filtered through.

"GO FUCK AWAY!"

The gathered crew burst into laughter, interspersed with applause.

"And that," Bette proclaimed, "is how you deal with monstrous egos."

"Jesus, Bette!" Bogie had found his voice at last. "I always suspected you had bigger balls than King Kong."

"It's not about having big balls, although I accept that as a compliment." She turned her huge Davis eyes on her audience. "It's about deciding what you're willing to put up with. And I don't just mean grossly inappropriate behavior such as what Curtiz thinks he's entitled to. It's about taking a stand and refusing to accept no for an answer." She gave Bogie the once-over as though he were an old Cadillac she was thinking of selling. "Tell Paul I said hello."

When the side door slammed behind her, the company turned back to the office door as Curtiz finished the job with a farrago of gasps, grunts, and Hungarian mutterings.

"Thanks for stepping in just now." Bogie had played every

variation of tough guy, street fighter, and punk with a Colt .45, and yet an actress had the power to render him mute as a log.

"I'm surprised you find her intimidating," Luke told him. "You've had your share of troublesome women. Including the one you're married to."

Bogie toyed with his hat. "Whenever Bette Davis talks to me, I feel like she's got a gun pointing at my manhood."

"You should've thanked her for improving your prank."

The office door swung open and Curtiz stepped out. "What is this?" he sputtered.

The company stood still, staring at him in reproving silence.

Al Alleborn, the unit production manager, stepped forward. "Somehow a live microphone ended up in your office—"

"So you all listened to me—"

"Everybody heard everything."

"This is outrage."

The young redhead, hair slightly mussed and her suit wrinkled in places where it had been pressed half an hour ago, stepped past him, her eyes glued to the floor, as a deep blush filled Curtiz's face.

Bogie headed toward the set.

Luke followed him. "And Huston?"

"What about him?"

"You still up for taking him to the cleaners?"

"Yes," Luke said. "But I have a stipulation."

Luke returned Bogie's telephone to its cradle as Bogie walked into the living room holding two tumblers. Luke could smell the whiskey before Bogie handed it to him. Old Forester, if he wasn't mistaken.

"How many times is that?" Bogie asked.

"Five." He clinked his glass against Bogie's and took a slug. Yep. Old Forester. "Still no answer."

"Maybe she doesn't feel like talking."

"Wilda loves nothing more than conversation."

"She must have gone out. She's the social butterfly type, isn't she?"

One of Bogart's black Scottie dogs planted herself at Luke's feet. He petted the top of her silky head, which felt almost as good as the whiskey. "She sent me out here with a phony falcon that turns out to be both hollow *and* empty. Simon sends me to a guy who looks like me, who has the same type of color blindness, and who draws lighthouses in his spare time, just like I do. Everything points to the all-too-real possibility that my mother might not be my mother."

"You deserve an explanation."

"But the only person who can give it to me isn't answering."

It was so unlike Wilda not to answer her phone or respond to telegrams. He wasn't one of those out-of-sight-out-of-mind fair-weather friends like the Chilean consul or the Madagascan can-can dancer. Not him. Not her darling Luke. But she did suffer from myocardial something-or-other.

"I feel so far away," he blurted out. "I want to jump on my bike, ride over to her apartment, bang on her front door. 'Spill the beans, old lady! Tell me everything because your silence is driving me bananas.'"

"Mayo informs me it's Steak Diane for dinner tonight."

"I'm sorry about this. I didn't mean to infringe on your evening."

"A bargain's a bargain. You take Huston for every cent, and I let you call Brooklyn, however long it takes. My wife isn't the most versatile cook in the world, but her Steak Diane's pretty good. Dinner's at eight, which gives you a whole hour yet."

"And if Wilda hasn't answered by then?"

"We'll sit down to dinner, have an enjoyable meal, and try again." Bogie drained the last of his Old Forester and checked

Luke's glass. "Tip the rest down your drainpipe and I'll fix us another."

Luke did as he was told. "Thanks, boss. If I outstay my welcome—"

"I'm a selfish asshole."

Bogie's admission slashed through the whiskey's soothing haze. "Because you ducked out of sight like a scared little panty-waist when Bette appeared?"

"No. Well, yes. What I mean is Mayo and me, we're a combustible couple. It doesn't matter where we are. We can't help ourselves—unless you're with us. We first noticed it that day on *Sluggy*. It was one of the most pleasant days we've ever spent." He got to his feet. "I'm a selfish asshole because tonight I don't have to worry that the evening will end with me crashing through the back door or getting knifed in the ass."

When Bogie left the room, Luke picked up the telephone and asked the operator to place a person-to-person call. He crossed his fingers. *Please pick up. Please be okay. Please have a reasonable explanation for this silence—and for everything else.* As Wilda's line rang, he noticed a mid-game chessboard on a small table. After fifteen rings, the operator told him the other party wasn't answering. He set the receiver back in the cradle, trying to ignore the cold finger of worry pressing the back of his neck.

Bogie returned with freshened drinks. "You still playing with Irving?" Luke asked.

"I didn't hear from him for the longest time. Chess-by-mail is a slow process, so I wasn't worried. A card arrived the night of our Pan-Pacific switcheroo."

Luke approached the table. "Which player are you? Black or white?"

Bogie pointed to the white pieces. "He's going to checkmate my king in two moves unless I stop him."

Luke set his tumbler on the tabletop. It hit the wood with a dull thud. "I'm an idiot!" He returned to the phone, snatched up the receiver and waited until the operator came on the line. "I need you to check with general information in New York for an Irving Kovner. His address is thirty-five Argyle Road, Brooklyn. Apartment G." He wished he hadn't abandoned his drink. Then again, if Irving was home, perhaps it was a good idea if Luke wasn't bombed.

"Sir, I have the number. It's Windsor 6-4456."

The palms of Luke's hands went clammy. "Please connect me." The line rang seven times before it picked up. "Irving? Irving?" Luke knew he was half-shouting; he didn't care.

"Yes, this is Irving Kovner. Who's calling, please?"

"It's me, Luke. In California."

"Luke, my boy. I'm so very glad to hear from you."

"I've been cabling and telephoning Wilda, but she's not answering."

"Telegrams? Hold on." A sharp crack shot down the line.

Bogie deposited Luke's whiskey on the telephone table. "At least he answered."

"He sounded surprised that Wilda hasn't responded to my telegrams. I think he's gone to check on her."

The ice in his glass tinkled as he picked it up. Whatever was coming, maybe being half-plastered wasn't such a bad idea.

After a thirty-second eternity, Irving came back on the line. "I have them here. Western Union just slipped them under her door."

"How come she's not home? Has she gone on vacation? I haven't heard from her in the longest time."

"Oh, Luke."

Two short syllables. But they were all Luke needed. He slumped into the chair, narrowly missing a Scottie, who yelped in protest. "What is it?" He could only manage a whisper.

"I would have contacted you as soon as it happened, but I only knew that you'd moved into a boarding house—"

"As soon as what happened, Irving?"

"Wilda had a heart attack. Real bad, it was. Not enough to finish her off, though."

Luke lurched forward, bending at the waist. His breath left his lungs in a raspy whoosh. "So she's all right? She'll be okay?"

Irving sighed. "It was worse than the doctors first thought. The damage was extensive and irreversible. It was simply too much."

Luke squeezed the armrest as hard as he could. "What are you saying?"

The pause that followed was interminably, unbearably long. "I'm sorry to have to tell you this, but our marvelous, magnificent Wilda passed away at five a.m. this morning. She's gone, Luke. We've lost her."

he side railing ran along the entire length of *Sluggy*. Luke gripped it with one hand and shielded his eyes from the sun with the other. "It must be a hundred degrees already. And it's not yet nine o'clock."

"It'll be cooler once we're out to sea," Bogie told him from the helm.

"I should have brought a hat with me."

Bogie opened the throttle and pulled *Sluggy* away from the dock. "Take your pick from under the breakfast nook."

Luke selected a fisherman's cap from the stash inside the bench. It smelled of briny sea air and had faded in streaky patches along the top. He put it on and rejoined Bogie on deck.

"Ah, the Cagney cap."

Luke tugged at the peak. "Jimmy?"

"He's got a schooner called *Martha*, and a fine one she is, too. Fir planking and Honduran mahogany interiors. The works."

Bogie swung *Sluggy* in a wide circle to the left—was that port or starboard? Luke couldn't remember. Beatrice had told him a quick mnemonic, but now he couldn't recall it, which in itself was cause for concern.

"Where are we patrolling?"

"The Coast Guard usually sends me south. Sometimes over to San Nicolas and San Clemente Islands. But today we're northbound, past Santa Monica, Malibu, and up to Port Hueneme, and home via the Channel Islands."

"What are we on the lookout for?"

"Rumrunners, buccaneers, smugglers, and the wiliest old sea dogs that ever sailed the seven seas."

"And Japs?"

"Aye, First Mate Vail. Them, too." Bogie dropped the B-picture pirate voice. "The truth is, I haven't seen one goddamned sign of Tokyo Joe."

"That's a good thing, right?"

He raised a sardonic eyebrow. "Is it?"

Nobody wanted a Pearl Harbor sequel playing out on the California coast. But Luke could tell that Bogie longed for any encounter with the enemy, no matter how insignificant or incidental.

Luke watched the Newport Yacht Club recede in the distance. *Fore is the front and aft is the back. But port and starboard? Why can't I remember which is which?*

Because, he told himself, your brain is a blurry bowl of mush.

Only raggedy scraps remained of the last forty-eight hours since Irving had said those three awful words. He had no memory of slumping to the floor, but he could feel the soft fibers of the Persian rug brushing his hands and the puff of Bogie's breath in his ear. Platitudes of sorrow and heartbreak, but none of the specific details. A bracing shot of whiskey. The fragile softness of a Kleenex in his hand. Bogie had driven him home, but the ride was a blur of neon signs and the wail of a fire engine until he was face down on his bed, breathing in Rinso fumes, his limbs, his chest, his head, everything heavy as bricks.

Wilda was gone. Wilda was gone. Gone. *GONE*. We've lost her. We've LOST her. We've lost *HER*.

The ribbon stretching from Brooklyn to Hollywood, binding him with home, had snapped. He felt untethered, left to drift amid the currents, powerless and alone. When Bogie had called by the boarding house and asked Luke—ordered him, really—to accompany him on patrol, it had felt like a life preserver.

"Hey, First Mate, how you doing over there?"

"Fine."

"No seasickness?"

Luke shook his head.

"You want to talk about it?"

"Seasickness?"

Bogie kept his gaze on the sleek horizon. "That, or what happened the other night."

"You're right. It's much cooler out here."

Bogie pointed to starboard. Or was it port? "Losing sight of the shore can give a guy perspective."

The coastline had narrowed to a hazy strip. Luke seized the railing, knuckles blanching as he watched the shore slip away. An image of Wilda flickered in its place. Lying on a bed. Her lips slightly parted. Calling his name. He closed his eyes, tightly as his muscles would allow, until he felt the thrum of the engine below his feet slacken to a leisurely chugga-chugga.

"Gonna puke?" Bogie asked.

"Nope."

"You're the color of dried glue."

Luke forced his eyes open. They were the only people, the only boat, the only signs of life in all directions. "I was thinking that this is the first time anyone in my family has seen the Pacific."

It was a selfish lie. Luke had taken the streetcar to Santa Monica during his first couple of weeks. He and Nell had spent a few Sunday afternoons strolling the pleasure piers and smooching behind the thick, wooden piles. He felt a trail of sweat dribble down his spine. *What a cretin you are. Bogie invited you out here for a change of scenery and you repay him with fiction.*

Bogie broke into a beaming smile. "We should take a photo. The studio lab will develop it for us. Maybe blow it up a little. Your folks'll get a kick out of seeing you here."

The hell they would.

Luke realized he was still riveted to the railing. He let it go and crossed his arms. "Nah. Thanks for the offer, but water's water, isn't it?"

Bogie revved the engine and propelled the boat forward. Soon, they were skimming across the surface. "Parents are a funny thing, aren't they?"

Luke craned his neck over the side and immediately wished he hadn't. The water was clear and, he assumed, a beautiful shade of blue. But he couldn't see the bottom the way he could at the yacht club. He reared backward, panic clutching at his throat.

"I admired my mother," Bogie continued. "Maud was an illustrator and commercial artist. Everybody knew her and would stop to say hello whenever we walked around the Upper West Side."

"You're from New York? You never told me that."

"Not much to tell."

"Your mom, she was talented?"

"Oh, yes. Very successful—at illustrating. But when it came to showing affection, she was wholly incapable. I missed out there."

The boat hit a wave, jolting Luke half an inch off the deck. It felt like three feet. How much water lay below them? Hundreds of feet?

"And your father?"

"Dr. Belmont DeForest Bogart—heck of a name, huh? He must have looked quite the catch. A doctor, rich, good-looking, avid huntsman, skilled sailor. But he had a violent temper."

Luke dropped onto the padded bench along the stern and kept his eyes trained on his bare feet. "That's an awful shame."

"It wasn't altogether his fault. A horse-drawn ambulance fell on him when he was not long out of medical school. His right leg copped some serious damage, and he got hooked on drugs to ease the pain. It was a terrible situation, but he never put his personal woes aside. Gosh, but I love it out here. A guy can be himself. No questions asked."

Out here, where? Out in California, or out on the open sea? Bogie kept his eyes fixed straight ahead of them, but Luke knew his attention was centered on him. He'd been distracting Luke, and it had worked. Sort of. But now Luke felt the lure of the ocean's depths pulling him.

He eased himself up and peered down into the Pacific's bottomless vastness. Was this how a lemming felt looking over the edge of a cliff?

"I'm no psychiatrist, but you're showing classic signs of thalassophobia."

Luke pushed against the railing. "Thala—what?"

"Thalassophobia. Fear of deep water. Terrified when you look into it but can't stop yourself."

Luke shook his head at the absurdity of it all. How long had he dreamed of escaping to Montauk? And now Humphrey Bogart was telling him that he was scared to death of the very thing he'd have been spending his life surrounded by?

"I'm glad to see you smiling," Bogie said. "Care to elaborate?"

"Did I ever tell you where I was headed before my California sidetrack?"

"You haven't told me much of anything about your past."

"I had applied to train as a lighthouse keeper. I was waiting to hear whether I'd been accepted when Wilda convinced me to return the hollow falcon."

"If she hadn't, you'd be a lighthouse keeper now?"

"We'll never know."

"D'you suppose she might have sent you out here to stop you from heading down that path?"

Montauk is not the solution. He could hear Wilda's voice as though she were standing right there next to him.

Sluggy hit a wave. Seawater splattered across the deck, sparkling in the summer sun.

"I think I screwed up." Bogie leaned on the steering wheel, his face contorted with angst. "I brought you out here to take your mind off your aunt."

"And I appreciate it."

"But now I've got you doubting the motives of someone you cared for."

"You gave me food for thought, that's all."

"Let me make it up to you. Keep your eyes port side." Bogie pointed toward the left. Beatrice's mnemonic came back to Luke: *Port is left because they both have four letters.* A smudge of dirt appeared on the far horizon. "Those are the Channel Islands. One of them has a lighthouse. Seeing as how you're a fan, I thought I'd take you to Anacapa."

The name dispelled his doubts over Wilda and fears of deep ocean water. "That lump? Is it Anacapa Island? I have a sketch of it hanging in my bedroom back in Brooklyn. It's my favorite."

"Of all the lighthouses on all the islands in all the world?"

The previous day, Nell had handed Bogie the revised pages for the scene they were to shoot on Monday. Disgusted at the endless revisions, Bogie had tossed them to Luke and asked if the new version was any better. There was a line in which Rick Blaine complained that of all the gin joints in all the towns in all the world, Ingrid Bergman had to walk into his. Luke had told him, "You can do a lot with a line like that."

"Anacapa is famous," Luke said.

"For what?"

"Ever heard of 'Whistler's Mother'?"

"Sure."

"Before Simon Whistler painted his mom, he was an engraver for the U.S. Coast Survey. One of his jobs was to prepare an engraving of Anacapa Island. He added some seagulls, but they fired him for taking artistic license."

"He did all right for himself in the long run. You will, too."

A sudden gust whipping over *Sluggy* almost swept away Bogie's gentle response as they approached Anacapa. Almost, but not quite. Luke caught the words, and the encouragement behind them.

The island was a flat plane that gave way to a steeply angled cliff, ending in a bridge before dropping into the water. Bogie cut the engine a couple of hundred feet from the shore and tossed the anchor overboard.

"I wish I'd brought my sketchbook." Luke's voice had dropped to an awed whisper.

"You sketch?"

"Seashores, rock pools, crashing waves."

"Any lighthouses?"

Luke smiled for what felt like the first time in living memory. "Mostly lighthouses."

"Well, well, well," Bogie said, lighting up. "I'm learning so many interesting nuggets today."

The hull beneath their feet rocked gently, like a huge cradle. The breeze had now dropped away, leaving the sun to prickle the skin along Luke's arms. "Boy howdy, this California heat." He pulled off his scruffy fisherman's cap and used it to fan his face. "It sure does sting."

"We could go for a swim."

The panic he'd felt earlier reared up again, throttling his breath, pressing against his chest. "What was that word? Fear of deep water?"

"Thalassophobia."

"Yeah, that." Luke felt the mesmerizing pull. Take a peek at me, it seemed to say. What harm can come from looking? Plenty, Luke told it. "Not a chance in hell I'm going into the drink. I don't care how refreshing it is."

"In that case." Without warning, Bogie grabbed Luke by the top of his Bermuda shorts and the collar of his shirt, hoisted him off his feet, and thrust him over the side of the boat and into the ocean.

The Pacific swallowed him whole; its icy chill pulled the breath from his lungs. He surfaced gasping for air, his hands flailing. "WHAT THE—?"

Bogie's roar of laughter shot out. "You can swim, can't you?"

Panic choked Luke's throat. Salt water slopped into his mouth. The Atlantic was like bath water compared to this. His fingertips grazed the weathered wood as the engine sputtered to life. The boat chugged away, leaving behind a cloud of acrid exhaust.

"YOU BASTARD!" This was the sort of mean-spirited trick his brothers might have pulled. Especially the meanest of the bunch. Tony would have pranked him like this and laughed the rest of the day. "YOU PIECE OF SHIT BAG OF SHIT SACK OF SHIT ASSHOLE."

Bogie cut *Sluggy*'s engine.

Luke wiped the seawater out of his eyes. Forty feet? Fifty, maybe. He could swim fifty goddamned feet.

Or could he? His clothes were soaked through. The muscles in his arms were giving out.

Don't be a wimp. Don't be a baby. Don't let this prick get the better of you.

He kicked his legs as hard as he could. One arm over the other. One, two, one, two, breathe. One, two, one, two, breathe.

His fingers pressed against the hull. He looked up to see Bogie peering down at him, a smug, taunting grin plastered across his face.

"You're one mean son of a bitch, you know that?"

"Better men than you have told me so." Bogie extended his hand down toward Luke. "I can't have a First Mate who's afraid of the water."

"Fair enough." Luke grabbed hold of Bogie's forearm. "On

second thought—" He yanked hard, pulling his boss ass over teakettle.

Bogie broke the surface of the ocean like a dead walrus, slapping it with a loud thwack. "Touché, jackass!"

Luke hoisted himself into the boat. By the time he had peeled off his sopping shirt, he'd caught Bogie's infectious laughter. "Need any help, chrome dome?"

Bogie barked out a foghorn of a laugh. "Yeah, shitheel, I do."

Luke grabbed hold of Bogie's extended hand and hauled him onto the deck. They fell into a soggy heap.

"The look on your face when you came up for air is the funniest damned sight I've seen all year."

"I'm glad my nearly drowning brought some hilarity into your life."

"If that treatment is good enough for Jimmy Cagney, it's good enough for you." Bogie unbuttoned the fly on his dungarees and wriggled out of them. "First day out on that yacht of his, he got seasick like you wouldn't believe. So I gave him a nickname: 'Captain Hates the Sea.' He didn't know he loathed it until he got out here; you didn't know you feared it until you did the same thing." He wrung out his pants and laid them in the sun to dry.

Luke followed suit. "Pushing him in the drink—did it work?"

Bogie cracked a new version of his droll wisenheimer grin. "You tell me."

Luke crept on all fours to the edge of the boat, clutched the railing until his knuckles blanched, then leaned over.

They were closer to the Anacapa shoreline now. A sea turtle emerged from under the boat about ten feet down. Beyond it, a school of halibut. Deeper still, a bed of seaweed carpeted the floor.

A lone cormorant perched itself on the rock bridge at the island's eastern extremity and stared at Luke. He pictured Wilda standing next to it, stroking its head, saying nothing. She just looked at him with loving approval as though he had finished a tune at the piano, note-perfect for the first time.

The engine sputtered to life as Bogie cranked the anchor out of the water. *Sluggy* cut a wide circle around the rock bridge, and a whitewashed lighthouse came into view. Smaller than the one at Montauk, it looked every bit as sturdy.

The cormorant took flight; Luke followed its trajectory overhead. "I wonder if they need a lighthouse keeper."

24

*B*ogie slammed his fist on the table hard enough to jostle the bottle at his elbow and delivered his "gin joints" line.

"CUT!"

"Dammit, Mike," Bogie yelled, "what the hell was wrong with that?"

"I want more darker around you. Rick is in the torment."

"So am I." Bogie stormed toward the back of the set to find a corner of solitude.

"What's up with him?" Nell asked.

The first sign of Bogie's foul mood had surfaced earlier that morning when he had walked into the dressing room and found five bags of fan mail. "Get these out of here!"

"I'm too afraid to ask." Luke added an autographed photo to the 'done' pile and picked up the next one.

The lighting guy shouted, "I need Luke at the desk."

Nell followed him onto the set. "Didn't you guys have an enjoyable time out on patrol?"

"It was exactly what I needed after—" His voice dried up

before he could say Wilda's name out loud. "He's happiest when he's out there on the open sea."

She shifted to one side. "Should you ask him what's on his mind?"

"God, no!" Bogie's leave-me-the-hell-alones were the easiest to recognize: hunched shoulders, averted eyes, chain-smoking. "Are we having dinner tonight?"

"Mondays are my bandage-rolling night. The Red Cross now lets Austrian refugees help. Paul Henreid's wife joined us last week. Lisl, her name is. Real nice, too."

"What time do you finish?"

"Not till ten."

Somber shadows clotted most of the background behind Rick's desk. Bogie paced the rear wall. Back and forth. Back and forth. Luke suspected this sour mood was Mayo-related. It wasn't a hard call to make—most of Bogie's surliness tracked back to his wife. He needed someone—that much was obvious, even to a guy as new to dating as Luke. But it ought to be the right someone, and Mayo didn't come close.

Luke had been reluctant to join Bogie on the boat. He would have preferred to lie in bed, blinds drawn, and wallow in the suffocating quicksand his life had become. Sea breezes and swooping cormorants? No thanks. But Bogie had known what he'd needed, and now Bogie was down in the dumps. Wasn't it Luke's turn to lift *his* spirits?

Curtiz called his star back to his mark. "We take it from Mr. Dooley asking Rick if he's going to bed."

Bogie took his seat and wrapped his fingers around the liquor bottle. "Can we start already? The genuine stuff is waiting for me in my dressing room."

Luke squirmed in his chair. "I'm glad you've got bandages to roll tonight," he told Nell. "I'll be here a while."

. . .

By eight p.m., Luke had signed every photo. He had also typed out replies to the more interesting fan mail letters the publicity department had sent over. And he'd dragged everything to the mail room.

As everyone had been preparing to leave for the day, Bogie had told Luke he "needed some peace and quiet," which was code for "I'll be in my dressing room having a few stiff drinks so make sure nobody comes in—including you." But 'a few stiff drinks' usually meant forty-five minutes. Not two hours.

Luke waited until the second hand on his watch ticked past twelve. "Knock, knock!" Silence. "I'm coming in, ready or not."

Bogie sat at his makeup table with his right hand wrapped around an empty whiskey bottle. "Excellent timing." Luke slid Bogie's jacket off the coat rack. Bogie hauled himself to his feet. "Did you know that Hal Wallis wanted to cast a girl piano player?"

"Sam was a woman?"

"He saw this incredible pianist, Hazel Scott. Plays jazz and classical like you wouldn't believe. He got to thinking maybe this *Casablanca* picture would be more interesting if Rick's sidekick was a colored girl. But Hazel was contracted to play Café Society through the summer, so he found someone else."

Luke found the keys to Bogie's Packard in an inside pocket and nudged Bogie out of the soundstage. He rattled them. Hint, hint. "Who?"

"Terrific singer. Lena Horne. Been playing a Cotton Club–style revue up on the Strip. Mayo and I went to see her. What a knockout."

Those swanky Sunset Strip nightclubs were beyond Luke's financial reach. "And we're talking about her—why?"

"She moved into a house down the street from us. I've got a hunch the neighbors are going to get ugly about it. Felix Young, he runs the Trocadero. She's about to perform there. He hadda sign her rental agreement, and she hadda move in during the middle of the night. I tell you, it chafes my ass to see prejudice play out like this. On my own street." Bogie slid onto the passenger seat and pulled a hip flask out of the glove compartment. "This girl, she has a special sort of glow you don't see too often. But she can't even sign a lease. That's not right."

Luke started the engine and pointed the car toward Gate Two. "Is this what's been bugging you? Yesterday you were so calm, so relaxed and at peace."

"I feel the same as Hemingway about the sea." Bogie's voice was wistful now. "It's pure. One of the last few free places on earth."

Luke wished the rest of the world could have seen yesterday's Humphrey Bogart. No flattering costume or painstaking lighting. No platforms strapped to his shoes, no toupée glued to his skull. Just the California sun warming his bare legs, briny wind to his back, and a mile-wide smile splitting his face. Was there a happier person in the whole world? The trappings of fame—the money, the adoration, the best table at Perino's, and front row at the Academy Awards—were they worth it if all you needed was a cabin cruiser, a swath of empty ocean, and squawking seagulls to keep you company?

"And then I have to come to work on this baloney. Boy-loses-girl, boy-finds-girl-again, boy-loses-girl-again—or gets her. Ilsa stays in Casablanca or gets on the plane for Lisbon. Maybe by the time we're done, Ilsa leaves Rick and Victor for a half-witted camel with lumbago and a yen for Swedish meatballs." Luke turned right into the Cahuenga Pass. "Where're you going?"

"I'm taking you home."

"Let's go to your boarding house."

"Why?"

"So that you don't have to walk home. I'll drive myself."

"Not with a bottle of Canadian Club inside you."

"I'm the boss."

The long route via Hollywood Boulevard would give him a chance to sober up a little. "All righty, then."

"And another thing."

"There's more?"

"Track down whatshisname."

"Could you be more specific?"

"That Navy guy you impressed at the Romanoff's fundraiser."

"Captain Stamina?"

Bogie slapped his thigh. "That's the one. Didn't he say he could get your 4-F reversed?"

"He indicated he might—"

"We need to nudge the situation."

Luke turned onto Highland Avenue and headed south toward the Hollywood Hotel. The windows were blacked out, making it look more like a deserted haunted house than the welcoming place where he'd landed seven months ago. "His instructions were 'Don't call me, I'll call you.'"

"That girl he's banging, can she get a message to him?"

"Dunno. Maybe?"

"We need to ask her. *Carpe diem*, and all that."

We? When did this opportunity with Captain Stamina become a 'we'? "I appreciate you wanting to help."

"My motives aren't so hot." The citywide blackouts had relaxed into dimouts. Neon lights and billboards were prohibited, but streetlamps could stay on as long as they had black sleeves pulled over the top of them. The light from one of these lamps reached Bogie's face as they passed by. "I was classified I-A-H, which means I'm physically fit, but I'm also 43, which translates as 'Too damned old.' And you can't fix old. But your situation is different. Nothing would give me greater pleasure than to see you qualify. I read a quote from Alexander the Great the other day. 'There is nothing impossible to him who will try.' So let's try."

A block down from the Hollywood Theatre, a line of people outside a new Western Union office overflowed down the sidewalk. A single bulb lit up a large sign.

SHIFT WORKERS
WIRE YOUR MONEY HOME
WE'RE OPEN 24 HOURS

Luke had overheard talk in the studio commissary about how war factory workers were making double what Bogie was paying him. Up to triple for those working the graveyard shift from midnight to eight. When fifty-dollar-a-week paychecks were low-hanging fruit, was it any wonder people were flooding into town?

Luke stared at the line outside Western Union and wondered if it was too soon to send Wilda another telegram until a jolt in his chest reminded him it was too late for that. How long would it take him to remember that she was gone? Luke felt foolish even asking himself that question. It'll take as long as it takes, boyo, and until it recedes, you're just going to have to live with the aching regret that you weren't there at the end.

Bogie's remedy of pushing him into the sea hadn't plugged the hole that Wilda's death had gouged out of his heart. But it had handed him a memory of lying on Humphrey Bogart's deck, soaking wet, dungarees off, and laughing hard enough to scare wildlife. But later that night in bed, reliving the overwhelming panic he hadn't seen coming, Luke had understood it wasn't the bottomless Pacific he was afraid of. It was the unmoored feeling that had swamped him. Wilda had been his anchor. The one dependable sanctuary he'd ever known. And now, that last weak link in the anchor chain had broken, casting him adrift.

Bogart's right. Wilda's voice whispered in his ear. *Carpe the hell diem, my boy.*

Luke rounded the corner onto Whitley Avenue and headed up the hill. "I could slip a note under her door."

Bogie pushed his fedora off his forehead and yawned. "What note under what door?"

"Beatrice. If she's not home for dinner, I could slip her a note telling her to wake me no matter what time she gets in."

"Now you're talking. Say, what's going on up there?" He pointed toward the far end of the street, where a hazy light quivered in the dusk. It was bright, too. Or did it only seem like that because of the dimout? It was hard to be sure these days.

A siren kicked into gear.

A fire truck raced past them.

And then another.

It wasn't until they reached the Padre Terrace corner that Luke saw flames licking the sky.

Luke hit the gas harder, his breathing growing more labored as the incline steepened. He could make out people standing around. Had the entire neighborhood turned out to watch—

No. NO. *NO!*

A white Cord Phaeton screeched away from the curb. Luke parked in the space it had left behind and raced across the street. He elbowed onlookers out of the way until he reached the front of the crowd, just as a loud crack rang out. Heat stung his face.

Another crack, louder this time. Shattered glass showered the porch roof.

"Stand back." A fireman pressed a firm hand to Luke's chest.

"But I live here."

"Not anymore. I'd say it's about to—"

A burst of flames roared out of Beatrice's window. The crash of splintering wood filled the smoky air.

"That was the stairs, I reckon," Bogie said behind Luke. "Won't be long now."

Luke looked left and right, scanning a sea of horrified faces. Beatrice? Edith? Seymour? Minerva? Tristan?

Another explosion of glass split the night air. The flames grew brighter, hotter. Luke lifted his hand to shield his face. The house shuddered, then teetered like an old lady on high heels.

The widow's walk was the first to disappear, then the chimney.

Bricks smashed through the floorboards one after the other until the walls disintegrated, and Whitley Manor collapsed in on itself, unable at last to resist the inferno.

* * *

Mayo stood outside in a bathrobe and hair curlers as Bogie pulled into the driveway. "It's after midnight. You might have phoned—" She caught sight of Luke climbing out of the passenger seat. "What the hell happened to you?" She sniffed at the air. "Why do you both reek of smoke?"

"Luke's boarding house," Bogie said. "It burned down."

"Aw jeez, kiddo. What a tough break. How bad?"

"The whole thing's gone. He's lost everything."

It was the first time Luke had heard those ghastly words: *lost everything.*

Mayo patted Luke's shoulder. "You poor thing."

Bogie nudged them toward the front porch. "I've offered him our guest room."

"Of course. You're welcome to stay as long as you want."

Luke let Bogie lead him down the hallway to a nautically decorated room. A pattern of three-sail sloops dotted the wallpaper in two-foot intervals; matching curtains bracketed the window. A large framed poster for *Captain Blood* hung on one wall. In one corner Flynn had scrawled *From one captive to another.*

"I'm going to take a shower," Bogie said. "You should too. We're stinking up the joint. I'll get towels from the linen press." He disappeared up the corridor.

Mayo sighed and turned to Luke. "You haven't said a word yet."

There was a hardness to her face Luke hadn't noticed before. When did she get those lines around her eyes? Her mouth? And so deeply etched, too. All the facials in the world behind Elizabeth Arden's red door wouldn't rid her of them. Booze and resentment had taken their toll. Still, she was sober and sympathetic.

"You never think about how you can lose everything until it goes."

Her expression took on a glum wistfulness. "Trust me, honey, I know all about how everything goes away."

Was she talking about her career? Her marriage? Her looks? On some other day Luke might have asked. But night stretched before him, bleaker than a Brooklyn winter. He was clean out of empathy.

Mayo fetched a large cardboard box from the wardrobe and hoisted it onto the bed. "Hump's old clothes and castoffs. I've been meaning to take them to the Salvation Army." She pulled out a fistful of shirts and dropped them on the patchwork coverlet. "Lucky for you, I'm lazy as a sloth."

The word 'lucky' made Luke flinch. He checked the labels: Brooks Brothers, Mullen and Bluett, Desmonds, I. Magnin, Bullocks—fancy stores he couldn't afford, but of course none of them bore Wilda's color-matching code. Were there pants inside the box too? Did any of them match these shirts? What choice did he have but to eeny-meeny-miny-moe it and risk looking like a garish circus clown? That's what happens when you're a charity case.

Charity case. The words conjured up dusty Okies fleeing the Dust Bowl. Hungry faces of the jobless standing in soup kitchen lines during the Depression. He reassured himself he wasn't *that* desperate—except that he was. No clothes. No belongings. Nothing to call his own. Not even a toothbrush. Other than his wallet, all he had was the latchkey to a house that no longer existed.

At least the firemen had confirmed they'd found no dead bodies in the smoky remains—he'd take whatever silver lining he could grab hold of. After the fire department and policemen had left and the neighbors had dispersed, Luke had kicked around some scraps of curtains, a shoe heel, and one of Edith's skillets, and waited for his neighbors. But none of them had shown up. Where had they all been? Taken to a hospital? Or worse?

Mayo looked around the room. "Early in our marriage, I fantasized this would be the Bogart nursery." She smoothed out the bedspread. "I realize now how foolish that was." She had to be staring down the barrel at forty. Too late to be starting a family. Especially for a couple who kept a supply of doors in their garden shed. Her blue eyes glazed over. "Thank you for looking after Hump. You do a better job than me."

"I'm sure that's not true."

She stared back at him with weary eyes that seemed to say, *We both know it is.*

Bogie appeared with a set of towels in his hand. "The guest bathroom's to the right. If you need anything, just yell." He shot Luke an impish wink. "We're used to yelling around here."

25

*L*uke could still smell the Lux soap and Drene shampoo from the harsh scrubbing he'd given himself a few hours earlier. Hours that felt like days.

Each time he closed his eyes, the movie projector in his head cranked to life. The flames, the cracking wood, the sirens.

Ugh.

Stop.

Enough.

He planted his feet on the oval rug with the Spanish galleon motif and dug his big toe into its crow's nest. Bogie had given him the day off, but what good could come from reliving the ordeal over and over? He needed distraction.

That night at the Brown Derby, when Ingrid had told him she preferred to stay at the studio twenty-four hours a day, he'd been puzzled, wondering whether she had no better place to go. He understood what she meant now.

He grabbed the first Salvation Army shirt and trousers his hands touched. They were dark, which was as close to matching as he could manage. He got dressed and walked into the kitchen where Mayo was stirring a large pot on the stove.

"I'm heading to the studio."

She looked up, surprised. "The grocer sold me his last bag of cauliflower so I'm making soup."

Luke spied a tumbler on the counter near her elbow. She had filled it with ice and something. Mostly something.

"My mind's a crazy mixed-up whirligig."

"We could play cards. Not poker, though. I hear you're too good at it. A few rounds of canasta?"

Luke thought of Gus filling in for him on Stage Eight. That guy was like a ship rat—always around, always scheming. "Maybe some other time. Can I call for a cab?"

Luke entered the soundstage as the bell rang, alerting the cast and crew that Bogie and Ingrid were ready for another take. Gus retreated to Luke's chair and parked himself beside Luke's girl-friend. Ingrid held a revolver in her hand. Curtiz called "Action!" She gave Bogie his cue about Victor Laszlo dying here if they didn't get out. He said his line about how Casablanca was a good place to die.

Luke's knees buckled. He grabbed at a papier-mâché palm tree labeled "Airport scene, *Casablanca*." He gripped the trunk and tried to steady his breath. What if he hadn't needed to drive Bogie home last night? What if he'd gone to bed early instead? He was a heavy sleeper. The smell of smoke wouldn't have woken him up.

"Cut and print!" Curtiz's voice rang across Rick Blaine's apart-ment. "Set up for Miss Bergman."

Luke let go of the palm tree and shook his head to clear it of the what-ifs bombarding him. The slap of running footsteps grew louder. Nell enveloped him in her arms. "Bogie told me what happened. I can't believe it!"

He pressed his face to her shoulder and buried himself in the familiar scent of her lavender shampoo. "One of the firemen said that after sixty or seventy Californian summers, those old Victorian houses are drier than a Mormon Christmas party."

Bogie approached them, still smoking the cigarette he'd lit during the take. "What are you doing here?"

"I'd much rather be busy."

"We're zipping through today's schedule so fast that we'll be done in a few hours."

"In that case, can we swing by the boarding house? I need to see it in the daylight."

Nell took his hand. "Can I come too?"

"I don't know what I expect to find," Luke told them, "but I'd rather not face it alone."

* * *

The ashes were still warm. Luke dug through them a little deeper. "I made six sketches of the Anacapa lighthouse and kept them in an old leather satchel Edith had in storage." Luke barely recognized his own voice; it sounded so far away. "I thought there might be a chance it survived."

Bogie nudged a blackened plank with his boot. A patch of brass the size of a quarter caught the late-afternoon sun. "A doorknob isn't much of a souvenir."

"IT'S YOU!"

Tristan sprinted along the sidewalk, his arms outstretched like he was Scarlett returning to Tara. "I'm so relieved. I was just saying to Sabine, if you're not here, what'll we do? She suggested sending a wire to Warners, which—" He caught sight of Bogie. "Hello there."

"You remember Tristan as Trixie Bagatelle from that fundraiser," Luke explained, and turned to greet Sabine, whose progress up the hill had been slower. "So?" he asked them. "Do you know what happened?"

"It was one of those rare nights when none of us were home,

but thank God I'd knocked off early. I found Edith passed out on the floor. I dragged her into the yard and ran next door to raise the alarm. The ambulance arrived real fast, even before the fire engines. They strapped her in and let me ride along."

"How's she doing?" Luke asked.

Tristan see-sawed his hand. "We'll all visit her when the doctors say it's okay."

"And now? You got a place to live? Accommodation is so scarce these days."

"A pal of mine is one of those girls Howard Hughes keeps stashed in an apartment. She barely hears from him, so she's lonely as all get-out. Lucky for me it's a two-bedroom. I'm taking her up on the offer she hasn't made yet." He looked out across the charred rubble. "All my costumes, my wigs, shoes, jewelry. Trixie's going into forced retirement."

"Trixie's a ton of fun," Bogie said. "You know how to command a stage."

"Thank you, Mr. Bogart. I appreciate that." Tristan's already pale face turned even more wan. "I'm looking at it as a sign. Time for a change. Don't ask me what, though. I'm still taking all this in."

"And you, Sabine?" Luke asked.

She shrugged indifferently. "Me? I'm a nomad. I've learned to not grow attached to hats and dresses and purses."

"But you need a place to lay your head. Where did you spend last night?"

"I called Josef von Sternberg and—"

"You did?" Bogie asked. "I'm impressed."

"We renewed our acquaintance at the Hollywood Anti-Nazi League. I met him when he came to Berlin to work with Max Reinhardt. He has a house full of guests—refugees, natürlich—so he offered me his office sofa. It is uncomfortable and I shan't be able to bear it for more than a few nights. After that?"

Sabine shrugged again. This time, though, Luke detected a hint of despair. He turned to Bogie. "What about Peter Lorre?"

"After the success of that fundraiser, I'm sure he'll be happy to offer his guestroom."

"I was thinking more like applying to the European Film Fund for assistance."

Sabine emitted a little yip. "I would qualify?"

"I don't know how it works, but Peter would. He's due on the set tomorrow."

"OH MY GOD!" Beatrice came running toward them. She was still in her Kress uniform, but her hair had lost all semblance of the victory rolls she had taken to wearing lately. "What—what happened?"

"Fire." Luke expected her to burst into tears, but she surveyed the remains with self-contained detachment. "Where were you?"

"Last night I was volunteering at the USO club. One of the gals twisted her ankle, and I took her home on her bicycle's handlebars. It was late by the time we got there, so I bunked in. Lucky for me, considering . . ." She wafted a hand over the debris.

"What about tonight? Can you bunk in with your pal again?"

"Heavens, no! She works graveyard at Lockheed. She's already hot-bedding it with a day-shift girl."

"Hot-bedding?" Sabine asked. "What is this?"

"Two people working different shifts sharing the same bed. It's hard enough to juggle two people, but three? Not a workable situation. What about you?"

"Bogie and Mayo took me in." Luke looked over at Bogie; the poor guy had almost disappeared behind a cluster of autograph seekers. "Otherwise, I don't know what I would have done. Finding a place to live isn't easy."

"Something'll turn up, I'm sure."

But Luke wasn't. Not when there were people living in chicken coops. "What about your captain? I saw him at the 'Stars Over America' gala a couple of weeks ago."

"You did?" Beatrice's eyes widened with surprise.

"Call him. Perhaps he can pull strings." And after he was done pulling strings to find her a place to live, she could ask him to follow through on his suggestion to reverse Luke's 4-F status.

"Oh, but I couldn't cut in line ahead of someone needier than me."

"You just lost everything. Nobody is needier than you right now." Luke pressed a nickel into Beatrice's palm and told her to call him from the phone booth at the twenty-four-hour Western Union office. When she still hesitated, Nell grabbed her hand. "Come on, I'll go with you. Don't worry about me," she told Luke. "I'll find my own way home."

Luke, Tristan, and Sabine watched Bogie drown in fans. "I should rescue him," Luke said. "He turned into my savior just when I needed one."

Tristan sighed. "I wish I had a fairy godfather like that."

Fairy godfather. Hmmmm.

"Do you know how to sew?"

"Who do you think made Trixie's costumes, Edith Head?"

"What if I put in a good word for you with Orry-Kelly?"

"You'd do that?"

"He told me how hard it's becoming to find decent staff because everyone is getting drafted or paid better elsewhere."

"Imagine me riveting bolts into a Corsair?" Tristan pressed his hands to his chest. "I'll be forever in your debt, even if he says no."

"He can be flamboyant and prone to tantrums."

"I know how to handle prima donnas. Just get me in to see him. I'll take it from there."

Bogie's smile had taken on a flinty edge. Luke joined the perimeter of the crowd gathered around him. "Mr. Bogart! Your night shoot starts soon. Mr. Warner won't be happy if you delay production."

Bogie held up his hands in surrender. "Trust me, folks, you don't want to hear the words that come out of Jack Warner when a picture goes over budget." He shouldered through the cluster without letting his face drop until they were at the Buick. "Thank Christ you're a quick thinker, boyo. Where's Nell?"

"I suggested to Beatrice that her captain might help find her a place. Nell's gone with her."

Bogie pushed Luke to the passenger seat and jumped behind the wheel. "You're a good egg," he said, and pulled away from the curb. "Look at you taking care of your pals. You suggested how Lorre could help Sabine, and you urged Beatrice to call her captain. Tristan needs a job and you might pull that off, too."

"How could you have heard that over your adoring fans?"

"Actors develop a three-hundred-sixty-degree periscope so that we're aware of everything and everybody. If you think I'm good, you should see Bette Davis."

Luke wondered if he was, in fact, such a good egg. Would he have thought to urge Beatrice to make that call to Captain Stamina if he didn't have an ulterior motive? Maybe it didn't matter. If the good captain found her a place to live *and* a way to reverse his 4-F, was that so bad? Didn't that mean everybody won?

Luke's head felt heavier than a bowling ball. He rested it against the back of the car seat.

"You're looking green around the gills, son."

Luke wanted to lift his arm to give Bogie a thumbs-up, but it, too, felt sluggish. The road ahead sloped downhill toward Hollywood Boulevard. Luke closed his eyes. Just for a moment. Just until he felt human again.

26

*C*urtiz rolled his script into a truncheon and hurled it onto the floor. "Jesus fucking the Christ! Where is she?"

Luke looked up from the typewriter perched on the plank across his chair. His reply to Jacob Stein from Baltimore would have to wait.

Bogie lit a cigarette.

Oh boy, this was bad. Curtiz threw tantrums at the slightest provocation. Malfunctioning props. Flubbed lines. Missed cues. It didn't take much. But Bogie lighting up while in costume? That was a big no-no. Especially in a white dinner jacket. A stray flake of ash might burn a very noticeable hole.

"I must have my leading lady!" Curtiz bawled. "If this was the first day of shooting, I would put her in the sack!"

A quiet snicker trilled around the crew. Twenty years in America and he still hadn't learned the difference between sacking someone and getting someone into the sack. Ironic, considering they had recently overheard him screwing some unlucky redhead. At least being caught out had put an end to Curtiz's odious behavior.

"Maybe she's sick. Has anyone called her at home?"

Luke turned to see who had spoken, and his eyes narrowed. Him again? Did Gus O'Farrell have nothing better to do than loaf around film sets he wasn't working on?

Curtiz towered over his assistant. "Why haven't you made the telephone to her house? You want me to dial for you the number?"

"I don't have it," the poor kid said. "Maybe Personnel—"

"Hey Mikey!" An Epstein—Luke still couldn't tell them apart— sauntered up to the director. "We've rewritten the casino scene where Rick helps that young couple at the roulette table. We came up with an angle that'll slay you—"

"What?" Curtiz thundered. "With the roulette and the angles and the slaying!" He grabbed the pages out of Epstein's hand and catapulted them into the air.

Bogie lit up a fresh cigarette. One was bad enough, but two? Yikes.

On the drive to the studio this morning, Bogie had leapfrogged from one topic to another: the Doolittle Raid on Tokyo, the WACs and the WAVES, MGM's *Mrs. Miniver* and Goldwyn's *The Pride of the Yankees,* black-market nylons, German submarines off the coast of New York. It had been hard for Luke to keep up until he realized it wasn't his job to respond. He was there to listen as Bogie burned through his pent-up nerves. Ahead of him stretched an emotionally raw scene in which Ilsa tried to explain herself. Bogie needed to lay bare Rick's anguish if the scene were to ring with any sort of authenticity.

"Maybe there's a problem with Ingrid's costume," Luke whispered to Nell.

"I'd skedaddle over there myself, but I need to be here if she shows up."

This was the opportunity Luke had been hoping for. He approached Bogie. "I have an idea where Ingrid might be. How about I hightail it over to—"

"Yeah, yeah." Bogie waved away the rest of Luke's suggestion.

. . .

A potted ficus held open the door to Costuming to create a cross breeze. Anything to secure relief from another sweltering day. "I don't suppose Ingrid Bergman is here?" Luke asked the girl at the front desk. "Things are getting tense on the *Casablanca* set."

She looked up from the striped ribbon she was sewing onto a straw hat and pointed to the closed door behind her.

The hinges squeaked as Luke peeked inside.

At least Ingrid was in costume—a white knee-length coat, buttoned at the waist, and an extra-long chiffon scarf wrapped around her throat. She sat on a round ottoman, elbows on her knees, her face cradled in the palms of her hands.

Luke ventured into the fitting room. "Hello."

When she looked up at him, relief flickered across her pale skin. "I half-expected Mr. Curtiz to stampede in here like a wounded buffalo."

"Keep him waiting much longer and he might."

"I need a moment to gather my wits."

He sat down next to her. "What's going on?"

She raked her nails through her hair. "Paramount has cast Vera Zorina as María in *For Whom the Bell Tolls*."

"So the ballerina didn't fall off the stage after all."

A hint of a smile. "You're the sweetest kid on the whole Warners lot."

"Did you tell your husband what's happened?"

"He cares so little about the movies, or my career. He said, 'It's just one role. I don't know what you're crying for.' I told him the reason I've been able to make it through *Casablanca* has been the hope that I'd get María. We had an awful fight that ended with him hanging up on me."

Luke pictured the *Casablanca* cast and crew looking at their watches. "Okay, so Mr. Curtiz—"

"Has he thrown his script on the ground yet?"

"Fifteen minutes ago."

"Hell's bells. I'm almost too afraid to face him."

"You've faced worse this morning."

Orry-Kelly burst through the doorway holding a wide-brimmed hat. "I'm rethinking the long scarf. Oh, hello." The hat dropped to his side. "I suppose you're here for that trench coat. I would have had Bogie's costume ready, but the demands on my time grow ever more burdensome. Who knows when I'll get around to writing my fashion column for Hearst. And nobody misses a deadline for that blowhard."

Ingrid took the hat from him. "I'll let Mr. Curtiz decide between this and the scarf. I must go back to Perc for makeup repairs." She thanked Luke and hurried away.

"If you're short-handed," Luke said, "I might be able to help you out."

"You can sew?"

"No, but my friend Tristan can, and he needs a job."

Orry-Kelly's face lit up, his eyes wide as coconuts. "Trixie Bagatelle?!"

"He makes his own gowns, you know."

"My dear boy, that's what he's famous for. Tell him to be here first thing tomorrow. I'll be starting on *Old Acquaintance* soon. Juggling Bette Davis and Miriam Hopkins won't be easy, so I'm going to need help wrangling those two before they kill each other. You're a godsend, Luke Vail! As my granny would say, your blood's worth bottling."

Luke was drawing close to Stage Five, where Errol Flynn was filming *Gentleman Jim*, when he heard Gus O'Farrell shout "NO!" He ducked behind a plaster statue of Stonewall Jackson in time to see Gus stumble through an open doorway. An older guy stomped forward, his face dark with fury. It didn't take a genius to figure out who he was: Gus O'Farrell plus twenty-five years, plus forty pounds, plus two inches in height and ten around the chest.

Hell O'Farrell raised fists the size of Christmas hams and

shoved his son. Gus staggered backward until he hit the statue. "You wanna get ahead, you do it on the coattails of a rising star? I got you onto *High Sierra*. You were supposed to take it from there."

"I did what you said, Pop. I was Bogart's stand-in and stuntman on *The Maltese Falcon* and *All Through the Night*."

"Until along comes that pipsqueak nobody from Brooklyn. Jesus, you can't even suck up to a self-absorbed actor?"

"But the pipsqueak's the same size as Bogie. There's nothing much I can do about it if—"

"The opportunity to climb over him landed in your lap like a baseball. The timing couldn't have been better if I had orchestrated it myself."

"Did you do that, Pop? Did you send those G.I.s to Romanoff's?"

Luke peeped between Stonewall's legs to see Hell bite down on his lower lip as though to stop himself from blurting out a confession he'd later regret.

"You gotta get creative if you're gonna eliminate your enemies."

"Sure, Pop, but kicking the crap out of someone?"

"For years I dreamed of having an O'Farrell head up the stunt department of each studio the way those Westmore boys run every makeup department in town—but we'd do it with blood and guts and muscle. Each of your older brothers has flaked out on me. And that means you're my last chance of a legacy."

"Don't you think I know that? I'm stunting for Flynn now. He's the biggest star we have."

"Only because I temporarily put Buster Wiles out of commission."

A passing truck cloaked the gasp that flew from Luke. Buster was an experienced stuntman who knew how to handle himself. And if he fell prey to O'Farrell's lack of scruples, what chance did Luke have?

"You know what you need to do?"

"Yes, Pop." Gus stared at his feet.

"Get rid of that little shit from Brooklyn."

"But I—"

"There's no such thing as 'but.'"

"I know, Pop, but—"

Hell hauled back and struck his son square across the face with a meaty palm. A sickening thud rang out as his hand connected with Gus's right cheek.

Junior crumpled to the ground.

"I should've let the draft board accept you, but we know it wouldn't have taken two seconds for them to realize how useless you are. You're an *in*ept, *in*competent, *in*adequate embarrassment to the O'Farrell name." He flung open the soundstage door and disappeared inside.

Gus scrambled to his feet. "Pop! This Vail guy speaks *GERMAN*!"

Luke ducked down onto all fours. Had Hell O'Farrell finagled his son out of the draft? Luke was no fan of Gus, but his father was a whole other pot of Hoover stew. Had he been worried about the wrong O'Farrell?

"You snooping on me?"

Gus loomed over Luke, arms crossed over his chest.

He scrambled to his feet. "I know it looks that way, but—"

"I don't care what you think you saw or heard—"

"Does he often slug you?"

Gus lunged forward. His face was now inches from Luke's. "You wanna talk about fathers, huh? All right. Let's talk about yours."

"What does my father have to do with—"

"You know that missing falcon statue I found?"

Not 'found.' Stole. "What about it?"

"It was hollow."

Give him your best poker face. "So?"

"Little button near the bottom. Press it and a trap door pops open."

Don't blink. Don't budge. Don't even breathe. "I guess that makes you the puzzle king."

"The real puzzle was inside."

So it *hadn't* been empty when Wilda had handed him the statue along with her fishy story. And he'd had it right there by his side for days and days.

"You don't know what was there," Gus taunted, "because otherwise you'd have kept it."

If Luke were Rick Blaine and had some razor-sharp, Epstein-penned rejoinder to throw in Gus's face, he would have. But nothing came to him, so he stared at the guy, mute as a lump of coal.

"Birth certificate," Gus said. "Yours."

"Horse hockey! Mine is back in Brooklyn, so—"

"Your *first* one."

"Nobody has two birth certificates."

"You do, Mister Osterhaus." Gus's smirk blurred as Luke tried to digest the name. "I should say *Herr* Osterhaus. Makes you a Kraut, don't it?"

"I was born in Brooklyn. I'm as American as you are."

"Your name isn't Vail, either. It's Valenti. And that's Italian. Just like your father. Born in Lucca. Italy. And your mother is from Münster. Germany. Who we're at war with. Now I get why you can talk Kraut to those pathetic refugees and European Heebs in there. I bet you're all a bunch of Nazi spies, in cahoots, sitting around coming up with God knows what. Blayney Matthews will be real interested to hear of this. You know about his book, don't you? *The Specter of Sabotage?*"

Luke took an aggressive step forward, like he'd seen his father and his brothers do. Pop had always said it didn't matter if you was in the right: "It's about convincing the other guy you are. And if that doesn't work, punch him in the face." Luke had never followed Pop's advice, preferring instead to preempt a situation before things unraveled to the slugging stage. "So, you've got my birth certificate."

Gus nodded slowly, condescendingly. "You're surprised."

"I'm surprised you know what it says."

"Why wouldn't I?"

"You'd have to be able to read it."

Luke watched as Gus's cheeks darkened. "What sort of imbecile can't read?"

"Isn't that why you're still a civilian?"

"What? No!"

Gus fell back a step; Luke advanced.

"That's not what I heard."

"I'm not 4-F."

"What are you, then?"

"2-A-F. Deferred in support of the war effort. The Office of War Information says motion pictures are a vital part of it."

Twenty bucks said strings had been pulled. Another twenty said Hell O'Farrell had been the string-puller. Bogie had mentioned how chummy Hell and Blayney Matthews were, and that Matthews was ex-FBI *and* ex-DA. A guy like that would have connections.

Gus sneered at him. "If I can't read, how come I know what was on your birth certificate?"

It was a fair point that Luke hadn't considered. It looked like he'd been wrong that day under the trees. As he shouldered past Gus, Hell's bitter words came back to him. *It wouldn't have taken two seconds to realize how useless you are.* Luke Valenti might be a pipsqueak nobody from Brooklyn, but he knew what it was like to live in the shadow of a domineering father.

Ingrid flew through the door on the far side of the set, chiffon wafting in her wake.

"Good morning, everyone!" She marched up to Curtiz and cupped his face in her hands. "I've kept you waiting, and for that I'm so very, very sorry. Let's get to work."

Luke climbed into the seat next to Nell. "I got Tristan a job working for Orry-Kelly."

"How wonderful. But why do you look like someone just ran over your dog?"

The assistant director called for quiet on the set. Bogie and Claude Rains took their places at the table as the RICK'S CAFÉ AMÉRICAIN neon sign glowed white.

"Action!"

Bogie delivered his line telling Rains how he'd been misinformed about the health waters in Casablanca. It was a funny line that said much about Rick's unwillingness to share his background.

Luke sank into his seat.

Lukas Osterhaus sounded like somebody else. He might not be Luke Vail, but he was a Valenti through and through. God knows Pop had talked often enough about Lucca. Famous for its soaring towers and broad medieval city wall. The piazza that used to be a Roman amphitheater. A short drive to the Leaning Tower of Pisa. Not long after the Montauk vacation, Pop had sat Luke down at the dining table and unfolded a tattered map of Italy. He'd pointed to a spot that he had circled in red ink. "Lucca," Pop had said, his voice thick with pride. "This is where I am from. It's why we called you Luke."

Luke. Lucca. Lukas. Valenti. Vail. Osterhaus. How many versions of him were there?

Curtiz yelled cut and ordered the cameraman to reset for Rains.

Luke felt a tap on his shoulder. A studio messenger boy handed him a Western Union envelope. "I think this is for you."

Luke had accepted enough telegrams to know that 'for you'

meant 'for Mr. Bogart.' Luke thanked the kid and stuffed it into his pocket.

Nell asked, "Aren't you going to read it?"

Luke withdrew the envelope and thrust it toward her. "It's for Bogie."

She shook her head. "No, it isn't."

He flipped it over and read the addressee through the window. *Luke Valenti.*

Nobody in his family had bothered to spend two cents to mail him even so much as a postcard. They sure as hell wouldn't shell out for a telegram.

Unless someone else had died.

He ripped open the envelope.

WILL BE IN LA FOR 48 HOURS STOP
NEED TO SEE YOU GET CAUGHT UP STOP
MEET ME TOMORROW UNION STATION 9AM
SUPER CHIEF STOP
TONY STOP

Tony? Brother Tony? Biggest bully in the family, Tony? Meanest drunk south of 60th Street, Tony? The Tony who wrote him off as a fag because he'd never had a girlfriend? The Tony who rarely spoke to him, and if he did, it was nothing more engaging than 'Pass the potatoes'? *Tony* needed to see him?

"Good news or bad?"

Luke hadn't noticed Bogie was now standing in front of him. "I honestly don't know." He handed over the slip of paper.

Bogie read it. "Looks like you've got yourself an important date. You want to borrow my car, boyo?"

"Thanks, but no, I couldn't."

"He's the worst asshole in a big bowl of assholes, isn't he? This is your chance to impress him."

"You can tell him it's Humphrey Bogart's car," Nell added. "I don't care where you're from, a nugget like that is bound to dazzle."

27

*L*uke pulled into a parking space out front of Union Station.

He could drive away. He didn't owe Tony anything. He had no reason to show up here at nine on a Sunday morning. What the hell would they talk about, anyway? How much Nathan's were charging for a hotdog at Coney Island these days?

"Get caught up," he'd said. On what? He had never showed a soupçon of interest before, so why would he now? Yeah, Tony, 'soupçon' is a word. Look it up. It wouldn't hurt you to read a book once in a red-white-and-blue moon.

Nell had pointed out he'd sent the telegram from Dodge City, Kansas, while he was on the train. Had he planned on furtively slipping in and out of Los Angeles, but changed his mind?

Luke's hands gripped the steering wheel as though the engine would explode if he let go.

Tony could have said "want to see you." But that wasn't the same as "need to," was it?

. . .

The Super Chief pulled into platform eight amid a gush of steam and honked its whistle with three long blasts. Luke stood at the end nearest the exit so that all disembarking travelers had to pass him. Moreover, if he spotted Tony first and courage deserted him, he had an escape route. But when Tony planted himself in front of Luke as porters and luggage carts skirted around them, he was too shocked to move. "You're a Marine."

"Gunnery Sergeant Antonio Valenti at your service." How peculiar it was to see him grin. He looked almost humble. "I have to report in at the mustering station by eleven hundred hours."

"Where is it?"

Tony pulled a sheet of paper from his front jacket pocket and unfolded it. "Santa Monica. Can we make it?"

This version of Tony, with his uniform, garrison cap, duffel bag and eleven hundred hours, was someone Luke might not have recognized had they passed in the street.

"Plenty of time," he said. "Come on, the car's out front."

Tony reappraised him with a slow once-over. "You have a car?"

They weren't even out of the station, and already Tony was impressed. "You're in California now, Sergeant."

Luke figured a scenic drive down Wilshire Boulevard would give this gunnery sergeant he barely knew a taste of Los Angeles.

Luke gestured at the uniform. "How was Pop when you told him you weren't joining his beloved Army?"

"Took him a coupla weeks to come around. He walked in as I was packing my duffel bag. 'Well, son,' he said, 'being in the Marines beats not being in the military at all.'"

In other words, it was better than getting branded with a 4-F scarlet letter. It had taken Tony all of, what, ten minutes to bring up his status. Maybe he hadn't changed much, after all.

"The park we'll be cutting through soon used to be called Westlake, but they're changing it to MacArthur Park to honor

General Douglas MacArthur. Not long after that, you'll see a soaring tower ahead of us. That's the Bullocks Wilshire department store. Too rich for my blood, but the tearoom on the top floor is like a parade of famous faces."

When Tony failed to respond, Luke snuck a sideways peek. A layer of hesitation coated his brother's face. A Valenti stopping first to think about what he was going to say? This was unprecedented.

It took Tony two blocks to speak. "The morning I left New York, some old-timer knocked on my door. Said he was Irving Kovner."

"Irving? Came to see you?"

"He starts yapping about Wilda Doyle. Did you know she died?"

"I did." If Tony noticed how Luke could barely squeeze out the words, he gave no sign of it.

"Anyhow, he told me the old lady had started a letter to you but didn't get around to finishing it." Luke's foot slipped off the gas pedal. The Studebaker behind them honked its horn. "He hoped we knew where to send it on account of your rooming house burned down. Is that true?"

"The whole thing. From rafters to front porch."

"Jesus! Where are you living now?"

Luke paused for dramatic effect. "I'm living with Humphrey Bogart."

"You're putting me on."

"He and his wife have a guest room—"

Tony slapped the dashboard. "There's no fuckin' way you know Humphrey fuckin' Bogart."

"I work for him."

"Get outta here!"

Yes, that's right. I work for Humphrey fuckin' Bogart, the movie fuckin' star. How's them apples? Have I finally impressed you? "Where did you send that telegram?"

"To Warner Bro—oh! Where he stars in them pictures, right?"

Luke pictured Tony writing his first postcard home. *Folks, get a load of this: Luke works for Humphrey Bogart.*

"You were saying how Irving had Wilda's letter?"

"Right. So he asked me if we had your address. I said no, but I was about to ship out to the Pacific and was going to be in Los Angeles for a couple of days. He asked—it was more like pleadin'—if I could give it to you."

"But how did you know to wire me at the studio?"

"That was Pop's idea."

They were passing the new May Company store now. Nell had told him they'd painted its curved corner gold to catch the eye of potential shoppers. Sure enough, it glinted with shards of sparkling light in the sun. Luke would have taken a moment to point it out, but he struggled to focus on the traffic ahead of them. Pop knew that Luke was working at Warners?

"How did he know?"

"Search me. We were saying goodbye at the bus depot and I mentioned the letter that the old guy gave me. He said, 'Try Warner Brothers.' Kinda off-hand, y'know? Like it was just a thought."

Luke couldn't imagine Wilda going out of her way to contact Pop. However, it wasn't inconceivable they might have bumped into each other at Bobo's Bakery at 13th and 54th. Pop loved their babka, and Wilda had sworn theirs was the best pumpernickel south of The Battery. Wilda might have thrown him a haughty look and said, "On the off chance you're interested, your youngest is working at Warner Brothers studios in Hollywood."

"This letter from Wilda," Luke said, "where is it now?"

Tony unbuttoned the square pocket at the front of his coat and pulled out a wrinkled envelope. Wilda's scent, Le Jade, wafted through the cabin.

Fragments of memories cascaded through his head. The sound of her clapping when he'd mastered a new tune on the piano.

Those ridiculously enormous gingham napkins. The mahogany barrette she swore was a gift from the Maharaja of Jaipur.

"You wanna hear something funny?" Tony said. "It wasn't until I saw her handwriting on the front of this here envelope that I recollected we met her during that week we spent in Montauk. You probably don't remember much about it. You were just a little nipper."

Remember it? Luke wanted to yell. Not one week has passed by that I haven't thought about it, talked about it, drawn it in charcoal, over and over and over.

"It was late June, the summer of twenty-nine," Luke said. "I remember every bit."

"I'm sure that broad could tell you were getting underfoot, so she offered to look after you."

Luke had only blissful memories of that vacation: the bonfires on the beach, the bracing sea air, barbecued hotdogs, feeling the sunburn tighten along his arms, watching the fisherman land their boats on the shoreline. And, of course, the lighthouse with its two-toned paint job. But when every detail from that week was etched so vividly in his memory, how could he have forgotten that Wilda had been there?

Tony asked, "Ever heard of a guy called Boris Osterhaus?"

That name. Again. "*Boris* Osterhaus? No."

"He had it in for Pop. Real bad. Spread rumors that Pop was a two-bit bum. Went out of his way to put Valenti Construction out of business. Played real dirty, too. Sent street thugs to wreck Pop's construction sites, bankrolled the competition to underbid him. Nothing too big or too abrupt. Didn't use the same goons twice in a row."

"But it didn't work."

"It sure did. By the late 1920s, Pop started getting low on cash, so he got involved in rumrunning. His fleet of trucks, he had 'em fitted out with false bottoms where he could stash bottles. If not for Prohibition, we might've starved."

Learning that Wilda was at Montauk would have been enough to cause Luke to slam on the brakes. Then came news of this other Osterhaus. And now rumrunning? A layer of sweat broke out along Luke's hairline. He'd grown used to standing on the sidelines of this family; now he felt like he wasn't even in the ballpark. "Go on."

"Of course, he ran up against the mob—and I'm talking Dutch Schultz. Pop took it as long as he could. He wanted to get away from them and saw his chance when he heard about a big shipment coming in from those two islands off Newfoundland."

"St. Pierre and Miquelon." Luke had made sketches of each of their five lighthouses. One of his cherished dreams was to visit them once he'd moved to Montauk.

"Why am I not surprised you know their names?" Tony chuckled. "Must be them books you've always got your nose stuck in. Anyway, Pop struck a deal with Schultz. Handle this one shipment and he'd be free. Christ Almighty, you should have seen it. Wine, Champagne, all kinds of Canadian whiskey and rye. Boatloads of it. More than Pop and his crew could manage, so we trooped up to Montauk pretending to be on vacation."

Pretending?

Had he spent the last fifteen years drawing and redrawing the beach, the bonfire, and the lighthouse until he'd shaped that vacation into the fantasy he wanted? So much for a photographic memory.

"Oh, brother, what a week," Tony continued. "Unloading booze from the boats. Sticking it in the hidden compartments. Trucking to Sag Harbor, Amagansett, East Hampton, Oyster Bay. I lost track of how many bottles we moved. Thousands, there were. Do you remember that huge bonfire?"

Tony had no idea of the sketches stacked under Luke's bed in Brooklyn. Why would he? Luke had only ever showed them to Wilda. "I do."

"We were stuck with a mountain of hooch crates, so we threw a beach party and built a fire to get rid of the evidence."

Luke didn't know how much more he could take. He needed time alone. And space. Lots of space to put these pieces together. And to read Wilda's letter. It still sat there, radiating Le Jade. They were passing the old soldiers home now. He needed to hang on for another half-hour without blowing a gasket.

Tony started laughing.

"What's so funny?"

"The Feds came sniffing around. You know Pop, the original Mister Smooth Talker. He fed 'em some line about you breaking up those crates for pocket money, but you didn't think you could do it by yourself. Bingo! Those bozos helped you break up Dutch Schultz's bootleg crates. Ha! Did we ever have a good laugh after they left."

Luke could picture those two men in their dark suits and Panama hats as clearly as he could see Wilda's letter. They'd both worn mustaches, but the older one shouldn't have. His was a meager effort compared to the luxuriance of his partner's Victorian handlebar.

His shoulders sagged. His precious memory, the life raft he'd held onto during a lonesome childhood, had been nothing but a ruse to fool the authorities. Luke doubted he'd get any sleep that night.

"Where did you say the mustering station is?"

Tony produced his orders. "Next to University High School."

They swung onto Barrington. University High was only a block or two away. Time enough for just one question. "This Osterhaus guy. Why did he make trouble?"

Tony tapped Wilda's letter. "This explains."

Luke turned it over. The envelope was unsealed. This was more like it. Shameless Tony. Tactless Tony. Inconsiderate Tony who thought nothing of reading someone else's mail. "You read it?"

"Yeah, but kinda by accident."

A small building on the corner of the campus rolled into view. A two-foot-high banner hung across the front.

U.S. MARINE CORPS – SEMPER FI – MUSTER HERE

Luke swerved the car toward a vacant stretch of curb and pounded the brake pedal. "How do you accidentally read a letter?"

"Okay, look. The envelope was sealed, but it was hot in that train and the glue gave out. It's a long ride from Chicago. I got bored. And curious. You've always been like a secretive monk, sitting up there in your room by yourself."

Luke didn't know what to say. Or, if he started, he didn't know if he could stop. It was coming up to eleven o'clock, the mustering station was half a block away, and he had a letter to read. This wasn't the time to walk through the door Tony had just opened.

"Lookit," Tony continued, "if it makes you feel any better, I wish I hadn't. I thought the old broad was just going to write 'I went for clams at Lundy's' and 'I'd kill Eleanor Roosevelt for a new pair of nylons.' If I'd known she'd written to you about . . ." He abandoned the rest of his sentence in favor of a whimper of frustration. "Anyway, thanks for the ride."

About what? Luke kept his eyes on Wilda's angular handwriting. "Sure thing."

Tony pulled his duffel bag from the back seat. "I've got a day's shore leave tomorrow before we sail on Tuesday. I don't suppose you could—it's okay if you can't—but I thought I'd ask—if—maybe—" Luke had never heard his brother sound so timid, so sheepish. "What are the chances I could get a tour of your movie studio?"

If he'd had the presence of mind to fob Tony off with a reasonable excuse, he probably would have, but his brain swirled with questions he had no answers to.

"Sure," he said. "I don't have enough gas rations to pick you up, so you'll need to take the bus. Remember that big building we passed, the one with the gold front? It'll drop you on the corner. I'll meet you there at ten."

Bogie had mentioned the Bow and Arrow while driving home one particularly late night. "It's got the lowest lighting in Santa Monica, which is what you want when you're on a bender that could put W.C. Fields under the table."

The waiter told him they only served liquor in the Bow Room and jacked a thumb to the right, giving him a look that said *If you're drinking at eleven on a Sunday morning, maybe you shouldn't go in.*

Luke wasn't determined to tank himself into oblivion, but if Tony wished he hadn't read Wilda's final words to him, then Luke needed to read them with at least one hit under his belt. Probably more.

The Bow Room had a six-stool bar along one wall, and four booths along the other. Luke ordered a whiskey, any brand, on the rocks, make it a double.

Jack Daniel's seared his throat. The lowball glass hit the wood with a blunt crack. The bartender asked if he wanted another. Luke nodded and headed for the corner booth.

Dearest Luke,

This is a letter I've wanted to write for quite some time. In a way, I've waited your whole life. And now, finally, I can.

No doubt, you'll have discovered that the falcon was hollow, and that hidden inside it was your birth certificate. Are you mad at me for not telling you? If I could have, I would have. But I had promised to keep this information to myself, and I'm a woman of my word. However, that old buzzard has drawn his final, rasping breath, which means all bets are off.

Okay, so here we go:

Your father had himself a grand time keeping out of harm's way by building temporary hospitals during the Great War. When his troop ship arrived in New York a day early, he wasn't ready to return to the wife and kids. He and his buddies went on one last hurrah in some dive in Greenwich Village. That's where he met a nice girl who said yes when he suggested they get a hotel room. In the morning he caught the subway to Brooklyn and got on with his life.

Nine months later an angry man stormed into your father's office and plopped a picnic basket on his desk. He said his name was Boris Osterhaus, that he was the girl's father, that she'd fallen pregnant, had had the baby, but died in childbirth. He said, "Here you go, you over-sexed, irresponsible doughboy. This bastard is your responsibility." Or words to that effect. You get the gist, I'm sure.

There was a second page, but Luke couldn't take much more. Tony's revelations—rumrunning, bonfires, the Montauk vacation —had assailed him like a plague of locusts. And now this. He was an actual, real-life, honest-to-God bastard?

The bartender delivered the second double Jack Daniel's without comment. Luke ran his finger around the rim of the lowball.

Wilda's disclosures explained an awful lot. Why he'd never felt like a member of the family. Why his parents had seldom made much time for him. Especially his mother.

Sara Valenti wasn't his mother. She was the woman who had been forced to raise her husband's accidental child. She had swallowed her pride and done the right thing. Washed his sheets, cooked his dinner, darned his socks. But don't expect her to like the little brat. Or kiss him on the head. Or make a fuss over his straight A's. Or ask him along to the baseball season opening game at Ebbets Field.

Another slug of Jack. The dimly lit walls of the Bow and Arrow bar were closing in on him now. The air had grown thick and moist. Luke took a deep breath, but it didn't help. He had a whole other page to slog through. This wasn't the place to read it. He needed to feel sun on his face, wind in his hair, to hear seagulls squawking and smell the brackish seaweed.

He threw a couple of dollar bills at the bartender and charged out into the daylight. Twenty-six blocks was too far to walk. He jumped into Bogie's car and roared down Santa Monica Boulevard. A free parking spot opened up near the pier. Five minutes later he was shoeless, feeling the damp sand squelch between his toes.

You remember my poster of The Four Blooms? Your mother was one of them. Her name was Lily Osterhaus. I was boon companions with her mother, Edwina, and I was there when Lily first showed us she could sing. A natural! When she started performing with Violet, Jasmine, and Rose, I submitted them for the Coney Island talent contest that sent them on the vaudeville circuit.

Boris wasn't impressed by any of this nonsense (his word, not mine). But Lily was a headstrong girl, and he gave in when I agreed to be their chaperone. I suppose it was only natural that she conscript me into being the sacrificial lamb, tasked with telling her father that she was pregnant and the circumstances that led to it. Boris hit the roof and forced her into agreeing to put the baby up for adoption at the Livingston Street Foundling Home. It was the only feasible course of action. However, everything changed when poor Lily died.

Luke looked away from Wilda's spindly handwriting. A pair of towheaded boys were building a sandcastle in the shallows. They had built it too close to the shoreline, so the waves kept flooding it. They laughed every time it happened. Maybe that was part of the fun. But watching them provoked a memory from an afternoon he'd almost forgotten.

His mother had appeared at his bedroom door one Saturday and told him they were going to spend the afternoon at Brighton Beach and to put on his bathing suit. Mystified—nothing like this had ever happened before—he did as instructed. She had driven to the beach in silence. "Now, go and build a sandcastle or something." She had issued the instructions like they were a punishment for a misdeed he couldn't remember committing. He'd been proud of his first attempt, but her only comment had been "Time for a hotdog."

Had that odd day trip been at Pop's insistence? Or had Mom lost a bet, and taking the bastard child to the beach had been her penalty?

After Lily died, Boris went from angry to vengeful. I never figured out how he tracked your father down. Private eye, I suppose. Just like Sam Spade! To your father's credit, he didn't shirk his responsibility. After Enzo took you (and Sara too—let's face it, that can't have been easy), Boris and I came to an agreement that I would keep an eye on you. I lived in Brooklyn, so it made sense. I reported in every now and then, and in return, Boris paid me a generous monthly allowance. How do you think I've been able to afford the rent on my fabulous apartment all these years? But he swore me to secrecy lest Lily's disgrace get out among New York society. And by "secrecy" I mean a contract, with lawyers and witnesses and everything. If I ever blabbed, he could sue me for breach of confidentiality. And trust me, Boris Osterhaus was not someone you wanted to double-cross. Ever. He was that sort of man. Awful, awful, awful.

. . .

The question of Wilda's Prospect Park apartment had niggled at Luke for years. He had concluded that one or two especially appreciative gentlemen callers showed their admiration via their pocketbook. How else could a piano teacher afford that rent, French champagne, theater tickets, and dazzling wardrobe?

You were an adorable child. My darling Lily's little boy! But even from afar I could see you were lonely. I knew what Enzo was up to with the bootleg, and I suspected that something was happening in Montauk. Since when did that family take a vacation? And if they did, let's be honest, aren't they more the Atlantic City types? You took to me straightaway. Quite honestly, I think they were relieved. Sara might have guessed the full story, but she never let on. Nobody showed any surprise when I started insinuating myself into your life. Nor did they stop me. I want you to know that as time went on, I felt more and more guilty about not telling you the truth.

I didn't blame Lily's mother for turning to booze. She was a hopeless drunk, in and out of sanatoriums. Lily's death tipped her over the edge, leaving you with no one but me. But the contract Boris drew up prevented me from even so much as breathing a word to you. Even after his death. It was all so intimidating. But when he died, I couldn't stand it anymore. It wasn't fair. You deserve to know who you are and where you came from. So I decided that while I couldn't TELL you the truth, I could LEAD you to it. That's when the whole thing with the Maltese falcon came up. It seems so far-fetched and convoluted, but Boris's killer-hawk New York lawyers would have been on me like a shot otherwise. So I sent you off to Los Angeles and to your Uncle Avery, hoping you would put two and two together. I can't tell you what a tonic it's been for me to get this off my chest. I'm positively drained, so now I need to lay myself down for a nap and will finish after lunch.

. . .

Was that the nap Wilda had never woken up from? Had this letter to him been the very last thing she'd done in her life? He was willing to bet it was. So, in a way, he had been there with her at the very end, after all.

The heat of tears stung behind Luke's eyes. Pressing his palms to his face didn't work. Tears trickled down the insides of his wrists, past the cuffs of his shirt, and all the way to his elbows.

* * *

Bogie looked up from Wilda's letter. "Holy cow."

Luke had been pacing in front of the fireplace while Bogie read. He noticed a patch of sand still clinging to his sleeve and brushed it into the hearth. "My life now makes more sense than it ever has before."

Bogie crossed to the bar and unscrewed the top of a fresh bottle of Four Roses. "In a funny way, I think you're lucky." They clinked glasses and each took a sip. That familiar burn down Luke's throat felt more of a comfort than it had in Santa Monica. "I never felt close to my folks, either," Bogie said. "But you just got handed an explanation you can wave around and say, '*This* is the reason I've felt like an outcast.'"

Back on the sofa, Luke rested his head on the floral chintz. "I don't feel lucky. Wilda was the only person who took an interest in me, and now she's gone. My mother died giving birth. And my grandfather, this Boris Osterhaus, sounds like a heinous asshole."

"He may have been a son of a bitch, but forced your father to do the right thing, and then made sure someone kept an eye on you. All I had was myself, flailing about in the sea of life hoping to bump into a life raft."

Luke's limbs grew soft and rubbery. It may have been the booze, but more likely it was because Bogie had found the golden needle in this haystack of turmoil. And maybe the Four Roses helped.

"This brother of yours, am I going to meet him?"

"He asked for a tour of the studio. Can we get him on some sort of list?"

"We can do better than that." Bogie lit a cigarette and took a deep drag. "Let's put on a show."

28

*T*ony was waiting on the sidewalk, his uniform buttons gleaming in the California sunshine, when Luke pulled to the curb. He opened the passenger door and slid inside. "Punctual. I like that—" He swiveled a full one-eighty degrees when he detected the movie star obscured in a cloud of cigarette smoke in the back seat. "Holy cannoli!"

"Didn't your brother tell you he's my right-hand man?"

"He did, but—"

"You're a gunnery sergeant with the Marines. That's terrific."

"Gosh, Mr. Bogart, that sure is swell of you to say."

Luke could practically hear Tony's smile stretching ear to ear. "Bogie's a member of the Coast Guard. Goes out on patrol practically every weekend."

"It's just the auxiliary."

"Every bit helps, Mr. Bogart."

"Please, call me Bogie."

"Thanks—Bogie. So whatcha working on now?"

"A potboiler called *Casablanca*. Luke thinks it's an excellent picture."

"It is," Luke said.

"You ask a hundred guys to point out Casablanca on the map, how many of them would get it right?"

"Not me," Tony confessed.

Bogie chuckled. "Your brother here gave me a geography lesson. French Morocco. Spanish Morocco. Gibraltar. Marrakesh. Maybe he should direct it."

Luke and Tony sat near the camera when Nell approached them. She wasn't one for wearing lipstick, but she'd made an effort today. Perfume, too. And not just any perfume, but Evening in Paris, which he'd bought for her at Kress's with Beatrice's guidance. Luke's heart softened at the thought she'd made such an effort.

"Tony, this is Nell Davenport. She's our continuity girl." Luke leaned in more closely. "Also my girlfriend."

Tony's head whipped around.

That's right. I said 'girlfriend.' Be sure to put that into your letter home.

Nell sat down. "You've got good timing. We're filming a scene with most of the cast." She pointed to Peter Lorre. "Today's his last day on the movie."

Tony squinted at Lorre as though to say, *I think I recognize him in between necking in the back row of the Fox.*

Ingrid appeared, her snowy Scandinavian teeth gleaming in the lights. "What a smart uniform. You look very spiffy." She frowned. Luke could tell it was an act for the benefit of Tony's jaw, which had dropped below his stiff collar. "This is a proper English word, spiffy, yes?"

Tony bounced out of his chair. "It sure is, ma'am."

"Hello, I'm Ingrid Bergman."

Tony pumped her hand a little too enthusiastically.

"Take it easy," Luke said. "Ingrid's going to need that hand in a minute."

"Think nothing of it, soldier," Ingrid said. "Or are you a sailor?"

"Neither." Tony's chest swelled. "I'm a Marine."

The studio commissary was already more than half-full by the time Luke and Tony approached a center table with their pastrami sandwiches.

Tony pulled a paper napkin from the metal box. "So, the letter. You read it?"

"I did."

"I bet you got some questions."

"Only seven or eight . . . hundred."

Tony cocked his head back. "I never knew how funny you could be."

Luke had exaggerated, but not by much. He'd been awake all night, reading and rereading Wilda's letter until he felt as though she had fed him through the wringer at a Chinese laundry.

"Did you know about my beginnings?"

"Nope."

"What, so one day Mom wasn't pregnant and the next it's 'Hey everybody, I've had a baby'? Come on, it's not like you were in grade school."

"That was the year Mom was real sick. She spent months in bed. Doctor's orders."

This was news to Luke. "With what?"

"Women's stuff." Tony bit off a mouthful of pastrami. "They don't talk about it in front of guys. And anyway, I was busy humping every girl who stopped long enough for me to get my hands up her skirt, so don't bust my balls. Mostly I remember dinner was ho-hum for five months. Pop got some woman in to cook. She worked in the kitchens of that Methodist hospital way up on Sixth. She was okay, I guess, but she wasn't Italian, and she sure as hell couldn't cook like Mom. But we all got through it.

And when you came along, I figured it was on account of a tough pregnancy."

Luke nodded. "So nobody ever mentioned it?"

"What?"

"That I'm a—" The words 'love child' hardly fit. What was he, then? A 'sex child'? That was worse than 'bastard.' "—that I wasn't Mom and Pop's."

Tony put down his sandwich and wiped his hands on the napkin. "Swear to God, Luke. Nobody said nothin'. You looked like a Valenti. A little paler, now that I think about it, but that's all. Why would we question it? Maybe Sal figured it out, but back then Rico, Cal, and Vic wouldn't have known their keister from a French letter." He laid a hand on top of Luke's wrist. It was the first time Luke could recall his brother touching him. "It sure must have come as a shock. But what's done is done. What else do you want to know?"

"Montauk. Did it get Pop out from under Dutch Schultz?"

"Dutch's feud with Legs Diamond started heating up right afterward. Then the stock market crashed. Funny how things work out, ain't it? Because of the Schultz job, Pop had all this cash, so we were sitting pretty. When the Depression hit, he reinvented himself into a pillar of Italian Brooklyn."

"Is that why we turned our communal backyard into a vegetable garden?"

"Us Italians were lower than the Irish in the pecking order. Pop tried to change that. He worked so damn hard to put himself in the center of things, but after reading that letter, now I'm wondering if he wanted to prove to Osterhaus that he wasn't no two-bit bum. I lost sleep last night thinking about that name— Boris Osterhaus."

Tony had always struck Luke as the type to log eight straight hours of pillow time, no matter what was going on. "What about it?"

"Some years back, Dad and I were roofing an apartment

building near Amersfort Park. Out of the blue, he pointed to a house across the street and said it belonged to the provost of Brooklyn College. Yeah, like I knew what a provost was. And then he pulled out an article from the *Brooklyn Eagle*. It was a photo of a coupla stuffed shirts grinning like they was monkeys at the zoo. He said, 'That's the provost and that asshole is Boris Osterhaus.' I asked him why he was an asshole. Pop said, 'Because he got the provost to approve Luke's college scholarship, and I hate people who use inside influence.' He told me if I came across him, don't trust a word that comes out of his lying, crooked mouth."

"Did he ever mention Boris Osterhaus again?"

"Nope."

"So *this* is the Marine I keep hearing about."

Bette Davis was dressed in a floor-length gown of glistening white, her hair swept into a flattering up-do. She waved away Luke and Tony's efforts to stand.

"Bette," Luke said, "I'd like to introduce you to my brother, Tony."

"Ann Sheridan was right. You look spiffy in that uniform."

Tony swallowed a mouthful of sliced beef without chewing. "Ann Sheridan talked about me?"

"She got the 'spiffy' part from Ingrid. You shipping out soon?"

As Tony told her about how he was heading out the next day, Luke thought of his college years. They had been the happiest time of his life, but had he not won that full scholarship on his own merits?

"And tell me, Luke, how's *Casablanca*?" Bette asked.

Luke blinked away his mental tangent. "We're on our last week of filming."

"A good picture, you think?"

"I do. Bogie doesn't, though."

"As I recall, he thought *Dark Victory* was a stinker when we were making it, but look how well it turned out. You can never tell about these things. Oh, and I was sorry to hear about that dreadful fire. Is it true you lost everything?"

"Lucky for me, Bogie and I are the same size. I've inherited his castoffs."

"And how nicely they suit you, too." She clasped her hands together. "I must get back to Stage Five. I have an afternoon of emoting to do." She swept away from the table.

"I ain't seen any of her pictures," Tony said, his eyes still on her, "but the thought of Bette Davis stopping to say hello—wow."

"That's how I feel working here every day."

"It's great you found a home."

"I'm only staying in Bogie's guest room until I find some new digs," Luke said. "Housing in L.A. is getting tougher and tougher to find, so it might take a while. Anywhere'll do; I'm just here for the duration." Tony shook his head, like he wasn't buying a word Luke was saying. "I've got it all planned. I'm going to apply to the lighthouse training program. I want to become the lighthouse keeper. Preferably at Montauk. That's where my real home is."

Once upon a time, the name 'Montauk' had represented everything he wanted. It had kept him surefooted when the path ahead became shrouded in a fog of uncertainty. But now it sounded like a word from a foreign language he didn't speak.

"I'm not talking about Bogart's guest room, you little twerp." He traced an outstretched finger in a wide circle. "I mean here."

"The commissary?"

"Jesus! And I thought you were the family genius. This studio, your job, that girlfriend, the whole kit and caboodle. You're a different person here."

"Different how?"

"You're like those flowers that close up real tight in the winter, waiting for warmer weather so that they can relax their petals and open up."

This observation was poetic for someone who had never

displayed the slightest lyrical leaning. "You're saying Brooklyn is the winter and I'm a summer flower?"

"Even I can tell that, and I'm pretty thick sometimes." His smile fell from his face. "I gotta say, Luke, I'm kinda jealous."

"Of what?"

"You."

The innards of Luke's sandwich slipped from between his fingers. "Why on earth—?"

"You escaped being press-ganged into the Great Valenti Plan. Five boys, each with our own house on the compound, and with a specialty skill contributing to the family business. Our lives were mapped out. We had no choice. Maybe Sal and Rico and Cal and Vic are okay with it. Not me. Pop isn't someone you want to disappoint, though."

"But you're such a good carpenter," Luke said. "I'm the one who should be jealous."

"Don't be." Tony spat the words out like they were chunks of rotted pastrami.

"If the choice had been yours, what would you have become?"

"You'll only laugh."

"I won't."

"You will."

"I promise."

"Hairdresser."

Luke was too shocked to laugh. If he'd written out a list of guesses, 'hairdresser' wouldn't have made the top one thousand.

"I'm good with my hands, sure, but shaving wood isn't what I wanted to do with them."

"Is that why your wife's hair always looks so good?"

A coy warmth returned to Tony's smile. "Audrey's the only other person I've ever told."

"She's lucky to have you." They were five words Luke never thought he'd ever say to this brother sitting in front of him.

"You're the lucky one," Tony said. "You got to do whatever you wanted, and deep down I've always been jealous. I think that's why I drank so much. Drown my frustration."

"Gee, Tony, I had no idea."

He feigned a casual shrug and took a bite out of his pickle. "How could you?"

"Is this why you're not in the Army? Joining the Marines—is it a giant 'Fuck you' to Pop?"

A cheeky grin lit up his brother's face. "You *are* smart. Oh, and get this: Ever since I enlisted, my bottomless thirst has started to dry up. Go figure. Marching off to war might be the best thing that ever happened to me."

"I'm happy for you."

"Makes me kind of wish that you could have the same experience. Getting 4-F'd . . . That had to hurt."

"It did," Luke admitted, "but the good news is that it may get reversed. I know someone who knows someone in the Navy."

"Navy, huh? That'll stick in Pop's craw."

"I thought he'd be pleased. He took my 4-F real hard."

Tony planted his elbows on the table and leaned in. "That's because he took your rejection real personal. Like the military was rejecting *him*. He didn't think about how you felt. So, if you chase after this shot because you think it'll set things right in Pop's eyes, that's fine. It probably will. But now I see that you're a constant reminder of that time he screwed up. You can't do nothin' about it, and you sure as hell don't owe him nothin'. But if you go after it, do it because *you* want to feel good about doing your bit for the war. You got that?"

Tony grabbed his fork like it was a bayonet. He pushed strands of pastrami around his plate and forced out his breath in brief spurts. Luke didn't know his brother very well, but he could tell some sort of confession was looming. Whatever it was, maybe it was too formidable to admit face to face.

"You want to take a walk?"

Tony screwed his paper napkin into a ball and jumped up from the table.

Luke pointed to the right. "See those brownstones? That's where James Cagney, and Edward G. Robinson, and the Dead End Kids pretend to be in New York. Realistic, aren't they?"

Tony had been silent since they had left the commissary, so Luke doubted he was taking in any of the details on the backlot.

"Let's sit down." Tony slipped the garrison cap off his head and sat on the nearest stoop. "I probably shouldn't tell you this. In fact, I know I shouldn't. But I need to." He rolled the cap into a tight ball. "I'm headed to the Solomon Islands. They're down near Australia somewheres."

The Solomons were smack dab in the middle of nowhere. Didn't that put Tony *out* of harm's way? What was the big deal about heading for some backwater? Luke studied his brother more closely. He had seen triumph, hostility, fearlessness, grit, and gumption in his brothers' faces. But not fear. Never fear. But he saw it now, slathered on thick as marzipan.

"They never let you know where they're shipping you. I have this buddy, though. He's in deployment. Told me on the Q.T."

"Dangerous?"

The pall of silence over them grew as heavy as the concrete beneath their feet. "I just wanted someone to know. Guadalcanal. You might hear it on the radio."

"I'll be listening."

Barbary Coast showgirls—a parade of bold stripes, ruffled petticoats, and sparkling corsets—passed by. They were probably the last pretty faces Tony would see for some time; Luke hoped he was drinking them in.

"Listen," Tony leaned in closer, his voice hoarse with intensity. "That letter, I'm guessing it's stirred up all kinds of hurt and misery. Understandable. But nothing's going to change the past. If you want my advice—not that you asked for it, but here it is."

Brute strength had always been his brothers' strong suit. Throwing the first punch was where they shone. This Brooklyn-winter-summer-flower analogy coming from the least poetic brother in the bunch almost made Luke's head spin. And now he was going to hand out some advice? Luke braced himself.

"You've found your home, Luke," Tony said, "and it's here. *This* is your place. Whatever it is you want to do with your life, go out and do it. Whatever you want to get out of life, go out and get it."

29

*L*uke took a towel from the white-blond Scandinavian man behind the front desk of the Finlandia Baths and followed Bogie and Peter Lorre into the locker room. "What do we do, exactly?"

Bogie kicked off his scruffy brogues. "Sit in the steam room."

"And do what?"

"Nothing!" the two actors chorused.

"That's the beauty of this place," Bogie said. "No clanging telephones, no nagging wives, no directors wanting a forty-third take, no interviews with Louella or Hedda—or worse, *Modern Screen.*"

Lorre let his trousers drop to his ankles, revealing a pair of notably hairy legs. "'Humphrey Bogart's Fight for Happiness.'"

"'Fifteen Ways to Peter Lorre's Heart.'" Bogie pointed to the tiled floor. "This is where we leave that malarkey behind. Just sit and chat with your pals. Or don't. Unless you bump into Bing."

"Crosby?" Luke asked.

"He and his brother own the building. With these tiles, he loves the acoustics."

Lorre wrapped a towel around his middle. "You've never been to one of these places?"

Valenti Construction worked six days a week. Seven, if winter was coming. Nobody could spare the time to sit around and shoot the breeze. But Luke had information to dig for and didn't want to risk offending the two men most likely to tell him what he wanted to know. "If a place like this exists in Brooklyn, nobody's mentioned it to me."

Lorre opened a wooden door with a tiny window; a cloud of menthol-scented steam ballooned out. The wood-paneled room had seating on three sides. Luke breathed in deeply. Every orifice in his body felt like it had yawned for the first time in years. He bent forward and put his face between his knees, ignoring the good-natured chuckling next to him.

"I gotta ask, boyo." Bogie said. "Did something happen when your brother blew through town?"

Luke had needed a chance to digest those how-did-I-not-know revelations, each one hefty enough to knock Maxie Rosenbloom to his knees. By the time Luke had dropped Tony off in Santa Monica, he felt like he'd gone ten rounds with Joe Lewis. Fortunately, Bogie was more sensitive than the public would ever have guessed. He had given Luke a few days to sort through it all.

"Tony made an interesting observation."

Bogie fanned the steam from his face. "Yeah?"

Luke sat upright. "I was talking to him about going home to Brooklyn after the war and picking up where I left off."

"The lighthouse keeper plan?"

"He said to me, no, you're already home. You've found your place, and this is it."

Lorre turned to Bogie. "Ten bucks. Cash only. No checks."

Bogie chuckled. "Damn! With only three days to go."

"Why do I feel like I'm part of a bet?" Luke asked them.

Bogie wiped away the thick layer of sweat coating his brow. "When we first met, you were like some pale, scared little rabbit."

"Scared little rabbits don't yell at you like I did."

"Scared, but feisty. I liked that. But since then, I've seen you flourish into the California Promise."

Heat bloomed across Luke's face. All this menthol was making him woozy. "The what?"

"Here's the thing they don't tell you. California has this—" Bogie drew his hands toward his chest "—magnetic pull. Not for everyone, mind you, but certain people. I call them 'true Californians.' They think they're coming west to build a better life. And they are, but not for the reasons they believe. They come here to figure out who they really are."

"You don't choose California," Lorre added. "It chooses you."

"It's California's gift. The opportunity to become who you were meant to be. I've been here a decade and feel like I've only just now found my feet. Count yourself as one of the lucky ones."

Lucky? *Lucky?* Losing everything in a fire didn't sound so lucky to Luke. Nor did learning he was the result of a hotel-room fling. This "California chooses you" business sounded like claptrap to him. Maybe he'd change his mind later when he'd had time to think about it—Bogie and Lorre looked deadly serious—but coming on top of everything else, he didn't have enough room in the jumble sale of his brain to deal with it.

"What kind of promise did California make to Hell O'Farrell?"

Bogie leaned against the tile wall. "Why are you asking about him?"

"That day Ingrid was late to the set, I overheard Hell bawling his son out. Gus was supposed to ingratiate himself with you so that he could ride on your coattails now that you're scaling the heights of stardom."

Bogie frowned. "Oh, he was, was he?"

"Hell told Gus my attack outside Romanoff's was the sort of caper he should come up with if he wanted to—and I quote—'remove enemies from his path.'"

"Jiminy Christmas!" Lorre unhooked a large wooden ladle off the wall. He dipped it into a bucket of water and splashed its contents onto the mound of heated rocks. The steam sizzled as it gushed to the ceiling.

Sweat was now pouring off Luke like Niagara Falls. He wasn't sure how much more he could take. "Having somebody out to get you—is that part of the California Promise too?"

"The California Promise is one thing," Bogie said. "The Hollywood Promise is another. It promises there's someone gunning for what you want or what you have."

"Any advice?"

The two men sat in silence. The longer they took to answer, the lower Luke's hopes fell, until Bogie said, "Hollywood is a small town where everybody knows everybody else's business. You've got to play it smart, and that means keep your friends close, and your enemies closer."

Luke stood up. He needed to get out of here before he passed out. He'd been hoping for more personalized advice, but he could see now he wasn't going to get it.

"Can't stand the heat?" Lorre asked.

Luke shook off the sweat oozing down his arms. "I have a date with two girls."

"And that," Lorre said, with a laugh, "is the Los Angeles Promise."

* * *

Luke and Nell took the last seats at the end of the J.J. Newberry lunch counter.

Nell asked, "How come we're meeting here when she works next door at Kress's?"

"Her postcard said to order her a root beer and French fries on the dot of six." He signaled the waitress. They had finished placing their order when Beatrice came flying along the counter seating.

"It's so good to see you!" She pressed her cheek against his, then elbowed past him to squeeze Nell's hand. "I sure do miss our boarding house dinners, catching up with everyone. Now we're scattered to the winds. Oh, and before I forget, I bumped into Sabine on the dance floor at the Palladium. I was there with Keaton, and she was cha-cha-ing with some tall, dark, and handsome Army officer."

Keaton? Was that Captain Stamina's first name? If it was, this might be the neat segue Luke was looking for.

The waitress set down their root beers and told them the French fries wouldn't be long.

"So," Luke said, "I take it you found someplace to live?"

"Yes, oh yes!" Beatrice's eyes widened. "It was the most amazing thing. I didn't catch Keaton that night I rang from Western Union. Not that I expected to. He's a hard one to pin down. So I slept on the sofa in my boss's office for a couple of nights. But then I finally did speak with him. And when I told him about the fire, he cut me off, mid-word, and said 'I love you!' Blurted it out. Ain't that something?"

"What did you say?"

"I stood there, saying nothing like a dummy, and he kept telling me how much he cares for me, and how distraught he'd have been if anything had happened to me. And then he says, 'What do you need?' I managed to stammer that I'd lost everything, including the roof over my head. He told me to call back in an hour. So I did, and by that time he'd found me a lovely place over near Paramount."

"So everything worked out?" Nell exclaimed.

"Yes, yes, it did. But lately I've been thinking about joining the WACS. Or maybe the WAVES. I can't decide, and I want to know what you guys think."

"They're both fine organizations," Luke said, "but Keaton's with the Navy, so I'm sure he'd prefer you join their female corps. He'd probably be offended if you didn't join the WAVES."

Beatrice wrinkled her nose. "I haven't brought it up with him."

"Why not?"

"I doubt he'd approve."

"It's not his place to approve or disapprove," Nell said. "You're not married—are you?!"

"No, but we're in love. He found that gorgeous little apartment, and," she added sheepishly, "he does pay my rent."

Nell crossed her arms and jutted out her chin a little. "He's generous, I'll give him that, but isn't this your call?"

She shifted in her chair and gazed across the five-and-dime for a moment, then turned to Luke. "He asked about you the other day."

Luke ran his finger along his section of lunch counter, nonchalant as a day at the beach. "What about me?"

"He wanted to know the sort of person you are. I wasn't sure why he was asking, so I hope I said the right thing."

"What are the chances of you getting him and me into a room together?"

She narrowed her eyes theatrically. "Whatever for?"

"That night at Romanoff's, he indicated that he might get my 4-F changed."

"You never mentioned that. Neither did he." Beatrice tapped her chin. "We need to make that happen." Luke felt like Fred Astaire-ing an extravagant tap number on the striped linoleum. "He travels all over the West Coast. Leave it with me and I'll see what I can do."

The waitress arrived with their fries. As Luke leaned across to grab a ketchup bottle from the adjoining place setting, he spotted an abandoned *Examiner*. The headline read: *MARINES LAND IN SOLOMON ISLANDS*. A map in the center of the page featured the main island's name: *Guadalcanal*.

The article detailed how the 1st Marine Division had captured a Japanese-built airfield and speculated that holding the ground would be difficult in the face of an enemy land-sea-air onslaught. U.S. forces were going to send thousands of troops into a vicious, drawn-out battle that was likely to experience high casualties.

Tony had known what he was heading into—and that he might not come back. He could've posted Wilda's letter to the Warner studio. Or thrown it away. But instead, he'd sent that telegram. He'd wanted to see a member of his family one last time.

Unnerved and distracted, Luke returned to their shared patch of countertop. Beatrice's face had hardened. "What did I miss?"

She shredded the corner of her paper napkin. "Nothing."

Nell whispered, "Gus and his flunkies just walked in."

"The big guy with the crew cut?" Beatrice kept her eyes on the scraps of paper piling under her fingertips. "He told me his name was Dwayne."

"You know him?" Luke asked.

"That's one way of putting it."

"Why are you acting weird? You haven't slept with him, have you?"

"Not voluntarily."

Nell clamped her hand on Beatrice's wrist. "He forced himself?"

"No, no, nothing like that." She swept the shreds into the ashtray. "I need a decent hat. Let's walk up to The Broadway department store. They have a nicer range."

They headed out and began walking. Beatrice kept mum until they'd put a full city block between them and Gus. "Like every other girl out here, I came to L.A. looking for fame. Big surprise, I got nowhere. When I ran out of money, I found work as a taxi dancer."

Luke and Nell locked eyes. *Where is this leading?*

"It was nice enough as those joints go. But the place went out of business because the accountant was fiddling the books. The more experienced girls got snapped up, but not me. I had a lean couple of months until I bumped into a friend and she asked if I wanted a job. It wasn't until I got there that I realized it was—" she paused until a trio of petty officers had passed them by, then whispered "—a brothel! Naturally, I can't tell Keaton any of this."

"Oh, honey," Nell said, "you don't have to tell us if you don't—"

"I need to get this off my chest." She hooked them by the elbows and railroaded them along the sidewalk. "It was classy in an old-money kind of way. Madame Lucille offered me four times what I'd been making. I figured what the hell? There are only so many rice-and-beans dinners a girl can eat. And she promised me I could quit any time because she didn't want anyone to be there involuntarily, so I took the job."

"Not under your real name, I hope." Nell said.

"God, no!" Beatrice giggled. "I went by Bianca. I figured it sounded like a hooker with a heart of gold."

"It does at that."

"And guess who was a regular."

Luke ran through a roll call of likely candidates: Gable? Welles? Fonda? Cooper? He moved on to other possibilities. The chief of police? The mayor? MacArthur?

Nell slugged him in the chest. "She's talking about Gus, you nitwit."

Mister Big Man on Campus? Went to a brothel?

"As a matter of fact," Beatrice said, "Dwayne was quite sweet in the sack. Which is more than I can say for his father."

"HIS FATHER?" Luke prodded both girls into the empty doorway of a stationery store. "Skip *none* of the details."

"He was always liquored up, which the madam didn't like, but he was a big tipper. He had three favorites, so I paid him little mind—until the day they all called in sick with a stomach bug. Madame Lucille prevailed on me to substitute with the promise of a bonus over and above his tip. So, like a dummy, I said yes."

"Double the tips?" Nell asked. "Why did that make you a dummy?"

Beatrice's eyes wrinkled at the edges. "He was real nasty. Like he hated himself for wanting to do it, but hated how he hated himself, so he took it out on the girl."

"Rough stuff?" Luke asked.

Beatrice nodded. "I earned a hundred bucks that night, but I don't know how his regular girls put up with him. On the bright side, most guys fill the whole half-hour, but that pig took less than ten minutes. And oh brother, was it ever the longest ten minutes I'd ever spent outside the dentist chair. But Dwayne? He took his time, nice and slow. The type who likes to think he knows how to make a girl feel good. So I made the right moaning and groaning sounds. 'Oh, baby, nobody does it like you. You really know how to please a girl.'"

Luke's stomach turned. "Did he fall for it?"

"It's why guys like them go to places like that."

They were almost at Vine Street now. War factory shift workers in overalls, dungarees, and flannel shirts, their hair pulled back in bandanas, were cooing at the perfume, makeup, and jewelry in the window display.

"Why did you stop working there?" Luke asked. "Had enough?"

"We got raided on Halloween. The joint opened again a few days later, but a week after that, it burned down. And you know what? My first thought was how Dwayne's father hates himself so much he probably called the vice squad. And when that didn't solve the problem, he torched it."

"No!" Nell gasped.

"That's extreme," Luke added.

"If you want to hear about extreme details, I can tell you what happened once I got into that room with Hell O'Farrell."

"No, thanks."

"You know what?" Nell said. "I wouldn't put anything past that egotistical jackass."

"Not that I have any proof." Beatrice shrugged dismissively. "I should thank him. I don't miss those night hours. I'm more of a daytime girl, so this Kress job suits me fine." She nodded at the store's front doors. "You coming in?"

Luke shook his head. "It's a long walk to Bogie's."

Nell took his hand in hers. "I'll walk with you part of the way."

They hugged their goodbyes and watched her disappear inside.

Nell spun around. "Can you believe what we just heard? Hookers, brothels, madams. My head is fairly spinning."

"But what a piece of work Hell O'Farrell turns out to be," Luke said. "Burning down a brothel because you hate yourself for going to hookers?"

They rounded the corner on Vine Street and headed south toward Sunset. The sidewalk was less crowded than Hollywood Boulevard. It was a relief to get some thinking space.

There was a time when Luke had thought Gus O'Farrell was the one he needed to be wary of.

Keep your friends close, and your enemies closer.

Hell O'Farrell, the brothel burner, was nobody Luke wanted to befriend. But Gus? He was a whole different animal. The sort who took the time to please girls. Maybe he could be a halfway-decent human being if someone gave him a chance.

The lights of the Satyr Book Shop next to the Brown Derby flickered to life. Only half the bulbs glowed, to keep in line with the dimout regulations, but they shone bright enough for Luke to see their display: *The Song of Bernadette*, *King's Row*, and *Mission to Moscow*. He had read none of them yet.

"Are we going in?"

Luke stared at his girlfriend's puzzled face. He hadn't told her about Wilda's letter or any of the information it had divulged. He'd needed time to redraw the lines around who he was and how he saw himself. Not to mention coming to grips with Lukas Osterhaus.

He stroked the back of Nell's hand. "I'm glad it's a warm August night."

"Why is that?"

"We're going to be walking for a while."

30

*L*uke tied the belt of Bogie's trench coat. The snap-brim fedora Orry-Kelly had supplied didn't fit, but it was close enough. *Casablanca* was days behind schedule and they were only now shooting the airport climax; nobody had time to be fussy.

Or maybe it wouldn't be the climax. The Epsteins had already come up with two versions: Ingrid departs with Paul Henreid, or she doesn't. Given the chaos of this shoot, it wouldn't have surprised Luke if they burst onto Stage One yelling "Hold everything! We've had a great idea for a whole new ending!"

Luke searched the floor for a chalk X. "Hey Jasper, where do I stand?"

"Depends on the fog."

"Fog? In the Sahara?"

Jasper jutted his jaw toward a Lockheed Electra airplane near the back wall. Midgets in overalls sat on the ground in front of it. "We have to camouflage the fact that the Lisbon plane is made of cardboard. Let's hope the good folks in Dubuque and Dallas won't know that the real Casablanca never sees a lick of fog." He wiggled the unlit roll-your-own cigarette dangling from his mouth. "If you're a smoker, sneak one in now. Our fog is vaporized oil. Once we fill the stage with it, we need to be mighty careful. You've got about twenty minutes. And could you check with Bogie how he plans on wearing that collar? Down is fine, but if it's up, those lapels will catch the lights. I need to adjust for that." He disappeared into the shadows.

Bogie sat at his table, hunched over a chessboard.

"You and Irving playing again?" Luke asked.

He kept his eyes on his pieces. "Who said we ever stopped?"

His dark tone threw Luke. He had been quiet on the morning drive to the studio, but not belligerent. "I haven't seen your board around much. I figured—"

"You figured wrong."

Luke caught sight of two sets of scripts laid out on the vacant chair. Mystery solved. "You want to run lines?"

"I've got it. Both goddamned, lousy versions."

"Need anything else—"

"I need you to keep people from bothering me," Bogie snapped. "Including you."

Luke was outside the dressing room before he realized he hadn't asked about the trench coat. If he went back in now, he'd get his head bitten off. Better to give Bogie ten minutes to cool off.

The set smelled faintly of oil, but they still had a ways to go if they wanted to fool moviegoers with their cardboard cutout. The midgets in the mechanics' overalls might not have caught Luke's attention had it not been for the shadow cast over the line of runway lights stretching behind the plane and out into the distance.

He suppressed a double-take when he saw Gus at the rear of the plane. Luke hadn't spotted him hanging around the *Casablanca* set since the day of that ugly confrontation outside the *Gentleman*

Jim stage. So what was he doing here now? Was it too paranoid to wonder if it had to do with that damned birth certificate? What would Captain Stamina make of an Italian father and a German mother? Luke hadn't heard from Beatrice. It had only been a few days, he'd told himself. These things take time. But still. It was hard not to worry.

Screw it. Why wait for Gus to pounce? Element of surprise and all that.

Luke cut a wide path around the airport hangar until he reached the grove of papier-mâché palm trees positioned near the entrance. He waited until Gus disappeared behind the airplane and made sure he was standing near the cardboard propellers at the same time Gus emerged.

"You don't work on this picture. You have no reason to be here."

Gus reared back. "What are you, the studio police?"

"I need to know what you plan on doing."

"With what? The certificate I found inside that falcon? Got you running scared, have I?"

"Of you?"

Gus pulled back his lips in scorn. "You should be."

"Your father, maybe," Luke threw back. "I've seen what he can do with a right hook." The fog was thickening. Luke wasn't sure his wisecrack had landed until Gus inhaled sharply.

"Listen, you pipsqueak nobody, you ain't in no position to order me around when I got—"

"LUKE!" Jasper's voice rang out from somewhere near the palm trees.

"Run along, Brooklyn," Gus said. "Somebody needs you to stand under a light. It must be satisfying to know you're an important cog in the war effort."

Luke was more skilled at landing insults than uppercuts, but he would have taken a crack at slugging Gus in the breadbasket had Jasper not been waiting for him. A parting shot would have to suffice. "You'll keep . . . *Dwayne*."

Luke would have given his next paycheck to see Gus's face, but Jasper was not someone to keep waiting. When he arrived at the palm trees, it was not Jasper he found standing there but Bogie. He held up the trench coat and helped Bogie into it.

"Listen, boyo, I owe you an apology."

The key lights above them switched on and off.

"Collar," Luke said, "up or down?"

Bogie hitched it up. "I behaved like a prick. You didn't deserve it."

"Who did, then?" Luke could see the answer in Bogie's eyes. "Has Mayo stabbed you again?"

"Nah. But we haven't been getting along so well."

"Worse than usual?"

"We save it for when you're out with Nell or after you've gone to bed."

"Sure beats duking it out at Mocambo." Bogie cracked a sliver of a smile, but Luke could see it took some effort. "Is it me? Am I getting underfoot?"

"I enjoy having you around." Luke breathed a little easier. Offering to move out was the right thing to do, but decent places to live were growing rarer than a virgin at Madame Lucille's. "Seeing my career gain traction cuts Mayo to the quick."

"If your wife can't be happy for your success, maybe you've got the wrong wife."

It was a brash statement, especially as they'd just managed to get back on even footing. But Bogie didn't seem to take offense.

"Was that Gus I saw you going toe to toe with?"

"We were having a little spat."

"Always play the long game."

Luke gave the collar a final adjustment. "Looks good."

"Remember, boyo, the short game is for the shortsighted."

* * *

Nell sighed. "It's millinery perfection."

Luke folded the leaflet he'd been reading for a late-August premiere of *The Pride of the Yankees* and subsequent celebrations at Ciro's, which was to be a fundraiser for Bette Davis and John Garfield's Hollywood Canteen project. "What is?"

She pointed to Bogie and Ingrid standing in front of the camera, the fake fog swirling around them. "Her hat. Simple, clean lines, just like her. Orry-Kelly outdid himself." She gestured to the leaflet. "Want to go?"

"How? It's not even Warners."

"I have a pal who works in Publicity for Sam Goldwyn. He could swing us a couple of tickets to the premiere."

Luke crossed his arms. "Do you have pals every-damned-where?"

"Pretty much. Do we have a date?"

What a kick it would be to walk past the multitudes in the bleachers to his first big, splashy Hollywood premiere.

An assistant called out, "Quiet, please. We're going to roll again."

It was the scene where Rick had a long speech in which he told Ilsa that she was getting on that airplane and leaving him behind in Casablanca. It included a line that Luke especially liked about always having Paris. Would he and Nell have a Paris someday? Santa Barbara and Palm Springs, perhaps. They were hardly the same thing, but he'd happily have either of them.

As Rick was giving Ilsa the brush-off, Luke caught sight of Gus skulking in the shadows to the far left. He waited until Bogie said his final line—"Here's looking at you, kid"—and Curtiz yelled, "Cut," then slid off his chair.

Resentment was etched into every line and corner of Gus's face. "What do *you* want?"

Luke held his palms up. "I come in peace." Calling him Dwayne had been a low blow. Luke knew that now. No player of the long game would have blundered like that. "I want you to go outside with me. Will you do that?"

Gus turned his head slowly, wariness replacing resentment.

Luke headed into the baking heat. Across the way, a group of extras in Nazi uniforms were sucking on last-minute cigarettes before heading into Stage Nine, where Errol Flynn was filming *Edge of Darkness*. He found a patch of shade and hoped Gus had followed him.

"Three minutes." Gus jammed his hands into his pants. The gaberdine stretched across the knuckles of his fists.

"I've got an offer for you."

"Don't make me laugh."

"How about I teach you how to read?"

Not a twitch, not a shudder, not a tremor. Luke had to hand it to the guy: he had mastered his poker face.

"I hate the thought of you missing out on the wonderful things that reading brings. I could help with that."

Gus extracted his hands from his pockets. They were still fists. Was he going to throw a punch?

"I didn't get deferred from the military because of the reading thing."

"I made a rotten assumption," Luke said as evenly as he could. "And now I'd like to make up for it."

He looked away to give Gus the space he needed to weigh up an offer he hadn't seen coming. On the other side of the alley, the Nazis crushed their cigarettes beneath the heels of their jackboots.

"How would it work?" Gus's question came out a faint squeak. "When would—what would—?"

"We could start right now."

"Here? In front of everybody?"

Two hundred yards farther down the end of the alley, extras in Air Force pilot uniforms exited the soundstage where Howard

Hawks was filming his new war picture. Luke pulled the *Pride of the Yankees* handbill from out of his pocket and held it up for Gus to see. "Let's start with this."

"All them words? I can't learn—"

"Just this one." Luke pointed to the name "Ciro's." "Five letters. 'C' as in 'certificate of the birth variety.' 'I' as in 'I'm starting to read.' 'R' as in 'Rum tastes good with Coca-Cola.' 'O' as in 'Oh my God, it's Rita Hayworth!' And 'S' as in 'Sunset Strip.' Put them all together and you have C-I-R-O-S."

Gus stared at the sheet of paper, his chin trembling. "The nightclub?"

"That wasn't so hard, was it?"

Gus's eyes took on a faraway sheen as he mouthed each letter again.

"How about twice a week we steal away to those old oak trees overlooking the river?"

"I've always felt like such a dunce."

"You'll be the only student in this class, so we can take it real slow."

"I couldn't catch on as fast as the other kids."

Gus couldn't bring himself to meet him in the eye, but that was okay. Luke could see the dots connecting like Christmas lights. "Your days of feeling like a dunce are over."

"Thanks."

"Tell me, though, if you couldn't read, how did you know what my birth certificate said?"

"I showed it to my dad."

31

*L*uke pointed the Packard into Bogie's parking space without having uttered a word on the drive from Horn Avenue. Over the three weeks since he had moved into the guest room, the air in the Bogart household had grown thicker with tension. It only eased during dinner, but Luke put that down to their multiple double whiskeys. That morning, Bogie had chain-smoked seven cigarettes in distracted silence.

Luke got out of the car and felt the sun's heat on his scalp. "Going to be another scorcher."

"What's that?"

"Never mind. Is there anything you want me to do today? I'm caught up on your fan mail."

Bogie slammed his door shut. "You might go to Costuming. Milo said he's collected some hats for *Action in the North Atlantic*. We don't start filming for a few weeks, so no rush." He disappeared into the soundstage, where Verita would already be set up with her array of hairpieces.

Luke headed for Costuming, figuring he could pinch some sketch paper. Orry-Kelly made sure his department got the good stuff.

The reception desk was unattended, so Luke let himself into the fitting room. Ingrid stood in front of the full-length mirror wearing a Spanish peasant blouse of dark calico and an unflattering skirt that looked like merchandise Beatrice might sell at Kress's.

"That doesn't look very Ilsa Lund."

She clapped her hands together, her face split by a wide, white smile. "I've had the most wonderful news. Sam Wood is disappointed in Vera Zorina's daily rushes in *For Whom the Bell Tolls*! Isn't that marvelous!"

"Disappointed enough to—?"

"Mr. Selznick talked him into giving me a screen test."

"You've got your chance!"

"All I wanted was the opportunity to prove I could do it." She raised her arms. "Will this work?"

"I assume you purposefully look like you just staggered out of a bombed-out stable."

"María barely survives her parents' execution before a mob of Falangists gang-rapes her."

"Okay, so *Flying Down to Rio* it's not." He pointed to her feet. "You're going to audition barefooted?"

"Not after I've spent fifteen minutes digging through the ugliest shoes in Christendom." Tristan stood at the door, a pair of dilapidated slippers in his hands. He presented them to her. "Looks shabby, doesn't she? This might be my best work yet." He looked like a proud mother sending her daughter off to the high school prom."

"Things are going well?" Luke asked.

"Anything Orry-Kelly throws me, I make sure I do it thoroughly, without complaint, and on time. We've formed a sickeningly sweet mutual admiration society. How are those shoes, darling? Fit okay?"

"A little tight, but they'll do."

"When is your audition?" Luke asked.

"Ten o'clock."

"That's less than an hour."

"It is? Oh, crumbs! Could you drive me there? They don't want Vera to know about me, so it's a couple of blocks away from Paramount at the old Metro lot on Cahuenga."

"I'd feel better asking Bogie's permission."

"It's vital we keep this a secret. I suppose I could call a cab, but with gas rationing they're hard to get these days."

Drive now and ask questions later. "Grab your handbag. With any luck, we'll be back before Bogie misses me."

* * *

The traffic lights at Hollywood and Vine turned red. "Is that your audition script?" Luke asked. "I've gotten pretty good at running lines."

Ingrid laid the pages in her hand onto her lap. "It's all so last-minute; they don't expect perfection."

The signal changed. Luke hit the gas. "But *you* do."

She let out a surprisingly girlish laugh. "Is that so dreadful?"

"I love that you want this role so badly you're willing to throw a costume together, hijack Bogie's car, and run right over here as though your life depends on it."

"Oh, but it does!"

"You love to work, don't you?"

"It's always made me feel like an oddity. That is, until a couple of weeks ago. Bette Davis invited me into her dressing room for tea. We talked about acting, mostly. She's the same way. I can't tell you how much better it made me feel about myself."

Luke turned right onto Fountain and wondered if Bogie was looking for him. He'd been so taciturn on the drive to work. Even more than usual.

Ingrid stared at a pair of women dressed in theater usher uniforms. "Mr. Selznick wanted me to change my name. He thought nobody could pronounce Ingrid *and* Bergman because it sounded too German, which of course meant too Nazi. He also thought it sounded too Jewish."

"Even Selznick can't have it both ways."

"He thought Berriman would be better. Or my married name, Lindstrom, to capitalize on Charles Lindbergh's popularity."

"Did you remind him that Lindbergh is a pro-Nazi mouthpiece for the America First movement?"

"Nobody tells Mr. Selznick what to think." Another laugh, shy and self-effacing. "I realized that to make it in this business, I have to hack my own way through the jungle."

Luke nodded. If the boarding house hadn't burned down, he could have knocked on Beatrice's door after her bed springs had stopped squeaking so that he could approach Captain Stamina himself. But nothing was easy or convenient anymore. The woman sitting beside him hadn't given up hope, and now she was minutes away from winning the role she desperately wanted. Everybody had their own jungle to hack through, didn't they?

Luke pointed to the left. "Can we drive onto the lot?"

"Mr. Selznick said it's just a facility of small soundstages for rent. Nobody cares who comes and goes."

By the time Luke had parked the Packard, Ingrid had transformed into a meek, young girl, unsure of herself. Her hands trembled as she smoothed her skirt. "Wish me luck."

"Luck, schmuck. You've got one task: make them see that they should have cast you in the first place."

After Ingrid disappeared into Stage Two, Luke sat in the car until the August sun started to roast him. It wasn't any cooler outside, but a nearby elm tree offered shade. He leaned against its trunk and took stock of where he was.

Not much of anywhere, really. Three ramshackle soundstages squeezed together, a low-slung administration building, a few sickly palm trees dotted around a parking lot. None of the cars were expensive or well-maintained. What a difference from Warner Bros., where every car sparkled. This place looked like the graveyard where has-beens' cars came to give up the ghost.

Except for one.

Luke left the shade of the elm tree. The closer he drew, the more certain he became that he'd seen this convertible Cord Phaeton before. He remembered the external exhaust pipes and the wraparound grille. It had been too dark to see the pop-up headlights, but those whitewall tires were hard to miss.

It sure was a sleek beast. Probably purred like a lion.

He reached in and ran his finger over the soft leather upholstery, warmed by the sun. A recent *L.A. Times* lay on the passenger seat, folded at an article about the proposed ban on searchlights and marquees. If the city adopted it, the final extravagant Hollywood premiere of the war would be for *The Pride of the Yankees*.

A memory broke through. Luke blinked in the bright sunshine and examined the Phaeton with fresh eyes.

The night of the fire. Luke was driving up Whitley Avenue. Fire engines and wailing sirens. The glow of flames against the dusk. As they approached the boarding house, a car barreled away in the opposite direction. Luke took the parking space it had left vacant. He could see it now, though. Careening past them. A white Cord Phaeton.

He retreated to the sheltering elm. Most of the Phaetons around L.A. were black. Or dark, at least. But white? He hadn't seen too many of them. And even fewer convertibles.

A door in the administration building jerked open. Luke ducked behind the tree. A thick-set bruiser in a Hawaiian shirt and a Panama hat dashed outside. He ran to the Phaeton, leapt over the driver's door and dropped into the seat. The engine roared to life before plunging into reverse. The driver cut a wide arc over the cracked asphalt and sped through the front gate.

Luke sprinted after him, reaching the sidewalk in time to watch the Phaeton hurtle up Cahuenga Boulevard, leaving a trail of exhaust in its wake. The guy was a reckless driver, but that hadn't surprised him at all: the man behind the wheel was Hell O'Farrell.

* * *

Luke rounded the corner of the Warners transportation garage holding the list he'd made while waiting for Ingrid. "I wasn't sure you'd be here."

Gus tossed away his half-smoked cigarette onto the L.A. river's concrete embankment. "Wasn't sure myself. Pop's working on that Errol Flynn picture, but he was real late getting to work today. I could tell what Mr. Milestone was thinking: 'We'll have to get Junior to do the stunt.' But right at the last minute, Pop ran in, throwing apologies around like confetti."

"Your father doesn't strike me as the apologetic type."

"He's not. But he was rattled something terrible."

"Over what?"

"He's not the explaining type, either." Gus pointed at the paper in Luke's hand. "Is that for me?"

"I thought we'd start with words you'd find familiar, so here's a list of Warner pictures. I figured you've seen them written in various places. On the screen, in magazines, maybe on production schedules."

Gus stared at the page. "I ain't much of a magazine reader, let alone production schedules."

Luke pointed to *The Old Maid*. Three words, three syllables.

"It's 'the,' isn't it?"

"You know more than you think. The next word starts with a vowel. A, e, i, o, u."

"O or u. They're the curved ones."

"Correct. So which one is it?"

"Is it o?"

"We have a winner!"

When Gus smiled, he looked like a five-year-old who'd won a spin-the-wheel prize at a beachside boardwalk.

"Moving on," Luke said. "The last letter of the second and third words is the same."

"B?"

"Close. It's a d, which is like a b written backward."

Luke had been absent from shooting all morning and doubted that he could push his luck by staying away half the afternoon, too. And besides, this process was a heavier slog than he'd imagined. They would not get through his list of twenty films today. After Gus had puzzled through *The Old Maid*, Luke skipped over *The Adventures of Robin Hood* and went to *Yankee Doodle Dandy*. After crawling through *Meet John Doe*, they had time for only one more. Luke pointed to *Confessions of a Nazi Spy*.

"Let's start with the last word first. It contains a letter that sometimes acts like a vowel." When Gus parsed 'spy,' Luke suggested he tackle the word next to it. "This one you must have seen, if only in the papers. It's in the headlines so much it's become another word for 'German.'"

Gus looked at the word, color draining from his face. "This one says 'Nazi'?" His eyes darted back and forth like crazed bumble bees. A lone coyote trotted along the southern bank. It jerked its head to look at them as though it had only just now discovered that it wasn't alone in the world.

When Gus spoke again, his voice was nearly a whisper. "My father thinks you're a Nazi spy." Luke laughed out loud. His astonishment evaporated when he saw Gus wasn't kidding. "It's my fault. I told him I'd heard you speaking Kraut on the *Casablanca* set, so he came to see for himself. There you were, gabbing away with Paul Henreid and Ingrid Bergman and Peter Lorre and a bunch of other people."

Luke knew which conversation he was referring to. The four of them, along with Conrad Veidt and a couple of Austrian exiles, Helmut Dantine and Ludwig Stössel, had been talking about the recent curfew that prevented enemy aliens from leaving their houses between eight at night and six the following morning.

"*Casablanca* is filled with European refugees," Luke said. "Are they all Nazi spies?"

"Pop doesn't trust any of them either. But you're American, so he thinks it's very suspicious. You're from New York, where the Friends of New Germany and the German-American Bund held that pro-Nazi rally in Madison Square Garden. Plus, you're pals with Bogart."

"So now Bogie's a Nazi spy, too? Come on, that's ludicrous."

Gus was starting to look like a punctured tire leaking air. "A few years ago, the FBI investigated Commies in the Screen Actors Guild. They listed a whole bunch of people—Bogie included. He cleared his name. But when you came along, Pop went digging."

"For what?"

"You heard of someone called Vance? First name Keith, maybe . . .?"

"Keaton Vance." Luke's mouth dried up; he forced down a swallow. "How did he come up?"

"Pop's real pally with Blayney Matthews, who used to work for the FBI before he became the studio fixer. Pop must have asked him to snoop around, because Blayney came to the house last week. I overheard them talking about that Vance guy."

"Does Blayney think Bogie's a Commie? Or that I'm a Nazi? Or both?"

"He's straight-up decent, far as I can tell. More of an 'innocent till proven guilty' type. But Pop's different. His M.O. is 'Everybody's out to get you.' When I showed him your birth certificate, I could almost see him thinking 'Ah-ha! I knew it!' Like one of those thought bubbles in the newspaper funnies."

Luke's right knee started jiggling of its own accord. "Is your father out to get me?"

Gus chewed on his lip longer than Luke would have liked. "How does that Vance guy fit in?"

Luke looked into Gus's eyes to see if he could detect any chicanery. Had Hell sent his son to dig around in the dirt? Was Luke the enemy *they* were keeping closer? Who exactly was the spy here?

Working in a movie studio full of actors and posers had trained Luke's eye to discern artifice. But when he looked at Gus, he saw only naked candor. Junior was here to learn how to read.

"Keaton Vance is a Navy captain who might get my 4-F reversed."

"Jeepers! Wouldn't that be tremendous?"

"Not if that birth certificate ruins my chances."

"This Vance guy, is he in intelligence?"

"He is. Why?"

Gus crossed his arms against his chest with a steely determination that Jimmy Cagney couldn't match. "Pop hates you for getting in my way. But if you went into the service, you'd be out of here. Problem solved. On the other hand, if you got to work in some secret job, he'd see that as you worming into the heart of the military, where you could do far more damage."

"Which could explain why he thinks I'm a spy." Even saying the words out loud—*he thinks I'm a spy*—sounded like a scene out of an absurd B-grade double-feature filler. Luke consulted his watch. "I ought to get back to work." They got to their feet, brushing the dirt from their trousers. "Is there any reason your father would be on the old Metro lot on Cahuenga?"

"One of his old Army buddies runs it. Why?"

"I saw him there today."

Gus squeezed his eyes closed and jerked his head away as though Luke had kicked him in the shins. "Oh, shit!"

"What?"

"He and Pop met at a meeting of the Hollywood Anti-Nazi League. They thought they were going to uncover a nest of American Nazis. I remember him being real disappointed."

"You think he's still looking for his Nazi spy?"

Gus nodded.

They headed toward the soundstages, where circus clowns and Norwegian fisherman mixed with typing pool girls heading back from their lunch break. As they approached Stage One, Gus asked Luke if he could have the list of movie titles for practice. As Luke handed it over, he searched O'Farrell junior once more for signs of treachery or subterfuge. But nope. Nothing. A stolid poker face was one thing, but this was like looking into the face of Baby Peggy.

Inside the soundstage, the crew was prepping to shoot the ending where Victor flies off to Lisbon alone. It was the guy-gets-the-girl ending that virtually every Hollywood movie fed its audience, but Luke felt it risked leaving them unsatisfied. Wouldn't it be more inspiring for each member of this romantic triangle to do what was right instead of striving only to please middle-aged housewives who wanted to see Humphrey Bogart walk off into the Saharan fog with Ingrid Bergman?

A studio runner sprinted past Luke. "Sir? Oh, sir!" He had raised his hands in the air like a half-crazed cheerleader.

"What is it, boy?" Curtiz asked.

"I have a message from the front office," the kid panted. "Mr. Wallis, he wants you to be extra careful."

"With what?"

"Everything. There's been a terrible accident on the set of *Edge of Darkness*. Hell O'Farrell. He fell off a bridge. Thirty feet. Straight down."

"Jesus!" Bogie said. "Is he dead?"

"No, sir, but he probably broke a leg and bruised a few ribs into the bargain. The studio doc tended to him while they waited for the ambulance. Said he'll be out of action for weeks."

Luke bit back a smile. Such excellent timing! If O'Farrell senior was going to be out of commission, that would give Beatrice a chance to get him together with Vance. But first he needed to secure that damned birth certificate.

32

*L*uke threaded his fingers behind his head and stared up at the guest room ceiling. Was Hell O'Farrell in agony right now? Was his leg bound in tight bandages? Did his ribs hurt like blazes every time he breathed? Or worse, sneezed. How glorious it would be if that bastard caught a summer cold.

Three sharp raps on the bedroom door interrupted his thoughts. Bogie walked in holding a Western Union envelope. "The sender paid extra for it to be delivered this early."

Luke thought of Tony charging onto the beaches of Guadalcanal. Tony's wife would get that telegram, wouldn't she? He ripped open the envelope and unfolded its contents.

CAPT STAMINA HARRY DINE HWOOD BLVD 8AM TODAY

Luke threw back the covers. "It's from Beatrice. 'Captain Stamina' is our nickname for Keaton Vance because he—let's just say he's very fit." Luke checked his watch. "I have less than an hour to get over there."

"Harry Dine? Menswear store next to the Egyptian? Open this early?"

"I doubt he'll be shopping for vicuña sports jackets." The heat of panic crawled across Luke's scalp as he faced Bogie. "I can't not be there."

"You will be. And so will I."

"But today's your last day on *Casablanca*."

"They're shooting atmosphere around the Blue Parrot. I won't be needed until later. Unlike Gable, Stewart, and Niven, I'm too old to serve in this melee, so I'm living vicariously through you. I know how much you want this, and if I can help you get there, then I will. Am I clear, swabbie?"

Luke saluted. "Sir! Yes, sir!"

"While you're in the shower, I'm going to pick out a suit and tie for you to wear—*and* I'll drive you to Hollywood Boulevard, where you're going to impress Captain Staying Power—"

"Stamina."

"—Captain Screw All Night until he begs you to join the Navy."

Office clerks, factory workers, mothers with strollers, sailors and soldiers thronged the sidewalk along the boulevard. Western Union was no longer the only place that never closed. Angelenos who worked evening shifts and graveyard shifts and split shifts needed burgers or entertainment or neckties day and night.

Bogie pulled up at the Highland Avenue traffic signal. "Nervous?"

"This might be my only chance to impress him."

"You already have; otherwise, he wouldn't have asked to meet."

Bogie found a free space at the end of the street. It wasn't until he grabbed a pair of sunglasses from the glove compartment that it dawned on Luke what a tremendous show of support he was making. As the night of the boarding house fire had demonstrated, it was difficult for Bogie to walk around in public undetected these days.

"Thank you," Luke said.

Bogie peered over the top of his sunglasses. "For what?"

"Being in my corner."

He grunted as though to say *You'd do the same for me* and jammed his fedora on his head. "Let's go get you enlisted."

They passed the Egyptian Theatre, where *Arabian Knights* was on a double bill with *Tarzan's New York Adventure*. A stream of factory girls, their hair still tied away from their faces, poured into the forecourt. Bogie accelerated into Harry Dine's.

Even in a store that was busy with browsing customers, it wasn't hard to spot Vance's dashing figure. Standing at the necktie counter, he kept his back straight as a mast. A visible jolt ran through him when he spotted Bogie a half-step behind Luke.

"I wasn't expecting such a notable wing man."

"I hear this place stocks some fine vicuña jackets," Bogie said.

Wariness filled Vance's eyes, and Luke's heart sank. Bringing Bogie had been a mistake. Not everybody was impressed by a famous movie star.

"I hadn't anticipated this sort of crowd. I assumed we'd be safe to talk."

This meeting had been hard enough to pull off. God only knew when he'd get another chance. Panicked, Luke looked at Bogie.

Bogie lifted up his sunglasses. "So it's distraction you want?" He turned toward the front of the store, but then turned back and said, "Don't forget to tell him about that day with the Morse Code," before heading to a display of suspenders near the front window. "Can anybody help me here?" He sounded more like a Humphrey Bogart impersonator than the real McCoy. A flurry of activity filled the store as every shopper and salesclerk converged on him.

Okay, so maybe it hadn't been such a bad idea to bring along a movie star.

Luke cleared his throat. "He won't be able to keep them diverted forever."

"Right." Vance swung back. "Here's the situation: We were close to cracking the Japs' code when Pearl Harbor happened. Afterwards, they changed to a different one, which we're having a hard time breaking. We base codes on language. Japs, though, are a smart bunch. I'm nursing a theory that they're constructing a new code based on German syntax."

"But there must be tons of people who know German."

"There *were*—until the government designated ten thousand German-Americans as hostile aliens, and other German speakers got drafted. Let me be frank: I've tried several other fellows, but they've failed to cut the mustard."

Good news at last. "How come?"

"We share cramped quarters with the other team I'm responsible for. They're working on a brand-new apparatus called radar. It allows us to track incoming traffic long before we have visual confirmation. It has a huge panel with all sorts of lights and displays, which has undone your predecessors. I desperately need someone who can focus on one thing at a time and isn't distracted by a rainbow of flashing colors. It's harder than it sounds."

A lopsided grin contorted Luke's face. "I got 4-F'd because of an inherited eye condition called tritanopia. It causes almost complete color blindness."

Vance frowned. "When you reported for enlistment, did they know you speak German?"

"On the induction form, 'health' is listed above 'skills.' As soon as the doc saw my affliction, he reached for his stamp. I tried to tell him, but he wasn't interested. I got tossed into the alley with the other rejects."

An outburst of laughter chimed at the front of the store. Word had spread to the street that Humphrey Bogart was inside Harry

Dine's. Luke and Vance weren't going to enjoy their pocket of privacy much longer.

"And so, Captain, if you're looking for someone who won't be distracted by colors—" he jabbed his thumb to his chest "—I'm your man."

"I think you just might be." Vance tilted his head as he appraised Luke in a new light. "What did Mr. Bogart mean about the day with the Morse code?"

Had Bogie not been with him, Luke might not have thought to bring it up. This was going to sound like bragging, but if bragging got him in, then the end justified the means.

"When he was studying for his Coast Guard skipper exam, he had to learn Morse code and he needed me to test him on it. Which meant I had to learn it, too."

"You already know Morse code?"

"I learned it in about ten seconds."

"TEN? Oh, right—that photographic memory of yours. Most impressive."

"Thank you. From what I can gather, you're talking about a codebreaking job."

"I am."

"That night at Romanoff's, you talked about special dispensation."

"I can get it done via back channels."

"You're taking a chance with me, aren't you?"

"I am," Vance admitted. "But if I'm right about the Japanese-German code, it could be a turning point in the war."

Luke was so damned close he could almost taste the crummy food and feel the uniform scratching his skin. He longed to ask Vance, "What's next?" but his conscience got the better of him.

"I need to come clean with you, sir."

"I'm listening."

Luke stroked a polka-dotted necktie lying on the glass countertop. Its comforting silky softness somehow gave him the courage to forge ahead.

"I've recently discovered that my parentage isn't what I'd been led to believe."

"Son, if there are skeletons in the family closet, I need to know about them."

"My father was born in Italy, and my mother's from Germany."

Vance grimaced. "That's a complicating wrinkle."

"There's more. My mother was born in Homburg. Out of curiosity, I looked it up."

"And?"

Oh boy, this was going to be hard. As hard as it was when he'd put two and two together at the library.

"Turns out, Homburg is where Heinz Spanknöbel is from."

"Spanknöbel? Who formed the pro-Nazi German-American Bund?"

"'Fraid so." Luke whispered the words as though it might make them less of a threat.

"Did Spanknöbel and your mother know each other?"

"Very unlikely. But I was thinking that, in theory . . ."

Vance dragged his hand through his hair. "On paper, you would look like the perfect spy. Or double agent, even. How do I know you're not?"

"You approached me, not the other way around." Luke held his breath until he saw a glimmer of approval in the captain's eyes.

"Your birth certificate needs to be dealt with," Vance said. "Do you have it on you?"

Luke shook his head. "But I can get it."

Luke clasped his hands together to stop them from shaking. If Gus had shown it to his father, it was safe to assume that Hell now had it. But would Gus help him retrieve it? The guy was grateful for the reading lessons, but was that enough to go behind his father's back?

* * *

Bogie groaned when he saw the typed pages on his dressing room table. He wadded his jacket into a ball and threw it at them. "My last day of shooting and they're still futzing with the script."

Luke reached for a hanger on the coat rack in the corner. "If it makes for a better scene, does it matter in the long run?"

"It'd matter more if I were Errol Flynn making *Edge of Darkness*, or Fredric March in *The Adventures of Mark Twain*."

"You're not the Mark Twain type, though, are you?"

"The budgets of those pictures are a million and a half. Meanwhile, our story is set in a town nobody can point to on a map and doesn't even warrant a million. The bigger the budget, the bigger the investment, the bigger the publicity."

Luke wanted to remind Bogie that nobody had been able to point to Algiers until Charles Boyer and Hedy Lamarr had turned it into a hit movie for United Artists. But Bogie was in no mood to hear it. He scanned the pages. "It's the farewell scene. You now shoot Conrad Veidt so that Ilsa and Victor can escape."

"Say, that's not a bad idea." Bogie grabbed the script from Luke and ran his eyes down the top page. "The guy doesn't get the girl. Ballsy move. Speaking of ballsy moves, you must be pretty hopeful after what Captain Screw All Night said."

"If there's anyone more suited for the job he has in mind, I'd like to meet him."

"I'm pleased for you, Luke." The clanking and clunking of the crew working on the airport set almost drowned out Bogie's voice. "My next picture I get to play a lieutenant, reminding me, yet again, that I'm not *in* the Navy, just someone who pretends to be. Listen, boyo, when you trot off to war, I'm going to miss having you around."

A soft vulnerability shone through his dark eyes that Luke hadn't glimpsed before. Not even in his love scenes with Ingrid. "Maybe you can train Nell to forge your autograph."

"A smart kid, that girl. She'll catch on quick."

A knock on the door. "Luke's needed for lighting."

He grabbed Bogie's trench coat and fedora and walked onto the set. He positioned his toes against a chalk line and jammed the hat on his head.

Oh, God. Nell! He hadn't thought about how she might take the news. In all the times he'd talked to her about how Vance could be his way forward, she'd never tried to talk him out of it. She'll be fine. She's a trooper. She has to be. All girls have to be troopers these days.

"Pssssst!"

Luke kept his head still and looked to the left. Ingrid was standing just a few feet away, already in costume and makeup. A twisted smile played on her lips as she sidled up beside him.

"Don't react," she whispered. "I just got off the telephone with Mr. Selznick, who told me Vera is out. I'm María!'"

"Congratulations." Luke grabbed her gloved hand. "You must be over the moon. Why are we whispering?"

"I can't announce it until he sends out his press release. If it wasn't for you, I might never have made it to that screen test." Her eyes glistened. She pulled a delicate handkerchief from her small clutch purse and dabbed at the corners.

"I don't know about that," he told her. "In any event, you can pour all that fervor into saying goodbye to Rick." Luke wanted to tell her that he knew how she felt. That he was *this* close to getting what he craved, too. But until he could wrest that damned bit of paper away from Hell O'Farrell, he ought to keep his trap shut. "You'll break every heart in every movie palace in America."

After the cast and crew had finished the domestic champagne—the French stuff was as rare as nylon stockings these days—that Hal Wallis had dug up to celebrate Bogie's release from the film, Luke encountered Gus leaning on Bogie's Packard, a faraway look in his eye. He straightened up when he saw Luke and Bogie approach.

"Could we have a word?" he asked Luke.

"I need to speak to you, too."

Bogie told him to take his time. He hadn't decided on his next chess move, so he headed back to his dressing room.

"Let's walk through the backlot. Less chance anyone will over-hear us." Gus led Luke past the commissary and the studio school. They were heading toward the pirate ship before he spoke again. "How did you know about Dwayne?" He almost stumbled over his whorehouse nom de plume.

It took guts to bring up that cheap shot Luke had fired at him. He must have a good reason.

"The boarding house I used to live in—my next-door neighbor was the girl you knew as Bianca."

Gus stopped in front of the galleon. The guys in the scenery department had aged the carved figurehead to look as though she'd been plowing the Spanish Main for decades.

"I was with her when you walked into Newberry's the other day."

"Had a good laugh at my expense, I suppose."

"It wasn't like that."

He studied the figurehead while his fingers jangled loose change in his pockets. "She shops at Newberry's?" He sounded surprised.

"She likes their fries."

"They are good."

He started walking again, past the length of the pirate ship, and headed toward the boxing arena, where Warners filmed their fight pictures. "Dwayne was a kid from my elementary school. Used to pick fights. Insult everyone. Nobody liked him. I assumed guys who went to places like Madame Lucille's didn't use their real names, so I used his. I thought I was being clever, but I soon regretted it because that's what Bianca called me when we were—you know."

"Your father wasn't so discreet."

Gus turned to him. "What's he got to do with anything?"

"You weren't the only regular."

"POP?!" Across the far side of the boxing ring, a couple of crewmembers patching up the back of the Philadelphia Street façade looked up. "Went to Lucille's?" His bottom lip quaked.

"He had quite the reputation. Likes the rough stuff, is what Bianca said."

"She must be mistaken. Pop would never—" Gus pulled the boxing ring's ropes toward his chest, then let them go. They snapped back like taut rubber bands. "Rough stuff. That's a nasty accusation."

"She experienced it first-hand."

"Not Bianca." Gus's mouth sagged at the edges. "She was my favorite. You mean he—?"

"'Fraid so, pal."

Gus paced along the boxing ring. "God, how I hate that man. It's terrible to say, but if you only knew how he treats me. Never lived up to the O'Farrell name. Never strong enough. Brave enough. Smart enough. The other day he caught me practicing my letters. Truth be told, I let him catch me. I thought maybe, just maybe, he'd be pleased to see me reading. But all he did was sneer and make some sort of comment about too little too late. And now you tell me he goes to whorehouses? Gets his kicks roughing up the girls? Bianca?" He punched at the air. "I wanna go home and slug him. Slug him a whole bunch. See if he likes getting the treatment he dishes out."

The sky had paled as the first evening stars appeared. But even in this dim light, Luke could see the last of the hero worship Gus had for his father drain out. "I need you to do me a favor."

"Anything."

"That birth certificate. Do you still have it?"

"Pop does. In his study, probably."

"Can you get your hands on it?"

Gus winced. "He can't make it up the stairs, so we've set up a hospital bed there. He only leaves it for bathroom breaks. His daytime nurse, a big ol' battleax called Mavis, helps him. She could lift an ox if she needed to."

"What about during the night?"

"He's worn out poor ol' Mom with his cranky demands, so I've become his second-class slave."

"Where would he keep my certificate?"

"In the No-Go Drawer. That's the locked one where he keeps our valuable family papers."

"Where's the key?"

"Somewhere in the study. God forbid he should trust any of us enough to tell us where."

"Is he a sound sleeper?"

"Since the accident, he's needed sleeping pills." A hint of a smile bloomed across Gus's face. "And I'm the one who gives them to him at night. He doesn't look at them, just swallows them down."

"So if you slipped in an extra, he wouldn't notice?"

"Let's make it two, just to be sure."

33

From what Luke could see by the dim light of a waxing crescent moon, the O'Farrells' house on Toluca Lake Avenue was one of the Spanish-style homes that was so popular in Los Angeles. Multi-level sloping tiled roofs and circular air vents that looked like portholes.

The drapes across the front room window were drawn. "If the coast is clear," Gus had told him, "the bottom half of the window will be up. Knock three times."

Gus had failed to mention the trio of pygmy palm trees with fronds sharp as shark teeth. They scratched Luke's forearm as he tapped the glass.

Ten long seconds dragged by.

Gus whispered, "S'at you?"

"How do I get in?"

"The front door has developed a terrible squeak. Mom's a light sleeper and wakes up to every little sound."

The right-hand drape swung open. Luke braved the sharp fronds and hoisted himself through the window into a room that smelled of wood polish, carbolic acid, and Cuban cigars.

Hell's hospital bed lay against the left wall. The misshapen lump beneath the sheet belched deep, irregular breaths.

"How's his leg?" Luke asked.

"It ain't broken, so no cast. Badly sprained, though. Lots of bandages and a fair amount of pain. I gave him four sleeping pills." Gus contorted his face into a wince. "Too much?"

"I think it takes a whole bottle to do any serious damage."

An imposing mahogany desk sat diagonally in the corner. The only items on top were a blotter and a banker's lamp. Books of all types, thicknesses, and sizes filled two walls.

"Where's the No-Go?"

Gus pointed to a deep drawer. "I saw an Alan Ladd movie where the key to a safe was taped to the underside of the murderer's desk."

"Any luck?"

Gus shook his head. "We're not allowed in here, so I doubt he hides it in any super-secret place."

They searched behind the prints of four famous bridges and under a miniature globe of the world. In an ornately carved wooden box that held an assortment of foreign coins, paperclips, and fountain pen nibs. The trash can. The leather tufted sofa. The standard lamp. A framed, autographed photo of FDR. Luke suspected that Hell O'Farrell and Enzo Valenti would have had a lot to talk about.

Neither of them found a key.

Luke ran his finger along a bookshelf. *The Outline of History* by H.G. Wells. *Revolt in the Desert* by T.E. Lawrence. *The Mind in the Making* by James Harvey Robinson. *The Man Nobody Knows* by Bruce Barton. Hell O'Farrell had struck Luke as more of a doer than a reader, so this wide-ranging library came as a surprise—unless they were there purely for show. The next volume caught his eye.

The Specter of Sabotage by Blayney F. Matthews.

He pulled it from the shelf and cracked it open. The first page held a quote from George Washington: "Put none but Americans on guard." The dedication came on the next page.

To Harry M. Warner, Jack L. Warner, and Albert Warner, courageous and far-seeing Americans, who were among the first of the country's industrialists to recognize the menace of the Fifth Column, and to engage in a relentless fight against subversive elements.

Bogie was no fan of his overlords, but he respected how the brothers had been the first movie moguls to raise a screw-you middle finger to Hitler and Mussolini. They'd also pulled out of the European market while MGM, Paramount, RKO, and Columbia were still wringing their hands over lost revenue.

Luke flipped to the preface. Matthews talked about how sabotage was part of Hitler's blitzkrieg technique. It was no light read, and this wasn't the time to start. Luke went to slot it back into position when he noticed a length of cotton thread looped through the spine. When he tugged at it, he felt a slight weight where there shouldn't have been one. He tugged a little more firmly. The weight moved. A third tug broke the thread. As a frayed end slipped through his fingers, something clattered onto the parquet flooring.

He looked down to see a brass key between his shoes.

"Found it." Luke held up the book. "Is this why your father thinks I'm a Nazi spy? I'm out to subvert—what? Warners? Los Angeles? The U.S.?" He deposited *Sabotage* onto the edge of the desk and handed Gus the key. The lock offered no resistance; the drawer slid open.

Gus pulled out papers, files, and folders, dumping them into a messy pile until he paused. "Gotcha."

Hell twisted the sheets in his hands and muttered, "Wha . . .? Wha . . .?"

Luke waited until Hell had settled down, then flattened the folded sheet against the blotter.

CITY OF NEW YORK
Birth Certificate
Lukas Osterhaus
Born October 12th, 1919
Mother: Lily Frida Osterhaus,
born Homburg, Germany
Father: Enzo Francis Valenti,
born Lucca, Italy

It was true, after all. There in perfect copperplate handwriting. Signed by the doctor. Witnessed by the nurse. Officiated by hospital administration.

He hadn't fully believed it. Not down deep in his bones. Sure, it made sense. Explained a lot. But that had been in theory. On the say-so from someone who, until recently, he neither liked nor trusted, with a father whose throat he could punch right this very minute and feel no remorse.

But there was no pretending anymore. This was who he was. What he was. Like it or not. Luke inserted the certificate in his back pocket as Gus laid *The Specter of Sabotage* under the banker's lamp. Hell had underlined phrases and added exclamation points. He had scrawled words and arrows every which way.

Gus pointed to a phrase written in large block letters along the bottom. "What does that say?"

"'Exactly right. This is the truth.'" Hell had drawn another arrow to a paragraph he had circled twice. Luke read out loud, "'The perfect agent/saboteur is one who passes for an American. Indeed, might even be American. But dig a little and you'll find

ALL THE GIN JOINTS

reasons to question his loyalty. Ties to the motherland—Germany,
Italy, Japan.'" He looked up at Gus, who was staring back at him,
his nostrils flaring. "Does he mean me?"

Gus flipped over to the next page and pointed to two words in
the margin. "Is that a name?" Hell had scrawled *Paul Gallico*. Below
it, he had added *Born in New York. Father from Italy. Mother from
Austria.* "Who is it?"

"Paul Gallico, the sports writer." His eyes wandered to the
right, where Hell had written *Lou Gehrig, Pride of the Yankees.* "And
this is the book he wrote about that ball player who died last year.
They've turned it into a Gary Cooper movie."

Gus said, "Gallico's coming to L.A. for the premiere, the one
with the Hollywood Canteen fundraiser afterwards."

Luke parked his behind on the edge of the desk. Gallico was a
Nazi spy because his parents were born in Germany and Italy, just
like Luke's? This was all so nutty.

He flipped through the next few pages until he found a passage
Hell had pockmarked with yeses in big letters so sloppy they were
almost illegible. Luke read it out loud.

"'All recognized authorities admit that Hitler and his cohorts
are planning to direct a knockout blow through sabotage against
America's production facilities. It is my belief that Germany and
her Axis partners will not hesitate to employ these methods
against us if we decide such drastic measures are necessary to
ensure victory.'"

Gus strummed the blotter. "You don't think Pop would—?"

"With his sprained leg?" Luke replied. "I'd like to see him try."

"My father's got more determination than a Sherman tank."

Luke's eye fell on a phrase Hell had underlined twice. "OH
SHIT!" The words popped out of Luke more loudly than he
intended. Hell's hospital bed creaked under his shifting weight.
"Your father is losing his grip on reality."

Gus's eyes dropped to the spot where Luke's finger still rested.
"What does that say?"

"'A knockout blow through sabotage against America's production facilities.'"

"Meaning?"

"I hope I'm wrong, but I think your father believes I'm out to sabotage Warner Brothers."

* * *

Luke found Bogie sitting in the breakfast nook, wrapped in a fraying brocade bathrobe. Brandy fumes crowded out the scent of the vase of magnolias at the end of the table. The Sunday edition of the *L.A. Times* lay open to the latest war news.

ALLIES LAND ON SOLOMON ISLANDS
JAPS CAUGHT BY SURPRISE

"Good news?"

Bogie grunted, keeping his eyes on the paper. "It's where your brother said he was headed, isn't it?"

His words came out thick and slurred. Eight in the morning was early, even for a dedicated boozehound like Bogie.

A photo of fifty Marines resting in a shallow gully filled a sizable chunk of the page. Luke longed to check it for Tony's face; however, Bogie's hunched-over posture told him he'd have to wait.

"Mayo still in bed?"

"Went out."

Mayo wasn't a morning person, especially on a Sunday. "Couldn't sleep?"

"Neither of us could."

"Celebrating the end of *Casablanca*?"

"Nope."

Bogie wasn't snapping his words, exactly, but there was a curtness to the way he nipped them off at the ends.

Luke slipped his prize onto the table. "I had a momentous night."

"You and me both." Bogie eyed the folded paper. "What's that?"

"The birth certificate!" Bogie's eyes sharpened. Not a lot, but enough to let Luke know he was paying attention. "The thing is, getting hold of it isn't the climax of the story."

Hell's idea that he was an Axis collaborator was all so implausible that Luke had trouble taking any of it seriously. But Hell had no trouble at all. He might even try to return to the studio before he was healed.

Luke took Bogie through the events of the previous evening. When he was finished, Bogie leaned back, arms crossed and his mouth pressed into sullen disdain—a far cry from the wily skepticism Luke had expected.

"I bet you didn't suspect you were housing a fifth columnist intent on blowing up the studio, did you?" he said glumly. He sat in uneasy silence as Bogie folded up the *Times* with pensive deliberation. Surely, he didn't think there was weight to Hell's demented reasoning?

Bogie struck a match from a Ciro's matchbook and lit a Chesterfield. "We need to talk."

"I'm no Nazi!"

"Don't be an idiot. O'Farrell's obviously jumped off the deep end. I'm talking about what happened when I got home from work last night. Mayo was already blitzed."

"Ugly drunk?"

"Is there any other kind?" Bogie smiled for the first time. A contemplative smile, stippled with regret. "I wasn't three steps inside the front door when she asked if Coney Island was with me. That's our nickname for you."

"I could think of a hundred worse."

"I told her you'd taken off straight from the studio for parts unknown. That's when she hit me with the news. I'm sorry, boyo, but she wants you to go."

This was a plot twist Luke hadn't seen coming, but he should have. If he hadn't been so preoccupied with wresting his birth certificate from the crackpot who thought he was a Nazi spy, maybe he would have.

"She thinks you've mooched on us long enough." Bogie took a drag of his cigarette and twirled it back and forth along his fingertips. "As far as I'm concerned, you can stay as long as you want. I reminded her that finding a place these days is a tall order. She said that it wasn't her problem, which is when I told her she was a callous shrew with the heart of a marble statue."

"I bet that went over well."

"I should have hidden the carving knife when I had the chance." He pulled aside his bathrobe to reveal a square bandage above his hip. "At least she waited until I'd finished filming."

"Isn't this getting a little out of hand?"

"She was too stinko to do much damage. Barely even scratched me."

"What if she comes after you when she's stone-cold sober?"

"She only gets stabby when she's pie-eyed."

The prospect of finding somewhere to live in a city where no such places existed was daunting, but at least he didn't have to worry about a past-her-prime actress coming for him the next time she'd poured one too many Old Fashioneds down her gullet.

"Did she set a date?"

Bogie lit a fresh cigarette from the dying butt of his last. "We didn't get that far in the conversation on account of the carving knife an' all. Let's assume sooner is better than later."

"I can start packing right now if it'd help calm things down."

"You got somewhere to go?" An uneasy swirl of hope and lament flecked Bogie's question like splattered blood.

Maybe Tristan had a sofa he could cadge for a few nights.

"This wasn't supposed to be permanent. She just wants her privacy."

"What she wants is to make sure there are no witnesses when she stabs me for good."

"Jesus, Bogie, don't say that!"

He reached across the nook table and gripped Luke by the wrist. "You're still aces with me, boyo."

The two men didn't say anything, nor did they need to.

Bogie released his grip and tapped the birth certificate. "Seeing as how this thing stands between you and the military, I'm surprised you haven't set fire to it already."

The screw-you mockery of leaving a little heap of ashes in Hell O'Farrell's trash can held enormous appeal. If Luke had thought of it, he would have.

Bogie picked up the Ciro's matchbook. A fancy, curly border framed the nightclub's logo with the oversized C. "By burning Lukas Osterhaus, you're saying goodbye to the old Luke. In my opinion, you're ready, but it's not my call."

Seeing the certificate for the first time had felt like a slap across the face, followed by a punch to the chest, plus a well-aimed kick in the nuts for good measure. But in a funny sort of way, it had also felt like meeting a long-lost twin he'd never known existed. And now, twelve hours later, was he ready to say goodbye?

Captain Stamina had a job he was desperate to fill. The perfect person to fill it wasn't Lukas Osterhaus. It was Luke Valenti. There was no going forward without letting go.

"Let's burn it."

"You're a smart kid, but do you know your Emily Dickinson?"

"Try me."

Bogie pinched a corner of the paper between his thumb and forefinger and held it up. "Ashes denote that fire was / Respect the grayest pile."

Luke plucked a match from the Ciro's matchbook and grazed

it across the scratch pad. It flared to life, heating his cheek. "For the departed creature's sake; That hovered there awhile." He held the lit match along the bottom edge until the paper caught alight.

"Fare thee well, Lukas Osterhaus," Bogie said.

They said nothing as the flames consumed the birth certificate, leaving behind only cinders.

*N*ell and Luke stood on the sidewalk outside the Pantages Theatre and watched Rita Hayworth step into a limousine with Victor Mature.

"Do you think they're having an affair?" Nell whispered.

"Because they made *My Gal Sal* together?"

"Do you know how movies often get cast? Those front office guys picture potential co-stars going at it in bed. And when everybody in the room says, 'I can see those two humping,' bingo."

"Is that what they did with Bogie and Bergman?"

"You can bet someone did."

"Yeah," Luke said. "Mayo."

"Glad you're out of there?"

This conversation had strayed onto a subject that plucked at Luke's nerves. He had told no one where he was living now. Not even Nell. Not yet, anyway. Not until he had to.

Mickey Rooney emerged from the Pantages with Ava Gardner. As their limousine pulled to the curb and their driver ran around the car to open the door, Luke visualized the two of them messing up the sheets. Rooney looked like he would be energetic, bedroom-wise, but what she saw in him Luke couldn't guess.

A team of four started packing away the giant searchlights that had greeted the arriving stars earlier that evening. An older guy in overalls set up a ladder in front of the marquee.

TONIGHT! SPECIAL MOVIE PREMIERE!
SAM GOLDWYN PRESENTS
"THE PRIDE OF THE YANKEES"
STARRING GARY COOPER

"It won't be the same," Nell said. "Premieres with no searchlights, no buzz or glamor." She slipped her hand into his. He loved it when she did that without warning. It never failed to thrill him. "Here we are, all dressed up with nowhere to go. It feels like a waste."

"Are you up for an adventure?"

"Always!"

Luke looked back at the deserted theater. "Nothing happened at tonight's premiere, thank goodness."

"What did you think Hell would do? Totter down the aisle and beat Sam Goldwyn over the head with his walking stick?"

"It's Bette's fundraiser that worries me." They turned as a Red Car clattered along the boulevard. Luke hurried her to the Vine Street stop. "I want to be sure there's nothing suspect going on. Hell's scribblings in Blayney's book were the ravings of a crazy person."

Nell's eyes flew open. "You mean case the joint? How very Sam Spade of you."

"I was thinking of gatecrashing the party."

"You, sir, have turned out to be a delightful surprise."

"Bogie said there are no tickets for the canteen benefit. If we walk in like we belong there, who's to stop us?"

Nell ran her hands down the front of her ensemble. "This belongs to one of the girls at my boarding house. Is it dressy enough?"

Luke stood back and pretended to appraise the outfit. The jacket had three-quarter-length sleeves, a peplum around the bottom, and a matching ankle-length skirt. He had no idea what color it was. Blue? Green? Purple? Or whether the color suited her. All he knew was that the cut of it did, and how. The streetcar pulled to a stop. "Absolutely."

* * *

Cowls of heavy blackout material hooded the top halves of the Sunset Strip streetlights, throwing the boulevard into a murky gloaming. With half the lights from Ciro's portico removed, it, too, slumbered in a somber dusk. A husky doorman in a tuxedo a size too small for him gave Luke and Nell a once-over as they approached. He nodded and opened the door, releasing a volley of gay chatter and the Xavier Cugat Orchestra's jaunty version of "I've Got a Gal in Kalamazoo." Above the stage, a hand-painted sign implored the revelers to

REMEMBER OUR BOYS!
HOLLYWOOD CANTEEN!
GIVE! GIVE! GIVE!

Charles Boyer was leading Hedy Lamarr around the dance floor. He looked dashing in his white dinner jacket, but of course nobody was looking at him.

The only vacant seats were at the end of the bar. Upholstered in thick velvet, Ciro's stools were the most comfortable Luke had ever sat on. Not that he'd been anywhere near this classy. One day, he'd be able to afford to bring Nell here and not have to worry about how he would pay the check. After the war, maybe? Considering where he was living now? After the war, *definitely*.

The bartender, a dimple-jawed gent who probably made far more in tips than he ever had in acting, asked, "What'll it be?"

"A martini for me," he said.

"And make mine a Gibson." Nell turned away from the bartender. "I doubt I've got more than five bucks."

"Me either. Let's hope we've got enough to pony up when the check comes."

"We could pretend we're going to the restroom and slip out the back."

Luke wasn't sure if she was kidding until he glimpsed her cheeky smile. "Or lift someone's wallet. This place is teeming with the overpaid."

They surveyed the crowd.

"Not Jack Benny," Nell said.

"Babe Ruth was in tonight's movie. I hear he hands out money like he's got a printing machine in the basement."

The bartender placed their drinks between them. "Want me to start a tab?"

"Yes, please!" Nell raised her glass. "Here's to finding the back door."

"I want you to know that it won't always be like this."

"Listen, most guys' idea of a fun date is a burger and fries at Simon's Drive-In. But look at us. Rubbing shoulders with the rich and famous at the swankiest gin joint in town."

"May I have your attention?"

Bette Davis stood at the microphone in a floor-length gown made of striped organza. She raised her hands to quiet the crowd.

"I promise this won't take long." She paused to let the audience settle down. "As you might know, John Garfield and I have come up with what we think is a marvelous idea. Our brave lads are coming through town from all over, often with a one-day shore leave. But where are they supposed to go? L.A.'s a big city. Filled with famous people. Wouldn't it be a thrill if they had a chance to meet you, Rita? Or you, Ginger? I saw Dorothy Lamour earlier. What kid from Grand Rapids or Louisville wouldn't give his first month's pay to dance with The Sarong Girl?"

As the crowd whooped and hollered, Luke surveyed the room until he spotted Paul Henreid and Claude Rains seated at the same table. In a pinch, he could prevail on Victor Laszlo or Captain Renault to bail him out, couldn't he? Then again, sneaking out the back would make for a funny story over affordable drinks at the Seven Seas.

Rains shifted to his left and spoke into the ear of his neighbor. It was Casey Robinson, who had written *Now, Voyager* and most of *Casablanca*'s love story. Next to him was Lillian Hellman, who had written the play that formed the basis for Bette's next movie, *Watch on the Rhine*. Was it possible that Hellman was here with her live-in lover, who had written the screenplay?

Luke leaned to the left to see around Bob Hope. Yes! It was him!

"We've secured the perfect spot a few miles from here," Bette continued. "But to get this project up and running, we need money. You people—" she jabbed her finger at half a dozen faces she picked out of the throng "—have it and I want it! And so I'm sending everyone's favorite Hungarian around with a top hat. Peter Lorre's got a big head, so it's a big hat, and it needs filling. Okay?"

She waited until the crowd had yelled "OKAY!" back, then left the stage to Cugat, who led his orchestra into an invigorating "Let's Put the Axe to the Axis," which didn't strike Luke as a very danceable tune, but was bound to rouse dollar bills from every wallet in the room.

Nell asked, "Who are you staring at?"

"See that guy with the thick gray hair next to Lillian Hellman? That's Dashiell Hammett."

She took a tiny sip from her Gibson. "The guy who wrote *The Maltese Falcon*? You should go up and introduce yourself."

"What happened to our inconspicuous plan?"

"That went out the window once we started drinking these. Who knew cocktails in fancier places pack more of a wallop?"

"I'm going to say hello to Claude and Paul." Luke slipped off the stool. "Won't be long."

As he approached their table, Paul Henreid asked his wife to dance. Paul nodded at Luke en route to the dance floor. Paul's wife had been sitting next to Hammett, which meant he now had a vacant seat beside him. Perfect.

"I need you!"

He turned to see Bette Davis charging toward him, her right hand raised and her finger curling like a hook.

"I don't make much money—" Luke began.

"Are you doing anything?"

He looked at Hammett, who hadn't noticed him, then back at Nell, who held her empty coupe in the air. "Not especially."

She pinched the lapel of the tuxedo jacket he had appropriated from Costuming and pulled him closer. "I have an unanticipated dilemma. Peter Lorre's collected so much loot that I don't know what to do with it."

"Already?"

"He's been at it since people started arriving. Turns out he's unbelievably skilled at luring cash from people." She blew Franklin Pangborn a kiss. "I thought this was going to be a blood-from-stone proposition, but these people are handing it over by the fistful! The First National Bank of Hollywood is sending a couple of security men. Meanwhile, the loot is in the back room off the kitchen with no one to stand guard. Peter Lorre saw you sitting at the bar and said Bogie has mentioned how reliable you are. Could I prevail upon you to look after it until the goons arrive?"

Luke snuck a peek at the chair beside Hammett. Geraldine Fitzgerald had filled it, and the two of them were having an animated conversation using salt and pepper shakers as props. Opportunity lost. "Absolutely."

He waved for Nell to join them. Together they wended their way to the kitchen, where Bette opened a door into a small office containing a large desk and not much else besides a Seagram's whiskey box, a Piggly Wiggly supermarket paper bag, and a Smucker's strawberry jam jar. "The bank men will be here in about an hour. Meanwhile, the only people allowed in are me, Garfield, and Lorre."

Luke nodded, and she closed the door behind her as she slipped back out into the crowd.

Nell pinched Luke's chin. "You sure know how to treat a girl to an interesting date."

He pulled her to him close enough to feel the swell of her breasts against his chest. "How about a smooch?"

"Let's."

Her lipstick tasted of cinnamon and cream. Not that it lasted long. A few minutes of hair-mussing and clothes-disheveling took care of that. He had her pressed up against the wall when the door opened and Lorre strode in with an upturned top hat filled to the brim with money.

He grinned slyly. "*Excusez-moi, jeunes amants.*" He dumped the cash into a pile on the desk. "Fundraising is a piece of cake when you're asking drunk, rich people."

"Such a cynic," Nell said.

"They're falling over themselves to show everybody how generous they are supporting troops they don't have to join. Guilt money, and I'm happy to relieve them of it." He spun the top hat around a few times by its brim, "Is Bogie going to the *Casablanca* preview Wallis has scheduled in Pasadena?"

"I doubt it," Luke said. "He was glad to be done with filming."

"Wallis and Curtiz still aren't satisfied with the ending at the airport. They plan to reshoot it."

"Another ending?" Luke's eye twitched at the thought of having to tell Bogie he wasn't out of the Saharan desert quite yet.

"Hump doesn't know when he's got it good. I've been filming *The Boogie Man Will Get You* at Columbia with Boris Karloff." Lorre's already mournful face took on an extra layer of melancholy. "I was hoping I'd see him, Ingrid, or Sydney tonight. I need a poker game, or a Finlandia steam bath, or an epic bender. Preferably all three." He grabbed the door handle, then turned back. "You'll remember to tell him that later tonight?"

"I will." Luke closed the door behind Lorre.

Nell flicked through the bills Lorre had just offloaded. "Ones. Fives. Tens. Twenties. Even a couple of fifties! We should leave the monkey business till later." She shoved the cash into the Piggly Wiggly bag, then opened the top drawer of the desk, peeked inside, closed it again, and tried the next one. The second drawer proved empty, but she found what she was looking for in the third: a tablet of blank paper and freshly sharpened pencils. "I want you to sketch me one of your lighthouses. Let me see what you got, mister."

Nobody had ever asked to see his work. Granted, he hadn't told many people about his efforts to recreate that magical week at Montauk. But still. Her request melted his heart.

The tip of the pencil hovered half an inch above the paper. This would be the first lighthouse he'd drawn since learning the truth about Montauk. Would his sketch turn out anything like the others?

"The Montauk lighthouse is unusual," he said, beginning to sketch. "The top and bottom thirds are painted white. The middle one, however, is different. Somebody said to me once it's the color of Coca-Cola labels. So, whenever I draw it, I can almost taste that Coca-Cola flavor and feel the bubbles on my tongue. I hope that doesn't make me sound like some sort of peculiar misfit." *At least not enough to make you rethink this budding romance of ours.* He would have looked up at her but for the furious blush creeping across his face. "It's near Ditch Plains Beach, which I think is a terrible name. There's a nearby spot called Camp Hero Bluff. Hero Beach sounds better, don't you think?"

"Much."

He moved his pencil to the left. "This is the bonfire that my Pop got the Feds to help me build. Made of the wooden crates used to ship bootleg."

He must have drawn that bonfire at least fifty times, but tonight it wasn't coming out right. This one was too messy. Too sprawling.

"Luke," Nell said softly, "where are you living?" The pencil jerked off the page. "It's just that you haven't told me. Is it some dreadful hovel?"

"Nah. Nothing like that. As a matter of fact, it's very comfortable." He laid down the pencil and looked her square in the eye, exactly as she deserved. "It's also illegal."

She made a sound that came out like a cross between a gasp and a giggle. "Don't stop now."

"I looked everywhere. Called every classified ad in every paper. But all I heard was no, no, no. I got desperate."

"Desperate enough to do what?"

"Gus and I have this little spot where we've been meeting for our lessons. One day I noticed a gate in the wire fence, so I checked it out. I couldn't believe there was no lock."

"You broke in?" Nell looked scandalized, delighted, and thrilled in equal measure.

"Technically speaking, did I break in if the gate was unlocked?"

"Technically speaking, it makes you an illegal squatter."

"Details, details. I had planned to move into Rick Blaine's apartment, but they pulled down the set once filming was over. So I sniffed out a more permanent berth."

"Where?"

"The pirate ship on the backlot. Captain Blood's quarters are very comfortable."

Nell slid close enough for him to see that tiny freckle on her left earlobe that he found so appealing. "Is there room for two?"

"If we snuggle in close."

She grabbed a fistful of notes from the Seagram's box and tossed them in the air. As sawbucks and greenbacks cascaded around them like expensive snowflakes, Luke kissed her freckle.

"Yo, ho, ho," he whispered, "and a bottle of yum-yum-yum."

35

*L*uke stepped aside and let Bogie walk into the sound department. "Do you have the new page?"

"It's just one line." He crushed his half-smoked cigarette into a metal ashtray shaped into a Warner Bros. shield. "Or do you think those geniuses with the worn-out Remingtons will dream up yet another one?"

"Hal Wallis wrote it, so probably not. They have to lock the picture some time. The preview is coming up soon. Which reminds me, Peter Lorre wants to know if you're going."

Bogie curled a lip.

Luke wished his boss could see what he had seen in the dailies. "I'll bet you five bucks *Casablanca* out-grosses *Falcon*."

"I'll take that bet."

A kid around Luke's age in a striped sweater-vest poked his head through the doorway. "It'll be a couple more minutes. There's a problem with the mike in the booth. You got Mr. Wallis's rewrite?"

Bogie looked wistfully at the cigarette he'd stubbed out. "The one about the beginning of a beautiful friendship?"

The kid nodded. "Won't be long!" He disappeared back out the door.

"Couldn't Wallis have come up with it last week, when I was still here, instead of dragging me in again?"

He didn't know the half of it. In order to drive Bogie to the studio that morning, Luke had had to wake up before dawn, slink out the unlocked gate and down the concreted riverbank, hike up the hillside to the Cahuenga Pass streetcar, and take that streetcar to Hollywood Boulevard, where he'd taken a second streetcar as far as he could, then walk to Horn Avenue.

"How's Mayo?"

Bogie produced a sealed pack of Chesterfields and ran his finger back and forth along the top. "Without you around, we let it rip. I suspect it's why she wanted you out."

Luke was newer to relationships than he was to moviemaking, but even he knew that if a couple needed a third wheel to keep their outlandish behavior in check, getting rid of the wheel wasn't the solution.

"You haven't told me where you moved to."

He doubted Bogie would snitch to the studio brass about his illicit squatting on board Captain Blood's ship. But what if the Battling Bogarts worked themselves into a ferocious brawl and Bogie let it slip? Would Mayo rat him out? It wasn't out of the question. When Mayo Methot had a few slugs inside her, nothing was off limits.

"I got lucky," he told Bogie. "My new landlady was sticking her 'Room Available' sign in the window when I was walking past."

The kid appeared in the doorway again. "We're ready for you, Mr. Bogart."

* * *

Minerva lifted the plate she had smuggled into Warner Bros. without losing its contents. "I'm making no promises."

With only the light of a few hurricane lamps to go by, it was hard to see anything now that the sun had gone down. Luke sniffed at the stack. "Chocolate cake?"

"They call it Wacky Cake. No butter, no eggs, no milk."

Sabine squinted. "Does it qualify as cake?"

"It had better," Seymour said. "We used our sugar ration for this entire month and the last of our cocoa powder."

"But what more perfect reason than this little reunion?" Nell said.

Luke took the top slice. "There's no telling how much longer I'll be able to bunk down here."

"Until they throw you out, it's thrilling to be so clandestine. I almost feel like I'm part of the Resistance."

"We would have been happy to host," Seymour said, "but we're living in a basement. It's a decent size, but without windows or ventilation it's all rather claustrophobic."

"And my room is smaller than the one I had at Edith's." Sabine giggled. "And even if it wasn't, how can you beat a pirate ship?"

At first, stowing away on the *Arabella* had felt like an enthralling escapade. Who wouldn't enjoy having a whole brigantine to themselves? The new dimout regulations dictated that filming must halt by seven p.m., which meant the studio was deserted by eight. Consequently, Luke also had the entire lot to himself—and the commissary. Nobody thought to bolt the windows, so he had access to the kitchen as well as the pantry.

The first few nights he'd felt like Alice in Wonderland as he'd wandered down Viennese Street and around Dijon Square. One evening he'd eaten his cheese-and-tomato-sandwiches dinner on the Venice Canal; the next night, he'd sat on New York Street and pretended he was in Greenwich Village. Mostly, though, he'd thought about Tony.

However, it soon grew lonesome on the nights Nell couldn't join him. This mini-reunion had been her idea, even if it was a risk to sneak Sabine, Seymour and Minerva in like this. Luke doubted Edith could make it through what Luke now called "Smuggler's Gate," even if she had been doing better. But she was still in the nursing home, struggling with lungs that refused to heal.

Minerva's Wacky Cake was surprisingly moist. "No butter or eggs, you say?"

"Or milk." Minerva pressed her knuckles to her mouth. "Can you tell?"

"I can't believe how lusciously chocolatey it is."

"Who knew that vinegar brings out the taste?"

They speculated about how long it would take Bette Davis and John Garfield to get their canteen idea up and running. The Ciro's night alone had gathered over six thousand dollars. Had Luke not been facing the front lot, he might have missed the shadowy figure inching along the wall of Stage Sixteen.

Nell peered over the portside wood railing. "What are you looking at?"

"Somebody's out there."

"A patrolling security guard?" Seymour suggested.

"I've never seen a soul after nine. Even more intriguing is that he's—" Luke shot Nell a meaningful glare "—limping. Which doesn't add up, because Gus told me it was a real bad sprain and that he wouldn't be up and around for ages."

"That blowhard has an ego the size of Mount Whitney," she said. "A few years back, he threw himself off a runaway locomotive. When they didn't get the shot they wanted, he did it again. Only this time, he told them to make the train go twenty miles an hour faster. Why do you think they call him Hell O'Farrell?"

"Hell?" Sabine asked. "This is somebody's name?"

Luke stood up. "I'm going to see what he's up to."

"Me too." Nell got to her feet.

"Should we all come?"

"I'm no private eye, but I'd say five people tailing someone isn't a good idea."

By the time Luke and Nell reached Stage Sixteen, the murky figure had cut across to Avenue E. They kept their distance as he passed the schoolhouse, Brownstone Street, and the sound recording studio. They didn't know for sure who they'd been following until he stood in the pool of light at the entrance to Film Duplication. Those broad shoulders and the thatch of sandy blond hair were unmistakable.

Opening the heavy door took some effort, but he managed it and hobbled inside. Luke and Nell counted sixty seconds, then followed him. The door opened without a tattletale squeak. Inside, the clang of metal against metal echoed off the walls.

Luke mouthed, "Film cans?"

Nell pulled out a whistle hanging from a chain around her neck and whispered into his ear, "A girl can't be too careful with drunken servicemen roaming the city. When I blow on this, drop your voice low as you can. Sound like a guard." She counted backward from three and blew out a sharp trill.

"HEY! YOU THERE!" Luke yelled. "THIS LOT IS OFF LIMITS! IDENTIFY YOURSELF!"

Hell let loose a string of indistinct mutterings. Luke and Nell ducked behind a filing cabinet and listened to the tap of his walking cane as he stumbled out the door. They waited until silence filled the warehouse.

Roughly stacked film cans sat on a wide table near an open cabinet as tall as the ceiling. Luke picked up the top one and read the label out loud. "Final cut negative. *Casablanca*. Reel two. September 1, 1942. PCA approval still pending."

Nell picked up another can. "Final cut preview positive. *Casablanca*. Reel three." She gaped at Luke. "He was stealing it?"

"Looks like it. To do what, though?"

"None of your damned business."

Hell stood twenty feet away, his right hand gripping the walking stick, his lips contorted with scorn.

"What are you doing here?" Luke demanded.

"This studio lot is closed, so the question is what are *you* doing here?"

"Do the rules not apply to you?"

Hell dragged his damaged leg a few steps forward. "Which rules apply to me ain't for you to decide."

He was close enough now for Luke to see the untethered look in his eyes. And that suited Luke. Madmen were easier to provoke. "Are there rules that apply regarding which rules apply to whom? Because if there are . . ."

Hell gripped a filing cabinet to take his weight as he raised his walking stick and jabbed it in the air. "Don't fool yourself for a second that I'm not on to you."

"And you don't know the first thing about your own son, so what in blazes could you possibly know about me?" Go on. Say it, you unhinged maniac. In front of a witness. Say it out loud so that I can hear it directly from you.

"I know all I need to know."

"About what?" Luke rapped his knuckles on the top film can. "This movie? Bogie doesn't think it's anything special. Nor Ingrid. For Curtiz, it's been just an assignment to be completed on Wednesday so that he can start a new one on Thursday. But *you* know better. You, who didn't even work on it."

"I've got my finger in every pie getting baked around here. And the word is that this *Casablanca* picture is a one-in-a-million."

"But that's what Luke believes too," Nell put in. "He's been saying it all along."

"Oh, yeah, I just bet he has." Hell didn't bother to look at her. "It's why he connived his way onto the lot. And into Bogie's good graces."

Bogie had hired Luke long before anybody had heard of *Casablanca*, of course. But since when did crackpots need reason on their side?

"So you think my plan is to steal it?" Luke asked. "That's pretty rich coming from the guy who's just been caught stealing it."

"I was not!"

"It's ten at night and you're here by yourself."

"I was *saving* it."

"From who?" Luke demanded. "From what?"

"Your plan of sabotage."

There. He'd said it. "In that case, I'm not so hot at my job, am I? *Casablanca* got made despite my attempts to blow it up."

"So now your only move is to destroy the negative and the one working print used in the Pasadena preview. I came here tonight to make sure that doesn't happen."

This nonsense had gone on long enough. If Hell was sufficiently healed to get himself to the studio and steal the movie, what else might he be capable of? Convincing Hal Wallis? Jack Warner? The FBI?

"Mr. O'Farrell, you are way off target."

"You speak German, don't you?"

"Because I studied German philosophy in college."

"I've seen your birth certificate. Your parents are German *and* Italian. Plus, you got rejected for military service, which means you resent the U.S. government. It all adds up."

"IT ADDS UP TO NOTHING!" Luke slapped a flattened palm on the table. "Even Blayney Matthews would frown on employees taking valuable company property off the lot. So here's what's going to happen: You're going home, where I suggest you rethink everything. Meanwhile, Nell and I are going to put these cans back where they belong." Hell tried to respond, but Luke cut him off. "We won't tell anyone what you were trying to do. You've been with this studio for twenty-five years. It would be a shame to tarnish your towering reputation."

"You won't get away with this!"

Luke picked up the top can and slid it into the storage cabinet. "Go now before I kick that walking cane out from under you and throw it into that lake out there."

"You think you're so clever. Yeah, well, I'm on to you, you —you—"

"Pipsqueak nobody from Brooklyn?"

Hell muttered a stream of invective too low to make out, but his meaning was clear enough. He turned around and retreated out the door.

Nell handed him the next can. "That isn't the last we'll see of him."

Luke slotted it into the drawer. "No, but at least for now we've rescued *Casablanca* from the hands of a lunatic."

36

*H*umphrey Bogart, Mary Astor, Sydney Greenstreet, and Peter Lorre huddled together in the foyer of the Warner Bros. Theatre on Hollywood Boulevard, each of them nursing a last-minute cigarette. The face Luke hoped to see most, though, was nowhere in sight.

Lorre spotted Luke and Nell as they approached. "Our *Maltese Falcon* family is now complete."

"I was just the continuity girl." Nell's wide smile betrayed her.

"My dear Miss Davenport," Greenstreet boomed. "*The Maltese Falcon* may have been my first motion picture, but it took me no time to realize that everybody in the soundstage performs a vital role. And that includes the continuity girl."

"I'd argue *especially* the continuity girl," Mary put in. "Without your efforts, the audience's willingness to suspend disbelief is undermined."

"And when that happens, how likely are they to tell their next-door neighbor, 'You must see that new *Maltese Falcon* picture!'?" Lorre raised a hand toward a poster mounted on an easel inside the foyer. "Or *Across the Pacific*, as the case may be."

"I wouldn't get your hopes up for this *Falcon* retread," Bogie said, with a wary leer. "Same cast, same director, but if Warners is hoping for lightning to hit twice, they should have at least changed the title. Relocating the action meant none of us actually crossed the Pacific. A better name would be *Don't Let the Japs Blow Up the Panama Canal as Well.*

"Either way, the tagline still applies." Lorre quoted from the poster, "'Boy! When Bogart boffs those Japs or when he kisses Mary Astor, you can feel it *Across the Pacific.*'"

The foyer was filling up, making it harder for Luke to make out individual faces. After his encounter with Hell O'Farrell, he wanted to leave nothing to chance.

"I wish they wouldn't do that," Mary said. "How am I supposed to explain it to my ten-year-old daughter?"

A squad of older men wearing an assortment of military jackets, caps, and medals marched past.

"Who are they?" Luke asked.

"Warner employees who have served in the military." A wistfulness had replaced Bogie's earlier cynicism. "The group's called Warvets."

He crushed his cigarette into the terrazzo floor with more force than he needed to. "I will say this about J.W.: he is the most patriotic of all the studio heads."

"I enjoyed *Confessions of a Nazi Spy*," Greenstreet said. "We forget how brave he was. Everything was so different before Pearl Harbor."

"Before Pearl Harbor," Mary echoed. "Seems so long ago. I can barely remember what it was like not to worry about sugar lasting till the end of the month."

"I heard coffee rationing is next," Lorre said mournfully.

Gus walked into the foyer. With Bogie not starting work on *Action in the North Atlantic* until Monday, Luke hadn't seen him since the night he'd confronted Gus's father. Luke joined him in front of a *Coming Attractions* poster for a Barbara Stanwyck picture, *The Gay Sisters*. "I assume your dad told you about what happened the other night?"

"Which night?"

"Nell and I caught him stealing the *Casablanca* film cans."

"He what?! When was this?"

"A week ago."

Gus jawed the life out of a wad of spearmint gum for a moment or two. "Since his accident, he's been playing the tough-guy routine. 'I'll be back at work in no time,' and 'That old quack didn't know what he was talking about.' But lately he's been locking himself in the study." Gus leaned a shoulder against the glass pane of the *Coming Attractions* poster, frowning now, puzzled and worried. "You sure he was stealing them?"

"'Stealing' is my word; his was 'saving.'"

"From what?"

"From the Nazi spy intent on sabotaging Warner Brothers."

"But you stopped him, didn't you?"

"I scared him off."

"Pop isn't the type to back down."

On the other side of the foyer, a uniformed usher had opened the auditorium doors. "If you see him or hear anything suspicious, you'll let me know, right?"

Conflict crosshatched Gus's face. "I'm real sorry he's treating you like this."

"It's not your fault that he's losing his marbles."

"Yeah, but I wouldn't have planted the seed, bad-mouthing you night after night, if I knew he had bats in his belfry."

Gus kicked the tip of his canvas basketball sneaker against the wall. He looked as though he could do with some company.

"Everybody's going in now," Luke said. "Want to sit with us?"

Gus shook his head.

"Now that *Action in the North Atlantic* is in production, we can resume our reading lessons. Assuming you still want to—"

"Yes! I've missed them a lot." He gestured at the doors. "You should go in."

Jack Warner gripped the microphone stand. "Good evening, my fellow Warnerites, and thank you for turning out tonight. *Across the Pacific* is a fine picture, but first I want to share some exciting news with you. The 'Stars Over America' war-bond drive is nearing the end of its nine-month tour. What a grand success it's been! In September alone, it sold seven hundred and seventy-five million dollars' worth of bonds." He tapped his right temple. "And I got to thinking." The king of the Warner lot wore a well-cut, expensive suit, sported manicurist-buffed fingernails and a big, fat diamond pinkie ring that shone in the spotlight. He also displayed a dopey, self-satisfied grin.

Bogie squirmed in his seat. "Oh, jeez."

"It sure is a grand sum, but eight hundred million would be a nice, round figure to end the tour on. So we're bringing it back to Hollywood. Specifically, to our studio, where we'll have an exhibit like at the kick-off event, only this one'll have props and costumes solely from our movies. Instead of just a single Maltese falcon, all four. Tap shoes from *42nd Street*, Tommy guns from *Public Enemy*, Bette's scarlet dress from *Jezebel*. We're also going to reconstruct Rick's Café from *Casablanca*. Plus, we'll set up a makeshift theater and run a sneak preview of it. This'll take place on September twenty-second. Doesn't it sound like a real humdinger?"

His rhetorical question drew an enthusiastic thunderclap of applause.

"Naturally, we'll have our stars there." He pulled some paper from his inside breast pocket. "Just to give you a taste of who'll be there so that you can tell your friends and ballyhoo this thing, get a load of this: Errol Flynn, Bette Davis, John Garfield, Alan Hale, Al Jolson, Humphrey Bogart, Mary Astor, Sydney Greenstreet,

Peter Lorre, James Cagney, Paul Henreid, S.Z. Sakall, Olivia de Havilland, and—oh, you get the idea."

"It'd be nice to be asked first," Bogie muttered. "Maybe I'm not available."

Mary Astor leaned over. "It's a command performance, dear. Refusal is not an option."

"Our publicity department people will roam around taking souvenir photos with our stars. Ten dollars a pop." J.W. slapped his hands together and rubbed them like a kid at Christmas. "And the highlight will be an auction. What the hell do we need with four Maltese falcons? So we'll be auctioning one of them." He snapped his fingers as though he'd just thought of an idea. It was clear to Luke from his stiff and exaggerated gesture that this so-called spontaneous patter was a well-rehearsed act. "Say, folks, if we could persuade our hometown boy, Mr. Humphrey Bogart, to sign it, we could double the donation!" He gestured toward the tenth row, where *Across the Pacific*'s cast sat. "Bogie's with us tonight, so let's encourage him."

The crowd gave Bogie a louder round of howls and hollers than they had given the boss. Bogie swung to his feet, acknowledged their support with a cheery wave and strained smile. When he landed back in his seat, he whispered to Luke, "And you wonder why I don't like going to these things."

* * *

Nell hooked her arm through Luke's on their way out of the foyer. "What did you think?"

"Bogie dismissed it as a *Falcon* retread; it's hardly that." Luke spotted Gus loitering in front of the *Coming Attractions* poster, right where he'd been standing earlier. "It's perfectly fine until you stack it up against one of the best pictures ever made."

"Bogie was right, though. They barely even sail *on* the Pacific, let alone across it."

Gus approached them with a cigarette pinched between his fingers. A half-inch of ash teetered on the end. "Could we have a word?" He glanced at Nell. "Privately?" Luke told him he could speak freely. "Mr. Warner's war-bond rally on the twenty-second —it's got me worried.

"Why?"

Gus sucked on his cigarette, barely noticing that it threatened to burn his fingertips.

"They'll be showing *Casablanca*, if you catch my meaning."

"With tons of celebrities around," Nell said. "Not to mention the press. Your dad would have to be—" She caught herself before she spoke the obvious.

Nuts.

"What I didn't tell you is that Pop's been getting more and more unstable. Flies off the handle for no reason. Mom and I breathe a sigh of relief when he disappears inside his study."

The theater's brass-and-glass doors opened and Beatrice flew in from outside. "Thank God I haven't missed you!" she told Luke. "You need—" She saw Gus; a furious blush filled her face. "Um— hello." She turned back to Luke. "Am I interrupting?"

"Nah." Gus flicked the butt into the ashcan on the floor. "I was just leaving."

Beatrice waited until he'd exited onto the street. "You're coming with me." Her voice had taken on a low, breathy rasp. "I have a car waiting around the corner." She grabbed them both by the arms and frog-marched them outside.

"I don't understand," Luke said. "How did you know where to find us?"

Beatrice bustled them onto Wilcox Avenue, where a black Lincoln idled at the curb. She opened the passenger door. "Get in. He hasn't got all night."

* * *

The driver braked out front of an apartment building, two up, two down, in a Mexican adobe style.

Nell squinted through the window. "This is cute."

"He said to bring Luke alone," Beatrice said. "Harvey here can drive you home." She got out of the Lincoln.

Luke scooped up Nell's hand and pressed his mouth to her ear. "I'll tell you everything tomorrow." He climbed out of the car and gestured toward the apartment house. "You certainly lucked out."

Beatrice yipped. "One of Keaton's Navy officer friends kept a mistress here. The night before our boarding house burned down, the two of them had a knock-down, drag-out fight and she left him stuck with the lease. So, when Keaton called asking if he knew of a place . . ." She led him up the flagstone path. "Whatever he wants to talk to you about, I hope it's what you want, too."

He squeezed her wrist. "Thank you. For everything."

She wrinkled her nose in reply and pushed open the front door. "We're here." She pointed through an archway on the right and disappeared into a bedroom on the left.

Vance sat on a loveseat upholstered in tufted velvet. Three Tiffany lamps lit the room with muddy light designed for make-out sessions. A portrait of a voluptuous Spanish tango dancer hung over the fireplace. She wore a towering mantilla and a full-skirted dress layered with frilly petticoats, her neckline cut so low that her décolletage was all but falling out of it. The room smelled of scented cigarettes and vanilla and—Luke sniffed the air again—freesias.

Yes, oh yes, this place reeked of mistress.

Vance wore one of those Aloha shirts that had become so popular since Pearl Harbor. This one had Hawaiian tiki gods interspersed with frangipani leis. He looked more relaxed out of uniform, more approachable. "I'm very glad Beatrice located you."

"She didn't just happen to find me, did she?"

"I've been keeping tabs on you." Luke made out a hint of a smile playing on the man's lips as he gestured for Luke to join him on the sofa. "Out of necessity." He waited until Luke took a seat. "Things have changed with disquieting swiftness since last we spoke."

A statement like that would raise alarm bells during peace-time. But this was war, when developments moved faster than a De Havilland Hornet. Americans only had to look at the desperate situation unraveling in the Solomon Islands to know that.

"Specifically, I'm talking about North Africa. Roosevelt and Churchill have switched their focus. Specifically, French Morocco."

"*Casablanca?*"

"You keep your ear close to the ground. I'm impressed. Yes, Casablanca is going to be the western prong of the three-pronged attack, along with Oran and Algiers."

Oh. *That* Casablanca? He was talking about the actual city? Luke strained to maintain his composure.

"Beatrice tells me you're from Brooklyn?"

"Yes, sir."

"Familiar with the Navy Yard?"

"My aunt lived just off Prospect Park, not ten minutes away."

"And the general terrain of Long Island?"

"Yes, sir, I'm familiar with that, too."

"You're even more suited to the job than I dared hope."

Luke interlaced his fingers and pressed the sides of his hands to his kneecaps. Stay calm. Keep it together. Don't blow it now. "Job?"

"Once the three-pronged attack gets underway, warfare in the Atlantic will be emphasized. So we'll station you on Long Island."

We'll station you. That's what he said. Not 'we might.' Not 'we plan to.' Not 'I hope I can arrange.' Were there three more exquisite words in the English language than 'We'll station you'?

"The Navy has personnel along the entire eastern seaboard. But Montauk is important because once those ships start streaming out of the Brooklyn Navy Yard, German U-boat traffic will increase significantly. You ever been there?"

Luke struggled to find his voice. "Montauk? Yes, I have."

"We're going to be monitoring the airwaves twenty-four hours a day."

"From the lighthouse?"

"That would be too obvious. But one of our main northeastern facilities is close by. I need you to bank up hours of in-the-field experience, and this is a terrific place to get it. Especially seeing as how you'll skip basic training."

Close to the Montauk lighthouse was close enough. Luke gripped the armrest and kept himself upright solely through willpower. "Can you tell me anything else?"

"The hours will be long. You might be alone much of the time, especially on the night shift. You need to be able to concentrate without distraction. Let me ask you one more time: are you up for this?"

"Yessir!" Luke felt like he should be saluting.

"Glad to hear it. In order to complete the paperwork for your enlistment into Navy intelligence, I need that birth certificate you mentioned."

What? WHAT? No. No! NO! *NO!* "It gives me a German name, with parents from Germany and Italy. You said yourself that it made me look like the perfect double agent."

Vance ran a knuckle along the back of the sofa. "Navy intelligence can retroactively fix that. Nevertheless, it's still the Navy. I must follow strict procedures. Government oversight, and all. The brass hates any sort of formal enquiry second-guessing our decisions."

"But I have another birth certificate. The one I've always had."

"That's no good to me. It's the original that counts when it comes to adjusting the records. Harvey will run you home to pick it up."

Luke's eyes stung as he held back the tears. Just when he was so close. So very, *very* close. Go on. Say it. You have to tell him. Spit the words out. Fast. "We can't do that because I burned it."

"Please tell me you're joking."

"You said we'd have to deal with it. I thought you meant 'get rid of it.'"

"Son of a lousy *bitch*!" Vance jettisoned himself off the sofa and paced back and forth. "You don't know the hoops I've jumped through. Your skills are ideally suited to the work. I can't lose you now. Not because of a single goddamned sheet of paper."

The zaftig tango dancer seemed to look down at Luke, laughing at him. So close, *mi corazon*. And yet so far. *Qué lástima.* What a dreadful, luckless shame. It all slips through your fingers because of a piece of paper.

A piece of paper. Could he? Would he?

"How about a forged one?"

Vance stopped pacing. "Keep talking."

"I know a guy." Luke barely recognized his own voice. "He's expert in—"

"Good enough to fool military intelligence?"

Avery had said he wasn't an art forger but a duplicator. *You name it, I can copy it.* Did that include birth certificates? Luke mentally crossed his fingers and said, "Yes."

Vance headed to a briefcase on the dining table. He pulled a logbook from it. "I need someone in Montauk by October eighth. It takes two weeks to process the paperwork, which means I must have your birth certificate—*a* birth certificate—by September twenty-second. If you can't make it by then, I'll have to go with my number two choice."

Of course Vance had a backup plan. This was the military. There always needed to be a second choice. "How will I find you?"

"Drop it off at my office." Vance pulled a card out of his wallet and deposited it on the tabletop. "Do it personally."

"Okay."

"How long will it take?"

"I'm not sure."

"Any time before the twenty-second is fine, just as long as I have it when I leave that night on a late train for the East Coast."

Luke picked up the card. The address was at the top end of Hill Street in downtown. "Got it." He spotted a pen and notebook on the table next to him. "Tell me if I'm out of line, but—" he wrote *Gunnery Sergeant Antonio Valenti, Guadalcanal* on the top sheet of paper and tore it off "—I'd sure appreciate it if you could find out if this guy is okay."

Vance crammed the paper into his pocket without comment. Luke accompanied him to the sidewalk, where Harvey was perched on the front fender having a smoke.

"I'll hear from you, yes?" Vance asked, opening the passenger door.

"You will. And thank you."

Luke watched the Lincoln disappear into the night. He dragged the business card back and forth along his fingernails. Even if Avery could forge official papers, was he good enough to fool the Navy?

Luke felt a presence beside him. "God knows I tried to eaves-drop, but the walls in that apartment are thick as Fort Knox."

"I need to get some paperwork to him by the twenty-second."

"You're frowning," Beatrice said. "Is there a problem?"

"Nope. I should have what I need by then."

37

*T*ommy Dorsey led his orchestra into "The Darktown Strutters' Ball" on Stage Sixteen. As Dick Haymes sang about picking up his honey at 'bout half-past eight, Bob Hope blasted an enthusiastic whistle across the dance floor. Ginger Rogers cupped her hands around her mouth. "If you want to dance with a lady, don't behave like she's your prize St. Bernard."

"Make with the hoofs, sister!" Hope cha-cha'd onto the floor. "This might be your last chance."

"Why's that? It's not as though the military is likely to enlist you anytime soon."

He mimed taking a bullet to the chest as she joined him on the dance floor, where she swished the deep pleats of her dress across his face.

Luke watched this routine play out, but barely paid attention. He checked his watch again. Had it only been two minutes since the last time he'd looked?

"We could wait at the security gate?" Nell said.

He waved his hand at the Dorsey orchestra and the crowd of well-dressed studio people. "I need the distraction."

"I know this is cutting it too fine for comfort—"

"When Avery said he could counterfeit a New York state birth certificate, I was so relieved that it never occurred to me it'd take him ten days just to track down the right sort of paper."

"You'll be trying to fool smart people, so it has to be corr—"

"I figured four days' leeway was plenty of time."

"Except nowadays we're at war. Delays have become—"

"So when he said the twenty-second, I—"

"—blew a gasket. I was with you in the phone booth, remember?" She grabbed his hand and hauled him up Avenue E. "You won't relax until you have that certificate."

"Not until I put it into Vance's hands."

"Which is why we'll wait at the security gate."

Nell's shrill tone pulled him up short. "I'm acting like a screwball, aren't I?"

"Not without good reason. You've only got until midnight to hand it to Captain Stamina. At least Avery promised he'd deliver it in person."

"It's nearly seven o'clock."

"He said no earlier than seven. The ink needs to dry; otherwise, ain't nobody gonna be hoodwinked. Let's say he doesn't show until eight. It won't take us long to get downtown this time of night. You've got more leeway than you think."

"Four hours—"

"—is not ideal. But far from impossible." They walked past the gate and onto a deserted Olive Avenue.

A thought shuddered through Luke. What if the correct paper hadn't been the only hurdle? What if getting his hands on the right ink wasn't as easy as Avery had assumed? Almost everything else was rationed these days; why not ink too?

He shook his fingers to relieve the jangled nerves tingling his fingertips and pictured his pirate ship bunk. He hadn't slept well since that meeting at Beatrice's. What a relief it'd be to crawl into it tonight and sink into the sleep of the dead.

He approached the guard at the security desk. "How long does it take for a taxi to show up once you've called them?"

"These days? Two hours?"

"TWO?"

"According to the *Examiner*, over eighty percent of cab drivers are now in the military. They thought women would take over, but those war factory jobs pay better. It's a good thing we've got the world's biggest public transportation system."

Nell dragged him away from the window. "Bogie's here, and so is his car. He'll let you run downtown."

A pair of dimmed headlights emerged from the Hollywood Hills. *Please be him. Please, please, please.* "Let's stand under the streetlamp."

The driver blasted his horn; tires squealed as a beat-up Oldsmobile came to a stop. The door swung open and Avery leaped out. He handed over a sheet of thick paper folded into three.

Luke held it up to the streetlight.

"Well?" Nell demanded. "Will it pass?"

As far as he could tell, it was identical to the one he and Bogie had burned. No wonder it cost fifty bucks.

"I sat on it driving over here," Avery said. "Genuine twenty-five-year-old birth certificates are rarely pristine."

"I can't thank you enough."

"I don't suppose you could give us a lift into downtown?" Nell asked.

Thank God she had the presence of mind to think of the perfect solution.

But Avery was already back in his car. "No can do. I've got to be in Santa Monica by nine for a guy who wants to get *out* of the military." He threw the Oldsmobile into a U-turn. "Good luck!"

Luke inserted his certificate into his jacket pocket as they headed inside the studio. "That was a damn good idea you had, asking Avery for a lift."

ALL THE GIN JOINTS

"Like my mom has said a thousand times: Up there's for thinking, down there's for dancing. It's a shame we won't get to dance to Tommy Dorsey. I'd have liked that. Especially now that you're heading off to war."

The reality of what he was about to pull off hit him like a bag of marbles. How many more opportunities would he have to smell the lavender in her shampoo? He took her into his arms and pivoted her outside the firehouse.

"What are you doing, you big galoot?"

He kissed her on the neck, where her skin was kitten-tummy soft. "I'm going to foxtrot you to Stage Eleven, then we'll run the rest of the way. Bogie has to be on hand for the falcon auction." They danced east along Third Street until they reached the end. "Thank you, ma'am." They broke into a sprint. As they passed Fourteen, the opening strains of "Don't Give Up the Ship" floated over the air.

They rounded Sixteen's corner and almost ran into Louella Parsons, who had laid siege to Rita Hayworth and Victor Mature. Rita dazzled in white, but wore the look of a cornered gazelle. If Victor Mature couldn't rescue her, nobody could.

Luke pointed to the western wall, where the publicity team had arrayed the costumes and props. "I'm going to scout the room this way. You go that direction, and if you see Bogie, tell him to meet me at the *Falcon* display."

As he passed Dorothy Lamour and Sam Goldwyn deep in conversation, he came across Beatrice and Tristan. She wore a sleeveless white two-piece suit, with a horizontally striped short-sleeve blouse underneath. It was one of Orry-Kelly's costumes for Ingrid—a bold move considering they were both around here somewhere.

"Thank God we found you," Tristan exclaimed, bug-eyed and panting with dismay. "We spotted Hell O'Farrell."

That bastard was a human helium balloon. Punch him down and he popped right up again.

"Where?"

"He was skulking around Errol's General Custer costume," Beatrice said. "Next to that are Ruby Keeler's tap shoes. Then the falcons."

Luke patted the folded paper sitting inside his jacket. It was now seven-twenty. Over four and a half hours to get downtown. Plenty of time. Hypothetically. "Have you seen Bogie?"

"He and Errol and Alan Hale were posing for photos in front of the *Virginia City* stagecoach," Beatrice said. "It's not every day regular folks get to have their picture taken with the likes of them, so there's a ton of people surrounding them."

"Fan out and try to track down Nell," Luke said. "Tell her I'll be at the falcons or the stagecoach. I'm desperate to speak with Bogie."

They disappeared behind Eugene Pallette and S.Z. Sakall.

At the long display, the throng was thickest under a banner hanging from the rafters.

AUCTION TONIGHT
ORIGINAL MALTESE FALCON PROP
HELP US GET TO $800 MILLION
GOD BLESS OUR TROOPS & FDR

Jack Warner had dressed up in his Army Air Corps lieutenant colonel uniform and stood at the bandstand's edge. As Haymes finished up crooning about how fools rush in where angels fear to tread, J.W. checked his notes on little cards, his lips moving as he rehearsed. The guy was known for his rambling speeches, which would give Luke time to maneuver in and around the multitudes, find Bogie, get his keys, and head for downtown.

"Hey there! Put it back!" Peter Lorre's distinctive voice shot over the knot of people gathered near the *Maltese Falcon* display. "You might break it!"

Luke wedged through the crowd and peeked out from behind a hat covered in parrot feathers to see Hell O'Farrell hoist one of the falcons above his head. "This was never used in the production and I know who faked it!" He spotted Luke and pointed the statue at him. "AND THERE HE IS!" People stepped away from this ranting lunatic in their midst, leaving a space between the two of them. Hell brandished the falcon at Luke like it was a medieval bludgeon. "Nazi spy! Saboteur!"

A woman behind Luke laughed. "It's that new type of theater. 'Improvisation,' they call it. Yeah! Give the Nazi spy hell, Hell!"

A round of goading applause rippled through the crowd.

"*Jawohl!*" Luke pitched his voice high to make him sound like an Abbott and Costello villain. "*Ich bin ein* big bad Nazi villain!" The ring of spectators chorused back, "Oooooooo!" "You *amerikanisch dummkopfs*! You suspect nothing as I sneak around and poison your cocktails and deviled eggs. But not zee sauerkraut!" He thrust a finger into the air. "Sauerkraut is sacred!"

Their audience applauded Luke's attempt to banter out of this sticky situation.

"This is not a joke!" Luke could see now that Hell's injury had aged him. His hair was thinner and wilder. When was the last time he'd seen a barber? If he didn't want people to think he was a lunatic, he should've at least given himself a decent shave. "This is no stage play! This man is out to sabotage the studio and we must not let him get away with it!"

"But all the world's a stage, isn't it?"

Nell jabbed at the air, pointing to Luke's right. Her eyes were open as wide as they could go. And what was she doing with her mouth? She had distorted into a strange shape. He looked over his shoulder just in time to see Hell O'Farrell bring the Maltese falcon down in a dark blur and strike the side of his head.

* * *

Luke's head throbbed. Ba-dum, ba-dum. Prying open his eyes took more effort than it should have. He closed them again and heard Nell say, "I think he's coming to." Or was it Beatrice?

"Jeepers, I was getting worried." Tristan's voice was unmistakable.

He opened his eyes once more. Above him was—a lamp? He couldn't be sure. Whatever it was, it had holes in it, allowing light to escape.

Tristan's and Nell's faces appeared. He could tell they were frowning, but that was about it.

"Luke, honey?" Nell said. "Can you hear us?"

He lifted his hand to his temple, but she brushed it aside. "My head. Pounding."

"Daddy O'Farrell clobbered you."

The light fixture was one of the black-painted metal Moroccan lamp shades that dotted Rick's Café. "How long have I been out?"

"Everyone's watching the *Casablanca* preview now," Nell said. "They'll be flooding in here once the movie's over, but you've got some time. Can you sit up?"

The tom-tom inside his head eased. No giddiness or nausea. His right temple felt tender. A terrific bruise would appear tomorrow. He let Nell and Tristan help him onto a nearby chair. "What happened?"

"Hell whacked you with a falcon," Nell said. "I nearly died! But people thought it was part of the show, so they applauded."

"To be fair," Beatrice said, "most of them were on their fourth cocktail. Right after you dropped, Tommy Dorsey introduced Jack Warner, so they headed for the stage. And thank God, too, because it let us get you away from there. Luckily, Gus is one strong ox *and* knows how to do the fireman's lift."

"Where is he now?"

"Gone to find his dad."

"Do you think he'll be back?"

Nell shrugged. "There's no telling what that loon might do."

"There you are!"

Bogie ran to their table with Lorre in tow. "You okay? Peter tells me Hell had a go at you. Spouting his Nazi spy gibberish."

"Didn't you know I'm out to sabotage the studio?"

"Come on, boyo, let's get you home."

Luke hadn't wanted to make Bogie feel guilty for kicking him out, so he hadn't told him about stowing away on the *Arabella*. "It's only a couple of blocks. The walk will clear my head."

"Okay." Bogie frowned, unconvinced. "Before everybody comes to Rick's for a drink, J.W. has hoodwinked me into doing a shameless dog-and-pony. I'm off to get into that trench coat."

Luke's head pounded like a kettledrum. He patted his breast pocket to reassure himself. The paper crinkled. "Dammit," he muttered, "I should've asked him for his car keys."

"You're in no shape to drive, mister," Tristan said.

"He's certainly not," Nell said, "but I am."

Luke planted his hands on the table and hoisted himself to his feet. "Where do you think he went? His dressing room on the *North Atlantic* set?"

"Slimy little weasel." Hell O'Farrell stood a foot or two inside the soundstage, silhouetted by the lights bordering the elephant door behind him. "Think you're so damned clever." He pushed aside the first table as though it were balsa. Luke saw it for what it was: an intimidation tactic. *I may have hurt my leg, but there's nothing wrong with my biceps.*

A wave of fatigue rolled through Luke, leaving him woozy. "This idea that I'm a Nazi spy . . ." He leaned on the back of a chair to help keep him upright. "It's a fairy tale."

Two tables separated them now. Hell struck his walking cane against the top of the nearest one with a piercing thwack.

"Blayney's book lays it out! I'm here to ensure you don't get away with your attempt to sabotage the studio—including trying to get me out of the way."

"How did I do that?"

"You caused my accident." He underscored the word 'accident' by pushing the table aside.

"I was never near the *Edge of Darkness*."

Fury blazed in Hell's eyes. "Of course that's what you'd say."

"So I sabotaged *Edge of Darkness* to set you up, did I? Like what you did to Buster on *Gentleman Jim*?"

Hell blinked.

Luke slapped his hands on the table between them. "And I quote: 'That's only because I put Buster Wiles out of commission.'"

"I didn't say—"

"And what about 'You need to get rid of that little shit from Brooklyn'? Is that why you're here? Is this the part where you get rid of me?"

"Everything that comes out of your mouth is a pile of stinkin' baloney, ya Kraut wop fraud mongrel bastard."

The cords on Hell's neck strained as he wrapped his fingers around the table's edge. What was he planning to do? Flip it over? He had the strength to do it without blinking. Luke weighed his options. It wouldn't take much to ignite this tinder-dry bonfire. Insults would only add gasoline to the flames. But oh brother, that mongrel bit stung real bad.

Jaunty notes from the intro to "As Time Goes By" floated through the air. Tristan sat at Dooley's piano. Beatrice stood behind it, a lopsided smile skewering her face.

She started singing about how a kiss was just a kiss. She wasn't wholly on key, but she gave it her all. When she got to the part about two lovers wooing, Hell gave a roar of recognition and cut her off.

"You're that little whore from Lucille's!"

Beatrice ignored him until she finished the verse. "And *you* are the worst damned lay I ever had. Sex with you was ugly and vicious and left me so disgusted that I had to scrub myself raw to be rid of the revulsion."

"Who cares what you think? You're just a filthy tramp."

"That's not Gus's opinion."

Hell's jaw fell slack. "My son would never . . ."

"He's everything in the sack that you're not. Tender. Considerate. And he doesn't rush through it like he's competing for the hundred-yard dash at the goddamned Olympics."

"LIARS!" Hell bellowed. "Whores like you lie through your teeth every time you open your filthy mouths!" Hell pounded the table with both fists. "Guttersnipes like it rough. Pushed around. Treated like the dirt you are because deep down you know it's all you deserve."

"Stop it, Pop. Just stop it." Gus stood with his feet spread wide. "She's telling the truth. I visited her. A bunch of times. She treated me nicely, which is more than you ever did. I tried to please you, live up to your expectations. *Be* you. And where did it get me? Yelled at. Insulted. Bianca made me feel like a man." Gus pointed to Luke. "And you know what he's been doing? Teaching me to read. Yes, that's right, Pop. I can read now, thanks to him. It should be thanks to you, but you preferred to make me feel inferior just because I had a little trouble with my letters."

"This pipsqueak nobody doesn't care about you." Hell spat out each word with undisguised malice. "He's using you to get to me because he knows that I'm on to him. Don't let him fool you, son. These people, they have their wiles and their ways."

Twenty feet behind Hell, Nell crept forward with a rope curled around the crook of her left elbow. A length of fabric dangled from her right hand. She stretched it across her mouth for a moment.

"Wiles and ways?" Luke yelled. "Christ almighty, O'Farrell, you make it sound like I'm recruiting him."

"You'll need an army of disciples if you're going to sabotage the American way of life."

Nell raised up the gag. She would have to jump him to get it over his head. But as she crouched down, Hell jerked his body to the left. Whipping his outstretched walking stick as he spun around, he whacked her across the chest. The blow sent her reeling until she tripped on an upended table and sprawled to the floor.

Gus dropped to his knees, reaching out to help her.

Hell grabbed his cane at each end and slammed it down on his son's back. A loud crack rang out. The cane splintered in two. Gus collapsed. Hell reeled around to face Luke and shoved the table aside. Its feet scraped along the floorboards with the wail of a wounded banshee. Luke stepped backward. Hell charged forward. His fingertips missed Luke by mere inches. One step closer and he would have been able to sock Luke square in the throat.

This barroom brawler, Luke realized, is no different from my brothers. Go in swinging until they're the last man standing. But I'm not that kind of back-alley slugger, and I'll be damned if I let this monster turn me into one.

"I won't fight you."

"You can't," Hell sneered, "because you're a yellow-bellied sissy with cotton-candy fists and less spine than a jellyfish."

"No," Luke shot back. "It's because I can do this."

He pitched himself forward until they were chest to chest, then reached behind Hell, grabbed the hem of his jacket, and yanked it over Hell's head to cover his face, blocking his view. He yanked it again, harder this time, sending Hell onto all fours. Nell threw Luke the rope. He caught it in one hand, thought for a moment, then flung it down, hard as he could.

"If anybody's a saboteur around here, it's you, O'Farrell. Your son isn't stupid. He just didn't learn to read. And what was your solution? You just ran around saying, 'Be more like me! Be as good as I am!' How was he supposed to do that when you suck up most of the oxygen? You've got to let your son breathe. Let him be his own man."

Gus helped Nell to her feet. He looked at Luke, his eyes brimming with torment. He mouthed, "Thank you" and kneeled down to aid his father. But Hell pushed him away and scrambled to his feet. "Who do you think you are, telling me how to raise my own son?"

"Now that Gus is learning to read, he doesn't need you to cover for him. It won't be long before he doesn't need you at all."

Without warning, Hell catapulted himself upwards. Luke leaned back, but not far enough. Hell's fingers caught Luke's lapels and ripped at them as he lumbered to his knees. The jacket tore apart at the seams, revealing the inside pocket. Avery's faked certificate fluttered to the floor. Luke made a desperate grab, but Hell was closer and beat him to it.

Oh, no you don't. Not when I'm this close. I don't care if you're connected to every hotshot from here to the White House. I'll sprain that leg of yours all over again if that's what it takes.

Luke threw himself at Hell. They tussled on the floor, arms and legs flailing. Hell grunted each time he landed a punch on Luke's back. The rough stubble on his chin scraped against Luke's forehead as he kept the certificate out of reach. His breath stank of hard liquor. Whiskey or bourbon. The cheap stuff.

Rick's Café Américain rang with the sound of Gus's deep, forceful voice. "NO, FATHER! ENOUGH! HAND THAT PAPER TO LUKE."

Hell froze. "What did you just say to me, son?"

"You heard me, Pop."

"What gives you the unmitigated gall to speak to your father—"

"Because we all have our limits, Pop, and I reached mine tonight." Gus dropped his right hand and subtly flicked his fingers toward the certificate.

Luke grabbed it and clambered to his feet. Nell stood at the elephant door, pointing to her wristwatch. "It's eleven p.m. The preview will be out soon, and this place'll be crowded with people. Too late to catch Bogie. Once he's done with his dog-and-pony show, he'll have scrammed."

"Let's go back to the front gate. We might get lucky."

They dashed along Third Street, past the security barrier, and out onto Olive Avenue.

"There must be a thousand people in there," Luke panted. "You'd think one of them would have booked a cab we could steal. Or what about those messenger bicycles? Where do they keep them?"

"They mostly run errands for the executives, so outside the front office?"

A car rounded the curve and pulled up in front of them. The passenger window wound down as Peter Lorre poked his head into the night air. "Good God, Luke, your jacket! Did you get into a knife fight with George Raft?"

Luke bent down and looked inside the cabin. Bogie sat behind the wheel. "We're commandeering this vehicle."

"You're what?"

Luke opened the rear door and pushed Nell in. "We've got forty-two minutes to get to Navy headquarters."

Bogie turned around and eyed the paper in Luke's hand. "You still haven't delivered it to Captain Screw All Night?"

"Long story. North end of Hill Street. Downtown. GO!"

"We could take Riverside Drive to San Fernando Road to the top of Broadway, and from there into downtown."

"But," Lorre said, "the Cahuenga Pass to Hollywood Boulevard to Sunset will take us to Hill."

Bogie's tires squealed as he swung into a U-turn.

"Thanks for coming along when you did," Luke said. "I don't know what I would've done."

"This is more fun than Mayo hurling my bowling ball through our back door. Which reminds me, boyo, you need to come over and replace it again."

* * *

Bogie turned right onto Hill. "What number?"

"Two three five," Luke said.

Nell spotted the ten-story building with its address stenciled over the revolving door.

Bogie braked. "We'll wait."

Luke and Nell found a listing for "Department of the U.S. Navy" on the lobby directory and jumped into the elevator. Luke pushed the button for the fourth floor. "What time is it? I'm too scared to look."

"Eleven twenty-two. See? Tons of time to spare."

Not tons, but enough. Even so, the unrelenting tightness in Luke's chest wouldn't relinquish its grip until he'd planted the certificate in Vance's hands.

The elevator doors slid open. They spotted a sign at the end of the corridor and broke into a run. Luke threw himself at the door. As they burst in, a woman in her forties yelled, "Gadzooks! You could give a girl heart failure—"

"Captain Vance." Panting, Luke held up the paper. "He must have this before he catches his train tonight."

The woman got to her feet and pressed her hands to her hips. "You've missed him."

"What do you mean 'missed him'?"

"Change of orders."

Luke felt the blood drain from his face. "But—but midnight—"

"Military orders change all the time, no notice, no explanation. Try working under those circumstances." She paused. "Are you Luke Vail?"

"Yes!"

"He's been waiting for you."

"Oh, ma'am, you don't know what I've been through to get here."

"I'm sorry, but he couldn't wait any longer."

Luke turned to Nell, stricken and defeated. It had all been for nothing.

She gripped his arm. "Nobody can say you didn't give it the ol' college try."

"I shouldn't do this," the woman said, "wartime security and all. The captain was supposed to catch a regular train tonight, but they've put him on a military service one instead. Platform twelve. Pullman car number one, behind the locomotive. It leaves at eleven-forty-five."

Luke and Nell jumped into the car. "Union Station. We've got eleven minutes."

The traffic lights ahead of them changed to red. Bogie hit the gas. "Hold on to your wigs and bonnets." He swerved onto Temple Street. "It can't be more than six or seven blocks away. We'll make it or my name isn't Humphrey DeForest Bogart!"

The wail of a police car erupted half a block behind them.

Lorre let out a nervous snicker. "What's that you said about your name?"

Bogie pressed his pedal to the floor; the Packard sped past Broadway.

"You're not stopping for the cops?" Nell asked.

Bogie ignored the bright swirling lights that filled the cabin as

Spring and Main Streets flew by in a blur. "Sweetheart, there are times when this movie-star caper comes in handy. Few, I'll grant you. But soft-soaping members of the LAPD is one of them." His tires squealed as he rounded the Alameda Street corner.

Ahead of them Luke could make out Union Station's clock tower. He glanced through the back window. "They're gaining on us."

Bogie turned right onto the double-lane driveway and roared past the tall, thin palm trees. "Don't wait till I come to a complete stop. In three, two, one—" Bogie hit the brakes.

Luke and Nell shot out of the car.

A cop yelled "HALT!" and raced over to Bogie's car as they burst through the front doors of the station.

Inside the terminal, a huge circular clock above the ticketing booth read eleven thirty-nine. The vast waiting hall ahead was all but empty, leaving them a straight line to the platform concourse.

"My heels," Nell called out. "I can't run in them." Luke glanced over his shoulder. She was already ten feet behind. She waved him on. "I'll catch up."

Luke charged up the concourse and onto platform twelve. A few people milled about, but not many. Luke sprinted past them, ignoring his burning lungs. At the far end he could make out a lone figure. Military or porter? He couldn't tell. If it wasn't Vance, what then? Jump on board restricted transportation? There had to be a formal punishment for that. It might even wreck his chances of joining the Navy.

Tears seeped from the corners of his eyes and trickled down his cheeks. Don't start crying yet. Not until the train pulls out. The locomotive whistle blew three long, shrill blasts.

He could barely see the lone figure, but at least the guy was still there. "Vance? Vance!" Luke scarcely had enough breath left to make himself heard.

The figure waved.

Luke held the birth certificate aloft. "I've got it!"

A second whistle punctured the air. The loudspeaker crackled to life. "ALL ABOARD."

"You're cutting it damnably fine." Vance plucked it out of Luke's hand and jumped into the nearest train doorway. He produced an envelope from the front pocket of his uniform.

Luke took it from him as steam gushed around his feet.

The train shunted forward. Vance called out, "How do I contact you?"

Good question. 'Care of the *Arabella*, Warner Bros. Studios, Burbank,' was hardly a legitimate address. "BEATRICE!"

Vance nodded. "Welcome to the Navy, Ensign Valenti."

The train gathered speed and slipped away, leaving Luke glued to the platform. Ensign Valenti. That's what he'd said. He was an honest-to-goodness, pressed-uniform, brass-buttoned, cap-wearing, salute-your-superiors ensign of the goddamned U.S. Navy.

Fingers wrapped around his forearm. "You missed him?"

"Caught him with two seconds to spare."

"You gave it to him, right?"

"He called me Ensign Valenti."

"You're in the military!"

"I am! Can you believe it?"

Nell wiped the tears from his face. "We should celebrate."

"Bogie and Lorre are bound to know some place that'll be open."

"They're gone," Nell said. "After I told you to keep running, I looked back to see Bogie signing an autograph for the cop. He shook Bogie's hand, but it was obvious he was telling Bogie to be on his way." She nodded at the envelope in Luke's grip. "What's that?"

"Captain Stamina gave it to me just as his train was taking off." Luke examined it for the first time. "My reporting orders?" He ripped along the top, withdrew the message and read it out loud. "Gunnery Sergeant Antonio Valenti recuperating at U.S. Naval Hospital at Pearl Harbor, Oahu, Hawaii. Current status: serious but stable." Luke lifted his face until he met Nell in the eye. "I have to call the folks." The platform was deserted now. His voice sounded so far away, like someone else was talking. "Not right now, of course. It's the middle of the night. But in a few hours, maybe. They'll be worried about him."

Nell smiled. "And glad to hear from you."

A knowing look passed between them. Yeah, maybe.

Luke stuffed the Navy telegram into his pocket, then lassoed her arm and walked her along the platform. "There's a Harvey House restaurant around here somewhere. How about a late-night feast?"

"We could."

She didn't sound convinced. "Got a better idea?"

"I don't suppose you noticed what's playing at the Million Dollar Theater?"

"I've been a little preoccupied."

"They're now open twenty-four hours a day for shift workers. From midnight to eight, they play second-run movies for only a quarter."

"What's playing there now?"

Nell raised her eyebrows impishly. "*The Maltese Falcon.*"

"I hear it's pretty good."

"Who knows when you'll see another decent picture. Or," she added, "if you'll come back at all."

"Why wouldn't I?"

"We'll have the Axis on the run soon; this war won't last forever. They're stationing you at Montauk, so when it all ends, you'll be close enough to hitch a ride home."

Luke pulled her into an intimate alcove next to a closed news-stand. "Back East? It's not home any more. I knew that when I read the telegram. I thought, 'I need to call the folks,' not 'I need to call home.'"

Fear and uncertainty filled her eyes. "So when all this ugly madness is over . . .?"

"I'll be returning to Hollywood, to here, and to you." He leaned in and kissed her soft lips. This wouldn't be their final kiss, but they needed to make each one count. "Come on," he said, tugging her toward the exit. "We've got a date with a falcon."

THE END

Did you enjoy this book?

You can make a big difference.

As an independent author, I don't have the financial muscle of a New York publisher supporting me. But I do have something much more powerful and effective, and it's something those publishers would kill to get their hands on: a committed and loyal bunch of readers. Honest reviews of my books help bring them to the notice of other readers. If you've enjoyed this book, I would be so grateful if you could spend just a couple of minutes leaving a review.

Thank you very much,

Martin Turnbull

AUTHOR NOTE

The genesis of this novel came about when a fact and an idea converged on me at almost exactly the same time. I read an article about Humphrey Bogart's love of chess, and how he played chess-by-mail with a guy in Brooklyn who was the brother of someone who worked at Warner Bros. studios in Los Angeles. My writerly mind started to speculate over how that came about.

I had also been thinking about how so many Hollywood stories are, in some way or other, about people who want to come to Hollywood, ambitious to make their mark, to reinvent themselves, or to escape their past—or all three. What if, I pondered, I could write a story about a character who *didn't* want to go to Hollywood, but was unwillingly compelled to? And what if that character came to find his true way forward in life?

And that's how Luke Valenti's story came into being.

So, yes, Bogart did play chess-by-mail with Irving Kovner, who lived in Brooklyn, and whose brother worked at Warner Bros. I was unable to find out anything about the brother, so Simon was my invention.

The original sculptor of the 1941 Maltese falcon was, as mentioned in this book, a Los Angeles artist named Fred Sexton. As far as I can tell, four falcons were made for the movie.

(1) John Huston wasn't happy with the falcon made for the 1931 version, so he got Sexton to make a more "masculine" one.

(2) Warner Bros.' props department produced a more aged version. This one was made of hard plaster.

(3) At some point, Warner Bros. producer Henry Blanke went outside the studio to have a light resin version made.

(4) And finally, there was a much heavier, more solid copy made of lead.

The history of those four falcon props is filled with enough twists and turns to fill a novel. The best account of them that I could find is in a *Vanity Fair* article, *The Mystery of the Maltese Falcon, One of the Most Valuable Movie Props in History*, which is available online.

The fifth, hollow falcon was my invention, as was Avery Osterhaus, and, by extension Lily, Boris, and The Four Blooms.

The Hollywood War Activities Committee's "Stars Over America" tour was real, and culminated in a huge rally at Madison Square Garden. The L.A. event held at the Warner Bros. studios was my invention, but the timing of it—coinciding with the preparation of *Casablanca*'s release—is faithful to the historical timeline.

There was a European Film Fund that was established and functioned as described in this novel. The fundraiser at Romanoff's was my invention, but I imagine they held events like that to raise money. I chose to set that scene at Romanoff's partly because it was Bogart's favorite restaurant in Los Angeles and partly because he was one of "Prince" Michael's original backers. The two men were good friends in real life. If you'd like to know more about Romanoff's, I have an article about it on my website:

https://martinturnbull.com/hollywood-places/spotlight-romanoffs/

The scene where Bette Davis knocks on Michael Curtiz's door while he's having sex never happened, but it was based in truth. Michael Curtiz often used to take young women (read: aspiring starlets whose movie careers advanced no further) into his office for sex during filming. Bogie and Lorre, who loved a good practical joke, did set up a loudspeaker one day so that everyone on the set could listen to Curtiz's exploits. The sort of behavior Curtiz indulged in wasn't all that unusual during this era, especially for powerful men like him, one of Warner Bros.' most successful, prolific, and versatile directors. This is despite the fact that he never mastered the English language, and his ability to mangle it was well known around Hollywood. Curtiz directed Bette Davis in *The Private Lives of Elizabeth and Essex* (1939), and I read several reports stating that they didn't get along very well, so who better to interrupt his escapade than gutsy Bette?

Hell O'Farrell and his son, Gus, were my invention, but Buster Wiles, the stuntman mentioned several times in this narrative, was a real-life stuntman, one of the most respected in Hollywood. Most of his IMDB credits are in Warner Bros. movies - https://www.imdb.com/name/nm0928777/ - where he doubled for some of their biggest stars including Humphrey Bogart, Errol Flynn, George Raft, and Dennis Morgan.

Bogart had a genuine love for sailing and the open ocean. He did own a boat called *Sluggy*, which he named after his then-wife,

Mayo Methot. The couple fought constantly, both in private and out in public, giving rise to their nickname, The Battling Bogarts. According to one account I read, they did order their back doors in bulk. Another story recounted the time when Mayo got so mad she stabbed Bogie in the back, which gives us an idea of the chaotic nature of their home life. The beginning of the end of that troubled marriage came about early in 1944, when Bogart started filming *To Have and Have Not* with Lauren Bacall.

The Battle of Los Angeles took place on the night of February 24, 1942. You can read more about it here:

http://www.militarymuseum.org/BattleofLA.html

As mentioned in this novel, the head of Security at Warner Bros. was Blayney Matthews. He began his career as an FBI agent and later worked as the chief investigator for the Los Angeles district attorney from 1930 to 1935, before joining Warners. Those jobs probably helped him when he needed to paper over scandals or fix problems with the help of the LAPD. In late 1941, he published *The Specter of Sabotage*. The full text of this book is available on the hathitrust.org website.

For the scene at the premiere of *The Pride of the Yankees* and the subsequent fundraiser for the Hollywood Canteen at Ciro's, I merged two real-life events. *The Pride of the Yankees* was the last movie given the full-searchlight Hollywood premiere before strict wartime blackout and dimout rules took effect. The movie premiere that preceded the Hollywood Canteen fundraiser was a Cary Grant-Jean Arthur-Ronald Colman film from Columbia called *The Talk of the Town*. In reality, the two movies had their premieres within days of each other, but since *The Pride of the Yankees* is the better-remembered movie, I substituted one for the other.

The kick-off fundraiser for the Hollywood Canteen took place at Ciro's on August 28, 1942, and raised $6,500 seed money for the project that Bette Davis and John Garfield spearheaded. The canteen subsequently opened on October 3 of that year. It closed on November 2, 1945, after having welcomed nearly 4 million servicemen and giving out nearly 3 million packs of cigarettes, 6 million pieces of cake, 125,000 gallons of milk, and 9 million cups of coffee.

My depiction of the making of *Casablanca* was as true to life as I could make it, given the contours of the fictional story I wove through it. The picture had five different writers working on it, and the script changed almost every day. This was not Bogart's favorite way of working, so he wasn't very happy during production, and consequently didn't think the picture would amount to much. Neither did Ingrid Bergman, who also wasn't happy at the time. Her marriage was in trouble, she felt no connection with her co-star, and the role she really wanted— María in *For Whom the Bell Tolls*—had gone to Vera Zorina (until the dailies of that movie showed Zorina wasn't up to the task, paving the way for Bergman to be recast in the role). From what I gather, both Bogart and Bergman were surprised at how well *Casablanca* did at the box office, and were amazed at its enduring popularity.

Another reason for Bogart's unhappiness was the necessity of his wearing three-inch wooden platforms so that he was taller than Bergman, who was five foot nine. You can see a picture of Bogart's feet in those platforms on my website:

https://bit.ly/bogart-platforms

There are a number of books about the chaotic making of *Casablanca*, but in my opinion, the best of the bunch is: *The*

Making of Casablanca: Bogart, Bergman, and World War II by Aljean Harmet:

My favorite Bogart biography is *Bogart* by Ann Sperber and Eric Lax.

ALSO BY MARTIN TURNBULL

Chasing Salomé: a novel of 1920s Hollywood

The Heart of the Lion: a novel of Irving Thalberg's Hollywood

All the Gin Joints: a novel of World War II Hollywood (Book 1 in the Hollywood Home Front trilogy)

Thank Your Lucky Stars: a novel of World War II Hollywood (Book 2 in the Hollywood Home Front trilogy)

The Hollywood's Garden of Allah novels

Book 1 – *The Garden on Sunset*

Book 2 – *The Trouble with Scarlett*

Book 3 – *Citizen Hollywood*

Book 4 – *Searchlights and Shadows*

Book 5 – *Reds in the Beds*

Book 6 – *Twisted Boulevard*

Book 7 – *Tinseltown Confidential*

Book 8 – *City of Myths*

Book 9 – *Closing Credits*

Rave reviews for Martin Turnbull's *Hollywood's Garden of Allah* series:

What a marvelous series! I tore through all nine books in record time and plan to go back to the beginning and start over! Thank you so much for this grand treat!

I loved this whole series! I'm sorry it had to end, but the reading was worth it! One of the best book series I have ever read!

If you start The Garden of Allah series from the beginning you will be treated to not only a great story but an accurate history of Hollywood from the 1920's Silent Era through the mid-1950's. I highly recommend this series of books for your total enjoyment.

I would give every one of the nine books more than 5 stars. This was a wonderful series that I wish did not have to end. I LOVED reading this series! They were so well-written, thorough, detailed, and really really interesting. I would love to read more, as I enjoyed these characters so much, and loved learning about the development of the industry and the area.

Martin Turnbull not only entertained me, but he gave me a respect and love for movies, actors, actresses, writers, directors, studios, and everything that contributed to the development of our entertainment industry.

What a great series of books! Anyone who loves movie history has to read these. I really felt I was part of of the friendship with Marcus, Gwen, and Kathryn, and shared every emotional rollercoaster ride.

~oOo~

Be the first to hear about new books and other news - sign up to my mailing list - http://bit.ly/turnbullsignup

(I promise (a) I won't fill your inbox with useless drivel you don't care about, (b) I won't email you very often, and (c) I'll never share your information with anyone. Ever.

ACKNOWLEDGMENTS

My heartfelt thanks to the following, who helped shaped this book:

My editor: Jennifer McIntyre for her keen eye, unfailing humor, and the willingness to debate every last letter and comma placement.

David Leibowitz, who was my go-to guy for all things Brooklyn.

Andreas Wessel-Therhorn on whom I relied to translate the German sentences in this book.

My thanks, also, to Susan Milner and Andie Paysinger for providing verisimilitude. I can only dream of these lives, but Susan and Andie lived it.

TJ Edwards for his assistance in getting the promotional graphics for this novel exactly right.

Steve Bingen, who provided me with detailed photos and maps of the Warner Bros. studio lot in Burbank, California.

My beta readers: Vince Hans, David Fox, Beth Riches, Steven Adkins and Gene Strange for their invaluable time, insight, feedback and advice in shaping this novel.

My Proof Readers Extraordinaire with the best eagle eyes in the biz: Bob Molinari, Susan Perkins, and Leigh Carter

Book cover by Damonza

Cover photo credit: The airplane on the cover photo taken by Kogo

https://it.wikipedia.org/wiki/Lockheed_L-12_Electra_Junior#/media/File:Lockheed_12A_Electra_Junior.j

ABOUT THE AUTHOR

A lifelong love of travel, history, and sharing his knowledge with others has led Martin Turnbull down a long path to authorship. Having made the move to the United States from Melbourne, Australia in the mid-90s, Martin staked his claim in the heart of Los Angeles. His background in travel allowed him to work as a private tour guide--showing off the alluring vistas, mansions, boulevards, and backlots of the Hollywood scene. With stints in local historical guiding with the Los Angeles Conservancy as well as time on the Warner Bros. movie lot, Martin found himself armed with the kind of knowledge that would fly off the very pages of his future works. As a longtime fan of Hollywood's golden era and old films, Martin decided it was time to marry his knowledge with his passions and breathe life back into this bygone world.

The product of his passions burst forth in the form of Hollywood's Garden of Allah novels, a series of historical fiction books set during the golden age of Hollywood: 1927-1959. Exploring the evolution of Hollywood's most famous and glamorous era through the lives of its residents, these stories take place both in and around the real-life Garden of Allah Hotel on iconic Sunset Boulevard. Although Martin's heart belongs to history, his energy remains in the present, continuing to put his passions on paper and beyond.

CONNECT WITH MARTIN TURNBULL

Website
https://martinturnbull.com/
Facebook
https://www.facebook.com/gardenofallahnovels
Blog
http://martinturnbull.wordpress.com/
Goodreads
https://www.goodreads.com/author/show/
5444454.Martin_Turnbull

Be sure to check out the Photo Blog for vintage photos of Los Angeles and Hollywood on Martin's website:

https://martinturnbull.com/photo-blog/

Made in United States
Troutdale, OR
07/09/2023

11086417R00268